YEAR'S BEST FANTASY 7

Year's Best Fantasy 7

EDITED BY
DAVID G. HARTWELL
& KATHRYN CRAMER

TACHYON PUBLICATIONS · SAN FRANCISCO

Year's Best Fantasy 7
Copyright 2007 by David G. Hartwell & Kathryn Cramer

Cover illustration © 2007 by David M. Bowers
Cover design © 2007 by Ann Monn
Interior design & composition by John D. Berry.
The text is typeset in FF Quadraat & FF Quadraat Sans,
with FF Quadraat Display & FF Quadraat Sans Display.

Tachyon Publications
1459 18th Street #139
San Francisco, CA 94107
(415) 285-5615
www.tachyonpublications.com

Series Editor: Jacob Weisman

ISBN 10: 1-892391-50-3
ISBN 13: 978-1-892391-50-6

Printed in the United States of America by Worzalla

9 8 7 6 5 4 3 2 1

First Edition: 2007

CONTENTS

Introduction

WELCOME TO the seventh volume in this annual series.

When we launched the series, originally in mass market paperback, we said that in this anthology series we will use the broadest definition of genre fantasy (to include wonder stories, adventure fantasy, supernatural fantasy, satirical fantasy and humorous fantasy). We believe that the best-written fantasy can stand up in the long run by any useful literary standard in comparison to fiction published out of category or genre. And furthermore, that out of respect for the genre at its best, we ought to stand by genre fantasy and promote it in this book. Also, we believe that writers publishing their work specifically as fantasy are up to this task, so we set out to find these stories, and we looked for them in the genre anthologies, magazines, and small press pamphlets. Some fine fantasy writers will still be missing. And you will find a broader set of examples, even from the very fringes of genre, where some of the finest work is being done, in this new trade paperback volume. The new format gives us a bit more latitude to represent the edges.

In these days when there are a plethora of bests to choose from, we still maintain that genre-bending fiction is not superior to, or more interesting than, or better written than, genre fiction – except when it is so well-done that it expands the genre itself.

We like to provide fairly extensive and informative story notes, rather than a lengthy introduction promoting – or attacking – new trends, and do so in this volume.

We do wish we had space to include half a million words of fiction, and therefore many more long stories, that, if we included in this size book, would knock three or four others out. But we feel that we have to include at least twenty stories in order to give a fair representation of the varieties of good fantasy fiction out there.

Like the earlier volumes in this series, this book provides some insight into the fantasy field, who is writing some of the best short fiction published as fantasy, and where. We try to represent the varieties of tones and voices and attitudes that keep the genre vigorous and responsive to the changing realities out of which it emerges. This is a book about what's going on now in genre fantasy. The center of the field is still occupied by the few biggest genre magazines, *Asimov's SF*, *The Magazine of Fantasy & Science Fiction*, and *Realms of Fantasy*, with the newly redesigned *Interzone* and its sister publication, *The Third Alternative*, the *Strange Horizons* webzine, *Weird Tales*, *Fan-*

tasy *Magazine*, and a few smaller fry attendant. The other principal repository of new fantasy fiction is genre anthologies and collections, of which there are many. A few exceptional ones from 2006 are: *Elemental*, edited by Alethea Kontis and Steve Savile; *Firebirds Rising*, edited by Sharyn November; *Salon Fantastique*, edited by Ellen Datlow and Terri Windling; *Cross Plains Universe*, edited by Scott A. Cupp and Joe R. Lansdale; *The Line Between*, stories by Peter S. Beagle. There were also a large number of single author collections from the small presses, often with one original story included among many reprints. The other loci of quality were the zines, little magazines of literary ambition such as *Electric Velocipede*, *Trunk*, and *Alchemy*, most of them descended from, or in partial imitation of, Gavin Grant and Kelly Link's zine, *Lady Churchill's Rosebud Wristlet*, which is still a leader.

The stories that follow show, and the story notes point out, the strengths of the evolving genre in the year 2006. But it is fundamentally a collection of excellent stories for your reading pleasure. It is supposed to be fun.

David G. Hartwell & Kathryn Cramer
Pleasantville, NY

YEAR'S BEST FANTASY 7

Build-A-Bear

Gene Wolfe

Gene Wolfe (tribute sites include *www.ultan.org.uk*, *www.urth.net*, and *members.bell-atlantic.net/ffiuze2tmhh/wolfe.html*) lives in Barrington, Illinois. He has published many fantasy, science fiction, and horror stories over the last thirty years and more, and has been given the World Fantasy Award for Lifetime Achievement. Each year he publishes a few short stories, of which at least one is among the best of the year in one genre or another, sometimes several – 2006 was that kind of year, a vintage Gene Wolfe year. His most recent book is *Soldier of Sidon* (2006) a fantasy novel in the world of Latro, the Soldier of the Mist. His next is *Pirate Freedom*, forthcoming in 2007, a novel of the pirates of the Caribbean. Collections of his short fiction include *The Island of Doctor Death and Other Stories and Other Stories* (1980), *Storeys from the Old Hotel* (1988), *Endangered Species* (1989), *Strange Travelers* (2000), *Innocents Aboard* (2004), and *Starwater Strains* (2005). He is among the finest living writers in any genre. This is the first of two stories by Wolfe in this book.

"Build-A-Bear" was published in *Jim Baen's Universe*, a new online magazine launched in 2006, and this is perhaps its first time in print. On a cruise for singles – an ominous setting if there ever was one – Viola attends a workshop in which a woman named Bellatrix helps her design a pink teddy bear, the perfect companion.

SIGHING, VIOLA PICKED UP the yellow schedule of shipboard activities and glanced at her watch. It was three-thirty, still two and half hours till dinner.

"*Bermuda and the Bermuda Triangle*" *2 Explorers Lounge*. She had gone to that one yesterday, and they were into it already. Nothing had happened.

"*Line Dancing for Beginners*" *10 Gym*. She could line dance nicely already, thank you very much, and did not enjoy being laughed at. Surely there had to be something more interesting than looking at the Atlantic.

"*Talent Aboard – passengers display their musical skills.*" *4 Seaview room*. She shuddered.

"*Make Your Pet.*" *9 Captain's Club*. What in the world…?

"I'm sorry I'm late," Viola told the smiling young woman with the laptop. "I didn't even know there was a Captain's Club, and the steward I got to help me find it only made things worse."

"No fret. I'm just glad somebody came. Bellatrix." Rising, Bellatrix held out her hand. "I'm in the show. Did you see me last night?"

"Oh, yes!" Viola lied womanfully. "That was you! I thought you were won-derful." She accepted the hand, larger and harder than her own.

"Thanks. But I do this, too, and I get paid by the head. I'll have to scan your keycard."

Viola hesitated.

"You won't be charged. It's included in the cruise. It's just the way I get paid." Bellatrix smiled again. "We show folks always need more money."

"Thank you." She glanced at the card. "Viola. Sit down, Viola. First we need to talk. Why did you come?"

Wondering when her card would be scanned but happy to sit, Viola said, "It sounded like fun, that's all. A friend of mine went to something like this called Build-a-Bear, where they made teddy bears. She made her own bear. It's always in the living room, and she tells everybody who'll listen all about it. Oh, God! I'm just terrible!"

"That's good, Viola." Bellatrix returned the key card. "I like terrible peo-ple. What's your specialty?"

"So I thought I might build a bigger bear than Marian. A prettier one. It'll kill her."

"Great." Bellatrix punched keys on her laptop. "It's got to be a bear? You don't want to build a cat or a horse or anything?"

Viola shook her head. "A bear. Marian's is brown, so I thought maybe pink."

"Got it. You said big. How big?"

"About like this." Viola held her hands apart. "This long. That should be twice the size of hers."

"Ninety centimeters." Bellatrix punched more keys. "You want it to talk, don't you?"

"With one of those strings in back you pull? Yes, I'd like that."

"That will take a bit of doing. Wait a minute."

"I thought I'd have to sew, and – oh, I don't know. Pick out the eyes. Make it."

Still punching keys, Bellatrix said, "You will pick out the eyes. We can do that next. What kind would you like?"

"What color, you mean?"

"Right. More pink?"

Viola shook her head. "You wouldn't be able to see them."

"Oh, you would if you looked closely. And she'd be able to see you, of course."

"A girl bear?"

Bellatrix nodded. "That's what I thought. Because of the pink."

"With a hair ribbon."

"If you want. That would be no trouble."

"I – I don't." Viola felt her cheeks grow hot. "I – I..."

"You don't have to explain," Bellatrix told her.

"I want to. I want to get it off my – my shoulders. I went on this cruise to meet someone."

"They have singles cruises, too. That might be better."

"I thought this was one." For a moment, Viola was puzzled. "Anyway, here I am with you instead of line dancing, and Beverly and Marian both say that's typical of me. I don't meet men because I'm too feminine. I hate singles bars."

"So do I."

"And I went with Lucas for almost three years, but he played golf. I couldn't learn, and to tell you the truth I didn't want to. I didn't think that would break us up, but it did. He met a girl with a three handicap and I was – was history. Am I going to cry?"

Bellatrix studied her. "I don't think so."

"That's good. I...I've cried too much about Lucas already."

"How about a pink boy bear?"

Mutely, Viola nodded.

"Nice dark eyes, with just a touch of fire in them?" Bellatrix punched more keys. "We can put a little vest on him."

"A black vest," Viola muttered, trying to get into the spirit of the thing.

"Right, to go with his eyes. Now we get into the hard part. Character, and all that. You want him to need you, don't you?"

"Absolutely." Viola almost smiled. "I want a warm bear who wants to be cuddled, not just one who sits in the living room and stares at people."

"Good. I'm with you on that. Brave?"

"Very. He's a bear after all."

"Right you are. Smart, too, I'll bet."

"Very smart. Quiet, too, and thoughtful. A bear of few words."

"Strong?"

"Very strong, too." Viola was smiling now. "A regular grizzly."

More keys were punched. "Got it. If he's going to be strong, he shouldn't be too thin. But you want him cuddly, from what you said. We need a balance of characteristics. I'm good at that."

"His expression...?"

"Exactly. Strong but vulnerable. Also you'll want him to be soft when you hold him, without being too soft. Suppose somebody broke in? You'd want a pet who could protect you."

"You know," Viola said, "you're deeper into this than I am."

"Of course. You should see some of mine." Bellatrix punched more keys. "There! That should do it. He's pretty close to standard, really. Some deviations, but we can use a lot of the regular subroutines. What's his name, by the way?"

Viola considered. "Theodore."

"Theodore Bear?"

"Exactly. When will I get to see him?"

"He'll be delivered to your cabin just as soon as he's finished," Bellatrix promised. "I'm making him look just a touch old-fashioned, okay? You strike me as a conservative sort of person, a bit old-fashioned yourself."

"I am," Viola said, and knew it for the truth.

"Four-thirty," she said to herself, as she left the Captain's Club, "and the ship's rolling a little. I hope I'm not too seasick for dinner." It seemed odd that she had not noticed the roll while she was talking bears, but she left that unsaid.

A different and somewhat more Spartan elevator carried her from Deck Nine to Deck Five, where – eventually – she found her cabin. A large pink teddy bear in a black vest lay upon her bed, propped by two small pillows.

"Well, hello!" It did not seem possible. "Hello, Theodore!" Sitting on the bed, she picked up the pink bear. His expression, she decided, was indecipherable. From one angle he looked severe, from another he appeared to plead, from a third he smiled warmly; he was a bear of many moods.

His paws felt soft – yet hard at the ends. Looking more closely she found lifelike claws, not sharp but long and curved. Playing with his face did little to alter his expressions, but led to the discovering of actual bearlike teeth behind his furry lips. "I'm taking you to dinner, Theodore. I want to show you to whoever I'm seated with today."

Her questing fingers found a ring on the pink bear's back. She pulled it, but not too hard.

"I'd like that," the bear said distinctly; his voice was deepish with a squeaky "I," and gruff overall.

"Very apropos." Viola patted the bear's furry back below the ring. "Now then... You will have observed, Theodore my bear, that our cabin boasts a small porch, balcony, or outdoor viewing area, called by captain and crew a veranda. Besides a little table and a great big footstool, it includes two wicker chairs. The first is large, with a splayed back. Rather a peacock-tail back, actually. It's clearly intended for the gentleman. That's you."

The pink bear appeared to smile.

"You, that is to say, when you are not on my lap – I fear your fur may quickly prove over-warm in the salubrious air prevailing on our veranda. I shall occupy the other chair, a lesser seat of the wing-back persuasion. At times you may occupy it with me – not that I've a great deal of lap to offer. May I have your opinion of the arrangement I suggest?"

She pulled the string as before, and the bear said, "I'd like that."

Only one phrase. She felt a little disappointed. "Is that all you can say?"

"Two," the bear added equally distinctly. Or perhaps "too" or "to."

Violet sighed. "I hope that extra noise doesn't mean you're broken already."

The bear did not reply; and so, not knowing what else to do, she picked him up and carried him onto the veranda, plumping him down in the wide wicker chair before seating herself in the smaller wing-backed one.

Beyond the Plexiglas-faced railing, a sea impossibly blue spread small swells to the horizon. Over it arched a sky equally blue. Someone had told Viola once that the sky was blue only because it was reflecting the blue of all the world's oceans. Looking at that sea and that sky, she felt that it might almost be true. "Cities," she thought, "have scraped away the sky with their skyscrapers. I wonder why they wanted to?"

Five o'clock. The dining room would not open for dinner until six. She leaned back, and when her eyes chose to close themselves she let them.

She was awakened by a tickling nose. Dispatched to wipe the tickle away, her hand encountered something large and soft.

Her eyes opened. "Theodore my bear, please mind your fur...."

It took three moments and two blinks to bring the pink bear into focus. "Did I put you in my lap? Never mind." She glanced at her watch – six-thirty. Dinner would be in full swing. "What about it?" she asked. "I am going to get something to eat, Theodore. You may remain here if you prefer, or – "

He might blow away.

"Inside on my bed, I mean. Or you may escort me. Which will it be?"

She pulled the string.

"I'd like that," the pink bear said distinctly.

"I thought you would. Dinner it is."

The Grand Dining Salon (as the ship called it) was at the stern on Deck Two. It was, as its name implied, very grand indeed. Wide glass doors in a glass wall opened on a spacious chamber resembling an amphitheater, wherein white-coated gladiators wrestled valiantly with laden trays. Spotless white tablecloths were embraced by massive chairs of wood well-carved – chairs that should, as Viola reflected at each meal, make excellent life preservers.

Five persons were already seated at the table to which she was brought to fill the last chair. She glanced at the faces of the three men as she took her seat, expecting signs of disappointment. There were none, and she smiled.

A blonde smiled in return and offered her hand, "Lenore Doucette."

Viola accepted it and introduced herself.

"I love musical names," the other woman said. She was meager and almost swarthy, with the hard, secretive eyes of a professional gambler. "I have one, too. I'm Raga."

Bone and a hank of hair, Viola thought. Aloud she murmured, "Pleased to meet you, Raga."

Lenore was looking at the pink bear. "Do you always carry that with you?" Her somewhat attractive face had the tight-skinned look that bespeaks plastic surgery.

"Only on the ship. Theodore's my bodyguard."

"Since the men will not introduce themselves – "

"Perhaps he'll let me do it." Viola smiled again, more relaxed than she had been at any of her previous meals. "What about it, Theodore? May I introduce you?" She pulled the string.

"I am Viola's bear," the pink bear said distinctly. "You may call me Theodore."

"You've more vocabulary than I thought," Viola muttered from behind her menu.

The round-headed, round-shouldered man seated on the farther side of Lenore said, "Don Partlowe," as if he were a little ashamed of it, to which the big, heavily handsome man on his left added, "Blake Morrison."

The waiter arrived, and Viola told him, "Five oh five four, and I'll have the split pea and the roast beef."

The man to Viola's immediate right coughed. "T – Tim Tucker, Miss Neudorf." He was small and looked (Viola thought) like a spike buck caught in the headlights.

"You have to call her Viola," Lenore instructed him. "Rules of the ship."

Raga smirked. "Another rule of the ship is that no more than six may eat at one table. I'm afraid that means you're out of luck, Viola. What would your bear like?"

"Honey," Viola told her firmly. "As in mind your manners, honey."

There was a brief, pained silence before Don said, "That's not on the menu, Viola. I'm afraid you'll have to eat for him."

The big man, Blake, leaned toward her. "Can he say honey?"

"He doesn't have to. I know his tastes."

Lenore tapped her wineglass. "I believe the score is Viola three and Table nothing. Would anybody else like to try?"

"I would," Tim whispered. The whisper was so soft, and his lips were so near Viola's ear, that no one else could possibly have heard it.

When dinner was over and she returned to her cabin, Viola dropped the bear on the bed and kicked the door shut behind her. "I'm fed up," she told him, "and do you know who I'm fed up with?"

An accusatory forefinger stabbed at her considerable chest. "Me, that's who. "Baked Alaska! I ordered baked Alaska, and I ate it, too. When I had finished mine, I ate half of poor Tim's."

With a violence that threatened to tear it, she pulled her blouse over her head. "I should go to the show tonight and watch for Bellatrix, and what am I going to do instead? I'm going to sit right here, by myself, and hate myself."

A step took her to the mirror. "Look at that tummy! What's the use of paying a thousand dollars for a singles cruise with a tummy like that?" She was sitting on her bed trying to wipe away the tears when she felt a small, soft embrace. For the next two hundred rollings of the ship, she hugged her bear and, occasionally, sniffled.

When the hugging and sniffling were over, she sat the bear on her lap and addressed him in the tone those near to tears generally use. "I love you, Theodore. I do. You're a – a much nicer toy than anybody has a right to expect. I... Well, I didn't even know... You're the – the most wonderful bear in the whole darned world, and I certainly don't deserve you."

Quite distinctly, the pink bear's head moved from side to side.

"I don't! I – I want people to like me."

Soft pink paws touched the pink bear's own well-rounded middle.

"Yes, you do. I know that. You've proved it. Can – will you tell me what I can do to make other people like me, too?"

Kindly, dark eyes opened, closed, and opened again, and the bear's large, pink head nodded.

"You can?" Viola pulled the string.

Distinctly, the bear said, "Smile."

"I do! I did! I was smiling all through dinner and nobody liked me."

Again the bear's head swung from side to side.

"All right, Tim did, and I imposed on him. Nobody else."

No signed the bear, and Viola pulled the string again.

"Lenore likes you."

"I don't believe it." Another pull of the string.

"Don liked you, too," the bear said distinctly. "She did not like that."

"He did not!" Viola insisted.

There was a knock at her door.

"Wait a minute!" Her robe was pink, too. As she knotted the sash she wondered vaguely whether the bear would approve.

"Miss...Viola?"

It was Tim. She nodded, groped her mind frantically for something to say, and settled for "Hi."

"I... You're – uh – getting ready for bed? I, um, there's a nice little – uh – cocktail lounge. The Seastar. It's – uh..."

"On this deck." Viola felt the need to speed things up.

"And I – uh – thought perhaps... But you're – "

She gave the smile her best try. "Why I'd love to have you buy me a drink, Tim. Could I meet you there in ten minutes or so?"

Tim gulped audibly.

"I won't bring Theodore. That's a promise."

"Oh, no!" Tim's eyes had flown wide. "I didn't mean that at all. Bring him, please. I – uh – I – uh..."

Smile again, Viola told herself firmly. Remember what Theodore said. "Then we'll both meet you there in ten or twelve minutes."

Tim's words rushed upon her like terrified birds. "It's-not-him-I'm-scared-of-it's-you." And Tim fled.

"Toward the bar," Viola reflected. "I wonder how many he'll have before I get there."

It seemed wise to hurry and she did, resuming the blouse she had discarded and spending no more than five minutes touching up her hair and makeup.

Tim was at a table near the all-glass wall. He stood and waved the moment she came in, then pulled the table out for her. It was a very small table, bare save for an ashtray and an almost-empty glass that had probably held a Tom Collins. Smiling, she accepted the offered chair, arranged the pink bear on the chair next to her own, and smiled some more.

"You're such a nice person," Tim said without a single uh. "I wanted to tell you that, and at dinner I couldn't."

A soft paw tapped her thigh; and she nodded, although only very slightly. "I know how you feel," she told Tim. "It's hard say things like that to – to anybody. Hardest of all when you've just met the person. At dinner I had to try very hard to look at the others, and not just at you all the time."

What remained of the Tom Collins vanished in a single swallow that brought a bowing, foreign-looking waiter. Viola ordered Dry Sack up, while Tim handed over his glass and said (in a voice that squeaked a trifle), "Do it again."

He turned to Viola. "That was one thing I wanted to tell you. This is the other. I hated this cruise for the first two days. Hated it right up till dinner tonight. All these women shopping for men as if they were at a white sale. All these men hoping to get laid by a woman they can forget about as soon as the cruise is over. "I...I – uh – I came...I came looking for – uh..."

She whispered it. "Love."

"Yes. I knew you'd know. You – you're – you're not married?"

"No. Of course not." Viola held out her left hand.

Tim almost took it. "Neither am I. A lot of these men are. Did you know that?"

"Are they?" It was a new thought. "I thought they were divorced."

"There's a lot of that, too. A lot more, actually. And nearly all the women are divorced."

The question hung in the air until Viola said, "I'm not. I've never been married. Once I thought – but it didn't work out."

"I haven't been either." Tim's smile was small and brave. (Like Theodore, Viola told herself.) "I write software, Viola, and I'm good at it – really, I am. I'm not good with people." He drew a deep breath. "Even if this doesn't work, I'll always, always remember you the way you are right now with the purple sea behind you and stars in your hair and the moon building a road across the water to you that only angels can follow."

As their drinks arrived, Viola murmured, "You're good with me."

On their way back to her cabin, the pink bear had to nudge her twice and point to keep her from getting lost. "I'm high, Theodore," she told him as she slipped her key card into the lock. "One little glass of wine, and I'm higher than – than any angel."

Her cabin was in the same, rather confused, state she had left it, her pink robe flung on the bed and makeup scattered across the top of the tiny dresser. She dropped the pink bear on the bed, too, sat there herself in utter disregard of her robe, and positioned him on one crowded knee. "He's never been married, Theodore, he's not dating anybody, and he has his own little software company. Did you see the way he looked when I told him I was a systems analyst? Did you?"

Distinctly, the pick bear nodded.

"We go together like ham and eggs, milk and cookies, roast pork and apple sauce." Viola paused to consider the final pairing. "I'm the pork, but I don't care."

There was a sound behind her, which she ignored. "I'm going to quit my job and move to New Orleans, Theodore. I didn't tell Tim that, but I am. This is not going to slip away. I won't let it. I'm – "

"Going to get hurt if you scream." The voice was deep and soft, carried on a gust of warm sea air. Half the lights in the cabin came on as the veranda door closed.

For a second she failed to recognize the big man in the aloha shirt, perhaps because so much of her attention was focused on the blue steel automatic he held.

"You're keeping quiet," Blake Morrison said. "That's good. That's smart. Now just relax and let me tell you how it's going to be between you and me."

Viola held up both hands. "If you think I've got a lot of jewelry, you're wrong. You can take what I've got. I'll tell you where everything is."

If the big man with the blue steel automatic had heard her, he gave no sign of it. "You're going to take off your clothes. All of them. You're going to do everything I tell you – and I mean everything – and you're going to act like you enjoy it. You're going to beg for more. Have you got that?"

"I guess I do, Blake." She nodded reluctantly.

"I'm leaving the gun here." He laid it on the seat of the chair nearest the window. "That will let me use both hands on you. If you try to edge over toward this side of the bed, you're going to get hurt a lot worse than you would otherwise. And no ventriloquism, understand? You're good. I'll give you that. But nothing you try is going to fool me."

Where was Theodore? As inconspicuously as she could, Viola felt for him with her feet. Nothing.

The big man was unbuttoning his aloha shirt. "You think you're going to report all this when it's over?"

Sensing the safe reply, she shook her head.

"I'll say it was consensual. How many couples do think are having consensual sex on this ship tonight?"

Still wondering desperately what had become of the pink bear, she raised her shoulders and let them drop.

"Half. Maybe more. You and me will be in that half, just for tonight. But let me tell you this, if you do report it, something very, very ugly is going to happen to you. And quick. So you'd better take it like a little soldier and try to forget it as fast as you can. Maybe you're wondering how I found out which cabin you're in."

"No, Blake." She was trying hard to keep her voice from shaking, trying hard to blink away the tears. "You learned it the same way Tim did. You have to – I had to – give my cabin number to the waiter when I ordered." It seemed worth a try. "Tim has already been here tonight, and he's coming back."

"Sure he is. Noises off, as the actors say."

A plump pink arm was reaching for the blue steel automatic on the chair seat.

A half-step nearer than that blue steel automatic, the big man had dropped his jeans. "Take a look. You like it, right?"

Shuddering, she shook her head. "You want me scared, d – don't you? You want me t – terrified. Okay! Okay, I'm scared out of my wits. You did it. But – "

The big man edged nearer her, stepping out of the jeans and blocking her view of the empty chair. "Take off that skirt!"

Slowly she stood, finding her knees so weak she nearly fell, and fumbled with the hook and the zipper. "I'm f-f-fat. You'll see. I'm v-very f-fat and – and ugly."

"Look lower," the big man told her, "and you'll see somebody who doesn't think so."

As though conjured by the big man's words, the pink bear rose beside Viola. Both plump pink forepaws were wrapped around the blue steel automatic.

The big man's jaw dropped.

So did Viola, sitting on the bed once more. When she had caught her breath, she turned so she could watch the big man and said, "Theodore will shoot if I tell him to." Her voice, she found, had somehow steadied itself. "Maybe even if I don't."

The big man's mouth worked soundlessly.

"Maybe you should lie down on the floor, or maybe just go without making any more trouble. I'm not sure which."

"Please!" the big man said. "Oh, please!"

"Please is nicer, Blake." Viola's smile was shaky, but it was a smile. "I like please. Wait a minute. Let's see what Theodore has to say to you." She found the ring on the pink bear's back and pulled the cord.

The pink bear lifted the blue steel automatic an inch or so, aiming it or appearing to aim it. Quite distinctly he said, "Want to close your eyes?"

Pimpf

Charles Stross

Charles Stross (*www.antipope.org*) is a computer programmer and writer living in Edinburgh, Scotland. He has been publishing occasional SF and fantasy since the late 1980s, but burst into prominence at the beginning of the new millennium with a series of stories in *Asimov's* SF that were collected as his novel *Accelerando* (2005). Between 2001 and the present he contracted for fourteen novels and some are yet to be published. *The Atrocity Archive* (2002), Stross's first novel, is a Lovecraftian fantasy that was serialized in three issues of the British periodical *Spectrum* SF. The novel was later expanded into *The Atrocity Archives* (2005), combining it with "The Concrete Jungle," a novella that won the Hugo Award in 2005. His novel *Singularity Sky* (2003), was a Hugo Award nominee. *The Family Trade* (2004), a fantasy with SF attitude, launched his popular Merchant Princes series. *The Jennifer Morgue* (2006) is his latest Lovecraftian volume, which also contains "Pimpf." In an interview with Lou Anders, Stross makes a remark that resonates particularly well with this story: "I've been privileged to live and work for most of a decade inside an industry that really did seem as if it was slouching towards a singularity, with exponential change and an outlook that said 15% growth per year is stasis. I think I'm still assimilating some of those implications – and also the realization that core human personality types persist even if you change the environment so far that they're hopelessly ill-adapted."

"Pimpf" was first published in the new electronic magazine, *Jim Baen's Universe*, an ambitious attempt to replace now-defunct *SciFiction* as the top-paying market in the field. This story is an entertaining tale blending corporate realities, government bureaucracies, and fantasy role-playing games. Bob Howard (Robert E. Howard's centennial was 2006) works for the secret government department that prevents actual demons from entering online gaming worlds when a dungeon master using realistic incantations and methods summons one.

I HATE DAYS LIKE THIS.

It's a rainy Monday morning and I'm late in to work at the Laundry because of a technical fault on the Tube. When I get to my desk, the first thing I find is a note from Human Resources that says one of their management team wants to talk to me, soonest, about playing computer games at work. And to put the cherry on top of the shit-pie, the office's coffee percolator is empty because none of the other inmates in this goddamn loony bin can be arsed refilling it. It's enough to make me long for a high place and a rifle...but in the end I head for Human Resources to take the bull by the horns, decaffeinated and mean as only a decaffeinated Bob can be.

Over in the dizzying heights of HR, the furniture is fresh and the windows recently cleaned. It's a far cry from the dingy rats' nest of Ops Division, where I normally spend my working time. But ours is not to wonder why (at least in public).

"Ms. MacDougal will see you now," says the receptionist on the front desk, looking down her nose at me pityingly. " Do try not to shed on the carpet, we had it steam cleaned this morning." *Bastards.*

I slouch across the thick, cream wool towards the inner sanctum of Emma MacDougal, senior vice-superintendent, Personnel Management (Operations), trying not to gawk like a resentful yokel at the luxuries on parade. It's not the first time I've been here, but I can never shake the sense that I'm entering another world, graced by visitors of ministerial import and elevated budget. The dizzy heights of the *real* civil service, as opposed to us poor Morlocks in Ops Division who keep everything running.

"Mr. Howard, do come in." I straighten instinctively when Emma addresses me. She has that effect on most people – she was born to be a headmistress or a tax inspector, but unfortunately she ended up in Human Resources by mistake and she's been letting us know about it ever since. "Have a seat." The room reeks of quiet luxury by Laundry standards: my chair is big, comfortable, and hasn't been bumped, scraped, and abraded into a pile of kindling by generations of visitors. The office is bright and airy, and the window is clean and has a row of attractively un-browned potted plants sitting before it. (The computer squatting on her desk is at least twice as expensive as anything I've been able to get my hands on via official channels, *and it's not even switched on.*) "How good of you to make time to see me." She smiles like a razor. I stifle a sigh; it's going to be one of *those* sessions.

"I'm a busy man." *Let's see if deadpan will work, hmm?*

"I'm sure you are. Nevertheless." She taps a piece of paper sitting on her blotter and I tense. "I've been hearing disturbing reports about you, Bob."

Oh, bollocks. "What kind of reports?" I ask warily.

Her smile's cold enough to frost glass. "Let me be blunt. I've had a report – I hesitate to say who from – about you playing computer games in the office."

Oh. *That.* "I see."

"According to this report you've been playing rather a lot of Neverwinter Nights recently." She runs her finger down the printout with relish. "You've even sequestrated an old departmental server to run a persistent realm – a multiuser online dungeon." She looks up, staring at me intently. "What have you got to say for yourself?"

I shrug. What's to say? She's got me bang to rights. "Um."

"Um indeed." She taps a finger on the page. "Last Tuesday you played Neverwinter Nights for four hours. This Monday you played it for two hours in the morning and three hours in the afternoon, staying on for an hour after your official flexitime shift ended. That's six straight hours. What have you got to say for yourself?"

"Only six?" I lean forwards.

"Yes. Six hours." She taps the memo again. "Bob. What are we paying you for?"

I shrug. "To put the hack into hack-and-slay."

"Yes, Bob, we're paying you to search online role-playing games for threats to national security. But you only averaged four hours a day last week...isn't this rather a poor use of your time?"

Save me from ambitious bureaucrats. This is the Laundry, the last over-manned organization of the civil service in London, and they're *everywhere* – trying to climb the greasy pole, playing snakes and ladders with the org chart, running esoteric counterespionage operations in the staff toilets, and rationing the civil service tea bags. I guess it serves Mahogany Row's purposes to keep them running in circles and distracting one another, but sometimes it gets in the way. Emma MacDougal is by no means the worst of the lot: she's just a starchy Human Resources manager on her way up, sty-mied by the full promotion ladder above her. But she's trying to butt in and micromanage inside my department (that is, inside *Angleton's* department), and just to show how efficient she is, she's actually been reading my time sheets and trying to stick her oar in on what I should be doing.

To get out of MacDougal's office I had to explain three times that my anti-quated workstation kept crashing and needed a system rebuild before she'd finally take the hint. Then she said something about sending me some sort of administrative assistant – an offer that I tried to decline without causing mortal offense. Sensing an opening, I asked if she could provide a budget line item for a new computer – but she spotted where I was coming from and cut me dead, saying that wasn't in HR's remit, and that was the end of it.

Anyway, I'm now looking at my watch and it turns out that it's getting on for lunch. I've lost *another* morning's prime gaming time. So I head back to my office, and just as I'm about to open the door I hear a rustling, crunching sound coming from behind it, like a giant hamster snacking down on trail mix. I can't express how disturbing this is. Rodent menaces from beyond space-time aren't supposed to show up during my meetings with HR, much less hole up in my office making disturbing noises. What's going on?

I rapidly consider my options, discarding the most extreme ones (Facilities takes a dim view of improvised ordnance discharges on Government premises), and finally do the obvious. I push the door open, lean against the battered beige filing cabinet with the jammed drawer, and ask, "Who are you and what are you doing to my *computer?*"

I intend the last phrase to come out as an ominous growl, but it turns into a strangled squeak of rage. My visitor looks up at me from behind my monitor, eyes black and beady, and cheek-pouches stuffed with – ah, there's an open can of Pringles sitting on my in-tray. "Yuh?"

"That's my computer." I'm breathing rapidly all of a sudden, and I carefully set my coffee mug down next to the light-sick petunia so that I don't drop it by accident. "Back away from the keyboard, put down the mouse, and nobody needs to get hurt." And most especially, my sixth-level cleric-sorcerer gets to keep all his experience points and gold pieces without some munchkin intruder selling them all on a dodgy auction site and re-skilling me as an exotic dancer with chloracne.

It must be my face; he lifts up his hands and stares at me nervously, then swallows his cud of potato crisps. "You must be Mr. Howard?"

I begin to get an inkling. "No, I'm the grim fucking reaper." My eyes take in more telling details: his sallow skin, the acne and straggly goatee beard. *Ye gods and little demons, it's like looking in a time-traveling mirror.* I grin nastily. "I asked you once and I won't ask you again: *Who are you?*"

He gulps. "I'm Pete. Uh, Pete Young. I was told to come here by Andy, uh, Mr. Newstrom. He says I'm your new intern."

"My new what...?" I trail off. *Andy, you're a bastard! But I repeat myself.* "Intern. Yeah, right. How long have you been here? In the Laundry, I mean."

He looks nervous. "Since last Monday morning."

"Well, this is the first anyone's told me about an intern," I explain carefully, trying to keep my voice level because blaming the messenger won't help; anyway, if Pete's telling the truth he's so wet behind the ears I could use him to water the plants. "So now I'm going to have to go and confirm that. You just wait here." I glance at my desktop. *Hang on, what would I have done five or so years ago...?* "No, on second thoughts, come with me."

The Ops wing is a maze of twisty little passageways, all alike. Cramped offices open off them, painted institutional green and illuminated by underpowered bulbs lightly dusted with cobwebs. It isn't like this on Mahogany Row or over the road in Adminis-

tration, but those of us who actually contribute to the bottom line get to mend and make do. (There's a malicious, persistent rumor that this is because the Board wants to encourage a spirit of plucky us-against-the-world self-reliance in Ops, and the easiest way to do that is to make every requisition for a box of paper clips into a Herculean struggle. I subscribe to the other, less popular theory: they just don't care.)

I know my way through these dingy tunnels; I've worked here for years. Andy has been a couple of rungs above me in the org chart for all that time. These days he's got a corner office with a blond Scandinavian pine desk. (It's a corner office on the second floor with a view over the alley where the local Chinese take-away keeps their dumpsters, and the desk came from IKEA, but his office still represents the cargo-cult trappings of upward mobility; we beggars in Ops can't be choosy.) I see the red light's out, so I bang on his door.

"Come in." He sounds even more world-weary than usual, and so he should be, judging from the pile of spreadsheet printouts scattered across the desk in front of him. "Bob?" He glances up and sees the intern. "Oh, I see you've met Pete."

"Pete tells me he's my intern," I say, as pleasantly as I can manage under the circumstances. I pull out the ratty visitor's chair with the hole in the seat stuffing and slump into it. "And he's been in the Laundry since the beginning of this week." I glance over my shoulder; Pete is standing in the doorway looking uncomfortable, so I decide to move White Pawn to Black Castle Four or whatever it's called: "Come on in, Pete; grab a chair." (The other chair is a crawling horror covered in mouse-bitten lever arch files labeled STRICTLY SECRET.) It's important to get the message across that I'm not leaving without an answer, and camping my hench-squirt on Andy's virtual in-tray is a good way to do that. (Now if only I can figure out what I'm supposed to be asking...) "What's going on?"

"Nobody told you?" Andy looks puzzled.

"Okay, let me rephrase. Whose idea was it, and what am I meant to do with him?"

"I think it was Emma MacDougal's. In Human Resources." *Oops, he said Human Resources.* I can feel my stomach sinking already. "We picked him up in a routine sweep through Erewhon space last month." (Erewhon is a new Massively Multiplayer Online Role-Playing Game that started up, oh, about two months ago, with only a few thousand players so far. Written by a bunch of spaced-out games programmers from Gothenburg.) "Boris iced him and explained the situation, then put him through induction. Emma feels that it'd be better if we trialed the mentoring program currently on roll-out throughout Admin to see if it's an improvement over our traditional way of inducting new staff into Ops, and his number came up." Andy raises a fist and coughs into it, then waggles his eyebrows at me significantly.

"As opposed to hiding out behind the wet shrubbery for a few months before graduating to polishing Angleton's gear-wheels?" I shrug. "Well, I can't say it's a *bad idea* – " Nobody ever accuses HR of having a *bad idea*; they're subtle and quick to anger, and their revenge is terrible to behold. " – but a little bit of warning would have been nice. Some mentoring for the mentor, eh?"

The feeble quip is only a trial balloon, but Andy latches onto it immediately and with evident gratitude. "Yes, I completely agree! I'll get onto it at once."

I cross my arms and grin at him lopsidedly. "I'm waiting."

"You're – " His gaze slides sideways, coming to rest on Pete. "Hmm." I can almost see the wheels turning. Andy isn't aggressive, but he's a sharp operator. "Okay, let's start from the beginning. Bob, this fellow is Peter-Fred Young. Peter-Fred, meet Mr. Howard, better known as Bob. I'm – "

" – Andy Newstrom, senior operational support manager, Department G," I butt in smoothly. "Due to the modern miracle of matrix management, Andy is my line manager but I work for someone else, Mr. Angleton, who is also Andy's boss. You probably won't meet him; if you do, it probably means you're in big trouble. That right, Andy?"

"Yes, Bob," he says indulgently, picking right up from my cue. "And this is Ops Division." He looks at Peter-Fred Young. "Your job, for the next three months, is to shadow Bob. Bob, you're between field assignments anyway, and Project Aurora looks likely to keep you occupied for the whole time – Peter-Fred should be quite useful to you, given his background."

"Project Aurora?" Pete looks puzzled. *Yeah, and me, too.*

"What is his background, exactly?" I ask. *Here it comes...*

"Peter-Fred used to design dungeon modules for a living." Andy's cheek twitches. "The earlier games weren't a big problem, but I think you can guess where this one's going."

"Hey, it's not my fault!" Pete hunches defensively. "I just thought it was a really neat scenario!"

I have a horrible feeling I know what Andy's going to say next. "The third-party content tools for some of the leading MMORPGs are getting pretty hairy these days. They're supposed to have some recognizers built in to stop the most dangerous design patterns getting out, but nobody was expecting Peter-Fred to try to implement a Delta Green scenario as a Never-

winter Nights persistent realm. If it had gone online on a public game server
– assuming it didn't eat him during beta testing – we could have been facing
a mass outbreak."

I turn and stare at Pete in disbelief. "That was him?" *Jesus, I could have been
killed!*

He stares back truculently. "Yeah. Your wizard eats rice cakes!"

And an attitude to boot. "Andy, he's going to need a desk."

"I'm working on getting you a bigger office." He grins. "This was Emma's
idea, she can foot the bill."

Somehow I *knew* she had to be tied in with this, but maybe I can turn it
to my advantage. "If Human Resources is involved, surely they're paying?"
Which means, deep pockets to pick. "We're going to need two Herman
Miller Aeron chairs, an Eames bookcase and occasional table, a desk from
some eye-wateringly expensive Italian design studio, a genuine eighty-year-
old Bonsai Californian redwood, an OC3 cable into Telehouse, and gaming
laptops. Alienware: we need lots and lots of Alienware...."

Andy gives me five seconds to slaver over the fantasy before he pricks my
balloon. "You'll take Dell and like it."

"Even if the bad guys frag us?" I try.

"They won't." He looks smug. "Because you're the best."

One of the advantages of being a cash-starved department is that nobody ever
dares to throw anything away in case it turns out to be useful later. Another
advantage is that there's never any money to get things done, like (for example) refit old offices to comply with current health and safety regulations.
It's cheaper just to move everybody out into a Portakabin in the car park and
leave the office refurb for another financial year. At least, that's what they do
in this day and age; thirty, forty years ago I don't know where they put the
surplus bodies. Anyway, while Andy gets on the phone to Emma to plead for
a budget I lead Pete on a fishing expedition.

"This is the old segregation block," I explain, flicking on a light switch.
"Don't come in here without a light or the grue will get you."

"You've got grues? Here?" He looks so excited at the prospect that I almost
hesitate to tell him the truth.

"No, I just meant you'd just step in something nasty. This isn't an adventure game." The dust lies in gentle snowdrifts everywhere, undisturbed by
outsourced cleaning services – contractors generally take one look at the
seg block and double their quote, going over the ministerially imposed
cap (which gets imposed rigorously on Ops, freeing up funds so Human

Resources can employ plant beauticians to lovingly wax the leaves on their office rubber plants).

"You called it a segregation block. What, uh, who was segregated?"

I briefly toy with the idea of winding him up, then reject it. Once you're inside the Laundry you're in it for life, and I don't really want to leave a trail of grudge-bearing juniors sharpening their knives behind me. "People we didn't want exposed to the outside world, even by accident," I say finally. "If you work here long enough it does strange things to your head. Work here too long, and other people can see the effects, too. You'll notice the windows are all frosted or else they open onto air shafts, where there aren't any windows in the first place," I add, shoving open the door onto a large, executive office marred only by the bricked-up window frame in the wall behind the desk, and a disturbingly wide trail of something shiny – I tell myself it's probably just dry wallpaper paste – leading to the swivel chair. "Great, this is just what I've been looking for."

"It is?"

"Yep, a big, empty, executive office where the lights and power still work."

"Whose was it?" Pete looks around curiously. "There aren't many sockets..."

"Before my time." I pull the chair out and look at the seat doubtfully. It was good leather once, but the seat is hideously stained and cracked. The penny drops. "I've heard of this guy. 'Slug' Johnson. He used to be high up in Accounts, but he made lots of enemies. In the end someone put salt on his back."

"You want us to work in here?" Pete asks, in a blinding moment of clarity.

"For now," I reassure him. "Until we can screw a budget for a real office out of Emma from HR."

"We'll need more power sockets." Pete's eyes are taking on a distant, glazed look and his fingers twitch mousily; "We'll need casemods, need overclocked CPUs, need fuck-off huge screens, double-headed Radeon X1600 video cards." He begins to shake. "Nerf guns, Twinkies, LAN party – "

"Pete! Snap out of it!" I grab his shoulders and shake him.

He blinks and looks at me blearily. "Whuh?"

I physically drag him out of the room. "First, before we do anything else, I'm getting the cleaners in to give it a class four exorcism and to steam clean the carpets. You could catch something nasty in there." You nearly did, I add silently. "Lots of bad psychic backwash."

"I thought he was an accountant?" says Pete, shaking his head.

"No, he was in *Accounts*. Not the same thing at all. You're confusing them with Financial Control."

"Huh? What do *Accounts* do, then?"

"They settle accounts – usually fatally. At least, that's what they used to do back in the '60s; the department was terminated some time ago."

"Um." Pete swallows. "I thought that was all a joke? This is, like, the BBFC? You know?"

I blink. The British Board of Film Classification, the people who certify video games and cut the cocks out of movies? "Did anyone tell you what the Laundry actually *does*?"

"Plays lots of deathmatches?" he asks hopefully.

"That's one way of putting it," I begin, then pause. *How to continue?* "Magic is applied mathematics. The many-angled ones live at the bottom of the Mandelbrot set. Demonology is right after debugging in the dictionary. You heard of Alan Turing? The father of programming?"

"Didn't he work for John Carmack?"

Oh, it's another world out there. "Not exactly, he built the first computers for the government, back in the Second World War. Not just codebreaking computers; he designed containment processors for Q Division, the Counter-Possession Unit of SOE that dealt with demon-ridden Abwehr agents. Anyway, after the war, they disbanded SOE – broke up all the government computers, the Colossus machines – except for the CPU, which became the Laundry. The Laundry kept going, defending the realm from the scum of the multiverse. There are mathematical transforms that can link entities in different universes – try to solve the wrong theorem and they'll eat your brain, or worse. Anyhow, these days more people do more things with computers than anyone ever dreamed of. Computer games are networked and scriptable, they've got compilers and debuggers built in, you can build cities and film goddamn movies inside them. And every so often someone stumbles across something they're not meant to be playing with and, well, you know the rest."

His eyes are wide in the shadows. "You mean, this is *government* work? Like in Deus Ex?"

I nod. "That's it exactly, kid." Actually it's more like Doom 3 but I'm not ready to tell him that; he might start pestering me for a grenade launcher.

"So we're going to, like, set up a LAN party and log onto lots of persistent realms and search 'n' sweep them for demons and blow the demons away?" He's almost panting with eagerness. "Wait'll I tell my homies!"

"Pete, you can't do that."

"What, isn't it allowed?"

"No, I didn't say that." I lead him back towards the well-lit corridors of the Ops wing and the coffee break room beyond. "I said you *can't* do that. You're under a geas. Section 111 of the Official Secrets Act says you can't tell anyone who hasn't signed the said act that Section 111 even exists, much less tell them anything about what it covers. The Laundry is one hundred percent under cover, Pete. You can't talk about it to outsiders, you'd choke on your own purple tongue."

"Eew." He looks disappointed. "You mean, like, this is *real* secret stuff. Like Mum's work."

"Yes, Pete. It's all really secret. Now let's go get a coffee and pester somebody in Facilities for a mains extension bar and a computer."

I spend the rest of the day wandering from desk to desk, filing requisitions and ordering up supplies, with Pete snuffling and shambling after me like a supersized spaniel. The cleaners won't be able to work over Johnson's office until next Tuesday due to an unfortunate planetary conjunction, but I know a temporary fix I can sketch on the floor and plug into a repurposed pocket calculator that should hold "Slug" Johnson at bay until we can get him exorcised. Meanwhile, thanks to a piece of freakish luck, I discover a stash of elderly laptops nobody is using; someone in Catering mistyped their code in their Assets database last year, and thanks to the wonders of our ongoing ISO 9000 certification process, there is no legal procedure for reclassifying them as capital assets without triggering a visit by the Auditors. So I duly issue Pete with a 1.4 gigahertz Toshiba Sandwich Toaster, enlist his help in moving my stuff into the new office, nail a WiFi access point to the door like a tribal fetish or mezuzah ("this office now occupied by geeks who worship the great god GHz"), and park him on the other side of the spacious desk so I can keep an eye on him.

The next day I've got a staff meeting at 10:00 a.m. I spend the first half-hour of my morning drinking coffee, making snide remarks in e-mail, reading Slashdot, and waiting for Pete to show up. He arrives at 9:35. "Here." I chuck a fat wallet full of CD-Rs at him. "Install these on your laptop, get on the intranet, and download all the patches you need. Don't, whatever you do, touch my computer or try to log onto my NWN server – it's called Bosch, by the way. I'll catch up with you after the meeting."

"Why is it called Bosch?" he whines as I stand up and grab my security badge off the filing cabinet.

"Washing machines or Hieronymus machines, take your pick." I head off to the conference room for the Ways and Means Committee meeting – to investigate new ways of being mean, as Bridget (may Nyarlathotep rest her soul) once explained it to me.

At first I'm moderately hopeful I'll be able to stay awake through the meeting. But then Lucy, a bucktoothed goth from Facilities, gets the bit between her incisors. She's going on in a giggly way about the need to outsource our administration of office sundries in order to focus on our core competencies, and I'm trying desperately hard not to fall asleep, when there's an odd thudding sound that echoes through the fabric of the building. Then a pager goes off.

Andy's at the other end of the table. He looks at me: "Bob, your call, I think."

I sigh. "You think?" I glance at the pager display. *Oops, so it is.* "'Scuse me folks, something's come up."

"Go on." Lucy glares at me halfheartedly from behind her lucky charms. "I'll minute you."

"Sure." And I'm out, almost an hour before lunch. Wow, so interns *are* useful for something. Just as long as he hasn't gotten himself killed.

I trot back to Slug's office. Peter-Fred is sitting in his chair, with his back to the door.

"Pete?" I ask.

No reply. But his laptop's open and running, and I can hear its fan chugging away. "Uh-huh." And the disc wallet is lying open on my side of the desk.

I edge towards the computer carefully, taking pains to stay out of eyeshot of the screen. When I get a good look at Peter-Fred I see that his mouth's ajar and his eyes are closed; he's drooling slightly. "Pete?" I say, and poke his shoulder. He doesn't move. *Probably a good thing, I tell myself. Okay, so he isn't conventionally possessed...*

When I'm close enough, I filch a sheet of paper from the ink-jet printer, turn the lights out, and angle the paper in front of the laptop. Very faintly I can see reflected colors, but nothing particularly scary. "Right," I mutter. I slide my hands in front of the keyboard – still careful not to look directly at the screen – and hit the key combination to bring up the interactive debugger in the game I'm afraid he's running. Trip an object dump, hit the keystrokes for quick save, and quit, and I can breathe a sigh of relief and look at the screen shot.

It takes me several seconds to figure out what I'm looking at. "Oh you stupid, stupid arse!" It's Peter-Fred, of course. He installed NWN and the other stuff I threw at him: the Laundry-issue hack pack and DM tools, and the creation toolkit. Then he went and did *exactly* what I told him not to do: he connected to Bosch. That's him in the screenshot between the two half-orc mercenaries in the tavern, looking very afraid.

Two hours later, Brains and Pinky are baby-sitting Pete's supine body (we don't dare move it yet), Bosch is locked down and frozen, and I'm sitting on the wrong side of Angleton's desk, sweating bullets. "Summarize, boy," he rumbles, fixing me with one yellowing rheumy eye. "Keep it simple. None of your jargon, life's too short."

"He's fallen into a game and he can't get out." I cross my arms. "I told him precisely what not to do, and he went ahead and did it. Not *my* fault."

Angleton makes a wheezing noise, like a boiler threatening to explode. After a moment I recognize it as two-thousand-year-old laughter, mummified and out for revenge. Then he stops wheezing. *Oops*, I think. "I believe you, boy. Thousands wouldn't. But you're going to have to get him out. You're responsible."

I'm *responsible*? I'm about to tell the old man what I think when a second thought screeches into the pileup at the back of my tongue and I bite my lip. I suppose I *am* responsible, technically. I mean, Pete's my intern, isn't he? I'm a management grade, after all, and if he's assigned to me, that makes me his manager, even if it's a post that comes with loads of responsibility and no actual power to, like, stop him doing something really foolish. I'm *in loco parentis*, or maybe just plain loco. I whistle quietly. "What would you suggest?"

Angleton wheezes again. "Not my field, boy, I wouldn't know one end of one of those newfangled Babbage machine contraptions from the other." He fixes me with a gimlet stare. "But feel free to draw on HR's budget line. I will make enquiries on the other side to see what's going on. But if you don't bring him back, I'll make you explain what happened to him to his mother."

"His mother?" I'm puzzled. "You mean she's one of us?"

"Yes. Didn't Andrew tell you? Mrs. Young is the deputy director in charge of Human Resources. So you'd better get him back before she notices her son is missing."

James Bond has Q Division; I've got Pinky and Brains from Tech Support. Bond gets jet packs, I get whoopee cushions, but I repeat myself. Still, at least P and B know about first-person shooters.

"Okay, let's go over this again," says Brains. He sounds unusually chipper for this early in the morning. "You set up Bosch as a server for a persistent Neverwinter Nights world, running the full Project Aurora hack pack. That gives you, oh, lots of extensions for trapping demons that wander into your realm while you trace their owners' PCs and inject a bunch of spyware, then call out to Accounts to send a black-bag team round in the real world. Right?"

"Yes." I nod. "An internet honeypot for supernatural intruders."

"Wibble!" That's Pinky. "Hey, neat! So what happened to your PFY?"

"Well..." I take a deep breath. "There's a big castle overlooking the town, with a twentieth-level sorceress running it. Lots of glyphs of summoning in the basement dungeons, some of which actually bind at run-time to a class library that implements the core transformational grammar of the Language of Leng." I hunch over slightly. "It's really neat to be able to do that kind of experiment in a virtual realm – if you accidentally summon something nasty it's trapped inside the server or maybe your local area network, rather than being out in the real world where it can eat your brains."

Brains stares at me. "You expect me to believe this kid took out a *twentieth-level sorceress?* Just so he could dick around in your dungeon lab?"

"Uh, no." I pick up a blue-tinted CD-R. Someone – not me – has scribbled a cartoon skull-and-crossbones on it and added a caption: DO'NT R3AD M3. "I've been looking at this – carefully. It's not one of the discs I gave Pete; it's one of his own. He's not *totally* clueless, for a crack-smoking script kiddie. In fact, it's got a bunch of interesting class libraries on it. He went in with a knapsack full of special toys and just happened to fuck up by trying to rob the wrong tavern. This realm, being hosted on Bosch, is scattered with traps that are superclassed into a bunch of scanner routines from Project Aurora and sniff for any taint of the real supernatural. Probably he whiffed of Laundry business – and that set off one of the traps, which yanked him in."

"How do you get *inside* a game?" asks Pinky, looking hopeful. "Could you get me into Grand Theft Auto: Castro Club Extreme?"

Brains glances at him in evident disgust. "You can virtualize any universal Turing machine," he sniffs. "Okay, Bob. What precisely do you need from us in order to get the kid out of there?"

I point to the laptop: "I need *that*, running the Dungeon Master client inside the game. Plus a class four summoning grid, and a lot of luck." My guts clench. "Make that a lot more luck than usual."

"Running the DM client – " Brains goes cross-eyed for a moment " – is it reentrant?"

"It will be." I grin mirthlessly. "And I'll need you on the outside, running the ordinary network client, with a couple of characters I'll preload for you. The sorceress is holding Pete in the third-level dungeon basement of Castle Storm. The way the narrative's set up she's probably not going to do anything to him until she's also acquired a whole bunch of plot coupons, like a cockatrice and a mind flayer's gallbladder – then she can sacrifice him and trade up to a fourth-level demon or a new castle or something. Anyway, I've got a plan. Ready to kick ass?"

I hate working in dungeons. They're dank, smelly, dark, and things keep jumping out and trying to kill you. That seems to be the defining characteristic of the genre, really. Dead boring hack-and-slash – but the kiddies love 'em. I know I did, back when I was a wee spoddy twelve-year-old. Fine, says I, we're not trying to snare kiddies, we're looking to attract the more cerebral kind of MMORPG player – the sort who're too clever by half. Designers, in other words.

How do you snare a dungeon designer who's accidentally stumbled on a way to summon up shoggoths? Well, you need a website. The smart geeks are always magpies for ideas – they see something new and it's "Ooh! Shiny!" and before you can snap your fingers they've done something with it you didn't anticipate. So you set your site up to suck them in and lock them down. You seed it with a bunch of downloadable goodies and some interesting chat boards – not the usual MY MAG1C USR CN TW4T UR CLERIC, DOOD, but actual useful information – useful if you're programming in NWScript, that is (the high-level programming language embedded in the game, which hardcore designers write game extensions in).

But the website isn't enough. Ideally you want to run a networked game server – a persistent world that your victims can connect to using their client software to see how your bunch o' tricks looks in the virtual flesh. And finally you seed clues in the server to attract the marks who know too damn much for their own good, like Peter-Fred.

The problem is, BoschWorld isn't ready yet. That's why I told him to stay out. Worse, there's no easy way to dig him out of it yet because I haven't yet written the object retrieval code – and worse: to speed up the development process, I grabbed a whole bunch of published code from one of the bigger online persistent realms, and I haven't weeded out all the spurious quests and curses and shit that make life exciting for adventurers. In fact, now that I think about it, that was going to be Peter-Fred's job for the next month. Oops.

★

Unlike Pete, I do not blunder into Bosch unprepared; I know exactly what to expect. I've got a couple of cheats up my non-existent monk's sleeve, including the fact that I can enter the game with a level eighteen character carrying a laptop with a source-level debugger – all praise the new self-deconstructing reality!

The stone floor of the monastery is gritty and cold under my bare feet, and there's a chilly morning breeze blowing in through the huge oak doors at the far end of the compound. I know it's all in my head – I'm actually sitting in a cramped office chair with Pinky and Brains hammering away on keyboards to either side – but it's still creepy. I turn round and genuflect once in the direction of the huge and extremely scary devil carved into the wall behind me, then head for the exit.

The monastery sits atop some truly bizarre stone formations in the middle of the Wild Woods. I'm supposed to fight my way through the woods before I get to the town of, um, whatever I named it, Stormville? – but sod that. I stick a hand into the bottomless depths of my very expensive Bag of Holding and pull out a scroll. "Stormville, North Gate," I intone (*Why* do ancient masters in orders of martial monks always *intone*, rather than, like, speak normally?) and the scroll crumbles to dust in my hands – and I'm looking up at a stone tower with a gate at its base and some bint sticking a bucket out of a window on the third floor and yelling, "Gardy loo." Well, *that* worked okay.

"I'm there," I say aloud.

Green serifed letters track across my visual field, completely spoiling the atmosphere: WAY KOOL, BO8. That'll be Pinky, riding shotgun with his usual delicacy.

There's a big, blue rectangle in the gateway so I walk onto it and wait for the universe to download. It's a long wait – something's gumming up Bosch. (Computers aren't as powerful as most people think; running even a small and rather stupid intern can really bog down a server.)

Inside the North Gate is the North Market. At least, it's what passes for a market in here. There's a bunch of zombies dressed as your standard dungeon adventurers, shambling around with speech bubbles over their heads. Most of them are web addresses on eBay, locations of auctions for interesting pieces of game content, but one or two of them look as if they've been crudely tampered with, especially the ass-headed nobleman repeatedly belting himself on the head with a huge, leather-bound copy of *A Midsummer Night's Dream*. "Are you guys sure we haven't been hacked?" I ask aloud. "If you could check the tripwire logs, Brains..." It's a long shot, but it might offer an alternate explanation for Pete's predicament.

I slither, sneak, and generally shimmy my monastic ass around the square, avoiding the quainte olde medieval gallows and the smoking hole in the ground that used to be the Alchemists' Guild. On the east side of the square is the Wayfarer's Tavern, and some distance to the southwest I can see the battlements and turrets of Castle Storm looming out of the early morning mists in a surge of gothic cheesecake. I enter the tavern, stepping on the blue rectangle and waiting while the world pauses, then head for the bar.

"Right, I'm in the bar," I say aloud, pulling my Project Aurora laptop out of the Bag of Holding. (Is it my imagination, or does something snap at my fingertips as I pull my hand out?) "Has the target moved?"

No JoY, Bo8.

I sigh, unfolding the screen. Laptops aren't exactly native to NWN; this one's made of two slabs of sapphire held together by scrolled mithril hinges. I stare into the glowing depths of its screen (tailored from a preexisting crystal ball) and load a copy of the pub. Looking in the back room I see a bunch of standard henchmen, -women, and -things waiting to be hired, but none of them are exactly optimal for taking on the twentieth-level lawful-evil chatelaine of Castle Storm. *Hmm, better bump one of 'em*, I decide. *Let's go for munchkin muscle.* "Pinky? I'd like you to drop a quarter of a million experience points on Grondor the Red, then up-level him. Can you do that?" Grondor is the biggest bad-ass half-orc fighter-for-hire in Bosch. This ought to turn him into a one-man killing machine.

o|< DOOD.

I can tell he's really getting into the spirit of this. The barmaid sashays up to me and winks. "Hiya, cute thing. (1) Want to buy a drink? (2) Want to ask questions about the town and its surroundings? (3) Want to talk about anything else?"

I sigh. "Gimme (1)."

"Okay. (1) G'bye, big boy. (2) Anything else?"

"(1). Get me my beer then piss off."

One of these days I'll get around to wiring a real conversational 'bot into the non-player characters, but right now they're still a bit –

There's a huge sound from the back room, sort of a creaking graunching noise. I blink and look round, startled. After a moment I realize it's the sound of a quarter of a million experience points landing on a –

"Pinky, what exactly did you up-level Grondor the Red to?"

LVL 15 CORTE5AN. LOL!!!

"Oh, great," I mutter. I'll swear that's not a real character class. A fat, manila envelope appears on the bar in front of me. It's Grondor's contract, and from the small print it looks like I've hired myself a fifteenth-level half-orc rent-boy for muscle. Which is annoying because I only get one hench-thug per game. "One of these days your sense of humor is going to get me into *really* deep trouble, Pinky," I say as Grondor flounces across the rough wooden floor towards me, a vision of ruffles, bows, pink satin, and upcurved tusks. He's clutching a violet club in one gnarly, red-nailed hand, and he seems to be annoyed about something.

After a brief and uncomfortable interlude that involves running on the walls and ceiling, I manage to calm Grondor down, but by then half the denizens of the tavern are broken and bleeding. "Grondor pithed," he lisps at me. "But Grondor thtill kickth ath. Whoth ath you wanting kicked?"

"The wicked witch of the west. You up for it?"

He blows me a kiss.

LOL!!! ROFL!!! whoops the peanut gallery.

"Okay, let's go."

Numerous alarums, excursions, and open-palm five-punches death attacks later, we arrive at Castle Storm. Sitting out in front of the cruel-looking portcullis, topped by the dismembered bodies of the sorceress's enemies and not a few of her friends, I open up the laptop. A miniature thundercloud hovers overhead, raining on the turrets and bouncing lightning bolts off the (currently inanimate) gargoyles.

"Connect me to Lady Storm's boudoir mirror." I say. (I try to make it come out as an inscrutable monkish mutter rather than *intoning*, but it doesn't work properly.)

"Hello? Who is this?" I see her face peering out of the depths of my screen, like an unholy cross between Cruella De Vil and Margaret Thatcher. She's not wearing make-up and half her hair's in curlers – *that's odd*, I think.

"This is the management," I intone. "We have been notified that contrary to statutory regulations issued by the Council of Guilds of Stormville you are running an unauthorized boarding house, to wit, you are providing accommodation for mendicant journeymen. Normally we'd let you off with a warning and a fifty-gold-piece fine, but in this particular case – "

I'm readying the amulet of teleportation, but she seems to be able to anticipate events, which is just plain wrong for a non-player character following a script. "Accommodate *this!*" she hisses, and cuts the connection dead. There's a hammering rumbling sound overhead. I glance up, then take to my heels as I wrap my arms about my head; she's animated the gargoyles, and they're taking wing, but they're still made of stone – and stone isn't known for its lighter-than-air qualities. The crashing thunder goes on for quite some time, and the dust makes my eyes sting, but after a while all that remains is the mournful honking of the one surviving gargoyle, which learned to fly on its way down, and is now circling the battlements overhead. And now it's my turn.

"Right. Grondor? Open that door!"

Grondor snarls, then flounces forwards and whacks the portcullis with his double-headed war axe. The physics model in here is distinctly imaginative, you shouldn't be able to reduce a cast-iron grating into a pile of wooden kindling, but I'm not complaining. Through the portcullis we charge, into the bowels of Castle Storm and, I hope, in time to rescue Pete.

I don't want to bore you with a blow-by-blow description of our blow-by-blow progress through Cruella's minions. Suffice to say that following Grondor is a lot like trailing behind a frothy pink main battle tank. Thuggish guards, evil imps, and the odd adept tend to explode messily very soon after Grondor sees them. Unfortunately Grondor's not very discriminating, so I make sure to go first in order to keep him away from cunningly engineered deadfalls (and Pete, should we find him). Still, it doesn't take us too long to comb the lower levels of the caverns under Castle Storm (aided by the handy dungeon editor in my laptop, which allows me to build a bridge over the Chasm of Despair and tunnel through the rock around the Dragon's Lair, which isn't very sporting but keeps us from being toasted). Which is why, after a couple of hours, I'm beginning to get a sinking feeling that Pete isn't actually here.

"Brains, Pete isn't down here, is he? Or am I missing something?"

H3Y DONT B3 5AD DOOD F1N|< OV V XP!!!

"Fuck off, Pinky, give me some useful input or just *fuck off*, okay?" I realize I'm shouting when the rock wall next to me begins to crack ominously. The hideous possibility that I've lost Pete is sinking its claws into my brain and it's worse than any Fear spell.

OK KEEP UR HAIR ON!! 15 THIS A QU3ST?? DO U N33D 2 CONFRONT SOR-CR3SS 1ST?

I stop dead. "I bloody hope not. Did you notice how she was behaving?"

Brains here. I'm grepping the server logfile and did you know there's another user connected over the intranet bridge?

"Whu – " I turn around and accidentally bump into Grondor.

Grondor says, "(1) Do you wish to modify our tactics? (2) Do you want Grondor to attack someone? (3) Do you think Grondor is sexy, big boy? (4) Exit?"

"(4)," I intone – if I leave him in a conversational state he won't be going anywhere, dammit. "Okay, Brains. Have you tracerouted the intrusion? Bosch isn't supposed to be accessible from outside the local network. What department are they coming in from?"

They're coming in from – a longish pause – somewhere in HR.

"Okay, the plot just thickened. So someone in HR has gotten in. Any idea who the player is?" I've got a sneaking suspicion but I want to hear it from Brains –

Not IRL, *but didn't Cruella act way too flexible to be a 'bot?*

Bollocks. That *is* what I was thinking. "Okay. Grondor: follow. We're going upstairs to see the wicked witch."

Now, let me tell you about castles. They don't have elevators, or fire escapes, or extinguishers. Real ones don't have exploding whoopee cushions under the carpet and electrified door-handles that blush red when you notice them, either, or an ogre resting on the second-floor mezzanine, but that's beside the point. Let me just observe that by the time I reach the fourth floor I am beginning to breathe heavily and I am getting distinctly pissed off with Her Eldritch Fearsomeness.

At the foot of the wide, glittering staircase in the middle of the fourth floor I temporarily lose Grondor. It might have something to do with the tenth-level mage lurking behind the transom with a magic flamethrower, or the simultaneous arrival of about a ton of steel spikes falling from concealed ceiling panels, but Grondor is reduced to a greasy pile of goo on the floor. I sigh and do something to the mage that would be extremely painful if he were a real person. "Is she upstairs?" I ask the glowing letters.

SUR3 TH1NG DOOD!!!

"Any more traps?"

NO!!??!

"Cool." I step over the grease spot and pause just in front of the staircase. It never pays to be rash. I pick up a stray steel spike and chuck it on the first step and it goes BANG with extreme prejudice. "Not so cool." Rinse, cycle, repeat, and four small explosions later I'm standing in front of the doorway facing the top step. No more whoopee cushions, just a twentieth-level sorceress and a minion in chains. *Happy joy.* "Pinky. Plan B. Get it ready to run, on my word."

I break through the door and enter the witch's lair.

Once you've seen one witch's den you've seen 'em all. This one is a bit glitzier than usual, and some of the furniture is nonstandard even taking into account the Laundry hack packs linked into this realm. *Where did she get the mainframe from?* I wonder briefly before considering the extremely ominous Dho-Na geometry curve in the middle of the floor (complete with a frantic-looking Pete chained down in the middle of it) and the extremely irate-looking sorceress beyond.

"Emma MacDougal, I presume?"

She turns my way, spitting blood. "If it wasn't for you meddling hackers, I'd have gotten away with it!" *Oops, she's raising her magic wand.*

"Gotten away with what?" I ask politely. "Don't you want to explain your fiendish plan, as is customary, before totally obliterating your victims? I mean, that's a Dho-Na curve there, so you're obviously planning a summoning, and this server is inside Ops block. Were you planning some sort of low-key downsizing?"

She snorts. "You stupid Ops heads, why do you always assume it's about *you?*"

"Because – " I shrug. "We're running on a server in Ops. What do you think happens if you open a gateway for an ancient evil to infest our departmental LAN?"

"Don't be naïve. All that's going to happen is Pimple-Features here is going to pick up a good, little, gibbering infestation then go spread it to Mama. Which will open up the promotion ladder once again." She stares at me, then her eyes narrow thoughtfully. "How did you figure out it was me?"

"You should have used a smaller mainframe emulator, you know; we're so starved for resources that Bosch runs on a three-year-old Dell laptop. If you weren't slurping up all our CPU resources, we probably wouldn't have noticed anything was wrong until it was too late. It had to be someone in HR, and you're the only player on the radar. Mind you, putting poor Peter-Fred in a position of irresistible temptation was a good move. How did you open the tunnel into our side of the network?"

"He took his laptop home at night. Have you swept it for spyware today?" Her grin turns triumphant. "I think it's time you joined Pete on the summoning-grid sacrifice node."

"Plan B!" I announce brightly, then run up the wall and across the ceiling until I'm above Pete.

P1AN 8 :) :) :)

The room below my head lurches disturbingly as Pinky rearranges the furniture. It's just a ninety-degree rotation, and Pete's still in the summoning grid, but now he's in the target node instead of the sacrifice zone. Emma is incanting; her wand tracks me, its tip glowing green. "Do it, Pinky!" I shout as I pull out my dagger and slice my virtual finger. Blood runs down the blade and drops into the sacrifice node –

And Pete stands up. The chains holding him to the floor rip like damp cardboard, his eyes glowing even brighter than Emma's wand. With no actual summoning vector spliced into the grid it's wide open, an antenna seeking the nearest manifestation. With my blood to power it, it's active, and the first thing it resonates with has come through and sideloaded into Pete's head. His head swivels. "Get her!" I yell, clenching my fist and trying not to wince. "She's from personnel!"

"*Personnel?*" rumbles a voice from Pete's mouth – deeper, more cultured, and infinitely more terrifying. "*Ah, I see. Thank you.*" The being wearing Pete's flesh steps across the grid – which sparks like a high-tension line and begins to smolder. Emma's wand wavers between me and Pete. I thrust my injured hand into the Bag of Holding and stifle a scream when my fingers stab into the bag of salt within. "*It's been too long.*" His face begins to lengthen, his jaw widening and merging at the edges. He sticks his tongue out: it's grayish-brown and rasplike teeth are sprouting from it.

Emma screams in rage and discharges her wand at him. A backwash of negative energy makes my teeth clench and turns my vision gray, but it's not enough to stop the second coming of "Slug" Johnson. He slithers towards her across the floor, and she gears up another spell, but it's too late. I close my eyes and follow the action by the inarticulate shrieks and the wet sucking, gurgling noises. Finally, they die down.

I take a deep breath and open my eyes. Below me the room is vacant but for a clean-picked human skeleton and a floor flecked with brown – I peer closer – slugs. *Millions* of the buggers. "You'd better let him go," I intone.

"*Why should I?*" asks the assembly of molluscs.

"Because – " I pause. *Why should he?* It's a surprisingly sensible question. "If you don't, HR – Personnel – will just send another. Their minions are infinite. But you *can* defeat them by escaping from their grip forever – if you let me lay you to rest."

"*Send me on, then,*" say the slugs.

"Okay." And I open my salt-filled fist over the molluscs – which burn and writhe beneath the white powderfall until nothing is left but Pete, curled fetally in the middle of the floor. And it's time to get Pete the hell out of this game and back into his own head before his mother, or some even worse horror, comes looking for him.

Four Fables

Peter S. Beagle

Peter S. Beagle (*www.peterbeagle.com*) lives in Oakland, California. 2006 was a special year for him: he won his first Hugo Award for the novelette "Two Hearts" (which was in competition with a story by Howard Waldrop who also appears in this volume). Everything you might want to know about his work and upcoming publications (including seven books to be published in 2007!) can be found at his web site. His latest novel is *Tamsin* (1999), and his latest story collection is *The Line Between* (2006), so a year in which seven books are to appear is truly a wonderful surprise for fantasy readers. He has everything from a new novel, a young adult novel, a collection of essays, and another story collection to several chapbooks and a forthcoming *Star Trek* nonfiction book. This is evidently the Peter S. Beagle renaissance. In a *SciFi Dimensions* interview with him about his approach to myths, legends and folklore, he remarks, "One person's myth is another person's urban legend." Here we present his "Four Fables" for you to integrate into your psyche as you like.

"Four Fables" is from *The Line Between*, in our opinion the best fantasy story collection published in 2006, and a close call – see the M. Rickert story, later in this book. The fables remind us of the *Hieroglyphic Tales* of Horace Walpole. Beagle says, "'The Fable of the Moth'" was first published in the 1960s...and owes something to Don Marquis' tales of Archy and Mehitabel. The other three were written specifically for this collection. They tend to suggest a dark – even cynical – view of the human condition, but then it has always seemed to me that fables and fabulists mostly do that. Aesop was lynched, after all, according to Herodotus."

The Fable of the Moth

Once there was a young moth who did not believe that the proper end for all mothkind was a zish and a frizzle. Whenever he saw a friend or a cousin or a total stranger rushing to a rendezvous with a menorah or a Coleman stove, he could feel a bit of his heart blacken and crumble. One evening, he called all the moths of the world together and preached to them. "Consider the sweetness of the world," he cried passionately. "Consider the moon, consider wet grass, consider company. Consider glove linings, camel's hair coats, fur stoles, feather boas, consider the heartbreaking, lost-innocence flavor of cashmere. Life is good, and love is all that matters. Why will we seek death, why do we truly hunger for nothing but the hateful hug of the candle, the bitter kiss of the filament? Accidents of the universe we may be, but we are beautiful accidents and we must not live as though we were ugly. The flame is a cheat, and love is the only."

All the other moths wept. They pressed around him by the billions, calling him a saint and vowing to change their lives. "What the world needs now is love," they cried as one bug. But then the lights began to come on all over the world, for it was nearing dinnertime. Fires were kindled, gas rings burned blue, electric coils glowed red, floodlights and searchlights and flashlights and porch lights blinked and creaked and blazed their mystery. And as one bug, as though nothing had been said, every moth at that historic assembly flew off on their nightly quest for cremation. The air sang with their eagerness.

"Come back! Come back!" called the poor moth, feeling his whole heart sizzle up this time. "What have I been telling you? I said that this was no way to live, that you must keep yourselves for love – and you knew the truth when you heard it. Why do you continue to embrace death when you know the truth?"

An old gypsy moth, her beauty ruined by a lifetime of singeing herself against nothing but arc lights at night games, paused by him for a moment. "Sonny, we couldn't agree with you more," she said. "Love is all that matters, and all that other stuff is as shadow. But there's just something about a good fire."

MORAL: *Everybody knows better. That's the problem, not the answer.*

The Fable of the Tyrannosaurus Rex

Once upon a very long ago, in a hot and steamy jungle, on an Earth that was mostly hot and steamy jungle, there lived a youngish *Tyrannosaurus Rex.* (Actually, we should probably refer to her as a *Tyrannosaurus Regina*, since she was a female, but never mind.) Not quite fully grown, she measured almost forty feet from nose to tail tip, weighed more than six tons, and had teeth the size of bananas. Although no intellectual, she was of a generally good-humored disposition, accepting with equanimity the fact that being as huge as she was meant that she was always hungry, except in her sleep. This, fortunately, she had been constructed to deal with.

Thanks to her size this Tyrannosaurus was, without a doubt, the queen of her late-Cretaceous world, which, in addition to great predators like herself, included the pack-hunting *Velociraptor*, the three-horned *Triceratops*, the

Iguanodon, with its horse/duck face, and the long-necked, whiptailed *Alamo-saurus.* But the world was populated also by assorted smaller animals – much smaller, most of them – distinguished from one another, as far as she was concerned, largely by their degree of quickness and crunchiness, and the amount of fur that was likely to get caught between her fangs. In fact, she rarely bothered to pursue them, since it generally cost her more in effort than the caloric intake was worth. She did eat them now and then, as we snap up potato chips or M&M's, but never considered them anything like a real meal, or even so much as *hors d'oeuvres.* It was just a reflex, something to do.

One afternoon, however, almost absent-mindedly, she pinned a tiny creature to earth under her left foot. It saved itself from being crushed only by wriggling frantically into the space between two of her toes, while simultaneously avoiding the rending claws in which they ended. As the Tyrannosaurus bent her head daintily to snatch it up, she heard a minuscule cry, "Wait! Wait! I have a very important message for you!"

The Tyrannosaurus – an innocent in many ways – had never had a personal message in her life, and the notion was an exciting one. Her forearms were small and weak, compared to her immense hind legs, but she was able to grip the nondescript little animal and lift him fifteen feet up, where she held him nose to nose, his beady red-brown eyes meeting her huge yellow ones with their long slit pupils. "Be quick," she advised him, "for I am hungry, and where there's one of you, there's usually a whole lot, like zucchini. What was the message you wanted to give me?"

The creature, if somewhat slow of action, atoned for this failing by thinking far faster than any dinosaur. "A large asteroid is about to crash into the Earth," it chirped brightly back at the Tyrannosaurus. "So if you happen to be nursing any unacted desires, now would be the time. To act them out, I mean," it added, realizing that the Tyrannosaurus was blinking in puzzlement at him. "It'll happen next Thursday."

"Asteroid," the Tyrannosaurus pondered. "What is an asteroid?" Before the little creature she held could answer, she asked, "Come to think of it, what's Thursday?"

"An asteroid is a rock," the animal informed her. "A big rock up in the sky, drifting through space. This one is about half the size of that mountain on the horizon, the one visible over the trees, and it's heading straight for us, and nothing can stop it. You and most other life on Earth are doomed."

"My goodness," said the Tyrannosaurus. "I'm certainly glad you told me about this." After a thoughtful moment, she inquired, "What does it all mean?"

"For you and most of your kind, absolute annihilation," the animal piped cheerfully. "For mine – evolution."

"I'm not very good with big words," the Tyrannosaurus said apologetically. "If you could..."

"You'll all be gone," the little creature said. "When the asteroid crashes into the Earth, it will raise a vast cloud of dust and debris that will circle the planet for years, cutting off all sunlight. You dinosaurs won't be able to survive the drastic change in the climate – you'll mostly vanish within a couple of generations. Then – just as when the fall of great trees makes room at last for the small ones struggling in their shadow – then we mammals will take our rightful place in the returning sun." Observing what it took to be a stricken expression on the Tyrannosaurus's yard-wide face, it added, "I'm really sorry. I just thought you should know."

"And your sort," the Tyrannosaurus ventured, "you will...evolute?"

"*Evolve*," the creature corrected her. " That means to change over time into something quite different in size or shape, or in your very nature, from what you were originally. My friend Max, for instance – smaller than I am right now – Max is going to evolve into a horse, if you'll believe it. And Louise, who came out of the sea with the rest of us, in the beginning – Louise is planning to go back there and become a whale. A blue whale, I think she said. It'll take millions of years, of course, but she's never in a hurry, Louise. And me – " here it preened itself as grandly as anyone possibly can in the grasp of a Tyrannosaurus Rex, fifteen feet in the air. "Me, I'm a sort of shrew or something right now, but I'm on my way to being a mammal with just two legs that will write books and fight wars, and won't believe in evolution. How cool is that?"

"And me?" the Tyrannosaurus asked, rather wistfully. "Everything will be changing – everyone will be turning into something else. Don't my relatives and I get to evolve at all?"

"You won't. But there's a bigger picture," the shrew reassured her. "It will take a good while, but some of your kind are going to fly, my dear. Those of your descendants who survive will find their scales turning gradually to feathers; their mighty jaws will in time become a highly adaptable beak, and they'll learn to build nests and sing songs. And hunt bugs."

"Well," said the Tyrannosaurus. "I can't say I follow all of this, but I guess it's better than being anni...annihil...what you said. But where does this Thursday come into it? What exactly is a Thursday?" "Thursday – " began the shrew, but found itself at a disadvantage in trying to explain the arbitrary concept of days, weeks, months and years to a beast who understood nothing beyond sunrise and sunset, light and dark, sun and moon. He said finally, "Thursday will happen three sleeps from now."

"Oh, *three* sleeps!" the Tyrannosaurus cried in great relief. "You should have said – I thought it was *two*! Well, there's plenty of time, then," and she promptly gulped down the shrew in one bite.

Savory, she thought. Nice crunch, too. But then again, there's that hair. They'd be better without the hair.

Turning away, she caught the scent of a nearby triceratops on the wind, and was about to start in that new and tempting direction when she was hit squarely on the back of the neck by the asteroid, blazing from its descent through the atmosphere. As advertised, its impact killed her and wiped out most of the dinosaurs in a very short while, at least by geological standards. The shrew had simply miscalculated the asteroid's arrival time – which is hardly a surprise, as he didn't really have a good grasp on Thursdays, either.

MORAL: *Gemini, Virgo, Aries or Taurus,*
      knowing our future tends to bore us,
      just like that poor Tyrannosaurus.

The Fable of the Ostrich

Once upon a time, in a remote corner of Africa, there was a young ostrich who refused to put his head in the sand at the slightest sign of danger. He strolled around unafraid, even when lions were near, cheerfully mocking his parents, his relations, and all his friends, every one of whom believed absolutely that their only safety lay in blind immobility. "It makes you invisible, foolish boy!" his father was forever shouting at him in vain. "You can't see the lion – the lion can't see you! What part of Q.E.D. don't you understand?"

"But the lion *always* sees us!" the ostrich would retort, equally exasperated. "What do you think happened to Uncle Julius? Cousin Hilda? Cousin Wilbraham? What good did hiding their stupid heads do them?"

"Oh," his father said. "Them. Well." He looked slightly embarrassed, which is hard for an ostrich. "Yes," he said. "Well, it's obvious, they moved. You mustn't *move*, not so much as a tail feather, that's half of it right there. Head out of sight and hold still, it's foolproof. Do you think your mother and I would still be here if it weren't foolproof?"

"The only thing foolproof," the young ostrich replied disdainfully, "is the fact that we can outrun lions – if we see them in time, which we can't do with our heads in the sand. That, and the fact that we can kick a lion into another time zone – which we also can't do – "

"Enough!" His father swatted at him with a wing, but missed. "We are ostriches, not eagles, and we have a heritage to maintain. *Head out of sight and hold still* – that's our legacy to you, and one day you'll thank me for it. Go away now. You're upsetting your mother."

So the young ostrich went away, angry and unconvinced. He attempted to enlist others to his cause, but not one disciple joined him in challenging this first and deepest-rooted of ostrich traditions. "You may very well be right," his friends told him, "we wouldn't be a bit surprised to see you vindicated one day. But right now there's a big, hungry-looking lion prowling over there, and if you'll excuse us..."

And they would hurry off to shove their heads deep into the coolest, softest patch of sand they could find, leaving their feathered rumps to cope with the consequences. Which suited lions well enough, on the whole, but deeply distressed the young ostrich. He continued doing everything he could to persuade other birds to change their behavior, but consistently met with such failure that he was cast down into utter despair.

It was then that he went to the Eldest Lion.

The pilgrimage across the wide savannas was a hard and perilous one, taking the young ostrich several days, even on his powerful naked legs. He would never have dared such a thing, of course, if the Eldest Lion had not long since grown toothless, mangy and cripplingly arthritic. His heavy claws were blunt and useless, more of his once-black mane fell out every time he shook his head, and he survived entirely on the loyalty of two lionesses who hunted for him, and who snarled away all challengers to his feeble rule. But he was known for a wisdom most lions rarely live long enough to achieve, and the young ostrich felt that his counsel was worth the risk of approaching him in his den. Being very young, he also felt quick enough on his feet to take the chance.

Standing within a conversational distance of the Eldest Lion's lair, he called to him politely, until the great, shaggy – and distinctly smelly – beast shambled to the cave entrance to demand, "What does my lunch want of me? I must ask you, of your kindness, lunch, to come just a little closer. My hearing is not what it was – alas, what is? A little closer, only."

The young ostrich replied courteously, without taking a further step, "I thank you for the invitation, mightiest of lords, but I am only a humble and rather unsightly fowl, unworthy even to set foot on your royal shadow. Sir,

Eldest, I have come a far journey to ask you a single simple question, after which I promise to retire to the midden-heap my folk call home and presume no more upon your grace." His mother had always placed much stress on the importance of manners.

The Eldest Lion squinted at him through cataract-fogged eyes, mumbling to himself. "Talks nicely, for a lunch. Nobody speaks properly anymore." Raising his deep, ragged voice, he inquired, "I will grant your request, civilized lunch. What wisdom will you have of me?"

For a moment the words he had come such a distance to say stuck in the young ostrich's throat (it is not true that ostriches can swallow and digest anything); but then they came tumbling out of him in one frantic burst. "Can you lions see us when we bury our heads in the sand? Are we really invisible? Because I don't think we are."

It seemed to the young ostrich that the Eldest Lion – most likely due to senility – had not understood the question at all. He blinked and sneezed and snorted, and the ostrich thought he even drooled, just a trifle. Only after some time did the ostrich realize that the Eldest Lion was, after his fashion, laughing.

"Invisible?" the ancient feline rumbled. "Invisible? Your stupidity is a legend among my people. We tell each other ostrich jokes as we sprawl in the sun after a kill, drowsily blowing away the feathers. Even the tiniest cub – even an ancestor like myself, half-blind and three-quarters dead – even we marvel at the existence of a creature so idiotic as to believe that hiding its head could keep it safe. We regard you as the gods' gift to our own idiots, the ones who can't learn to hunt anything else, and would surely starve but for you."

His laughter turned into a fusillade of spluttering coughs, and the young ostrich began to move cautiously away, because a lion's cough does not always signify illness, no matter how old he is. But the Eldest Lion called him back, grunting, "Wait a bit, my good lunch, I enjoy chatting with you. It's certainly a change from trying to make conversation with people whose jaws are occupied chewing my food for me. If you have other questions for me – though I dare not hope that a second could possibly be as foolish as that first – then, by all means, ask away." He lay down heavily, with his paws crossed in front of him, so as to appear less threatening.

"I have only one further question, great lord," the young ostrich ventured, "but I ask it with all my heart. If you were an ostrich – " here he had to pause for a time, because the Eldest Lion had gone into an even more tumultuous coughing spasm, waving him silent until he could control himself. "Tell me, if you were an ostrich, how would you conceal yourself from such as yourself? Lions, leopards, packs of hyenas and wild dogs...what would be *your* *tactic?*" He held his breath, waiting for the answer.

"It is extremely difficult for me to conceive of such an eventuality," the Eldest Lion replied grandly, "but one thing seems obvious, even to someone at the very top of the food chain. To bury your head while continuing to expose your entire body strikes me as the height of absurdity – "

"Exactly what I've been telling them and telling them!" the young ostrich broke in excitedly.

The Eldest Lion gave him a look no less imperious and menacing for being rheumy. "I ate the last person who interrupted me," he remarked to the air.

The ostrich apologized humbly, and the Eldest Lion continued, "As I was saying, the truly creative approach would be to reverse the policy, to keep the *body* hidden, leaving only the head visible – and thus, I might add, much better able to survey the situation." He paused for a moment, and then added thoughtfully, "I will confide to you, naïve lunch, that we lions are not nearly as crafty as you plainly suppose. We are creatures of habit, of routine, as indeed are most animals. Faced with an ostrich head sticking out of the sand, any lion would blink, shake his own head, and seek a meal somewhere else. I can assure you of this."

"Bury the *body*, not the head! Yes...yes...oh, *yes!*" The young ostrich was actually dancing with delight, which is a rare thing to see, and even the Eldest Lion's wise, weary, wicked eyes widened at the sight. "Thank you, sir – sir, thank you! What a wonder, imagine – you, a lion, have changed the course of ostrich history!" About to race off, he hesitated briefly, saying, "Sir, I would gladly let you devour me, out of gratitude for this revelation, but then there would be no one to carry the word back to my people, and that would be unforgivable of me. I trust you understand my dilemma?"

"Yes, yes, oh, *yes*," the Eldest Lion replied in grumbling mimicry. "Go away now. I see my lionesses coming home, bringing me a much tastier meal than gristly shanks and dusty feathers. Go away, silly lunch."

The two lionesses were indeed returning, and the young ostrich evaded their interest, not by burying any part of himself in the sand or elsewhere, but by taking to his heels and striding away at his best speed. He ran nearly all the way home, so excited and exalted he was by the inspiration he carried. Nor did he stop to rest, once he arrived, but immediately began spreading the words of wisdom that he had received from the Eldest Lion. "The *body*, not the head! All these generations, and we've been doing it all wrong! It's the *body* we bury, not the head!" He became an evangel of the new strategy, traveling tirelessly to proclaim his message to any and every ostrich who would listen. "It's the *body*, not the head!"

Some time afterward, one of the Eldest Lion's lionesses, who had been away visiting family, reported noticing a number of ostriches who, upon sighting her, promptly dug themselves down into the sand until only their heads, perched atop mounds of earth, remained visible, gazing down at her out of round, solemn eyes. "You've never seen anything like it," she told him. "They looked like fuzzy cabbages with beaks."

The Eldest Lion stared at her, wide-eyed as one of the ostriches. "They bought it?" he growled in disbelief. "Oh, you're kidding. They really...with their heads *really* sticking up? All of them?"

"Every one that *I* saw," the lioness replied. "I never laughed so much in my life."

"They bought it," the Eldest Lion repeated dazedly. "Well, I certainly hope you ate a couple at least, to teach them...well, to teach them *something*." He was seriously confused.

But the lioness shook her head. "I told you, I was laughing too hard even to *think* about eating." The Eldest Lion retired to the darkest corner of his cave and lay down. He said nothing further then, but the two lionesses heard him muttering in the night, over and over, "Who knew? Who knew?"

And from that day to this, unique to that region of Africa, all ostriches respond to peril by burying themselves instantly, leaving only their heads in view. No trick works every time; but considering that predators are almost invariably reduced to helpless, hysterical laughter at the ridiculous sight – lions have a tendency to ruptures, leopards to actual heart attacks – the record of survival is truly remarkable.

MORAL: *Stupidity always wins, as long as it's stupid enough.*

The Fable of the Octopus

Once, deep down under the sea, down with the starfish and the sting rays and the conger eels, there lived an octopus who wanted to see God.

Octopi are among the most intelligent creatures in the sea, and shyly thoughtful as well, and this particular octopus spent a great deal of time in profound pondering and wondering. Often, curled on the deck of the sunken ship where he laired, he would allow perfectly edible prey to swim or scuttle by, while he silently questioned the *here* and the *now*, the *if* and the *then*, and

– most especially – the *may* and the *might* and the *why*. Even among his family and friends, such rumination was considered somewhat excessive, but it was his way, and it suited him. He planned eventually to write a book of some sort, employing his own ink for the purpose. It was to be called *Concerns of a Cephalopod*, or possibly *Mollusc Meditations*.

Being as reflective as he was, the octopus had never envisioned God in his own image. He had met a number of his legendary giant cousins, and found them vulgar, insensitive sorts, totally – and perhaps understandably – preoccupied with nourishing their vast bodies; utterly uninterested in speculation or abstract thought. As for his many natural predators – the hammerhead and tiger shark, the barracuda, the orca, the sea lion, the moray eel – he dismissed them all in turn as equally shallow, equally lacking in the least suggestion of the celestial, however competent they might be at winkling his kind out of their rocky lairs and devouring them. The octopus was no romantic, but it seemed to him that God must of necessity have a deeper appreciation than this of the eternal mystery of everything, and surely other interests besides mating and lunch. The orca offered to debate the point with him, from a safe distance, before an invited audience, but the octopus was also not a fool.

For a while he did consider the possibility that the wandering albatross might conceivably be God. This was an easy notion for an octopus to entertain, since he glimpsed the albatross only when he occasionally slithered ashore in the twilight, to hunt the small crabs that scurried over the sand at that hour. He would look up then – difficult for an octopus – and sometimes catch sight of the great white wings, still as the clouds through which they slanted down the darkening sky. "So alone," he would think then. "So splendid, and so alone. What other words would suit the nature of divinity?"

But even the beauty and majesty of the albatross could never quite satisfy the octopus's spiritual hunger. It seemed to him that something else was essential to fulfilling his vision of God, and yet he had no word, no image, for what it should be. In time this came to trouble him to the point where he hardly ate or slept, but only brooded in his shipwreck den, concerning himself with no other question. His eight muscular arms themselves took sides in the matter, for each had its own opinion, and they often quarreled and wrestled with each other, which he hardly noticed. When anxious relatives came to visit, he most often hid from them, changing color to match wood or stone or shadow, as octopi will do. They were strangers to him; he no longer recognized any of them anymore.

Then, as suddenly as he himself might once have pounced out of dark-

ness to seize a flatfish or a whelk, a grand new thought took hold of him.
What if the old fisherman – the white-bearded one who sometimes rowed
out to poke around his ship with a rusty trident when low tide exposed its
barnacled hull and splintered masts – what if he might perhaps be God? He
was poorly clad, beyond doubt, and permanently dirty, but there was a certain dignity about him all the same, and a bright imagination in his salt-red-
dened eyes that even the orca's eyes somehow lacked. More, he moved as
easily on the waters as on land, both by day and night, seemingly not bound
to prescribed sleeping and feeding hours like all other creatures. What if,
after all the octopus's weary time of searching and wondering, God should
have been searching for him?

Like every sea creature, the octopus knew that any human being holding
any sharp object is a danger to everyone within reach, never to be trusted with
body or soul. Nevertheless, he was helpless before his own curiosity; and the
next time the fisherman came prowling out with the dawn tide, the octopus
could not keep from climbing warily from the ship's keel...to the rudder...
then to the broken, dangling taffrail, and clinging there to watch the old
man prying and scraping under the hull, filling the rough-sewn waterproof
bag at his belt with muddy mussels and the occasional long-necked clam.
He was muddy to the waist himself, and smelled bad, but he hummed and
grunted cheerfully as he toiled, and the octopus stared at him in great awe.

At last it became impossible for the octopus to hold his yearning at bay
any longer. Taking his courage in all eight arms, he crawled all the way up
onto the deck, fully exposed to the astonished gaze of the old fisherman.
Haltingly, but clearly, he asked aloud, "Are you God?"

The fisherman's expression changed very slowly, passing from hard,
patient resignation through dawning disbelief on the way to a kind of worn
radiance. "No, my friend," he responded finally. "I am not God, no more
than you. But I think you and I are equally part of God as we stand here,"
and he swept his arm wide to take in all the slow, dark shiver of the sea as it
breathed under the blue and silver morning. "Surely we two are not merely
surrounded by this divine splendor – we both belong to it, we are of it, now
and for always. How else should it be?"

"The sea," the octopus said slowly. "The sea..."

"And the land," said the fisherman. "And the sky. And the firelights glittering beyond the sky. All things taken together form the whole, including things like an octopus and an old man, who play their tiny parts and
wonder."

"My thoughts and questions were too small...I have lived in God all my life, and never known. Is this truly what you tell me?"

"Just so," the old man beamed. "Just so."

The octopus was speechless with joy. He stretched forth a tentative tentacle, and the fisherman took firm hold of it in his own rough hand. As they stood together, both of them equally enraptured by their newfound accord, the octopus asked shyly, "Do you suppose that God is aware that we are here, within It – part of It?"

"I have no idea," the fisherman replied placidly. "What matters is that *we* know."

There was a rough thump as the boat tilted suddenly starboard and nose down, its gentle rocking halted. The sea lowered, falling away from the boat in a great rush, exposing faded paint and barnacles to the air. Shifting gravel and rock clawed at the hull and rudder. The octopus, automatically exerting his suckers against the deck, was unmoved, but the fisherman went tumbling, and above and below and around them the world itself seemed to open a great mouth and draw breath ever more steadily toward the west.

"And that?" the octopus inquired. He pointed with a second tentacle toward the naked expanse of ocean floor over which the tide had withdrawn almost to the horizon – surest sign of an approaching tsunami. "Is that also part of God, like us?"

"I am afraid so," replied the old fisherman, braced now against the slanting rail. "Along with typhoons, stinging jellyfish, my wife's parents and really bad oysters. In such a case, I regard it as no sin to head for the high ground. The shore is far, true, but I was fast on my feet as a young man and this life has kept me fit. I will live, and buy another boat, and fish again."

"I wish you well," said the octopus, "but I am afraid my own options are somewhat more constrained. For escape I require the freedom of the deep sea, which is now entirely out of reach. No. God's great shrug will be here soon enough. I will watch it come, and when it arrives I will give it both our greetings."

"You'll be killed," said the fisherman.

The octopus was hardly equipped to smile, but the fisherman could hear one in his voice all the same. "I shall still be with God."

"That particular form of deep metaphysical appreciation will come to you soon enough without the help of fatalism or fifty-foot waves," said the fisherman, pulling the half-filled canvas bag from his belt. "Besides, *our* conversation has just begun."

Quick as the eels he was so good at catching, the fisherman slid over the rail and dropped to the exposed seabed. Once there he knelt down and pulled the open canvas bag back and forth through the silty, cross-cut shallows, losing his catch, but harvesting a full crop of seawater.

"Well? Are you coming?" the fisherman shouted up to the octopus. He held out the brimming bag exactly like the promise it was. "Time and tide, my many-armed friend. Time and tide!"

In the years that followed – and these were many, for the fisherman and the octopus did survive the tsunami, just – these two unlikely philosophers spent a great deal of time together. The fisherman found in the octopus a companion who shared all his interests, including Schopenhauer, Kierkegaard (whom the octopus found "a trifle nervous"), current events both above and below the water, and favorite kinds of fish. The octopus, in turn, learned more than he had ever imagined learning about the worlds of space and thought, and in time he even wrote his book. After suffering rejections from all the major publishing houses, it finally caught the attention of an editor at a Midwestern university press. That worthy, favoring the poetic over the literal, tacked *Eight Arms to Hold You* above the manuscript's original title – *Octopoidal Observations* – advertised the book as allegory, and watched it enjoy two and a half years on the New Age bestseller lists. Every three months he dutifully sent a royalty check and a forwarded packet of fan letters to a certain coastal post office box; and if the checks were never cashed, well, what business was it of his? Authors were eccentric – no one knew that better than he, as he said often.

The octopus's book found no underwater readership, of course, since in the ocean, just as on land, reviewers tend to be sharks. But the one-sidedness and anonymity of his fame never troubled him. When not visiting the fisherman, he was content to nibble on passing hermit crabs and drowse among the rocks in a favorite tide pool (his own sunken hulk having been smashed to as many flinders as the fisherman's old boat), thinking deeply, storing up questions and debating points to spring on his patient and honorable friend.

And he never asked if anyone or anything was God, not ever again. He didn't have to.

MORAL: *The best answer to any question? It's always a surprise.*

The Potter's Daughter

Martha Wells

Martha Wells (*www.marthawells.com*) lives in College Station, Texas. She has published eight novels to date, seven of which are fantasy, as well as a number of short stories. The most famous of her novels are *The Element of Fire* (1993), which was nominated for several awards and introduced her fantasy world of Ile-Rien, and *The Death of the Necromancer* (1998), which was a Nebula Award nominee for best novel. She is a very active science fiction fan and was the chairman of the Texas convention AggieCon 17.

"The Potter's Daughter" is the first of several stories in this book from *Elemental*, edited by Alethea Kontis and Steven Savile, and one of the best anthologies of the year. This is a prequel story to *The Element of Fire*. Kade, who is to become a central character of that book, is a girl, half-human, half-fairy. Wells says, "One of the themes of *The Element of Fire* is Kade coming to terms with the fact that she's more human than fairy... 'The Potter's Daughter' is about the thing that really made her start to confront those feelings." But there is also a darker side to the story: an author's coming to terms with the fact that some people may not *have* feelings for the people who care about them.

THE POTTER'S DAUGHTER sat in the late afternoon sun outside the stone cottage, making clay figures and setting them out to dry on the flat slate doorstep. A gentle summer breeze stirred the oak and ash leaves and the dirty grey kerchief around her dirty blond hair.

Someone was coming up the path.

She could hear that he was without horse, cart, or company, and as he came toward her through the trees she saw that he was tall, with dark curly hair and a beard, with a pack and a leather case slung over one shoulder. He was unarmed, and dressed in a blue woolen doublet, faded and threadbare, brown breeches and brown top boots. The broad-brimmed hat he wore had seen better days, but the feathers in it were gaily colored. Brief disappointment colored her expression; she could tell already he wasn't her quarry.

Boots crunched on the pebbles in the yard, then his shadow fell over her and he said, "Good day. Is this the way to Riversee?"

She continued shaping the wet clay, not looking up at him. "Just follow this road to the ford."

"Thank you, my lady Kade."

Now she did look up at him, in astonishment. Part of the astonishment was at herself, that she could still be so taken by surprise. She dropped the clay and stood, drawing a spell from the air.

Watching her with delight, he said, "Some call you Kade Carrion, because that is the sort of name given to witches. But the truth of the matter is that you are the daughter of the dead King Fulstan and Moire, a woman said to be the Dame of Air and Darkness of the fayre." He was smiling at her. His eyes were blue and guileless, and he had a plain open face.

Kade stopped, hands lifted, spell poised to cast. Names could be power, depending on how much one knew. But he was making no move toward her. Intrigued, she folded her arms and asked, "Who soon to be in hell are you?"

"I know all the tales of your battle with the court, the tricks you play on them," he told her, his expression turning serious. "But the story I tell of you is the one about the young gentlewoman of Byre, who died of heartbreak in the Carmelite Convent's spring garden when the prince of a rival city took her maidenhead and mocked her for it afterwards."

Kade lifted an ironic brow. "I remember the occasion. I didn't realize how entertaining it was. Finding an untidy dead woman in my favorite garden was not the high point of my day." It was incredible that he had recognized her; no one in their right mind would expect a half-fay half-human witch to be barefoot and wearing a peasant's muddy dress. As a rule the fay were either grotesquely ugly or heartbreakingly beautiful. Kade was neither. Her eyes were merely grey, her skin tended to brown or redden rather than maintain an opalescent paleness, and her features were unfashionably sharp. She had never looked like anyone expected her to look and this was why she had never expected anyone to recognize her when she didn't want to be recognized.

Oblivious, he continued, "You took on the appearance of the poor lady and waited there, and when the prince returned – "

"He found me instead, and we all know what happened to him then, don't we?"

"Yes," he agreed readily. "You found that the little idiot had consented, and that she had been as guilty of bad judgment and weak nature as he was guilty of being a rake. So instead of killing him you cursed him with a rather interesting facial deformity to teach him better manners."

Kade frowned, startled in spite of herself. She had never heard anyone tell the incident in that light. It was astonishingly close to her own point of view. "And what does that tell you?"

"That you have a sense of justice," he assured her, still serious. "I've told many stories of you, and it's one of the things about you that always impressed me."

Kade considered him carefully. He evidently knew his danger and didn't shrink from it, though he hadn't exactly dared her to be rid of him. It had been a long time since anyone had spoken to her this way, with a simple fearless acceptance. Kade found herself saying, "She didn't perish dramatically of heartbreak, you know. She killed herself."

He shifted the pack on his shoulder and shook his head regretfully. "It's all the same in the end." He looked up at her, his gaze sharp. "But I'm here now to tell the story of the potter of Riversee who was murdered, and how you avenged her. I'm Giles Verney, a balladeer."

The balladeer part she could have guessed, but she still wasn't sure what to make of this man. *Surely he can't be simply what he seems,* she thought. People were never what they seemed. "Very well, Giles Verney, how did you know me?"

"There's a portrait of you in the manor at Islanton. It's by Greanco, whom you must remember, as he was court artist when – "

"I remember," she interrupted him. The only other portrait of her had hung in the Royal Palace in Vienne, and was probably long destroyed. Greanco was a seventh son and had the unconscious ability to put a true representation of the soul of his subject into his work. Kade could weave glamour into an effective disguise, but hadn't bothered for the inhabitants of Riversee, who had never seen her before. "You came here for the story of the dead potter."

Giles looked toward the door of the cottage. "I was in Marbury and heard about it from the magistrate there." He shook his head, his mouth set in a grim line. "It's a shocking thing to happen."

Maybe if I show him exactly how shocking it is he'll go away, she thought. She said, "See for yourself."

He followed her into the cottage with less hesitation than she would have expected, but stopped in the doorway. It was dark and cool and flies buzzed in the damp still air. The plaster walls were stained with dried blood and the rough plank floor littered with the glazed pieces of the potter's last work, mixed with smashed furniture and tumbled cooking pots. After a quiet moment he asked, "Do you know what did this?"

She hesitated, but his story of the gentlewoman of Byre alone had bought him this answer. "Yes."

Giles stepped forward, stooping to pick a piece of wooden comb out of the rubble. His face was deeply troubled. "Was it human?"

"I don't know. But you'd be surprised how often something like this is done by a man, despite the number of tales where giant hands come down chimneys." Kade rubbed the bridge of her nose. She was tired and the whole long day had apparently been for nothing. She made her voice sharp, wanting to frighten him. "Now why don't you go away? This isn't a game and I'm not known for my patience."

He looked up at her, the death in the poor little room reflected in his eyes. As if it was the most self-evident thing in the world, he said patiently, "There has to be an end to the story, my lady."

Stubborn idiot, if you are what you seem, Kade thought wearily. "There might be no end. I've waited all day here and all I caught was you, a human mayfly."

His expression turned quizzical. "You're pretending to be another potter?"

"Clever of you to notice." Kade regarded the thatched ceiling sourly. The inhabitants of Riversee knew her only as the potter's daughter, come from another village to see to her mother's body and continue her craft. But now Giles' recognition of her made her wonder. Had she fooled anyone? Did the whole village whisper of it behind her back?

"Do you know why it was done?" Giles dropped the comb and got to his feet, dusting his hand off on his doublet.

She wouldn't give him that answer. "No."

"She was killed because potters are sacred to the old faith, or you wouldn't be here." Giles glanced around the room again, frowning in thought. "Could it have been the Church?"

Kade shrugged, scratching her head under the kerchief. "The local priest is about as old as his god's grandfather. I'm not discounting misplaced religious fervor, but he hasn't the strength or the temperament." As for the rest of Riversee, they might be baptized in the Church and pay their tithes regularly, but they still left fruit and flowers for the nameless spirits of the water and the wood, as well as the fay. Then she glared at him, because he had drawn her in again and she had hardly noticed.

Giles nodded. "That's well, but as you say, it's best not to discount it altogether. What do you plan next?"

She stared at him incredulously. "Are you mad?"

He smiled, with the air of someone waiting for a joke to be explained so he could laugh too. "Why do you say that?"

Kade clapped a hand to her forehead in exasperation. "In all the stories you've supposedly told of me, did it ever occur to you that I'm easily angered and don't appreciate human company?"

Apparently this hadn't occurred to him. He was aghast. "Don't you want the truth told?"

"Not particularly, no." Kade waved her arms in frustration. She still couldn't believe she was having this conversation.

"Why?" he demanded.

"Because it's my concern," she said pointedly.

"My concern is to tell tales. This would make a very good tale," he assured her, all earnest persuasion.

Gritting her teeth in frustration, Kade pulled a bit of yarn off her belt and knotted it into a truthcharm. The strands held together and she knew he believed what he said, and she was enough of a judge of character to know that he wasn't merely overdramatizing himself. She took a deep breath, flicking the charm away, and tried to reason with him. "That's all well and good, Giles, but I've made this my battle, and I don't need interference."

"People will tell things to a balladeer they wouldn't think of saying to any other stranger," he persisted. "I could be a great help to you."

Apparently reason worked as well with him as it would with the birds in the trees. "I don't need help, either." Exasperated, she stepped out of the shadowed cottage into the bright sunlight of the dirt yard.

He followed, the leather case he carried bumping against the doorframe with a suspicious twang. Kade hesitated, her attention caught. "What's in there?" she asked warily.

He patted it fondly. "A viola d'amore."

Despite her best intentions, she found herself eyeing the case, torn between caution and greed. Like all her mother's people, she had a weakness for human music. She conquered it and shook her head, thinking, *If I wanted to trap myself, I would send just such a man. Inoffensive and kind, easy to speak to, with a legitimate purpose for being here.* "I want you to leave, on your own, or I'll make you."

"Is it trust? Wait, here's this." Giles set his pack on the ground, knelt to fish a small fruit knife out and used it to cut off a lock of his hair. He held it up to her. "There's trust on my part. This should be enough to show you that there can be trust on yours."

She took it from him mechanically. That was trust. For a man without any magical knowledge it was also the greatest foolishness. For someone who knew as much about her as he plainly did it bordered on insanity.

She sighed. He might have a touch of the sight; the best balladeers did.

Whatever it was, she really couldn't see her way clear to killing him.

No need to tell him that immediately. She lifted a brow, regarding him thoughtfully. "Did you ever hear the story of the balladeer who spent the rest of his life as a tree?"

Kade led Giles through the crumbling town walls and into the cluster of cottages that surrounded Riversee's single inn. The small houses on either side of the rough cart track were made of piled stone with slate or thatched roofs, each in its own little yard with dilapidated outbuildings, dung heaps, and overgrown garden plots. The ground was deeply rutted by wagon wheels, dusty where it wasn't muddy with discarded slops. The nearby post road made Riversee more cosmopolitan than most villages, but the passersby still watched Giles narrowly. They had become used to Kade, and a few nodded greetings to her.

As they passed under the arched wagongate of the inn's walled yard, Kade said quietly, "Tell your stories of someone else, Giles. I can be dangerous when I'm embarrassed." She added ruefully, *And I've embarrassed myself enough, thank you, I don't need any help at it.*

He smiled at her good-naturedly, not as if he disbelieved her, but as if it was her perfect right to be dangerous whenever she chose.

The inn was two stories high, with a shaded second-story balcony overlooking outside tables where late afternoon drinkers gathered with the chickens, children, and dogs in the dusty yard. A group of travelers, their feathered hats and the elaborate lace of their collars and cuffs grimy with road dust, argued vehemently around one of the tables. To the alarm of bystanders, one of them was using the butt of his wheellock to pound on the boards for emphasis. Kade recognized them as couriers, probably from royalist troops engaged in bringing down the walls of some noble family's ancestral home. Months ago the court had ordered the destruction of all private fortifications to prevent feuding and rebellious plots among the petty nobility. This didn't concern Kade, whose private fortifications rested on the bottom of a lake, and were invisible to all but the most talented eyes.

Kade took a seat on the edge of the big square well to watch Giles approach the locals. The men seated at the long plank table eyed him with suspicion as the balladeer started to open the leather case he carried. The suspicion faded into keen interest as Giles took out the viola d'amore.

Traveling musicians were usually welcomed gladly and balladeers who could bring news of other towns and villages even more so. Within moments they would be fighting to tell him their only news – the grim story of the potter's death, or at least what little they knew of it. Kade stirred the mud near the well with her big toe. She was disgusted, mostly with herself. She knew why the potter had been killed well enough – to attract her attention.

In the old faith, the villages honored the fay in the hopes that the erratic and easily angered creatures would leave them alone. Riversee was dedicated to Moire, Kade's mother, and Kade could only see the death of the village's sacred potter as a direct challenge. A few years ago it might have pleased her, this invitation to battle, but now it only threatened to make her bored. She wasn't sure what had changed; perhaps she was growing tired of games altogether.

That night, seated atop one of the rough tables in the inn's common room, Giles picked out an instrumental treatment of a popular ballad, and watched Kade. She sat near the large cooking hearth in the center of the room, regarding the crowd with an amused eye as she tapped one bare foot to the music. The inn was crowded with a mix of locals and travelers from the nearby post road. Both the magistrate and the elderly parish priest were in attendance; the first to count the number of wine jugs emptied for the Vine-growers' Excise and the second to discourage the patrons from emptying the jugs at all. Smoke from clay pipes and tallow candles and the heat of the fire made the room close and muggy. The din of talk and shouted comments almost drowned the clear tone of the viola, but whenever Giles stopped playing enraged listeners hurled crockery at him.

If Giles hadn't known better he would've thought the dim flickering light kind to the rather plain woman who called herself the old potter's daughter. But when firelight glittered off a wisp of pale hair as she leaned forward to catch some farmer's joke, he saw something else instead. *The daughter of the spirit dame of air and darkness, and a brute of a king*, Giles thought, and added a restless undercurrent to the plaintive ballad. Smiling at his folly, he bent his head over the viola.

Over the noisy babble and the music there were voices in the entryway. Two men with a party of servants entered the common room. One was blond and slight, with sharp handsome features and a downy beard. His manner was offhand and easy as he said something with a laugh to one of the servants behind him. His companion could not have been a greater contrast if nature had deliberately intended it. He was tall, muscled like a bull, with dark greasy hair and rough features. Both men were well-turned out, though not in the latest city style, and Giles labeled them as hedge gentry.

He also had a good eye for his audience, and saw tension infect the room like a plague in the newcomers' wake. There was muttering and an uneasy shifting among the local people, though the travelers seemed oblivious to it. In Giles' experience the nobility of this province were little better than gentlemen farmers and usually got on quite well with their villages and tenants, except for the usual squabbles over dovecotes and rights to the mill. Obviously the relationship in Riversee was somewhat strained.

Seated at the table Giles was using as a stage were the grizzled knife-grinder who worked in the innyard, a toothless grandmother that might have been a hundred years old, and a farmer in the village to sell pigs. Giles nodded toward the new arrivals and asked softly, "And who is that?"

The knife-grinder snorted into his tankard. "The big one is Hugh Warrender. Some distant kin of the Duke of Marais."

"Fifth cousin, twice removed," the piping voice of the old woman added.

The farmer said, "Fifth cousin...? Quiet, you daft old – "

"The boy is Fortune Devereux," the knife-grinder continued, oblivious to his companions' comments. "He's a brother from the wrong side of the bed, come up from Marleyton."

"From Banesford," the old woman put in, almost shouting over the farmer's attempts to keep her quiet.

"He first came here two years ago." The grinder shrugged. "Warrender's not well thought of, but Devereux' not so bad."

"Wrong!" The old woman glanced suspiciously around the room and lowered her voice to a shriek. "He's worse, far worse!"

Kade watched as a table was cleared for Warrender and his men near her seat beside the hearth, a process which involved a good deal of shouting, jostling, and imprecations. As the group argued with the landlord, her eyes fell on the blond Devereux. He was an attractive man, but she wasn't sure that was what had drawn her eye. There was something else about him, something in his eyes, the way he moved his hands as he made a placating gesture to the ruffled landlord. Whatever the something was, it made the back of her neck prickle in warning. She was so occupied by it that she was caught completely unawares when Warrender turned with a growl and backhanded a grubby potboy into the fire.

No time for thought or spell, her stool clattered as Kade launched herself forward. She landed hard on her knees, catching the boy around the waist before he stumbled into the flames.

Thwarted, Warrender snarled and lifted a hand to strike both of them. Kade knelt in the ashes, the fearful boy clutching a double handful of her hair. "Yes, it would hurt me," she said quietly to the madness in Warrender's face. "But it would also make me very, very angry."

Something in her face froze Warrender. He stared at her, breathing hard, but didn't drop his arm. The moment dragged on.

Then Fortune Devereux stepped forward, catching his brother by the shoulder. Past Warrender's bulky form Kade met the younger man's gaze. Though his expression was sober, his eyes danced with laughter. *Yes*, she thought, her grip on the boy unconsciously tightening, *Oh yes. And now I know.*

The tension held as Warrender hesitated, like a confused and angry bull, then he laughed abruptly and let Devereux lead him away.

Kade felt the potboy shiver in relief and released him. He scrambled up and darted away through the crowd. She was aware that across the room Giles was on his feet, that an older man had him by the wrist, trying to pry a heavy wooden stool out of his hand. As Warrender and the others moved away, Giles forced himself to relax and let the man take the makeshift club. He retrieved the viola from the table where he had dropped it and sat down heavily on the bench. She saw his hands were shaking as he rubbed at an imperfection on the instrument's smooth surface.

As the rest of his party took their seats, Devereux strolled over to the balladeer's table. He spoke, smiling, and tipped his hat. Giles looked up at him warily, gave him a grudging nod.

Kade looked away, to keep from betraying any uneasiness. Devereux had marked Giles' reaction, had seen him ready to leap to her defense. *That*, she thought, *cannot mean anything good.*

"What did he say to you?" Kade's voice floated down from the cavernous darkness of the stable's loft.

"Nothing." Giles had finished wrapping the viola d'amore in its oiled leather case. He was not sure when Kade had gotten into the loft or how. The stable, the traditional sleeping place of itinerant musicians and entertainers, was warm and dark except for the faint glow of moonlight through the cracks in the boards. The horses and mules penned or stalled along the walls made a continuous soft undercurrent of quiet snorts and stamping as they jostled one another. Straw dust floated down from above and into Giles' hair. He stretched slowly, trying to ease the knots out of his aching back. This had not been one of his better nights.

He knew he was a fool, but he would rather no one else know it; when Warrender had been a breath away from knocking Kade into the fire, he had come dangerously close to exposing his feelings. *She's the most dangerous woman in Ile-Rien*, he told himself ruefully. *She doesn't need your defense*. Except in his songs maybe, that spoke the truth about her when others lied.

"I know he said something to you, I saw his lips move," she persisted impatiently.

"Nothing that meant anything. Only gloating, I think. He said he was sorry for the disturbance." Giles hesitated. "What would you have done?"

"When?"

Irritated, he replied more sharply than he meant to. "When that hulking bastard was about to push you into the fire, when do you think?"

"I wouldn't turn to dust at the first lick of flame, you know." There was a pause. "I did have in mind a certain charm for the spontaneous ignition of gunpowder. And considering where he carried his pistol – " She added, "Devereux made his brother do it, you know."

Giles turned to look up at the dark loft, startled. "What?"

"Warrender's under a binding spell. You could see it in his eyes."

"Devereux is a sorcerer?" Giles frowned.

Her voice was lightly ironic. "Since he can do a binding spell, it's the logical conclusion."

"But why would he do that? Did he kill the potter?"

"Assuredly."

Giles gestured helplessly. "But why?"

She sounded exasperated. "I'm only an evil fay, ballad-maker, I don't have all the answers to all the questions in the world."

Giles drew a deep breath, summoning patience. Then he smiled faintly to himself. "My lady Kade, the playwright Thario always said that it was how we behave in a moment of impulse that told the true tale of our souls. And you, in your moment of impulse, kept a boy from being pushed into a fire. What do you say to that?"

An apple sailed upward out of the loft, reached the peak of its ascent, then dropped to graze his left ear. There was a faint scrabble and a brief glint of moonlight from above as a trap door opened somewhere in the roof. "My mother was the queen of air and darkness, Giles," her voice floated down as if from a great height. "And darkness...."

Giles rolled over, scratching sleepily at the fleas that had migrated from his straw-filled pallet. The stable had become uncomfortably warm and the summer night was humid. The sound of a woman sobbing softly woke him immediately. Wiping sweat from his forehead, he sat up and listened. It was coming from the stableyard, the side away from the inn.

He pushed to his feet and pulled his shirt on. Moonlight flickered down through the cracks in the high roof. As he crossed the hay-strewn floor a horse stretched a long neck over a stall and tried to bite him.

The sobbing was slightly louder. It seemed to blend with the whisper of the breeze outside, forming an ethereal lament. Giles stopped, one hand on the latch of the narrow portal next to the large wagon door, some instinct making him wary.

Even through tears, the voice was silvery, bell-like. Odd. If the woman was under attack by whatever had killed the potter, she wouldn't be merely crying quietly.

On the chance that this was some private lover's quarrel and that interruptions, no matter how well-meant, would be unwelcome, he groped for the rickety ladder in the darkness and climbed to the loft. The window shutters were open to the breeze and the big space was awash in moonlight. The hay-strewn boards creaked softly as Giles crossed it and crouched in front of the window.

A woman was pacing on the hardpacked earth in front of the stable, apparently alone. Her hair was colorless in the moonlight, and she wore a long shapeless robe of green embroidered with metallic threads. She swayed as the wind touched her, like a willow, like tall grass. Behind her the empty field stretched out and down toward the trees shadowing the dark expanse of the river.

The woman tilted her head back and the tears streamed down her face, into her hair. Giles had one leg out the window when Kade caught the collar of his shirt and jerked him back. He sat down hard and looked up to see her standing over him.

He shook his head, dizzy and a little ill, suddenly aware his mind had not been his own for a moment. His gut turning cold, he looked out at the weeping woman again, but this time saw her gliding progress as strange and unnatural. "What is it?" he whispered, prickles creeping up his spine.

Kade knelt in the window, matter-of-factly knotting her hair behind her head and tucking it into her kerchief. "A glaistig. Under that dress it's more goat than human and it's overly fond of the taste of male blood. They usually frequent deep running water. Someone must have called her up from the river."

Giles looked down at the creature again, warily fascinated.

Kade said grimly, "Mark it well for your next ballad, that's your killer."

"Devereux controls it?" Giles guessed, thinking of the red ruin of the potter's house. "He made it kill the potter?"

"He must have. It wouldn't attack an old woman unless it was forced."

"But why send it here?"

Kade threw him an enigmatic look. "There's been too much happenstance already tonight. She's not trying to seduce a pack mule. She's after you."

"Me?" he said, startled, but Kade was already gone.

Kade closed her eyes and pulled glamour out of the night air and the dew, drawing it over herself. It was a hasty job, and it wouldn't have fooled anyone in daylight, but the creature below was not intelligent and the dark would lend its own magic.

She grabbed the tackle that hung from the loft and swung down, the heavy rope rough against her hands and bare feet.

The glaistig turned toward her, smiling and stretching out its arms. It would see a young man, in shirt and breeches, barefoot, details of feature and form hidden by the barn's shadow. Kade moved toward it, dragging her feet slightly, as if half-asleep. She was thinking through the rote words of a binding spell, to tie the glaistig to her and let her call it whenever she chose. The difficulty was that she had to touch the creature for the binding to take effect.

Within touching distance the glaistig hesitated, staring at her. Its eyes threw back the moonlight like the glassy surface of a pool, but Kade could read confusion and suspicion there.

Before it could flee, Kade leapt forward and grabbed its hands. It shrieked in surprise, the shrill piercing cry turning into a growl. It tried to jerk free and only succeeded in dragging Kade across the dusty yard.

Kade stumbled, the gravel tearing into her feet. The glaistig was a head taller than she and heavier. She dug her heels in and gasped, "Just tell me why he sent you after my new favorite musician and we'll call this done."

"Let go!" Far gone in rage, the creature's voice was less alluringly female, but far more human.

Straining to stay on her feet, Kade hoped it didn't get the idea to slam her up against the barn or the stone wall of the innyard, but the creature seemed just as bad at advance planning as she was. "I'm giving my word. Tell me why he sent you and I'll let you go!"

The glamour had dissolved in the struggle, and the residue of it lay glit-

tering on the earth like solid dewdrops. The glaistig abruptly stopped struggling to peer at her, confused. "What are you?"

"I've power over all the fay and if you don't tell me what I want to know
now I'll bind you to the bottom of the village well in a barrel with staves and
lid of cold iron. Does that tell you who I am?" Kade snarled. She had no idea
if that would tell the glaistig who she was or not. And with her spell trembling like sinew stretched to the breaking point she couldn't have bound a
compass needle to true north.

The glaistig shivered. "He didn't tell me."

"Oh, come now, you can do better than that." Sweat was dripping into
Kade's eyes.

"I don't know, I don't know," it wept, sounding like a human woman
again. "I swear, he told me to come here after the music-maker, he didn't tell
me why. Do you think he would tell me why? Let me go."

Kade released the spell in relief and the glaistig flung away from her. It
stumbled, then fled toward the river in an awkward loping run. Kade sat
down heavily on the hard-packed earth. She realized Giles was standing
beside her, that he had been outside watching nearly the entire time.

He said, "You could have been killed."

She got to her feet, legs trembling with strain. "No, only nibbled on a little." She shook the dust out of her hair. "I can call that glaistig back whenever I want it. Though I'm not sure why I would. This all started out in a very
promising way, but Devereux hasn't tried to fight me, or set me any puzzles
to solve."

There was a moment of silence, then Giles said, "What do you mean?"

Something in his voice made Kade reluctant to answer. She watched the
glaistig disappear among the trees near the river. Beautiful as it was, it was
still just as empty-headed and perverse as the rest of the fay. It might guide a
child out of the forest or care for elderly fishermen, but it would certainly kill
any young man it could catch.

Giles asked, "Did he have any reason at all to kill the potter?"

"No." She could all but hear him drawing that last conclusion. If Giles
Verney, balladeer, knew enough about Kade Carrion to realize that killing
the village potter would bring her here, than surely the local sorcerer would
realize it as well.

"The potter did nothing to him, knew nothing about him?"

Kade looked at him, his face a white mask in the moonlight. "What did
you think this was?" she asked quietly.

"I didn't think it was a game. I didn't think he did it just to get your attention." He didn't sound shocked, only resigned.

With a snort of irony, Kade said, "It's what we do, Giles." She drew the fallen, scattered glamour around her to cloak herself in moonlight and shadow, and walked away.

Later in the night, when the moon was dimmed by clouds, Kade walked up the cart track to the gates of the Warrender manor house. The walls were crumbling like those around the village, too low to attract royal attention and be torn down. The house was small by city standards, but it was better than anything anyone else in Riversee had. It was two stories, with high, narrow windows shuttered against the darkness.

It had never mattered before what anyone else thought of her. The fay disliked each other as a matter of course, and Kade had never regarded her relatives on either side of the family with anything but anger or contempt. Having Giles' idealistic vision of her shattered shouldn't twist in her heart. But she hadn't chosen this game, Devereux had; she would find out what he wanted and end it tonight, one way or another.

Two servants were sleeping in a shabby outbuilding that housed the dovecote; she heard one cough and stir sleepily as she passed the door but neither wakened.

As she had hoped, there was a doorway near the back of the house, open and spilling lamplight. A postern door here would make a convenient exit for someone who wanted to leave or enter late at night without drawing attention.

The dry grass caught at her skirt as she stepped up to the open door. The room inside was low-ceilinged and cluttered with the debris of sorcery. Two long tables held heavy books, clouded glass vessels, curiously shaped and colored rocks or fragments of crystal. Wax had collected at the bases of the candles, their wan light revealing bare stone walls and soot-stained rafters. Fortune Devereux stood at the far end of the room, his back to her, leaning over an open book.

Kade held out a hand, took a slow breath, tasting the aether carefully. There was nothing, no wards that would set off nasty spells if she touched the doorsill. She took the last step forward and leaned in the doorway, saying, "Now what do you need this mess for?"

Devereux turned, his smile slow and triumphant. His doublet and shirt were open across his chest and she saw again that he was a very attractive man. "I didn't think you'd come."

She added that smile to what she knew of sorcerers and thought, *So this room is warded.* She tested the aether again and felt the tug of the spell this time. *Damn.* She hadn't felt it outside because it wasn't set to stop her from entering the room; it was set to stop her from leaving. *Idiot. Overconfidence and impatience will kill you without any help from Devereux.* She didn't like stepping into his trap, but she still thought her power was more than equal to this mortal sorcerer's. If he struck at her directly, he would find that out. She smiled back, making it look easy. "I've only just gotten here and you're lying already."

His expression stiffened.

"You bound a glaistig and killed an old potter in the village you know by tradition I consider my property. Simply to get my attention. But you expected me not to take the bait and appear? Really, that makes you something of a fool, doesn't it?"

Devereux lifted a brow. "I misspoke. I didn't think you would come tonight, since you were occupied with your musician."

"I see." She nodded mock-complacently. "Jealousy, and we've only just met. Did it ever occur to you that all I had to do was point you out to the villagers, explain how you used the glaistig to kill the old potter, and this house would be burning down around your ears now?"

He laughed. "And I thought your loyalty to these people was as fickle as that of the rest of the fay. I didn't realize you were so virtuous."

Kade lifted a cool brow, though for some reason the jibe about loyalty had hit home. "My loyalty is fickle, but at least they gave me fruit and flowers. What did you ever do for me?"

"I have an offer for you." Devereux took a step forward. "You could benefit from an alliance with me."

"Benefit?" She rolled her eyes. "I repeat, what did you ever do for me?"

"It's what I can do for you. I can give you revenge."

This was new. No one had ever offered that before. Kade watched his calm face carefully, intrigued. "Revenge on who?"

"The court, the king. The tricks you play on them, however deadly, aren't worthy of you. With my help, and the help of others that I know – "

"You want to use me against my royal relatives," Kade shook her head, disappointed, and added honestly, "It's an audacious plan, I'll willingly give you that much. No man's had the courage to suggest such a thing to me before."

His face had hardened and she knew it had been a long time since anyone had refused him anything. "But it is not to your taste, I take it."

Kade shrugged. "If I really wanted to kill my mortal brother I could have done it before now. What I want to do is make him and his mother suffer, and I don't think you or your supporters would agree to that. And as soon as I wasn't useful to you anymore one of you would try to kill me, then I'd have to kill one or more of you, and the whole mess would fall apart." She hesitated, and for some reason, perhaps because he was so comely, said, "If you had approached me as a friend, it could have been different. Perhaps we could have worked something out to serve your end."

But from his angry expression he didn't recognize it as the offer it was, or he felt it was a lie or a trap. *Maybe it was,* Kade admitted to herself. Maybe what she really wanted was something else entirely, something Devereux simply hadn't the character to offer her.

"I suggest you reconsider," Devereux said, his voice harsh.

She said dryly, "I suggest you stick to sorcery and leave politics to those with the talent for it."

He stepped back, giving her a thin-lipped smile. "You can't leave. This room is warded with a curse. If you break the barrier, the creature that loves you most in the world will die."

Relieved, Kade laughed at him as she slipped out the door. Fay didn't love each other, and there was no mortal left from her childhood who didn't want to see her dead. He had chosen this spell badly. "Curse away. I've nothing to lose."

"I think you have!" Kade heard him call after her as she ran through the tall grass. As she came around the side of the house there was a shout. Ahead in the darkness she saw moving figures and the glow from the slow match of a musket. She swore and ducked.

The musket thundered and there was a sharp crack as the ball struck the stone wall behind her. *If they hit me with that thing,* Kade thought desperately, *we're all going to find out just how human I am.* The musket balls were cold iron, and her fay magic could do nothing to them.

But that protection didn't extend to the gunpowder inside the musket. She covered her head with her arms and muttered the spell she had considered using on Warrender in the inn.

There was an explosion and a scream as someone's wheellock pistol went off, then a dozen little popping sounds as the scattered grains of powder from the musket's blast ignited.

Kade scrambled to her feet. The grass near the gate had caught fire and she was forgotten in the face of that immediate threat. She ran to the back wall with its loose bricks and crumbling mortar and climbed it easily. At the top she paused and looked back. In the glow of the grass fire she could see

Devereux walking back and forth, shouting at the servants in angry frustration. Revenge against her royal relatives would have been sweet. *But it would
never have worked, not with him, anyway,* she thought with a grimace. *Too bad.*

It was barely dawn when she reached the inn, and through the windows she
could see that candles had been lit in the common room. From just outside
the door she thought there was more noise than seemed normal at this hour,
especially after last night's drinking bout.

When she stepped inside, she heard a woman say, "Must have died in his
sleep, poor thing."

The morning was well advanced when Kade waited for the glaistig beneath a
bent aging willow in a stretch of forest near the river.

It dropped a lock of golden hair into Kade's palm.

"Did he notice?" Kade asked, looking up at the creature.

The glaistig's eyes were limpid, innocent. "I did it while he slept."

"Very good." She should have treated Devereux' curse with more caution,
she had said that to herself a hundred times over the rest of the long night.
And you should have known. All those brave stories Giles had told of her, his
audacity in coming here to find her, should have said it plainly enough. She
had also said that she didn't care, but no amount of repetition could make
a lie the truth. *Giles knew I was dangerous company to keep.* Yes, he knew, but he
had kept it anyway. And that made it all the worse.

She added the hair to a small leather pouch prepared with apricot stones
and the puss from a plague sore, then sat down on a fallen log to sew it up
with the small neat stitches she had learned as a child.

"The sorcerer was lovely," the glaistig said regretfully, watching her.

"He was lovely," Kade agreed. "And cunning, like me. And I would trade a
hundred of both of us to know that one unlovely ballad-singer was still alive
somewhere in the world."

Kade left Riversee after that. She had thought to stay to see the result of her
handiwork but she had discovered that knowing was enough.

Gray clouds were building for a storm, and she might have summoned
one of the many flighted creatures of fayre and ridden the wind with it, but
she had also discovered that she preferred to walk the dusty road. Some
things had lost their pleasure.

Thin, On the Ground

Howard Waldrop

Howard Waldrop (*www.sff.net/people/Waldrop*) lives in Austin, Texas. He was a member of the original 1970s Turkey City Writers Workshop that included Lisa Tuttle, Bruce Sterling, Lewis Shiner, Leigh Kennedy, among others, and lived in recent years in rural Washington State, fishing a lot, before returning to Austin. Eileen Gunn says, on Waldrop's web site: "Amid such celebrity, Waldrop himself continues to live below poverty level, volunteering for a top-secret study that helped determine the nutritional limits of using integrity as Hamburger Helper. As part of this historic experiment, he once pulled a story that had already sold to a big-bucks market in order to place it elsewhere for half the price." He is an extraordinary writer of SF and fantasy, an original in a field of pinnacle originals, situated somewhere among Avram Davidson (a writer of almost suicidal principles), R. A. Lafferty (a brilliant stylist respected by his peers), and Philip K. Dick (especially his generosity and legendary poverty) in the pantheon of weirdest genre heroes. His cult reputation is based on his quirky, intelligent, charming short stories. He has appeared often since the mid-1970s on genre award ballots, and the bulk of his early stories are reprinted in his collections, *Howard Who?* (1986), *All About Strange Monsters of the Recent Past: Neat Stories* (1987), *Night of the Cooters: More Neat Stories* (1990), *Going Home Again* (1997) and *Custer's Last Jump and Other Collaborations* (2003).

"Thin, On the Ground" is from the original anthology, *Cross Plains Universe*, edited by Scott A. Cupp and Joe R. Lansdale, a collection of stories by Texas writers in honor of the centennial of the birth of Robert E. Howard. It is a story of supernatural menace with a light touch. Two teenagers cross the border into Mexico and encounter the world of Magic Realism. In an interview with *Locus*, Waldrop remarked, "...there's got to be a better world than this one. Look at it! I wouldn't be writing about an alternate world if I liked the one I was in – I'd be writing stories set in the *wonderful* here and now."

THERE'S A SAMPLER on Gramma's wall that says: "You don't have to look for Trouble: It's looking for you." – Uncle Brock

Of course, they tell me he always also said: "If unarmed and assaulted, pull a tree out of the ground and flail away."

We weren't looking for trouble. We were going to Mexico to celebrate graduation from high school, class of 1962.

I was the third person in my family to make it all the way through school. We were me and Bobby Mitchell, my absolute best friend since first grade.

We got in the 1953 Ford pickup we owned together, way before dawn of the morning after we graduated; it was so early the big comet everyone was talking about was blazing across the sky.

Bobby, who's a lot smarter than me, said it was called Comet 1962 IIB and had a Norwegian and a Japanese guy's names after it.

I just thought it was big and pretty.

We drove off under it, heading south. The stoplight on the highway was still on blink.

We'd bought the truck back in January, and we'd stood in line like everyone else in Texas, at the courthouse over in Crosley on April 1st to get our new black number on white background plates to replace the 1961 white-on-black plates: and then we'd flipped a nickel and called it and Bobby had slept in the truck down at the service station the night of April 14th to be in line to get a new inspection sticker which everyone had to have on April 15th. We were new to truck ownership but we knew there was a better way to do it than that...

That was all behind us, and we were heading south. On our dashboard was a glow-in-the-dark Jesus Bobby's sister had won in Sunday school, way back in the third grade, for reciting all the books of the Bible, pretty much in one breath. When we bought the truck, Bobby convinced her to sell us the statue for a whole dollar. She didn't want to sell it; she kept it on top of her chest of drawers in her bedroom. "We can drive it all over the world," he said. "What are you gonna do, take your dresser out for a drive?"

Bobby was looking at the plastic Jesus. He started singing:

"My name is Jesus, the son of Joe:
Hello-hello-hello..."

And kept singing it as we passed through Rising Star as the east was beginning to lighten.

We'd left home before sunup and we pulled up at the parking lot at the bor-der-town (it was called Bordertown, Texas) at 6 p.m. on a blazing hot May day. Even from here, you could hear the sounds of Tex-Mex music coming across the Rio Grande, which was about forty feet wide here.

"Not so grande," said Bobby, who spoke some Spanish.

We walked across the wooden bridge and a vista opened up before us – a whole town of one-story buildings spread out before us as far as the eye could see – the only thing taller was a miniature Eiffel-tower-looking thing with an umbrella and chair on top and a man asleep in it.

"The ever-alert fire lookout," said Bobby. "The *bomberos* – firemen."

We nodded at the Mexican border guards. They waved back. "Keep out of *real* trouble," said a dapper-looking one to us in English.

The bridge emptied onto what looked like the main street. There was a big sign just as you came to it: Official Exchange Rate Today (and a space for a chalked message which today said $1.00 US = 12 Pesos).

"Think of everything as eight cents," said Bobby. "If it's too expensive at eight cents, it's too expensive in pesos."

Guys, like carnival barkers, were lined up in front of all the shops, which looked like used record stores to me. "Bargains galore!" they yelled. "No down payment to GI Joe!" they said to a couple of soldiers. "Your uniform is your collateral!" I wondered what the hell they could be selling in *installments.* "Shopper's Paradise; a consumer's Eden!" yelled another.

We came to a store. There was a guy standing in front of it like the others, but with his arms crossed and not saying anything.

As we got to him he said, "Please come in and buy some junk so I can close early."

Well, *honesty* is the best policy.

We got a gold-plated machete and a red-and-white striped *rebozo* and a two-gallon purple piggy-bank with a comical expression on its face. The bank was covered with painted green and orange flowers.

"Where's Boy's Town?" asked Bobby.

"This *whole* town's Boy's Town," said the man, "but the second street to the left" – he pointed – "is what *you* want."

"Do you have a sack for this stuff?"

"Here's how we do it." He put the machete and piggy-bank inside the *rebozo,* made a couple of folds, and handed the neat package, square and tight, by the *rebozo*-hood handle, to Bobby.

"Could you do that *again?*" asked Bobby, his eyes wide.

"No, I cannot," said the shopkeeper. "I can only make a package that neat once a day. Your pardon."

As we left the shop he was putting up the Closed sign on the door. We heard the wire security gate scraping down behind us.

Imagine an endless honky-tonk. The street looked like the inside of a juke-box – colored lights, noise and music everywhere, neon beginning to come on, and more guys yelling. The blinking lights said "Girls! Girls!! Girls!!!"

And "30 Lovely Senoritas – 18 Beautiful Costumes!" and "This is the place!"

It was starting to get dark and the outline of the comet appeared with the first stars. Bobby said tonight was going to be about the brightest it would get, and it would fade over the next month or two.

A guy came toward us, singing:

"*Me nombre Jésus, hijo de José*:

Hola-hola-hola..."

He passed us by, a broad grin on his face. A crowd of guys and soldiers headed down the street. We started to join them.

Then I thought I heard crying. I looked over a couple of streets, and a woman was walking away toward the river. The sound was coming from her, and it was the most heart-wrenching thing I'd ever heard.

"Hey!" I said. "That lady's in *trouble*."

Bobby held up his *rebozo*-package like a shield. "It's probably a scam. We go help her and we get jumped."

"That's *real* crying." I said. "That's not fake."

We hurried to help her.

She had gone out onto the river shore. She was wearing a long black dress and a cape like Little Red Riding Hood, only in the fading light it looked blue. Her crying rose in pitch and force.

I saw that there were two kids on the Texas side and they were holding their arms out toward her.

A guy with a fishing pole was coming up the riverbank toward us on our side. He stopped and dropped the pole and a couple of Rio Grande perch he had on a stringer.

"*¡Caramba!*" he yelled. "*¡La LLorena!*" and ran away.

The woman's crying never stopped. The kids were crying too, holding out their hands.

The woman turned toward us. Inside the hood was the head of a horse.

When we stopped running we were in front of a place called *Salon de Baile*.

"You look like you've seen a ghost," said the guy out front.

"Don't ask," said Bobby.

It was a real dance hall with a *conjunto* band and actual couples dancing, and a stag-line, and on the other side of the room, women waiting to be asked to dance.

"Hey. This place is *legit*," said Bobby. "There are two *duennas* with the women."

"What a let-down," I said.

Bobby ordered two beers from the waiter. We drank them in a few seconds. I was still breathing hard from the run from the river.

We watched the couples dance. They were dressed for a Saturday night (which is what it was) in their finest. There were even one or two guys in *vaquero* outfits, the full thing; one guy who was dancing had on a powder-blue outfit with silver trim and back at the table he'd come from was a big blue and silver sombrero across the back of a chair.

"It's *different* here," I said to Bobby. "A guy can go out on a Saturday night in a powder-blue suit."

The band played faster and the dancers swirled around.

Then there was a scream, and a woman collapsed and everyone ran to her. They stirred the air near her with their fans and their *mantillas*. She screamed from the floor.

"¡El hombre pie de gallo!" she yelled. "¡El hombre pie...*"

Bobby went over to listen. He came back.

"She was dancing with the guy in the blue suit," he said. "*Muy suavecito* as she described him, very dapper. She was *really* dancing with the music; she looked down and instead of boots, he had the feet of a rooster. A sign of the devil."

I looked over. The guy in the blue and silver outfit was gone, and so was his hat. I hadn't seen anyone leave.

"Let's go *somewhere else*," I said.

We were outside. The comet was so bright it lit the place up like there was a full moon, though I knew that wouldn't be until the middle of next month.

A wagon rolled down the street. It was the first wagon I'd seen in years, drawn by two mules. One had a child's sombrero on its head, with holes cut out for its ears. I saw it by the neon lights of the joint next door.

There was a woman standing outside, smoking a cigarette. A guy on a horse rode up, big sombrero, silver studs sparkling off the saddle from the strings of colored lights in the street.

He asked for a light; he held a *cigarillo* down towards her.

She looked up. She dropped the Zippo she'd taken out of her handbag and began to scream: "¡Aaiiee! ¡Aaiiee!"

A guy came out of the bar, stopped, and yelled: "¡Caracoles! ¡El jinete sin cabeza!" And ran off. So did the woman.

I looked up. Between the collar of the horseman's jacket and the brim of his hat, I could see the top of a tree three blocks away, silver in the comet's light.

The guy shrugged his shoulders, turned his horse around and went off down the way. I watched the scenery through his invisible head. He turned left two streets down.

We ran into the bar.

It was very late. We were drunk. The street had about four or five people on it. The barkers had all gone inside, and some of the colored lights and neon signs had been turned off. If I weren't so drunk it would have looked sad.

We made our way as best we could down the street. The comet blazed away, taking up half the sky.

"This stuff's getting heavy," said Bobby. "Take it for a while." He handed me the wrapped-up *rebozo*.

He was right. It was heavy.

We were looking for a place with nothing but red lights out front. We came to the corner of a cross street.

There was a well-dressed man standing in the diagonal corner; formal wear, shiny cufflinks, cummerbund and all. Another guy was walking toward him on the side street, whistling. There was some conversation between them – the walking man slowed and answered as he neared.

I'd swear the comet-light brightened then dimmed then brightened again *by a half*. I looked up, then back. Where the formally dressed man had been was a seedier-looking individual. His clothes had changed, his hair was wilder, he looked like a gargoyle Betty Boop; his head was as wide as his shoulders. There was a thing like a butterfly's tongue under his chin, and it uncurled like an elephant's trunk and went up the other guy's nose; there was a sucking sound we heard from across the corner, and the other guy's head deflated like a punctured beach ball and the light from the comet pulsed *on and off, on and off*. The other guy dropped straight down like a dead weight and the guy with the big head was wiping grey stuff off his extended snout with both hands before curling it back under his chin.

Then he looked over at us.

Someone had come up behind us we hadn't heard. We jumped a foot when he yelled: "¡Mierda! ¡El Baron! ¡El Brainiac!"

We heard footsteps running away.

And then the baron was on us.

He grabbed Bobby by the shoulders.

If I weren't drunk I'd be thinking faster. I remember great-great granduncle Brock's admonition about assailants and trees. The nearest one was three blocks back and at least fifty feet tall.

I swung the *rebozo*-package into the baron, hard enough to shatter the piggybank. The baron lurched back, then got a more secure grip on Bobby.

The gold machete dropped out of the *rebozo*. I picked it up. The baron's face was closer to Bobby's and the snout-tongue was unfolding and going toward his nose. Beyond Bobby I could see the dead guy lying crumpled on the opposite corner.

The tongue was an inch from Bobby's nose. The comet pulsed overhead.

I swung the machete and chopped off the snout-tongue as close to the baron's face as I could. The baron's tongue hit the ground, writhing like a run-over snake. The baron squealed then, a cross between a feral hog and a giant bat that started a ringing in my ears.

The baron ran away, gouts of blood splashing onto the street, to the south.

We ran north.

We were still running when we reached the bridge. A party of Mexican citizens was starting over the bridge toward the US. One of them played a guitar and a few of them were singing.

I'd put the machete back in the *rebozo* with the broken bank. We ran past the singing party, and Bobby yelled to the border guards on the Mexican side: "¡Adiós! ¡Gracias!"

We ran up to the US station. "Make way for a couple of Americans!" I yelled.

The US guards were laughing. "Had enough of Mexico, boys?"

I stopped and turned to the party of Mexican citizens who'd followed us onto the bridge.

"How do you people *live* in that country!?" I yelled.

We ran for the truck and made for home at a hundred miles an hour.

Pol Pot's Beautiful Daughter (Fantasy)

Geoff Ryman

Geoff Ryman (*www.ryman-novel.com/info/about.htm*) is a Canadian-born writer who moved to the USA at age eleven, and has been living in England since 1973. He began publishing SF stories in the mid-1970s, and wrote some SF plays, none published but most performed, including a powerful adaptation of Philip K. Dick's 1982 novel, *The Transmigration of Timothy Archer*. Ryman's third novel, *The Child Garden* (1989), won the Arthur C. Clarke Award and the John W. Campbell Memorial Award, and confirmed him as a major figure in contemporary SF. He has worked with computers for nearly two decades; he published a hypertext novel, *253* (1996; *www.ryman-novel.com*), and *Air* (2004), which is about the future of the internet, and the winner of the British Science Fiction, Arthur C. Clarke, and James Tiptree, Jr. awards, yet he also chooses not to have a personal web site. A majority of his work in the last decade or more is not genre, though he has continued to publish excellent genre short fiction throughout. He travels frequently to Cambodia, where his forthcoming mainstream novel, *The King's Last Song*, is set. In an essay on Cambodian writers published in *The Guardian*, Ryman described the paradoxes of life in Cambodia during and after its "autogenocide": "Pal Vannarirak, the host of a new Cambodian TV show about books and authors, has written more than 100 short stories and 40 novels. Having survived the Khmer Rouge, Vannarirak found work for the Vietnamese-backed government – as a censor. She had to ban her own novels. 'Because I knew the kinds of books I was hunting, I knew the kind of books I was not supposed to write. So I wrote them.'"

"Pol Pot's Beautiful Daughter (Fantasy)" was published in *The Magazine of Fantasy & Science Fiction*, and is a fantasy set in contemporary Cambodia, in the generation after the death of one of the twentieth century's most prominent political monsters, while the ghosts of his horrible crimes still linger. It is a story about redemption.

IN CAMBODIA PEOPLE ARE USED TO GHOSTS. Ghosts buy newspapers. They own property.

A few years ago, spirits owned a house in Phnom Penh, at the Tra Bek end of Monivong Boulevard. Khmer Rouge had murdered the whole family and there was no one left alive to inherit it. People cycled past the building, leaving it boarded up. Sounds of weeping came from inside.

Then a professional inheritor arrived from America. She'd done her research and could claim to be the last surviving relative of no fewer than three families. She immediately sold the house to a Chinese businessman, who turned the ground floor into a photocopying shop.

The copiers began to print pictures of the original owners.

At first, single black-and-white photos turned up in the copied dossiers of aid workers or government officials. The father of the murdered family had been a lawyer. He stared fiercely out of the photos as if demanding something. In other photocopies, his beautiful daughters forlornly hugged each other. The background was hazy like fog.

One night the owner heard a noise and trundled downstairs to find all five photocopiers printing one picture after another of faces: young college men, old women, parents with a string of babies, or government soldiers in uniform. He pushed the big green off-buttons. Nothing happened.

He pulled out all the plugs, but the machines kept grinding out face after face. Women in beehive hairdos or clever children with glasses looked wistfully out of the photocopies. They seemed to be dreaming of home in the 1960s, when Phnom Penh was the most beautiful city in Southeast Asia.

News spread. People began to visit the shop to identify lost relatives. Women would cry, "That's my mother! I didn't have a photograph!" They would weep and press the flimsy A4 sheets to their breasts. The paper went limp from tears and humidity as if it too were crying.

Soon, a throng began to gather outside the shop every morning to view the latest batch of faces. In desperation, the owner announced that each morning's harvest would be delivered direct to *The Truth*, a magazine of remembrance.

Then one morning he tried to open the house-door to the shop and found it blocked. He went 'round to the front of the building and rolled open the metal shutters.

The shop was packed from floor to ceiling with photocopies. The ground floor had no windows – the room had been filled from the inside. The owner pulled out a sheet of paper and saw himself on the ground, his head beaten in by a hoe. The same image was on every single page.

He buried the photocopiers and sold the house at once. The new owner liked its haunted reputation; it kept people away. The FOR SALE sign was left hanging from the second floor.

In a sense, the house had been bought by another ghost.

This is a completely untrue story about someone who must exist.

Pol Pot's only child, a daughter, was born in 1986. Her name was Sith, and in 2004, she was eighteen years old.

Sith liked air conditioning and luxury automobiles.

Her hair was dressed in cornrows and she had a spiky piercing above one eye. Her jeans were elaborately slashed and embroidered. Her pink T-shirts bore slogans in English: CARE KOOKY. PINK MOLL.

Sith lived like a woman on Thai television, doing as she pleased in lip-gloss and Sunsilked hair. Nine simple rules helped her avoid all unpleasant-ness.

1. Never think about the past or politics.

2. Ignore ghosts. They cannot hurt you.

3. Do not go to school. Hire tutors. Don't do homework. It is disturbing.

4. Always be driven everywhere in either the Mercedes or the BMW.

5. Avoid all well-dressed Cambodian boys. They are the sons of the estimated 250,000 new generals created by the regime. Their sons can behave with impunity.

6. Avoid all men with potbellies. They eat too well and therefore must be corrupt.

7. Avoid anyone who drives a Toyota Viva or Honda Dream motorcycle.

8. Don't answer letters or phone calls.

9. Never make any friends.

There was also a tenth rule, but that went without saying.

Rotten fruit rinds and black mud never stained Sith's designer sports shoes. Disabled beggars never asked her for alms. Her life began yesterday, which was effectively the same as today.

Every day, her driver took her to the new Soriya Market. It was almost the only place that Sith went. The color of silver, Soriya rose up in many floors to a round glass dome.

Sith preferred the 142nd Street entrance. Its green awning made everyone look as if they were made of jade. The doorway went directly into the ice-cold jewelry rotunda with its floor of polished black and white stone. The individual stalls were hung with glittering necklaces and earrings.

Sith liked tiny shiny things that had no memory. She hated politics. She refused to listen to the news. Pol Pot's beautiful daughter wished the current leadership would behave decently, like her dad always did. To her.

She remembered the sound of her father's gentle voice. She remembered sitting on his lap in a forest enclosure, being bitten by mosquitoes. Memories of malaria had sunk into her very bones. She now associated forests with nausea, fevers, and pain. A flicker of tree-shade on her skin made her want to throw up and the odor of soil or fallen leaves made her gag. She had never been to Angkor Wat. She read nothing.

Sith shopped. Her driver was paid by the government and always carried an AK-47, but his wife, the housekeeper, had no idea who Sith was. The house was full of swept marble, polished teak furniture, iPods, Xboxes, and plasma screens.

Please remember that every word of this story is a lie. Pol Pot was no doubt a dedicated communist who made no money from ruling Cambodia. Nevertheless, a hefty allowance arrived for Sith every month from an account in Switzerland.

Nothing touched Sith, until she fell in love with the salesman at Hello Phones.

Cambodian readers may know that in 2004 there was no mobile phone shop in Soriya Market. However, there was a branch of Hello Phone Cards that had a round blue sales counter with orange trim. This shop looked like that.

Every day Sith bought or exchanged a mobile phone there. She would sit and flick her hair at the salesman.

His name was Dara, which means Star. Dara knew about deals on call prices, sim cards, and the new phones that showed videos. He could get her any call tone she liked.

Talking to Dara broke none of Sith's rules. He wasn't fat, nor was he well dressed, and far from being a teenager, he was a comfortably mature twenty-four years old.

One day, Dara chuckled and said, "As a friend I advise you, you don't need another mobile phone."

Sith wrinkled her nose. "I don't like this one anymore. It's blue. I want something more feminine. But not frilly. And it should have better sound quality."

"Okay, but you could save your money and buy some more nice clothes."

Pol Pot's beautiful daughter lowered her chin, which she knew made her neck look long and graceful. "Do you like my clothes?"

"Why ask me?"

She shrugged. "I don't know. It's good to check out your look."

Dara nodded. "You look cool. What does your sister say?"

Sith let him know she had no family. "Ah," he said, and quickly changed the subject. That was terrific. Secrecy and sympathy in one easy movement.

Sith came back the next day and said that she'd decided that the rose-colored phone was too feminine. Dara laughed aloud and his eyes sparkled. Sith had come late in the morning just so that he could ask this question. "Are you hungry? Do you want to meet for lunch?"

Would he think she was cheap if she said yes? Would he say she was snobby if she said no?

"Just so long as we eat in Soriya Market," she said.

She was torn between BBWorld Burgers and Lucky7. BBWorld was big, round, and just two floors down from the dome. Lucky7 Burgers was part of the Lucky Supermarket, such a good store that a tiny jar of Maxwell House cost US$2.40.

They decided on BBWorld. It was full of light and they could see the town spread out through the wide clean windows. Sith sat in silence.

Pol Pot's daughter had nothing to say unless she was buying something. Or rather she had only one thing to say, but she must never say it.

Dara did all the talking. He talked about how the guys on the third floor could get him a deal on original copies of Grand Theft Auto. He hinted that he could get Sith discounts from Bsfashion, the spotlit modern shop one floor down.

Suddenly he stopped. "You don't need to be afraid of me, you know." He said it in a kindly, grownup voice. "I can see, you're a properly brought up girl. I like that. It's nice."

Sith still couldn't find anything to say. She could only nod. She wanted to run away.

"Would you like to go to K-Four?"

K-Four, the big electronics shop, stocked all the reliable brand names: Hitachi, Sony, Panasonic, Philips, or Denon. It was so expensive that almost nobody shopped there, which is why Sith liked it. A crowd of people stood outside and stared through the window at a huge home entertainment center showing a DVD of Ice Age. On the screen, a little animal was being chased by a glacier. It was so beautiful!

Sith finally found something to say. "If I had one of those, I would never need to leave the house."

Dara looked at her sideways and decided to laugh.

The next day Sith told him that all the phones she had were too big. Did he have one that she could wear around her neck like jewelry?

This time they went to Lucky7 Burgers, and sat across from the Revlon counter. They watched boys having their hair layered by Revlon's natural beauty specialists.

Dara told her more about himself. His father had died in the wars. His family now lived in the country. Sith's Coca-Cola suddenly tasted of anti-malarial drugs.

"But...you don't want to live in the country," she said.

"No. I have to live in Phnom Penh to make money. But my folks are good country people. Modest." He smiled, embarrassed.

They'll have hens and a cousin who shimmies up coconut trees. There will be trees all around but no shops anywhere. The earth will smell.

Sith couldn't finish her drink. She sighed and smiled and said abruptly, "I'm sorry. It's been cool. But I have to go." She slunk sideways out of her seat as slowly as molasses.

Walking back into the jewelry rotunda with nothing to do, she realized that Dara would think she didn't like him.

And that made the lower part of her eyes sting.

She went back the next day and didn't even pretend to buy a mobile phone. She told Dara that she'd left so suddenly the day before because she'd remembered a hair appointment.

He said that he could see she took a lot of trouble with her hair. Then he asked her out for a movie that night.

Sith spent all day shopping in K-Four.

They met at six. Dara was so considerate that he didn't even suggest the horror movie. He said he wanted to see *Buffalo Girl Hiding*, a movie about a country girl who lives on a farm. Sith said with great feeling that she would prefer the horror movie.

The cinema on the top floor opened out directly onto the roof of Soriya. Graffiti had been scratched into the green railings. Why would people want to ruin something new and beautiful? Sith put her arm through Dara's and knew that they were now boyfriend and girlfriend.

"Finally," he said.

"Finally what?"

"You've done something."

They leaned on the railings and looked out over other people's apartments. West toward the river was a building with one huge roof terrace. Women met there to gossip. Children were playing toss-the-sandal. From this distance, Sith was enchanted.

"I just love watching the children."

The movie, from Thailand, was about a woman whose face turns blue and spotty and who eats men. The blue woman was yucky, but not as scary as all the badly dubbed voices. The characters sounded possessed. It was though Thai people had been taken over by the spirits of dead Cambodians.

Whenever Sith got scared, she chuckled.

So she sat chuckling with terror. Dara thought she was laughing at a dumb movie and found such intelligence charming. He started to chuckle too. Sith thought he was as frightened as she was. Together in the dark, they took each other's hands.

Outside afterward, the air hung hot even in the dark and 142nd Street smelled of drains. Sith stood on tiptoe to avoid the oily deposits and cast-off fishbones.

Dara said, "I will drive you home."

"My driver can take us," said Sith, flipping open her Kermit-the-Frog mobile.

Her black Mercedes Benz edged to a halt, crunching old plastic bottles in the gutter. The seats were upholstered with tan leather and the driver was armed.

Dara's jaw dropped. "Who...*who* is your father?"

"He's dead."

Dara shook his head. "Who was he?"

Normally Sith used her mother's family name, but that would not answer this question. Flustered, she tried to think of someone who could be her father. She knew of nobody the right age. She remembered something about a politician who had died. His name came to her and she said it in panic. "My father was Kol Vireakboth." Had she got the name right? "Please don't tell anyone."

Dara covered his eyes. "We – my family, my father – we fought for the KPLA."

Sith had to stop herself asking what the KPLA was.

Kol Vireakboth had led a faction in the civil wars. It fought against the Khmer Rouge, the Vietnamese, the King, and corruption. It wanted a new way for Cambodia. Kol Vireakboth was a Cambodian leader who had never told a lie or accepted a bribe.

Remember that this is an untrue story.

Dara started to back away from the car. "I don't think we should be doing this. I'm just a villager, really."

"That doesn't matter."

His eyes closed. "I would expect nothing less from the daughter of Kol Vireakboth."

Oh for gosh sake, she just picked the man's name out of the air, she didn't need more problems. "Please!" she said.

Dara sighed. "Okay. I said I would see you home safely. I will." Inside the Mercedes, he stroked the tan leather.

When they arrived, he craned his neck to look up at the building. "Which floor are you on?"

"All of them."

Color drained from his face.

"My driver will take you back," she said to Dara. As the car pulled away, she stood outside the closed garage shutters, waving forlornly.

Then Sith panicked. Who was Kol Vireakboth? She went online and Googled. She had to read about the wars. Her skin started to creep. All those different factions swam in her head: ANS, NADK, KPR, and KPNLF. The very names seemed to come at her spoken by forgotten voices.

Soon she had all she could stand. She printed out Vireakboth's picture and decided to have it framed. In case Dara visited.

Kol Vireakboth had a round face and a fatherly smile. His eyes seemed to slant upward toward his nose, looking full of kindly insight. He'd been killed by a car bomb.

All that night, Sith heard whispering.

In the morning, there was another picture of someone else in the tray of her printer.

A long-faced, buck-toothed woman stared out at her in black and white. Sith noted the victim's fashion lapses. The woman's hair was a mess, all frizzy. She should have had it straightened and put in some nice highlights. The woman's eyes drilled into her.

"Can't touch me," said Sith. She left the photo in the tray. She went to see Dara, right away, no breakfast.

His eyes were circled with dark flesh and his blue Hello trousers and shirt were not properly ironed.

"Buy the whole shop," Dara said, looking deranged. "The guys in K-Four just told me some girl in blue jeans walked in yesterday and bought two home theatres. One for the salon, she said, and one for the roof terrace. She paid for both of them in full and had them delivered to the far end of Monivong."

Sith sighed. "I'm sending one back." She hoped that sounded abstemious. "It looked too metallic against my curtains."

Pause.

"She also bought an Aido robot dog for fifteen hundred dollars."

Sith would have preferred that Dara did not know about the dog. It was just a silly toy; it hadn't occurred to her that it might cost that much until she saw the bill. "They should not tell everyone about their customers' business or soon they will have no customers."

Dara was looking at her as if thinking: This is not just a nice sweet girl.

"I had fun last night," Sith said in a voice as thin as high clouds.

"So did I."

"We don't have to tell anyone about my family. Do we?" Sith was seriously scared of losing him.

"No. But Sith, it's stupid. Your family, my family, we are not equals."

"It doesn't make any difference."

"You lied to me. Your family is not dead. You have famous uncles."

She did indeed – Uncle Ieng Sary, Uncle Khieu Samphan, Uncle Ta Mok. All the Pol Pot clique had been called her uncles.

"I didn't know them that well," she said. That was true, too.

What would she do if she couldn't shop in Soriya Market anymore? What would she do without Dara?

She begged. "I am not a strong person. Sometimes I think I am not a person at all. I'm just a space."

Dara looked suddenly mean. "You're just a credit card." Then his face fell. "I'm sorry. That was an unkind thing to say. You are very young for your age and I'm older than you and I should have treated you with more care."

Sith was desperate. "All my money would be very nice."

"I'm not for sale."

He worked in a shop and would be sending money home to a fatherless family; of course he was for sale!

Sith had a small heart, but a big head for thinking. She knew that she had to do this delicately, like picking a flower, or she would spoil the bloom. "Let's...let's just go see a movie?"

After all, she was beautiful and well brought up and she knew her eyes were big and round. Her tiny heart was aching.

This time they saw *Tum Teav*, a remake of an old movie from the 1960s. If movies were not nightmares about ghosts, then they tried to preserve the past. *When, thought Sith, will they make a movie about Cambodia's future? Tum Teav* was based on a classic tale of a young monk who falls in love with a properly brought up girl but her mother opposes the match. They commit suicide at the end, bringing a curse on their village. Sith sat through it stony-faced. *I am not going to be a dead heroine in a romance.*

Dara offered to drive her home again and that's when Sith found out that he drove a Honda Dream. He proudly presented to her the gleaming motorcycle of fast young men. Sith felt backed into a corner. She'd already offered to buy him. Showing off her car again might humiliate him.

So she broke rule number seven.

Dara hid her bag in the back and they went soaring down Monivong Boulevard at night, past homeless people, prostitutes, and chefs staggering home after work. It was late in the year, but it started to rain.

Sith loved it, the cool air brushing against her face, the cooler rain clinging to her eyelashes.

She remembered being five years old in the forest and dancing in the monsoon. She encircled Dara's waist to stay on the bike and suddenly found her cheek was pressed up against his back. She giggled in fear, not of the rain, but of what she felt.

He dropped her off at home. Inside, everything was dark except for the flickering green light on her printer. In the tray were two new photographs. One was of a child, a little boy, holding up a school prize certificate. The other was a tough, wise-looking old man, with a string of muscle down either side of his ironic, bitter smile. They looked directly at her.

They know who I am.

As she climbed the stairs to her bedroom, she heard someone sobbing, far away, as if the sound came from next door. She touched the walls of the staircase. They shivered slightly, constricting in time to the cries.

In her bedroom she extracted one of her many iPods from the tangle of wires and listened to *System of a Down*, as loud as she could. It helped her sleep. The sound of nu-metal guitars seemed to come roaring out of her own heart.

She was woken up in the sun-drenched morning by the sound of her doorbell many floors down. She heard the housekeeper Jorani call and the door open. Sith hesitated over choice of jeans and top. By the time she got downstairs she found the driver and the housemaid joking with Dara, giving him tea.

Like the sunshine, Dara seemed to disperse ghosts.

"Hi," he said. "It's my day off. I thought we could go on a motorcycle ride to the country."

But not to the country. Couldn't they just spend the day in Soriya? No, said Dara, there's lots of other places to see in Phnom Penh.

He drove her, twisting through back streets. How did the city get so poor? How did it get so dirty?

They went to a new and modern shop for CDs that was run by a record label. Dara knew all the cool new music, most of it influenced by Khmer-Americans returning from Long Beach and Compton: Sdey, Phnom Penh Bad Boys, Khmer Kid.

Sith bought twenty CDs.

They went to the National Museum and saw the beautiful Buddha-like head of King Jayavarman VII. Dara without thinking ducked and held up his hands in prayer. They had dinner in a French restaurant with candles and wine, and it was just like in a karaoke video, a boy, a girl, and her money all going out together. They saw the show at Sovanna Phum, and there was a wonderful dance piece with sampled 1940s music from an old French movie, with traditional Khmer choreography.

Sith went home, her heart singing, Dara, Dara, Dara.

In the bedroom, a mobile phone began to ring, over and over. Call 1 said the screen, but gave no name or number, so the person was not on Sith's list of contacts.

She turned off the phone. It kept ringing. That's when she knew for certain.

She hid the phone in a pillow in the spare bedroom and put another pillow on top of it and then closed the door.

All forty-two of her mobile phones started to ring. They rang from inside closets, or from the bathroom where she had forgotten them. They rang from the roof terrace and even from inside a shoe under her bed.

"I am a very stubborn girl!" she shouted at the spirits. "You do not scare me."

She turned up her iPod and finally slept.

As soon as the sun was up, she roused her driver, slumped deep in his hammock.

"Come on, we're going to Soriya Market," she said.

The driver looked up at her dazed, then remembered to smile and lower his head in respect.

His face fell when she showed up in the garage with all forty-two of her mobile phones in one black bag.

It was too early for Soriya Market to open. They drove in circles with sunrise blazing directly into their eyes. On the streets, men pushed carts like beasts of burden, or carried cascades of belts into the old Central Market. The old market was domed, art deco, the color of vomit, French. Sith never shopped there.

"Maybe you should go visit your mom," said the driver. "You know, she loves you. Families are there for when you are in trouble."

Sith's mother lived in Thailand and they never spoke. Her mother's family kept asking for favors: money, introductions, or help with getting a job. Sith didn't speak to them any longer.

"My family is only trouble."

The driver shut up and drove.

Finally Soriya opened. Sith went straight to Dara's shop and dumped all the phones on the blue countertop. "Can you take these back?"

"We only do exchanges. I can give a new phone for an old one." Dara looked thoughtful. "Don't worry. Leave them here with me, I'll go sell them to a guy in the old market, and give you your money tomorrow." He smiled in approval. "This is very sensible."

He passed one phone back, the one with video and email. "This is the best one, keep this."

Dara was so competent. Sith wanted to sink down onto him like a pillow and stay there. She sat in the shop all day, watching him work. One of the guys from the games shop upstairs asked, "Who is this beautiful girl?"

Dara answered proudly, "My girlfriend."

Dara drove her back on the Dream and at the door to her house, he chuckled. "I don't want to go." She pressed a finger against his naughty lips, and smiled and spun back inside from happiness.

She was in the ground-floor garage. She heard something like a rat scuttle. In her bag, the telephone rang. Who were these people to importune her, even if they were dead? She wrenched the mobile phone out of her bag and pushed the green button and put the phone to her ear. She waited. There was a sound like wind.

A child spoke to her, his voice clogged as if he was crying. "They tied my thumbs together."

Sith demanded. "How did you get my number?"

"I'm all alone!"

"Then ring somebody else. Someone in your family."

"All my family are dead. I don't know where I am. My name is – "

Sith clicked the phone off. She opened the trunk of the car and tossed the phone inside it. Being telephoned by ghosts was so...unmodern. How could Cambodia become a number one country if its cell phone network was haunted?

She stormed up into the salon. On top of a table, the $1500, no-mess dog stared at her from out of his packaging. Sith clumped up the stairs onto the roof terrace to sleep as far away as she could from everything in the house.

She woke up in the dark, to hear thumping from downstairs.

The sound was metallic and hollow, as if someone were locked in the car. Sith turned on her iPod. Something was making the sound of the music skip. She fought the tangle of wires, and wrenched out another player, a Xen, but it too skipped, burping the sound of speaking voices into the middle of the music.

Had she heard a ripping sound? She pulled out the earphones, and heard something climbing the stairs.

A sound of light, uneven lolloping. She thought of crippled children. Frost settled over her like a heavy blanket and she could not move.

The robot dog came whirring up onto the terrace. It paused at the top of the stairs, its camera nose pointing at her to see, its useless eyes glowing cherry red.

The robot dog said in a warm, friendly voice, "My name is Phalla. I tried to buy my sister medicine and they killed me for it."

Sith tried to say, "Go away," but her throat wouldn't open.

The dog tilted its head. "No one even knows I'm dead. What will you do for all the people who are not mourned?"

Laughter blurted out of her, and Sith saw it rise up as cold vapor into the air.

"We have no one to invite us to the feast," said the dog.

Sith giggled in terror. "Nothing. I can do nothing!" she said, shaking her head.

"You laugh?" The dog gathered itself and jumped up into the hammock with her. It turned and lifted up its clear plastic tail and laid a genuine turd alongside Sith. Short brown hair was wound up in it, a scalp actually, and a single flat white human tooth smiled out of it.

Sith squawked and overturned both herself and the dog out of the hammock and onto the floor. The dog pushed its nose up against hers and began to sing an old-fashioned children's song about birds.

Something heavy huffed its way up the stairwell toward her. Sith shivered with cold on the floor and could not move. The dog went on singing in a high, sweet voice. A large shadow loomed out over the top of the staircase, and Sith gargled, swallowing laughter, trying to speak.

"There was thumping in the car and no one in it," said the driver.

Sith sagged toward the floor with relief. "The ghosts," she said. "They're back." She thrust herself to her feet. "We're getting out now. Ring the Hilton. Find out if they have rooms."

She kicked the toy dog down the stairs ahead of her. "We're moving now!"

Together they all loaded the car, shaking. Once again, the house was left to ghosts. As they drove, the mobile phone rang over and over inside the trunk.

The new Hilton (which does not exist) rose up by the river across from the Department for Cults and Religious Affairs. Tall and marbled and pristine, it had crystal chandeliers and fountains, and wood and brass handles in the elevators.

In the middle of the night only the Bridal Suite was still available, but it had an extra parental chamber where the driver and his wife could sleep. High on the twenty-first floor, the night sparkled with lights and everything was hushed, as far away from Cambodia as it was possible to get.

Things were quiet after that, for a while.

Every day she and Dara went to movies, or went to a restaurant. They went shopping. She slipped him money and he bought himself a beautiful suit. He said, over a hamburger at Lucky7, "I've told my mother that I've met a girl."

Sith smiled and thought: and I bet you told her that I'm rich.

"I've decided to live in the Hilton," she told him.

Maybe we could live in the Hilton. A pretty smile could hint at that.

The rainy season ended. The last of the monsoons rose up dark gray with a froth of white cloud on top, looking exactly like a giant wave about to break.

Dry cooler air arrived.

After work was over Dara convinced her to go for a walk along the river in front of the Royal Palace. He went to the men's room to change into a new luxury suit and Sith thought: he's beginning to imagine life with all that money.

As they walked along the river, exposed to all those people, Sith shook inside. There were teenage boys everywhere. Some of them were in rags, which was reassuring, but some of them were very well dressed indeed, the sons of Impunity who could do anything. Sith swerved suddenly to avoid even seeing them. But Dara in his new beige suit looked like one of them, and the generals' sons nodded to him with quizzical eyebrows, perhaps wondering who he was.

In front of the palace, a pavilion reached out over the water. Next to it a traditional orchestra bashed and wailed out something old fashioned. Hundreds of people crowded around a tiny wat. Dara shook Sith's wrist and they stood up to see.

People held up bundles of lotus flowers and incense in prayer. They threw the bundles into the wat. Monks immediately shoveled the joss sticks and flowers out of the back.

Behind the wat, children wearing T-shirts and shorts black with filth rootled through the dead flowers, the smoldering incense, and old coconut shells.

Sith asked, "Why do they do that?"

"You are so innocent!" chuckled Dara and shook his head. The evening was blue and gold. Sith had time to think that she did not want to go back to a hotel and that the only place she really felt happy was next to Dara. All around that thought was something dark and tangled.

Dara suggested with affection that they should get married.

It was as if Sith had her answer ready. "No, absolutely not," she said at once. "How can you ask that? There is not even anyone for you to ask! Have you spoken to your family about me? Has your family made any checks about my background?"

Which was what she really wanted to know.

Dara shook his head. "I have explained that you are an orphan, but they are not concerned with that. We are modest people. They will be happy if I am happy."

"Of course they won't be! Of course they will need to do checks."

Sith scowled. She saw her way to sudden advantage. "At least they must consult fortunetellers. They are not fools. I can help them. Ask them the names of the fortunetellers they trust."

Dara smiled shyly. "We have no money."

"I will give them money and you can tell them that you pay."

Dara's eyes searched her face. "I don't want that."

"How will we know if it is a good marriage? And your poor mother, how can you ask her to make a decision like this without information? So. You ask your family for the names of good professionals they trust, and I will pay them, and I will go to Prime Minister Hun Sen's own personal fortuneteller, and we can compare results."

Thus she established again both her propriety and her status.

In an old romance, the parents would not approve of the match and the fortuneteller would say that the marriage was ill-omened. Sith left nothing to romance.

She offered the family's fortunetellers whatever they wanted – a car, a farm – and in return demanded a written copy of their judgment. All of them agreed that the portents for the marriage were especially auspicious.

Then she secured an appointment with the Prime Minister's fortuneteller.

Hun Sen's *Kru Taey* was a lady in a black business suit. She had long fingernails like talons, but they were perfectly manicured and frosted white.

She was the kind of fortuneteller who is possessed by someone else's spirit. She sat at a desk and looked at Sith as unblinking as a fish, both her hands steepled together. After the most basic of hellos, she said. "Dollars only. Twenty-five thousand. I need to buy my son an apartment."

"That's a very high fee," said Sith.

"It's not a fee. It is a consideration for giving you the answer you want. My fee is another twenty-five thousand dollars."

They negotiated. Sith liked the Kru Taey's manner. It confirmed everything Sith believed about life.

The fee was reduced somewhat but not the consideration.

"Payment up front now," the Kru Taey said. She wouldn't take a check. Like only the very best restaurants she accepted foreign credit cards. Sith's Swiss card worked immediately. It had unlimited credit in case she had to leave the country in a hurry.

The Kru Taey said, "I will tell the boy's family that the marriage will be particularly fortunate."

Sith realized that she had not yet said anything about a boy, his family, or a marriage.

The Kru Taey smiled. "I know you are not interested in your real fortune. But to be kind, I will tell you unpaid that this marriage really is particularly well favored. All the other fortunetellers would have said the same thing without being bribed."

The Kru Taey's eyes glinted in the most unpleasant way. "So you needn't have bought them farms or paid me an extra twenty-five thousand dollars."

She looked down at her perfect fingernails. "You will be very happy indeed. But not before your entire life is overturned."

The back of Sith's arms prickled as if from cold. She should have been angry but she could feel herself smiling. Why?

And why waste politeness on the old witch? Sith turned to go without saying good-bye.

"Oh, and about your other problem," said the woman.

Sith turned back and waited.

"Enemies," said the Kru Taey, "can turn out to be friends."

Sith sighed. "What are you talking about?"

The Kru Taey's smile was as wide as a tiger-trap. "The million people your father killed."

Sith went hard. "Not a million," she said. "Somewhere between two hundred and fifty and five hundred thousand."

"Enough," smiled the Kru Taey. "My father was one of them." She smiled for a moment longer. "I will be sure to tell the Prime Minister that you visited me."

Sith snorted as if in scorn. "I will tell him myself."

But she ran back to her car.

That night, Sith looked down on all the lights like diamonds. She settled onto the giant mattress and turned on her iPod.

Someone started to yell at her. She pulled out the earpieces and jumped to the window. It wouldn't open. She shook it and wrenched its frame until it reluctantly slid an inch and she threw the iPod out of the twenty-first-floor window.

She woke up late the next morning, to hear the sound of the TV. She opened up the double doors into the salon and saw Jorani, pressed against the wall.

"The TV..." Jorani said, her eyes wide with terror.

The driver waited by his packed bags. He stood up, looking as mournful as a bloodhound.

On the widescreen TV there was what looked like a pop music karaoke video. Except that the music was very old fashioned. Why would a pop video show a starving man eating raw maize in a field? He glanced over his shoulder in terror as he ate. The glowing singalong words were the song that the dog had sung at the top of the stairs. The starving man looked up at Sith and corn mash rolled out of his mouth.

"It's all like that," said the driver. "I unplugged the set, but it kept playing on every channel." He sompiahed but looked miserable. "My wife wants to leave."

Sith felt shame. It was miserable and dirty, being infested with ghosts. Of course they would want to go.

"It's okay. I can take taxis," she said.

The driver nodded, and went into the next room and whispered to his wife. With little scurrying sounds, they gathered up their things. They sompiahed, and apologized.

The door clicked almost silently behind them.

It will always be like this, thought Sith. Wherever I go. It would be like this with Dara.

The hotel telephone started to ring. Sith left it ringing. She covered the TV with a blanket, but the terrible, tinny old music kept wheedling and rattling its way out at her, and she sat on the edge of her bed, staring into space.

I'll have to leave Cambodia.

At the market, Dara looked even more cheerful than usual. The fortunetellers had pronounced the marriage as very favorable. His mother had invited Sith home for the Pchum Ben festival.

"We can take the bus tomorrow," he said.

"Does it smell? All those people in one place?"

"It smells of air freshener. Then we take a taxi, and then you will have to walk up the track." Dara suddenly doubled up in laughter. "Oh, it will be good for you."

"Will there be dirt?"

"Everywhere! Oh, your dirty Nikes will earn you much merit!"

But at least, thought Sith, there will be no TV or phones.

Two days later, Sith was walking down a dirt track, ducking tree branches. Dust billowed all over her shoes. Dara walked behind her, chuckling, which meant she thought he was scared too.

She heard a strange rattling sound. "What's that noise?"

"It's a goat," he said. "My mother bought it for me in April as a present."

A goat. How could they be any more rural? Sith had never seen a goat. She never even imagined that she would.

Dara explained. "I sell them to the Muslims. It is Agricultural Diversification."

There were trees everywhere, shadows crawling across the ground like snakes. Sith felt sick. *One mosquito*, she promised herself, *just one and I will squeal and run away.*

The house was tiny, on thin twisting stilts. She had pictured a big fine country house standing high over the ground on concrete pillars with a sunburst carving in the gable. The kitchen was a hut that sat directly on the ground, no stilts, and it was made of palm-leaf panels and there was no electricity. The strip light in the ceiling was attached to a car battery and they kept a live fire on top of the concrete table to cook. Everything smelled of burnt fish.

Sith loved it.

Inside the hut, the smoke from the fires kept the mosquitoes away. Dara's mother, Mrs. Non Kunthea, greeted her with a smile. That triggered a respectful sompiah from Sith, the prayer-like gesture leaping out of her unbidden. On the platform table was a plastic sack full of dried prawns.

Without thinking, Sith sat on the table and began to pull the salty prawns out of their shells.

Why am I doing this?

Because it's what I did at home.

Sith suddenly remembered the enclosure in the forest, a circular fenced area. Daddy had slept in one house, and the women in another. Sith would talk to the cooks. For something to do, she would chop vegetables or shell prawns. Then Daddy would come to eat and he'd sit on the platform table and she, little Sith, would sit between his knees.

Dara's older brother Yuth came back for lunch. He was pot-bellied and drove a taxi for a living, and he moved in hard jabs like an angry old man. He reached too far for the rice and Sith could smell his armpits.

"You see how we live," Yuth said to Sith. "This is what we get for having the wrong patron. Sihanouk thought we were anti-monarchist. To Hun Sen, we were the enemy. Remember the Work for Money program?"

No.

"They didn't give any of those jobs to us. We might as well have been the Khmer Rouge!"

The past, thought Sith, *why don't they just let it go? Why do they keep boasting about their old wars?*

Mrs. Non Kunthea chuckled with affection. "My eldest son was born angry," she said. "His slogan is 'ten years is not too late for revenge.'"

Yuth started up again. "They treat that old monster Pol Pot better than they treat us. But then, he was an important person. If you go to his stupa in Anlong Veng, you will see that people leave offerings! They ask him for lottery numbers!"

He crumpled his green, soft, old-fashioned hat back onto his head and said, "Nice to meet you, Sith. Dara, she's too high class for the likes of you." But he grinned as he said it. He left, swirling disruption in his wake.

The dishes were gathered. Again without thinking, Sith swept up the plastic tub and carried it to the blackened branches. They rested over puddles where the washing-up water drained.

"You shouldn't work," said Dara's mother. "You are a guest."

"I grew up in a refugee camp," said Sith. After all, it was true.

Dara looked at her with a mix of love, pride, and gratitude for the good fortune of a rich wife who works.

And that was the best Sith could hope for. This family would be fine for her.

In the late afternoon, all four brothers came with their wives for the end of Pchum Ben, when the ghosts of the dead can wander the Earth. People scatter rice on the temple floors to feed their families. Some ghosts have small mouths so special rice is used.

Sith never took part in Pchum Ben. How could she go to the temple and scatter rice for Pol Pot?

The family settled in the kitchen chatting and joking, and it all passed in a blur for Sith. Everyone else had family they could honor. To Sith's surprise one of the uncles suggested that people should write names of the deceased and burn them, to transfer merit. It was nothing to do with Pchum Ben, but a lovely idea, so all the family wrote down names.

Sith sat with her hands jammed under her arms.

Dara's mother asked, "Isn't there a name you want to write, Sith?"

"No," said Sith in a tiny voice. How could she write the name Pol Pot? He was surely roaming the world let loose from hell. "There is no one."

Dara rubbed her hand. "Yes there is, Sith. A very special name."

"No, there's not."

Dara thought she didn't want them to know her father was Kol Vireakboth. He leant forward and whispered. "I promise. No one will see it."

Sith's breath shook. She took the paper and started to cry.

"Oh," said Dara's mother, stricken with sympathy. "Everyone in this country has a tragedy."

Sith wrote the name Kol Vireakboth.

Dara kept the paper folded and caught Sith's eyes. *You see?* he seemed to say. *I have kept your secret safe.* The paper burned.

Thunder slapped a clear sky about the face. It had been sunny, but now as suddenly as a curtain dropped down over a doorway, rain fell. A wind came from nowhere, tearing away a flap of palm-leaf wall, as if forcing entrance in a fury.

The family whooped and laughed and let the rain drench their shoulders as they stood up to push the wall back down, to keep out the rain.

But Sith knew. Her father's enemy was in the kitchen.

The rain passed; the sun came out. The family chuckled and sat back down around or on the table. They lowered dishes of food and ate, making parcels of rice and fish with their fingers. Sith sat rigidly erect, waiting for misfortune.

What would the spirit of Kol Vireakboth do to Pol Pot's daughter? Would he overturn the table, soiling her with food? Would he send mosquitoes to bite and make her sick? Would he suck away all her good fortune, leaving the marriage blighted, her new family estranged?

Or would a kindly spirit simply wish that the children of all Cambodians could escape, escape the past?

Suddenly, Sith felt at peace. The sunlight and shadows looked new to her and her senses started to work in magic ways.

She smelled a perfume of emotion, sweet and bracing at the same time. The music from a neighbor's cassette player touched her arm gently. Words took the form of sunlight on her skin.

No one is evil, the sunlight said. *But they can be false.*

False, how? Sith asked without speaking, genuinely baffled.

The sunlight smiled with an old man's stained teeth. *You know very well how.*

All the air swelled with the scent of the food, savoring it. The trees sighed with satisfaction.

Life is true. Sith saw steam from the rice curl up into the branches. *Death is false.*

The sunlight stood up to go. It whispered. *Tell him.*

The world faded back to its old self.

That night in a hammock in a room with the other women, Sith suddenly sat bolt upright. Clarity would not let her sleep. She saw that there was no way ahead. She couldn't marry Dara. How could she ask him to marry someone who was harassed by one million dead? How could she explain I am haunted because I am Pol Pot's daughter and I have lied about everything?

The dead would not let her marry; the dead would not let her have joy. So who could Pol Pot's daughter pray to? Where could she go for wisdom?

Loak kru Kol Vireakboth, she said under her breath. *Please show me a way ahead.*

The darkness was sterner than the sunlight.

To be as false as you are, it said, you first have to lie to yourself.

What lies had Sith told? She knew the facts. Her father had been the head of a government that tortured and killed hundreds of thousands of people and starved the nation through mismanagement. I know the truth.

I just never think about it.

I've never faced it.

Well, the truth is as dark as I am, and you live in me, the darkness.

She had read books – well, the first chapter of books – and then dropped them as if her fingers were scalded. There was no truth for her in books. The truth ahead of her would be loneliness, dreary adulthood, and penance.

Grow up.

The palm-leaf panels stirred like waiting ghosts.

All through the long bus ride back, she said nothing. Dara went silent too, and hung his head.

In the huge and empty hotel suite, darkness awaited her. She'd had the phone and the TV removed; her footsteps sounded hollow. Jorani and the driver had been her only friends.

The next day she did not go to Soriya Market. She went instead to the torture museum of Tuol Sleng.

A cadre of young motoboys waited outside the hotel in baseball caps and bling. Instead, Sith hailed a sweet-faced older motoboy with a battered, rusty bike.

As they drove she asked him about his family. He lived alone and had no one except for his mother in Kompong Thom.

Outside the gates of Tuol Sleng he said, "This was my old school."

In one wing there were rows of rooms with one iron bed in each with handcuffs and stains on the floor. Photos on the wall showed twisted bodies chained to those same beds as they were found on the day of liberation. In one photograph, a chair was overturned as if in a hurry.

Sith stepped outside and looked instead at a beautiful house over the wall across the street. It was a high white house like her own, with pillars and a roof terrace and bougainvillaea, a modern daughter's house. What do they think when they look out from that roof terrace? How can they live here?

The grass was tended and full of hopping birds. People were painting the shutters of the prison a fresh blue-gray.

In the middle wing, the rooms were galleries of photographed faces. They stared out at her like the faces from her printer. Were some of them the same?

"Who are they?" she found herself asking a Cambodian visitor.

"Their own," the woman replied. "This is where they sent Khmer Rouge cadres who had fallen out of favor. They would not waste such torture on ordinary Cambodians."

Some of the faces were young and beautiful men. Some were children or dignified old women.

The Cambodian lady kept pace with her. Company? Did she guess who Sith was? "They couldn't simply beat party cadres to death. They sent them and their entire families here. The children too, the grandmothers. They had different days of the week for killing children and wives."

An innocent-looking man smiled out at the camera as sweetly as her aged motoboy, directly into the camera of his torturers. He seemed to expect kindness from them, and decency. *Comrades*, he seemed to say.

The face in the photograph moved. It smiled more broadly and was about to speak.

Sith's eyes darted away. The next face sucked all her breath away.

It was not a stranger. It was Dara, her Dara, in black shirt and black cap. She gasped and looked back at the lady. Her pinched and solemn face nodded up and down. Was she a ghost too?

Sith reeled outside and hid her face and didn't know if she could go on standing. Tears slid down her face and she wanted to be sick and she turned her back so no one could see.

Then she walked to the motoboy, sitting in a shelter. In complete silence, she got on his bike feeling angry at the place, angry at the government for preserving it, angry at the foreigners who visited it like a tourist attraction, angry at everything.

That is not who we are! That is not what I am!

The motoboy slipped onto his bike, and Sith asked him: What happened to your family? It was a cruel question. He had to smile and look cheerful. His father had run a small shop; they went out into the country and never came back. He lived with his brother in a jeum-room, a refugee camp in Thailand. They came back to fight the Vietnamese and his brother was killed.

She was going to tell the motoboy, drive me back to the Hilton, but she felt ashamed. Of what? Just how far was she going to run?

She asked him to take her to the old house on Monivong Boulevard.

As the motorcycle wove through back streets, dodging red-earth ruts and pedestrians, she felt rage at her father. How dare he involve her in something like that! Sith had lived a small life and had no measure of things so she thought: *It's as if someone tinted my hair and it all fell out. It's as if someone pierced my ears and they got infected and my whole ear rotted away.*

She remembered that she had never felt any compassion for her father. She had been twelve years old when he stood trial, old and sick and making such a show of leaning on his stick. Everything he did was a show. She remembered rolling her eyes in constant embarrassment. Oh, he was fine in front of rooms full of adoring students. He could play the bong thom with them. They thought he was enlightened. He sounded good, using his false, soft, and kindly little voice, as if he was dubbed. He had made Sith recite Verlaine, Rimbaud, and Rilke. He killed thousands for having foreign influences.

I don't know what I did in a previous life to deserve you for a father. But you were not my father in a previous life and you won't be my father in the next. I reject you utterly. I will never burn your name. You can wander hungry out of hell every year for all eternity. I will pray to keep you in hell.

I am not your daughter!

If you were false, I have to be true.

Her old house looked abandoned in the stark afternoon light, closed and innocent. At the doorstep she turned and thrust a fistful of dollars into the motoboy's hand. She couldn't think straight; she couldn't even see straight, her vision blurred.

Back inside, she calmly put down her teddy-bear rucksack and walked upstairs to her office. Aido the robot dog whirred his way toward her. She had broken his back leg kicking him downstairs. He limped, whimpering like a dog, and lowered his head to have it stroked.

To her relief, there was only one picture waiting for her in the tray of the printer.

Kol Vireakboth looked out at her, middle-aged, handsome, worn, wise. Pity and kindness glowed in his eyes.

The land line began to ring.

"Youl prom," she told the ghosts. Agreed.

She picked up the receiver and waited.

A man spoke. "My name was Yin Bora." His voice bubbled up brokenly as if from underwater.

A light blinked in the printer. A photograph slid out quickly. A young student stared out at her looking happy at a family feast. He had a Beatle haircut and a striped shirt.

"That's me," said the voice on the phone. "I played football."

Sith coughed. "What do you want me to do?"

"Write my name," said the ghost.

"Please hold the line," said Sith, in a hypnotized voice. She fumbled for a pen, and then wrote on the photograph Yin Bora, footballer. He looked so sweet and happy. "You have no one to mourn you," she realized.

"None of us have anyone left alive to mourn us," said the ghost.

Then there was a terrible sound down the telephone, as if a thousand voices moaned at once.

Sith involuntarily dropped the receiver into place. She listened to her heart thump and thought about what was needed. She fed the printer with the last of her paper. Immediately it began to roll out more photos, and the land line rang again.

She went outside and found the motoboy, waiting patiently for her. She asked him to go and buy two reams of copying paper. At the last moment she added pens and writing paper and matches. He bowed and smiled and bowed again, pleased to have found a patron.

She went back inside, and with just a tremor in her hand picked up the phone.

For the next half hour, she talked to the dead, and found photographs and wrote down names. A woman mourned her children. Sith found photos of them all, and united them, father, mother, three children, uncles, aunts, cousins and grandparents, taping their pictures to her wall. The idea of uniting families appealed. She began to stick the other photos onto her wall.

Someone called from outside and there on her doorstep was the moto-boy, balancing paper and pens. "I bought you some soup." The broth came in neatly tied bags and was full of rice and prawns. She thanked him and paid him well and he beamed at her and bowed again and again.

All afternoon, the pictures kept coming. Darkness fell, the phone rang, the names were written, until Sith's hand, which was unused to writing any-thing, ached.

The doorbell rang, and on the doorstep, the motoboy sompiahed. "Excuse me, Lady, it is very late. I am worried for you. Can I get you dinner?"

Sith had to smile. He sounded motherly in his concern. They are so good at building a relationship with you, until you cannot do without them. In the old days she would have sent him away with a few rude words. Now she sent him away with an order.

And wrote.

And when he came back, the aged motoboy looked so happy. "I bought you fruit as well, Lady," he said, and added, shyly. "You do not need to pay me for that."

Something seemed to bump under Sith, as if she was on a motorcycle, and she heard herself say, "Come inside. Have some food too."

The motoboy sompiahed in gratitude and as soon as he entered, the phone stopped ringing.

They sat on the floor. He arched his neck and looked around at the walls. "Are all these people your family?" he asked.

She whispered. "No. They're ghosts who no one mourns."

"Why do they come to you?" His mouth fell open in wonder.

"Because my father was Pol Pot," said Sith, without thinking.

The motoboy sompiahed. "Ah." He chewed and swallowed and arched his head back again. "That must be a terrible thing. Everybody hates you."

Sith had noticed that wherever she sat in the room, the eyes in the photo-graphs were directly on her. "I haven't done anything," said Sith.

"You're doing something now," said the motoboy. He nodded and stood up, sighing with satisfaction. Life was good with a full stomach and a patron. "If you need me, Lady, I will be outside."

Photo after photo, name after name.

Youk Achariya: touring dancer

Proeung Chhay: school superintendent

Sar Kothida, child, aged 7, died of "swelling disease"

Sar Makara, her mother, nurse

Nath Mittapheap, civil servant, from family of farmers

Chor Monirath: *wife of award-winning engineer*
Yin Sokunthea: *Khmer Rouge commune leader*
She looked at the faces and realized. *Dara, I'm doing this for Dara.*

The city around her went quiet and she became aware that it was now very late indeed. Perhaps she should just make sure the motoboy had gone home.

He was still waiting outside.

"It's okay. You can go home. Where do you live?"

He waved cheerfully north. "Oh, on Monivong, like you." He grinned at the absurdity of the comparison.

A new idea took sudden form. Sith said, "Tomorrow, can you come early, with a big feast? Fish and rice and greens and pork: curries and stir-fries and kebabs." She paid him handsomely, and finally asked him his name. His name meant Golden.

"Good night, Sovann."

For the rest of the night she worked quickly like an answering service. This is like a cleaning of the house before a festival, she thought. The voices of the dead became ordinary, familiar. Why are people afraid of the dead? The dead can't hurt you. The dead want what you want: justice.

The wall of faces became a staircase and a garage and a kitchen of faces, all named. She had found Jorani's colored yarn, and linked family members into trees.

She wrote until the electric lights looked discolored, like a headache. She asked the ghosts, "Please can I sleep now?" The phones fell silent and Sith slumped with relief onto the polished marble floor.

She woke up dazed, still on the marble floor. Sunlight flooded the room. The faces in the photographs no longer looked swollen and bruised. Their faces were not accusing or mournful. They smiled down on her. She was among friends.

With a whine, the printer started to print; the phone started to ring. Her doorbell chimed, and there was Sovann, white cardboard boxes piled up on the back of his motorcycle. He wore the same shirt as yesterday, a cheap blue copy of a Lacoste. A seam had parted under the arm. He only has one shirt, Sith realized. She imagined him washing it in a basin every night.

Sith and Sovann moved the big tables to the front windows. Sith took out her expensive tablecloths for the first time, and the bronze platters. The feast was laid out as if at New Year. Sovann had bought more paper and pens. He knew what they were for. "I can help, Lady."

He was old enough to have lived in a country with schools, and he could write in a beautiful, old-fashioned hand. Together he and Sith spelled out the names of the dead and burned them.

"I want to write the names of my family too," he said. He burnt them weeping.

The delicious vapors rose. The air was full of the sound of breathing in. Loose papers stirred with the breeze. The ash filled the basins, but even after working all day, Sith and the motoboy had only honored half the names.

"Good night, Sovann," she told him.

"You have transferred a lot of merit," said Sovann, but only to be polite.

If I have any merit to transfer, thought Sith.

He left and the printers started, and the phone. She worked all night, and only stopped because the second ream of paper ran out.

The last picture printed was of Kol Vireakboth.

Dara, she promised herself. *Dara next.*

In the morning, she called him. "Can we meet at lunchtime for another walk by the river?"

Sith waited on top of the marble wall and watched an old man fish in the Tonlé Sap river and found that she loved her country. She loved its tough, smiling, uncomplaining people, who had never offered her harm, after all the harm her family had done them. Do you know you have the daughter of the monster sitting here among you?

Suddenly all Sith wanted was to be one of them. The monks in the pavilion, the white-shirted functionaries scurrying somewhere, the lazy bones dangling their legs, the young men who dress like American rappers and sold something dubious, drugs, or sex.

She saw Dara sauntering toward her. He wore his new shirt, and smiled at her but he didn't look relaxed. It had been two days since they'd met. He knew something was wrong, that she had something to tell him. He had bought them lunch in a little cardboard box. Maybe for the last time, thought Sith.

They exchanged greetings, almost like cousins. He sat next to her and smiled and Sith giggled in terror at what she was about to do.

Dara asked, "What's funny?"

She couldn't stop giggling. "Nothing is funny. Nothing." She sighed in order to stop and terror tickled her and she spurted out laughter again. "I lied to you. Kol Vireakboth is not my father. Another politician was my father. Someone you've heard of...."

The whole thing was so terrifying and absurd that the laughter squeezed her like a fist and she couldn't talk. She laughed and wept at the same time.

Dara stared.

"My father was Saloth Sar. That was his real name." She couldn't make herself say it. She could tell a motoboy, but not Dara? She forced herself onward. "My father was Pol Pot."

Nothing happened.

Sitting next to her, Dara went completely still. People strolled past; boats bobbed on their moorings.

After a time Dara said, "I know what you are doing."

That didn't make sense. "Doing? What do you mean?"

Dara looked sour and angry. "Yeah, yeah, yeah, yeah." He sat, looking away from her. Sith's laughter had finally shuddered to a halt. She sat peering at him, waiting. "I told you my family were modest," he said quietly.

"Your family are lovely!" Sith exclaimed.

His jaw thrust out. "They had questions about you too, you know."

"I don't understand."

He rolled his eyes. He looked back 'round at her. "There are easier ways to break up with someone."

He jerked himself to his feet and strode away with swift determination, leaving her sitting on the wall.

Here on the riverfront, everyone was equal. The teenage boys lounged on the wall; poor mothers herded children; the foreigners walked briskly, trying to look as if they didn't carry moneybelts. Three fat teenage girls nearly swerved into a cripple in a pedal chair and collapsed against each other with raucous laughter.

Sith did not know what to do. She could not move. Despair humbled her, made her hang her head.

I've lost him.

The sunlight seemed to settle next to her, washing up from its reflection on the wake of some passing boat.

No you haven't.

The river water smelled of kindly concern. The sounds of traffic throbbed with forbearance.

Not yet.

There is no forgiveness in Cambodia. But there are continual miracles of compassion and acceptance.

Sith appreciated for just a moment the miracles. The motoboy buying her soup. She decided to trust herself to the miracles.

Sith talked to the sunlight without making a sound. *Grandfather Vireakboth. Thank you. You have told me all I need to know.*

Sith stood up and from nowhere, the motoboy was there. He drove her to the Hello Phone shop.

Dara would not look at her. He bustled back and forth behind the counter, though there was nothing for him to do. Sith talked to him like a customer. "I want to buy a mobile phone," she said, but he would not answer. "There is someone I need to talk to."

Another customer came in. She was a beautiful daughter too, and he served her, making a great show of being polite. He complimented her on her appearance. "Really, you look cool." The girl looked pleased. Dara's eyes darted in Sith's direction.

Sith waited in the chair. This was home for her now. Dara ignored her. She picked up her phone and dialed his number. He put it to his ear and said, "Go home."

"You are my home," she said.

His thumb jabbed the C button.

She waited. Shadows lengthened.

"We're closing," he said, standing by the door without looking at her.

Shamefaced, Sith ducked away from him, through the door.

Outside Soriya, the motoboy played dice with his fellows. He stood up. "They say I am very lucky to have Pol Pot's daughter as a client."

There was no discretion in Cambodia, either. Everyone will know now, Sith realized.

At home, the piles of printed paper still waited for her. Sith ate the old, cold food. It tasted flat, all its savor sucked away. The phones began to ring. She fell asleep with the receiver propped against her ear.

The next day, Sith went back to Soriya with a box of the printed papers.

She dropped the box onto the blue plastic counter of Hello Phones.

"Because I am Pol Pot's daughter," she told Dara, holding out a sheaf of pictures toward him. "All the unmourned victims of my father are printing their pictures on my printer. Here. Look. These are the pictures of people who lost so many loved ones there is no one to remember them."

She found her cheeks were shaking and that she could not hold the sheaf of paper. It tumbled from her hands, but she stood back, arms folded.

Dara, quiet and solemn, knelt and picked up the papers. He looked at some of the faces. Sith pushed a softly crumpled green card at him. Her family ID card.

He read it. Carefully, with the greatest respect, he put the photographs on the countertop along with the ID card.

"Go home, Sith," he said, but not unkindly.

"I said," she had begun to speak with vehemence but could not continue. "I told you. My home is where you are."

"I believe you," he said, looking at his feet.

"Then...." Sith had no words.

"It can never be, Sith," he said. He gathered up the sheaf of photocopying paper. "What will you do with these?"

Something made her say, "What will *you* do with them?"

His face was crossed with puzzlement.

"It's your country too. What will you do with them? Oh, I know, you're such a poor boy from a poor family, who could expect anything from you? Well, you have your whole family and many people have no one. And you can buy new shirts and some people only have one."

Dara held out both hands and laughed. "Sith?" *You, Sith, are accusing me of being selfish?*

"You own them too." Sith pointed to the papers, to the faces. "You think the dead don't try to talk to you, too?"

Their eyes latched. She told him what he could do. "I think you should make an exhibition. I think Hello Phones should sponsor it. You tell them that. You tell them Pol Pot's daughter wishes to make amends and has chosen them. Tell them the dead speak to me on their mobile phones."

She spun on her heel and walked out. She left the photographs with him.

That night she and the motoboy had another feast and burned the last of the unmourned names. There were many thousands.

The next day she went back to Hello Phones.

"I lied about something else," she told Dara. She took out all the reports from the fortunetellers. She told him what Hun Sen's fortuneteller had told her. "The marriage is particularly well favored."

"Is that true?" He looked wistful.

"You should not believe anything I say. Not until I have earned your trust. Go consult the fortunetellers for yourself. This time you pay."

His face went still and his eyes focused somewhere far beneath the floor. Then he looked up, directly into her eyes. "I will do that."

For the first time in her life Sith wanted to laugh for something other than fear. She wanted to laugh for joy.

"Can we go to lunch at Lucky7?" she asked.

"Sure," he said.

All the telephones in the shop, all of them, hundreds all at once began to sing.

A waterfall of trills and warbles and buzzes, snatches of old songs or latest chart hits. Dara stood dumbfounded. Finally he picked one up and held it to his ear.

"It's for you," he said, and held out the phone for her.

There was no name or number on the screen.

Congratulations, dear daughter, said a warm kind voice.

"Who is this?" Sith asked. The options were severely limited.

Your new father, said Kol Vireakboth. The sound of wind. *I adopt you.*

A thousand thousand voices said at once, *We adopt you.*

In Cambodia, you share your house with ghosts in the way you share it with dust. You hear the dead shuffling alongside your own footsteps. You can sweep, but the sound does not go away.

On the Tra Bek end of Monivong there is a house whose owner has given it over to ghosts. You can try to close the front door. But the next day you will find it hanging open. Indeed you can try, as the neighbors did, to nail the door shut. It opens again.

By day, there is always a queue of five or six people wanting to go in, or hanging back, out of fear. Outside are offerings of lotus or coconuts with embedded josh sticks.

The walls and floors and ceilings are covered with photographs. The salon, the kitchen, the stairs, the office, the empty bedrooms, are covered with photographs of Chinese-Khmers at weddings, Khmer civil servants on picnics, Chams outside their mosques, Vietnamese holding up prize catches of fish; little boys going to school in shorts; cyclopousse drivers in front of their odd, old-fashioned pedaled vehicles; wives in stalls stirring soup. All of them are happy and joyful, and the background is Phnom Penh when it was the most beautiful city in Southeast Asia.

All the photographs have names written on them in old-fashioned handwriting.

On the table is a printout of thousands of names on slips of paper. Next to the table are matches and basins of ash and water. The implication is plain. Burn the names and transfer merit to the unmourned dead.

Next to that is a small printed sign that says in English HELLO.

Every Pchum Ben, those names are delivered to temples throughout the city. Gold foil is pressed onto each slip of paper, and attached to it is a parcel of sticky rice. At 8 A.M. food is delivered for the monks, steaming rice and fish, along with bolts of new cloth. At 10 A.M. more food is delivered, for the disabled and the poor.

And most mornings a beautiful daughter of Cambodia is seen walking beside the confluence of the Tonlé Sap and Mekong rivers. Like Cambodia, she plainly loves all things modern. She dresses in the latest fashion. Cambodian R&B whispers in her ear. She pauses in front of each new waterfront construction whether built by improvised scaffolding or erected with cranes. She buys noodles from the grumpy vendors with their tiny stoves. She carries a book or sits on the low marble wall to write letters and look at the boats, the monsoon clouds, and the dop-dops. She talks to the reflected sunlight on the river and calls it Father.

The Osteomancer's Son

Greg van Eekhout

Greg van Eekhout (*www.sff.net/people/greg*) lives in Tempe, Arizona. He is an instructional designer and multimedia developer for Arizona State University. His stories have appeared in *The Magazine of Fantasy & Science Fiction*, *Asimov's Science Fiction*, *The Year's Best Fantasy and Horror*, *Starlight 3*, and other places. He maintains a blog at *writing-andsnacks.com/blog*. In a recent interview published on LitHaven.com, he describes his approach to writing: "I'm very instinctual in my approach. I never set out to write, for example, a plotless present-tense story employing recursive narratives in the Aeolian mode that might be right for a small press, nor a traditional quest story with a stoic hero and a quipping sidekick that might be right for a big market. I usually start off with a core idea, and some neat stuff I want to fit in, and something that's harder to define – a general shape, or a color, or a tone, that I want to capture."

"The Osteomancer's Son" was published in *Asimov's Science Fiction*, which has drifted into the same publishing space as *The Magazine of Fantasy & Science Fiction*, but reversed. F&SF publishes a preponderance of excellent fantasy and some fine SF and horror, while *Asimov's* publishes a similar mix (without the horror), emphasizing SF. This tale is hard fantasy in the mode of Michael Swanwick's Iron Dragon stories (see the Swanwick story note later in this book), dark and brutal, technological, magical, and political. This kind of world is becoming one of the standard settings of fantasy. Here, Daniel, a thief and the son of an osteomancer, who knows a lot more about bone magic than is safe, is caught in a magical struggle.

THE BUS COMES TO A STOP at Wilshire and Fairfax, just a few blocks from the La Brea Tar Pits. When the doors hiss open, the tar smell washes over me. Thick and ancient, it snakes through my sinuses and settles in the back of my brain like a ghost in the attic.

"Get off or stay on," the driver says, impatient. So I step off into the haunted air.

The walk to Farmer's Market is too short. Not enough time for me to change my mind. For a moment, I wonder if looking at my wallet photo of Miranda would give me some more courage. I know every detail by heart: She's smiling and squinting into the camera, her face sun-dappled and brilliant. The ice cream cone I bought her on her third birthday is a pink smear across her face.

It's easier to think of her that way than to contemplate the handkerchief inside my bowling bag and the small bone contained within its linen folds.

I put my head down and keep walking, entering a maze of stalls and awnings, of narrow paths crowded with bins and baskets and little old ladies with sharp elbows. Shopping carts bark my shins and roll over my toes. Ranchero music and some kind of Southeast Asian pop bounces off my head.

"Hey, you got problem?" A man behind the counter beckons with a hooked finger, his face brown and creased like a cinnamon stick. "You got problem, yeah. I can tell. I got just what you need." With a knife, he sweeps bright orange dust into a little paper envelope. It looks like that the dehydrated cheese powder that comes with instant macaroni.

"What's that?" I ask.

His smile reveals several gold teeth. "Come from dragon turtle. You see giant dragon turtle wash up in San Diego? You see that on news?"

"I'm not really up on current events." Especially not as regurgitated by state-controlled news organizations.

He nods enthusiastically and edges more powder into the envelope. "This come from San Diego dragon turtle. Wife's younger brother, he lifeguard. He scrape some turtle shell before Hierarch's men confiscate whole carcass."

"What's it for?" I ask, indicating the powder-filled envelope.

"All sorts of stuff. Rheumatism, kidney stones, migraine, epilepsy, bedroom problems... All sorts."

"No, thanks," I say as I try to shoulder my way back into the crowd.

"Get you girls," he calls after me. "Make you animal! Guaranteed!"

Dragon turtle can't do any of those things, of course. Not that it's genuine turtle he's selling. I figure it for flour and sulfur, with maybe the tiniest pinch of rhinoceros horn thrown in. You can't even put a street value on the genuine stuff these days.

I know. I've experienced the genuine stuff. It's in my bones.

One Sunday afternoon I found a piece of kraken spine while walking down Santa Monica Beach with Dad. It was a cold day, the sand a sloping plain of gray beneath a slate sky, and we were both underdressed for the weather. But it was Sunday, the one day of the week we had together, and I had wanted to go the beach.

I spotted the spine in the receding foam of the surf. It was just a fragment, like a knitting needle, striped honey and black. I showed it to Dad.

"Good eye," he said, resting his hand on my shoulder. "I don't see many of these outside a locked vault." In his white shirt and gray slacks, he looked like one of the seagulls wheeling overhead. I imagined him spreading his long arms to catch the wind and float to the sky.

I, on the other hand, took after my mom – short and stocky, skin just a shade paler than terra cotta. "Your father is made of air," Mom once told me. "That's why he's so hard to understand; he's not always down here with us. But you and me, kid, you and me are plain as dirt."

Dad held out his hand for the spine. "Kraken live in the deeps," he said. "They hunt for giant squid and sperm whale. Sometimes, in a fight, the spines break off and they wash ashore." He smelled the spine, inhaling so deeply it was almost an act of aggression. "You've found good bone, Daniel. Better than mammoth tusk."

"Really?" John Blackland had never been known to lavish idle praise.

"Better than all the La Brea stuff, in fact. The kraken is even older. Smarter."

I waited while my father's thoughts followed their own silent paths. Then, brightly, he told me to find a shell. "Abalone would be perfect, but I'll take anything from the sea I can use as a crucible."

Within a few minutes I'd located half a mussel shell. We sat on the sand, the shell between us, and Dad cooked the tip of the kraken spine over the flame of his Zippo. Thin tendrils of smoke rose from the spine, smelling of salt and earth and dark, deep mud.

When a single drop of honey-colored fluid oozed from the tip of the spine into the shell, Dad killed the flame. "Okay," he said. "Good. Now, do like me." He lifted the shell to his mouth and lightly touched his tongue to the fluid. I did the same. It burned, but not more than a too-hot mug of cocoa. The oil tasted exactly as it smelled, like something that had come from dark and forgotten places, but also from inside me.

"Quick, now, Daniel. Hold my hand."

For a few moments, the waves crashed ashore and the gulls cried overhead and I shivered in the cold. Then it started. A prickling sensation ran across my skin, raising goose bumps. The tiny hairs on my arms stood at attention. Then it was popping in my body, as though my blood were carbonated. It hurt, and I felt it in my lips and eyes, a million pinpricks.

I looked at Dad. His face was a blur. He was actually vibrating, and I realized I was, too, and he smiled at me. "Don't be afraid," he said, his voice shuddering. "Trust me."

I wasn't afraid. Or, rather, the scared part of me was smaller than the part that was thrilled at the power of my father, the power of the kraken, the power inside me.

Lightning struck. Silver-white, cracking bursts.

Pain took me. I screamed, desperately trying to let some of it out, but there was only more. My body was a sponge for it, with limitless capacity. Pain replaced everything.

When my world finally stilled and my eyes could once again see, Dad and I were surrounded by a moat of liquefied sand. Black, gooey glass smoked and bubbled.

"The kraken is a creature of storms," Dad said. "Now, a part that will always rage inside you. That's the osteomancer's craft: To draw magic from bones, to infuse it into your own." He looked at me a long time, as if to see if I understood.

The pain was over, but the memory of it roiled inside and around me, like smoke from a fire.

Trust me, he'd said.

"Don't tell your mom about this. That kraken spine could have paid for your college education."

Farther back in the recesses of Farmer's Market, closer to the Tar Pits, the smell of asphalt clogs the air. Black ooze seeps through cracks in the alley, and when I walk, my shoes stick to the ground. There's black tar under the pavement. Pockets of gas lurk beneath the sidewalks like jellyfish.

Storage sheds and small warehouses line the alley, guarded by guys, teenagers, just a few years younger than me. They conceal their hands in the pockets of their roomy pants and watch me make my way down a row of cinderblock structures. I stop before a building with a steel roll-down door, and four guards converge on me, forming a diamond with me at the center.

"You must be lost," one says.

They all have eyes the color of coffee ice cream and the same face. Not just similar in appearance, but identical. Maybe they're quadruplets, but more likely they're mirror-spawn. It takes pretty deep magic to create them, but when it comes to the Hierarch and his interests, no expense is ever spared. These guys aren't just rent-a-cop security. These guys are weapons.

"Are these warehouses?" I say, waving vaguely at the buildings around us.

The four share a look and nod in unison.

"Then I think I'm in the right place."

"You'd have been better off lost," says the one behind me. "What's in the bowling bag?"

"A bowling ball."

"What kind?"

"Brunswick." That's the name written on the bag.

"I like to bowl," they all say together. Then, just the one behind me: "Let's take a peek inside."

Two of them unzip the bag, while the other two keep their eyes on me. I reach into my coat pocket and all four get ready to pounce. "Relax," I say, pulling out my leather glasses case. "Just putting on my shades."

Which, really, is all I do.

Frowns form on the faces of the four mirror-spawn. They blink. They work their lips a little. "What are you looking at?" they all ask of each other.

"Nothing," they all decide.

Their diamond formation loosens, and they go back to whatever they were doing before I showed up. I take my bowling bag and continue looking for the right warehouse.

When my first baby tooth fell out I tucked it under my pillow, just as Mom had told me to. The next morning the tooth was gone but I found no coin. Mom and Dad were arguing in the living room. I wanted to go out and see Dad, but not until the fight was over.

I read some comics.

I glued plastic tusks on my Revel Colombian Mammoth model.

With my tongue, I probed the empty socket where my tooth had been.

Finally, the noise in the other room died down, and I heard the front door open and shut. Moments later, a car started and drove away: Dad going back to his apartment.

"From now on," Mom said, standing in the doorway, "when you lose a tooth, put it in an envelope for your father."

"What for?"

She gripped the doorjamb so tight her hand shook. "So he can eat them."

By that age, I already knew Dad worked for the Hierarch – the most powerful osteomancer of all – and I knew that made my father a very important man.

It wasn't until years later, until after the Night of Long Knives, that I knew Dad was a traitor.

This, I found out from Uncle Otis, my father's brother, who took me in after Dad was murdered and Mom defected to Northern California.

I'd left Otis when I turned sixteen and had nearly no contact with him until two weeks ago. I knew he helped out Connie and Miranda with money, dropped in on their little apartment in Boyle Heights to make sure they were okay, but I'd never asked him to do that and I refused to be grateful.

The door jingled as I entered his shop for the first time in seven years.

"You never got tall," he said by way of greeting.

He wasn't alone. On a stool behind a glass display counter of jewelry and cigarette cases and Zippo lighters sat a thin-shouldered man in a sweater the color of wilted lettuce. He gave me a smile with his lipless turtle mouth and took a sip from a Dodgers coffee mug.

"Nice to meet you, Daniel."

I took note of the turtle man's skin, teeth, fingernails. They were by no means healthy colors, but neither were they the deeply embedded telltale brown of a practicing osteomancer. I figured him for a supplier, like Otis.

I should have turned around, gone back home. Trafficking in osteomancy had been a bad idea since the Night of Long Knives – I was surprised Otis hadn't been caught yet – and I always got the feeling the Hierarch's eyes were on me, being the son of John Blackland.

Otis tried to introduce me to the turtle man. "Daniel, this is Mr. – " But the turtle man cut him off with a sharp look. Otis settled on telling me he was a friend of my father's.

I took "friend" as a codeword for former co-conspirator. Dad had been a darling of the Hierarch until he'd decided there was too much power concentrated in the Hierarch's hands, and he hadn't been alone in this belief. Magic wants to be free. But after the Night of Long Knives, what had been the seeds of a revolution had degenerated into merely a black market for osteomantic materials. Now, it was just about skimming a bit off the Hierarch's profit.

I wanted no part of it. Not a sliver. But there was the lure of money and pangs about how little I was doing for Miranda. "Is this a bag job?"

Otis nodded. "The sort of thing you're good at."

I had kept myself out of the family business, but that didn't mean I'd been walking the straight and narrow. Part of the reason I'd left Otis's care was because I felt he wasn't dealing fairly with me when fencing stuff I'd boosted from houses and businesses.

"It's a tricky job, in a place hard to get into and even harder to get out of."

"Government warehouse, I suppose?" Which was tantamount to a suicide mission.

The turtle man looked at me with dark eyes. I recognized that look. In his head, he was stripping me of clothing and skin. He was wondering what my skeleton looked like. "It's not just any government warehouse, Daniel. We're sending you into the Ossuary itself."

The Ossuary. The dragon's greatest treasure trove. The Hierarch's own private stash.

I didn't bother explaining what an impossible task that would be. These guys were veterans. They wouldn't risk exposure in a pointless exercise. But they would risk my life to get their hands on the Hierarch's riches.

I, on the other hand, would not. "Thanks, Otis," I said, turning my back and heading for the door. "Don't call me ever again."

I heard the turtle man's coffee cup clank against the glass counter. "You haven't even heard our terms."

"And I'm not going to," I said. "My daughter deserves a living father."

"Daniel, I have something for you." I stopped and watched Otis place a folded handkerchief on the glass counter. The look on his face was infinitely sad as he peeled back the corners of the handkerchief and revealed a small distal phalanx. A finger bone. A child's finger bone, not white, but already turning brown. The bone of a child who has been fed bone. When I was a kid, that's what my bones would have looked like, because even then, Dad was preparing me.

"It belongs to Miranda," the turtle man said. "Do the job or we'll piece her out, bit by bit."

Dad lived in the back of his osteomancer's shop, and that's where I spent most of my time with him during weekend visits. Six years after that afternoon on the beach, I was in his workroom, watching a pair of horn-rimmed glasses bob inside a kettle of boiling oil. The lenses were blanks, but the frames were special, carved from the vertebrae of a Choctaw sint holo serpent. I was certain that Dad didn't have legal access to such materials. He'd probably obtained it in one of the back-alley exchanges he'd become increasingly involved with. Things had been different for him, lately. Once one of the Hierarch's chief men, he was more and more on the fringes of things.

Dad stirred the oil with a copper spoon, sniffing the vapors that rose from the pot. He quizzed me: "Any idea what these glasses will do?"

I was bored. Only eight blocks away there was a mall full of video games and CDs to shoplift and girls. I couldn't remember the last time Dad and I had talked about anything other than bones and oils and feathers and powders. Dad's world was full of dead things that stank.

"I have no idea what they do," I said. It was true, but it wasn't what Dad wanted to hear.

He breathed a small sigh. "Smell it, Daniel. You can tell by smell. Smells are ghosts. Let them in and they'll talk to you."

He wouldn't give up until I did as he asked, so, sullenly, I admitted the phantoms. Figuring out what they were trying to tell me was a process requiring the kind of patience and attention I could seldom be bothered to exhibit. I lowered my nose to the kettle.

First, there were my father's tells, not just because he was in the room, but because the kettle contained his magic. There was clean sweat. Old Spice. And tar. Deeply embedded, way down to the marrow of Dad's bones. My father's living ghost. And also something of me. Maybe some of my baby teeth. The smells were all mixed up, and I couldn't tell where he ended and I began.

"What do you think?" Dad whispered, bending close to my ear.

"It's like...something I can't hold onto. Like confusion."

Dad straightened. "It's in your bones, now, Daniel. You know how to let the old bones inside you. You only need to listen to them, and they'll tell you how to do whatever you need to do. That's osteomancy. That's deep magic." He gestured at his work counter, littered with jars and vials and little envelopes. "All else is merely recipe."

From outside, the sound of a helicopter rotor pounded the air. The phone rang. Dad went to the front room to answer it, and I stayed behind, eavesdropping on his conversation.

"Not a good time, Otis." Then, his voice dropped. "Yes, I've got something cooking right now."

The sound of the helicopter grew closer, and now it sounded as though there were more than one. I went to the door and saw the look on Dad's face, the way the lines deepened, the haunted shadows of his eyes. "Who else did they get?" he said into the receiver, craning his neck to peer out the living room window. Dad listened to whatever Otis's answer was, his eyes shut tight. When he opened them, he saw me standing in the doorway. "Will you take care of him, Otis? Will you promise me?" There was a pause, and then he put the receiver back in its cradle.

Out on the street, car doors slammed. Dad came over to the workroom doorway and pushed me back inside. "The glasses aren't ready yet," he said. "Wait as long as you can before putting them on. Don't come out till you've heard the thunder. When you walk, make no noise." With that, he shut the door on me.

A few moments later, I heard shouting in the living room, a scuffle. And then cracks of thunder, so close, like bombs detonating in my head. The loudest thing I'd ever heard.

Silence followed, broken by soft footsteps outside the workroom. The doorknob jiggled. Another beat of silence, and something impacted the door. Wood splintered.

I ran to Dad's work counter. The glasses still tumbled inside the boiling oil. With a pair of copper tongs, I lifted out the glasses and put them on, hissing in pain as I burned my fingers and temples and the backs of my ears and the bridge of my nose. My skin blistered, and whatever substance Dad had used to fashion the frames leeched into me.

With another blow the door gave, hanging on one hinge, useless as a broken arm. Half a dozen cops surged in. A gray-haired man in a blue windbreaker, marked with the Hierarch's skull insignia, pushed to the front of the group. I backed up against the workbench. The man in the windbreaker was close enough to touch. He looked at me, right at me, and raised his hand as if to reach out and grab my throat. I remained silent, and he only blinked stupidly in my general direction.

My heart pounding, I forced myself to walk slowly past the cops, who flinched as though brushed by cobwebs. In the living room were four charred bodies. The flesh on their faces and hands bubbled, black and red. The room stank of ozone and meat and kraken.

Dad hadn't managed to get them all. He was on his back. Three cops were cutting the skin off of him with long knives. They'd already flayed his arm, exposing the deep rich brown of his radius and ulna. And they'd peeled his face back to expose his coffee-brown skull.

That night, I ran. Away from Dad's place, away from the rotor blades and searchlights. I ran until I could only walk, walked until I could only stumble, stumbled until I could only crawl. When morning broke, I woke up in wet sand and bathed myself in the cold waves that rolled in on the edge of a winter storm. I will live here, I thought. I will live here on the beach, and I will never take off these glasses, and I will live here as a ghost.

He was already dead, I told myself. When the men cut open Dad to take his bones, he was already dead.

I would keep telling myself that until I could believe it.

The route to the Hierarch's ossuary takes me through a network of tunnels buried so deep beneath the city that, after a while, I can no longer feel the rumble of traffic from Wilshire Boulevard. The stench of tar and magic is almost a solid wall here, the ghosts so thick I can practically scoop them out of the air with my hands. Using the turtle man's collection of lock picks, stolen keys, alarm codes, passwords, and my father's glasses, I eventually find myself at the threshold of the Hierarch's ossuary.

Let's say you're sickeningly wealthy. And let's say what you're rich in is gold, and you want a big room in which to hoard your treasure. What could be more fitting, then, than a room built of solid gold bricks? The Hierarch's ossuary is kind of like that, only it's built of bone. The walls are mammoth femurs stacked end-to-end. The floor, a mosaic of various claws and delicate vertebrae and healing jewels pried from the heads of Peruvian carbuncles. Overhead, mammoth tusks form the domed ceiling. And from the dome hangs a chandelier of unicorn horns, white as snow.

I remind myself to breathe.

Six sentries carry bayonets with basilisk-tooth blades. They exchange uneasy glances as I step deeper into the room. I've been warned by Otis and the turtle man that anyone I encountered this far inside the Hierarch's stronghold will have received advanced training. They will have tasted deep-magic bone.

"Hoss, you okay?" says one of the sentries.

Another shakes his head, looking directly at me. "Nope. Something's creeping me out."

"Yeah, me too. Think we should get the hound in here?"

"Yeah." The sentry reaches for a wall-mounted phone.

I unlace my boot and pry it off. With everything I've got, I chuck it up at the unicorn chandelier. The horns shatter like glass, the sound of children shrieking. I backpedal to avoid the rain of shards.

The sentries look up in horror. They're in charge of protecting a lot of money, and something's just gone dreadfully wrong. They flutter about the mess like maiden aunts over a collapsed soufflé.

I retrieve my boot and make a dash for a passageway into an even larger room.

The entrance of bone was made to impress. This place, large enough to berth an ocean liner, houses yet greater wealth. Floor-to-ceiling shelves occupy most of it, but there are also fully assembled skeletons in chain-link cages: a serpent at least one hundred yards long, a feline body as large as an elephant with a boulder-sized skull. And suspended overhead looms a kraken – flat, shovel-shaped head, tail half the length of a football field, and running down the tail, dozens of spines as long as jousting lances. The stench of its power makes my stomach churn.

There is really only one reason Otis and the turtle man chose me for this job. One thing I can do better than anyone else. There's a scent I'm sensitive to, one I can pick out like a bright white stripe on a black highway. I follow it to a row of towering shelves and bring over a ladder on wheels. I climb.

Stacked on the shelves are long cardboard boxes. In front of my face is the one containing my father's bones.

His remains are powerful weapons. I understand why Otis and the turtle man and whoever else is in their cabal wants them.

Most of Dad is missing. Probably sold off. All that's left are some of the small bones of his hands, and some ground powder, just a pinch, in a glass vial. I unzip my bowling bag and dump the remains inside.

A voice from below: "Come down off that ladder, son."

In a linen button-down shirt and tailored black slacks, the Hierarch isn't exactly what I expect, but I recognize his face from coins and postage stamps. He's thin and dark as bones from the tar pits, his fingernails, teeth and eyes saturated with magic.

"Those glasses of yours are very clever," he says, inhaling deeply. "Sint holo serpent bones and Deep Rhys herbs. Two sources of invisibility, mixed together, along with your own essence. That's good work. But it's not fooling me, so you might as well come on down now."

I grip the ladder to keep my hands from shaking. I can smell him. His magic is old. "So, you really hang out in your own warehouse? Don't tell me you drive the forklifts."

He smiles indulgently. "No, that takes special training I lack. But when thieves get this far past my defenses, I take personal interest. Now, please, come down."

"Not just yet. I like the view from up here. You have a lot of nice things. Is that really a sphinx?" I wonder if he's noticed my legs shaking.

"Yes. One of only three ever found."

"Where are the other two?"

"I smoked them." And he spits at me. He fires up a dark brown glob that splatters on my cheek. It burns me like acid, hurting so bad, filling me with pain and surprise, that I can't even scream.

A curtain of gray descends over my vision, and I lose balance, falling off the ladder, eight feet down to the concrete floor. I huddle there at the Hierarch's feet, struggling not to give in to the tempting relief of unconsciousness. My cheek burns. And I think I've broken my right arm. But somehow – reflex, dumb luck, who knows? – I've managed to hold onto the bowling bag containing Father's bones. Some of the bones have fallen out. The vial of powder lies shattered, its contents spilled.

I have to get to my feet. I can do this. I can make myself do this. Using my good arm to push myself up, I manage to drive my palm into the tiny shards of glass from the broken vial.

"Are you okay?" the Hierarch asks. I can hear the flesh on my face sizzle. I try to say "fine," but the word won't come out.

"So, who's that in the bowling bag?"

"John Blackland," I rasp. "He was an osteomancer."

The Hierarch puts his hands in his pockets and bounces on the balls of his feet, as if stretching out his calf muscles. "This entire section of the ossuary is full of osteomancers. It's the osteomancy section. I suppose you're John Blackland's son?"

The Hierarch's spit continues to burn. "Yeah," I gasp. "Daniel Blackland."

It feels like someone's drilling into the cracked bones of my right arm. And my cheek...the air hits exposed bone.

The Hierarch squints at the hole in my face as if checking out a door ding on a parked car. "If it's any comfort, you got farther than most. No doubt you've come equipped with some powerful osteomantic weapons. But look at me." He holds his brown hands up toward my face. "I've smoked, eaten, inhaled, and injected more ancient and secret animals than anyone alive. I'm the Hierarch."

"How could I have done this better?" I ask.

"I do make public appearances, you know. You could have tried a car bomb. Or a high-powered rifle. You revenge-obsessed boys have extraordinary passion, but it seems to get in the way of achieving practical goals."

He thinks this is about vengeance, not simple theft. I'm out of courage, and hope, and pretty much everything. But then Dad talks to me. He begins softly, through weak and subtle scents that waft up from his scattered bones: tar, the salt tang of kelp, and a trace of something clean and dark and old from the sea bottom.

That's the osteomancer's craft. To draw magic from bones, to infuse it into your own.

My father turned me into a weapon. And while I was off, screwing around, I let inheritors of my father's noble cause turn Miranda into a weapon. I've still got her in my bowling bag. I am a vessel carrying three generations of power. But I'll die before I use my daughter in that way.

Broken arm. Face being eaten away. Glass splinters in my good hand. I put my palm to my ruined cheek. Screaming, I rub residue of my father's ground-up bones into my raw flesh.

Firecrackers pop under my skin.

The Hierarch sees what I've done, and he begins to exude something. A toxic stench, thick as mud, fills my head, more and more until I hear myself shrieking with blind pain.

The Hierarch coughs, and he coughs and coughs, and his eyes never leave mine. His jaw unhinges like a snake's, and brown fluid gushes out of him. Where it hits the floor, concrete liquefies and boils away.

"If there's anything left of you," he says, his voice gargly, "I'll drink it with green tea."

I don't know if I'll live, but I know the Hierarch has lost. Because, overhead, the spines of the kraken skeleton vibrate and sing. And just before the Hierarch unleashes another torrent of magic from inside, the storm I called with Dad strikes. The bolts come down. The bolts come out of me. They come from Dad's bones, soaked with Dad's magic, mixed in my blood. They come from spirits and memories.

When it's over, the Hierarch's charred body melts into a puddle of brown, sizzling fluid.

Ding-dong, dead.

I should just walk out of here. With my glasses, I can get past the guards and get as far from the ossuary as a guy with a broken arm and a ravaged face can get.

But the residue of the Hierarch is thick, powerful magic. There's got to be a sponge and bucket around here somewhere.

We've been driving all day and all night and have been for a few days. Connie rides with Miranda in the back, singing Spanish lullabies, trying to get her to stop crying. I cooked up a salve for her hand, and I don't think it hurts her any longer, but the girl misses the tip of her finger. Of course she does. How could she not? When she's older, maybe I'll give it to her and she can wear it on the end of a necklace.

And once that thought is complete, I want to hit myself. Isn't that the sort of thing Dad might do?

At least once every hour I'm tempted to turn the car around and head back to Los Angeles. There's a fight being waged there between high-ranking ministers and osteomancers, between freelancers and opportunists and twisted idealists like Otis and the turtle man. I shouldn't be tempted to head back and join in, but I am. I'm pretty sure I would prevail. After drinking the Hierarch's remains, I may well be the most powerful osteomancer in all the Californias. Possibly the most powerful on the entire continent. Part of me wants that power. There's something in my bones that craves it.

But then, when the hunger gets too strong, I lean back and get a whiff of Miranda. She carries the taint of magic, a scent much older than she is, and I won't stop driving, till all I can smell is baby powder and shampoo and clean, soft skin.

Yours, Etc.

Gavin J. Grant

Gavin J. Grant (*www.lcrw.net/gavinjgrant/index.htm*) lives in Northampton, Massachusetts, with his wife, Kelly Link. He moved to the USA in 1991 from Scotland. He worked in bookshops in Los Angeles and Boston, and then while living in Brooklyn, worked for *BookSense.com*, a web site for independent bookshops. He is the publisher of Small Beer Press and, since 1996, editor and publisher of *Lady Churchill's Rosebud Wristlet*, a twice-yearly small press zine. With Ellen Datlow, he and Kelly Link co-edit *The Year's Best Fantasy and Horror*, a distinguished competitor of this book. While Grant's publication credentials are impressive and easy to come by when researching him, he is notably shy about revealing his much about himself. His author photo on the Endicott Studios web site shows him peeking out from behind some rocks, which, we think, says it all.

"Yours, Etc.," a strange surrealistic ghost story of upscale suburban life, was published in *Salon Fantastique*, edited by Ellen Datlow and Terri Windling, one of the most distinguished original fantasy anthologies of the year. This tale is an ambiguous construction that evokes echoes of the great fantasy story by Charlotte Perkins Gilman, "The Yellow Wall-Paper." It is about the inner life of someone who might *appear* to be normal.

SHE WAS WRITING to one of the dead girls again while he walked around the house. He walked solidly, stolidly, muddily, froggily. He was lost in a wordless daydream where words came up with his steps, lost their meaning, bled into others. He was lost but he knew where he was going. He had passed the front door – the outside light on, he knew what was on the other side. So now thought four left turns. Four more left turns, he thought, and the front door would appear again. But he knew his house was not square, that he could not take four more lefts unless he acquired the dead girls' ability and began walking through walls. He walked and walked and the dead girls did what they always did. Nothing.

His wife had finished writing and was chopping something in the kitchen when he passed the windows. He knew she couldn't see him through the night-black glass. He imagined it was onions that she was chopping but the word became something else. Bunions. Blisters. Corns. Vegetables that grew off the corpse. Mushrooms, always it came back to mushrooms. Was there nothing else that grew off the rot? He would take his flashlight and look under the hedgerows.

He stopped walking. The ghosts came a little closer. He had neither flashlight nor hedgerow. He grew neither mushrooms nor corn. He was an empty man with an empty garden. His father told him he had a beautiful lawn. He didn't know why his father would say that. A team of men came once a week and took care of it. Made the lawn green, short, rolling. Sometimes his wife talked to them on the phone for hours and they'd come back again and again until whatever it was she wanted was done.

She'd pretend she wanted something new. Perhaps some landscaping. She'd scatter catalogs and her voice would grow deep with longing. Her calls were always returned.

She'd moved him out of the house without him really noticing. He was tied up at work. Or, wearing a tie and working. Then his home office had been moved from the back room to the basement and then out over the garage. He'd liked that. Until the first winter.

It wasn't that the house was done in chiffon or some other unrecognizable substance. It had been Crate and Barrel. Then Williams-Sonoma. Then she'd moved away from mall stores. She kept ahead of his position, his credit cards. She said it was important for their house to look the part. He thought maybe it would be nice to look the part of a beach bum in Jamaica for a week. She told him they couldn't afford it even as he was wondering if a resort in Jamaica was really all he could imagine.

He'd given up on the garden when the cupola went up. He'd enjoyed getting into his old trousers – which she'd probably thrown out – and getting dirt under his nails.

It was winter and he was walking widdershins around the house, and he was aware now that it wasn't the first time he'd done it. Light from the windows washed over him, spilled over him, slicked him down, sucked him in and spat him out. He crept, he leapt, he kept his balance. And all the while he wife was writing to a dead girl. He had taken off his shoes. His trousers were wet where he had been sitting under the pine tree near the front door. He had left his shoes there. He crept out from under the tree and crept around the house. Everything was different, new parts were sore, when he went around on hands and knees. Every five steps – shuffles? – he tried to meow like a cat. He heard rustlings around him and knew it was the dead. He was pulling all his history behind him, tying them in knots around his house like a fishing line with more tangles than straights.

He lived in a house and he drove a car and he worked in an office. When he was a child he had been raised by raccoons at night, feral cats by day. When he was a child he had built a sleeping platform in the trees and stayed there summer after summer. He did not remember his childhood rightly. He remembered the roads melting softly in the sun and he thought about global warming and how perhaps the roads would melt and sink into the earth. He had loved the outdoor world and now Monday through Friday he might never step outside, other than walking to and from his car.

So now he walked around the house. He could not walk around his neighborhood. The roads had no sidewalks. The cul de sacs and gated communities did not welcome walkers. There was an asphalt path around the lake. His garden, so controlled, so manicured, was all his wildness now.

A dead girl had moved in with them, once. It wasn't anyone they knew. Just a dead girl. The husband hadn't been as good at seeing ghosts then. He couldn't hear when she explained why she was there. Couldn't hear what she said to his wife. He could barely see her. He didn't know how or why she had died. But his wife knew; she could see all of these things.

That was why they had moved. The two of them were rattling around their McMansion by themselves but it was newly built when they bought it and his wife said it would take years for a ghost to work its way in.

He could tell his wife where the ghosts' late night murmurings were becoming entangled in a fir tree. But he didn't tell her about the line of history he was walking into the ground around the house. He couldn't.

At their old house, the dead girl had been persistent. This was why his wife still wrote to her. He thought she missed her. He knew the dead girl missed his wife. He could feel the dead girl coming closer. Or, that could be cold. His body felt it differently now. Old age. Death's winged Cadillac hurrying near.

He reminded himself he could feel and it didn't have to be only the dead girl's tiny steps. But she *pushed* through the ether and he felt the vibrations.

His mother had always called him sensitive and he had laughed it off. He was a jock. A smart jock, able to work in an office, but still a jock. He was fully rounded. More so then than now, he thought. More so now than then, too.

He was walking around the house again, circling, drawing the ghosts into his path and away from the house when he saw the antlers in front of him. He lifted the antlers and put them on his forehead. He bent forward to take the weight on his shoulders. He had to keep watching the ground in case he tripped. He had to watch the mulch he'd spread by the wall. He had to watch the mud he had made walking around the house.

"The antlers are a gift from Herne the Hunter," the dead girl said. She was there walking beside him. If he looked straight at her he could see her shrinking back through time. But she only went so far. Back to her birth, forward to her death. There was an emptiness where her future should have been. That was part of her bespecteredness. The missing, slightly plump fifty-two-year-old teacher she would have been. The annoyingly perky cheerleader with the B+ average.

She told him she haunted her own future looking for herself, and when she couldn't find it she would come back and tell him what she missed about herself. And when she was bored with that she might tell him lies about himself, about everyone he knew.

She was dead and so knew things he could not know so he could not tell what were lies, what weren't.

"The Hunter loves you because you live in the city but you're walking the darkness," she said.

She said, "You should be glad to be loved by the Hunter." And, "The Hunter doesn't love anyone so you should be careful."

He walked and walked. He had a pedometer sitting in his briefcase and he imagined it unhappy at being unable to count his steps.

The girl said she hated herself for the things she had never done. And it wasn't sex or drugs or drinking. She boasted unconvincingly of doing her share of partying. She hated not having ever had a dog. Not taking the hostess job at Vegedilla's when she had the chance. Not dyeing her hair any color ever but New Summer Sun.

He wore the antlers all that night and his shoulders sank into knots. He found his shoes under the fir again. He went in the back door, ducking into the house. His wife had gone to bed. He considered all the places he could sleep. On the couch. In the basement. In a guest bedroom. In his office. But he loved his wife and wanted to sleep with her. He thought she would not mind the antlers.

In the morning he left before his wife was up. He wore the antlers to work and no one said anything. He began to get used to them. He wore them home and when he went out that night to look at the stars he bent his head back carefully and breathed deeply of the air. He was conscious of his neck straining and he tipped himself backward but he could not make himself fall. Instead he began to walk around the house again. Wearing his antlers and tying the ghosts into his tread, he walked and walked around the house.

★

Dead girls ran in his family but he hadn't known this until they had gotten one of their own. The dead run in every family but no one ever wants to talk about it. They'd been married, the husband, the wife, in a tiny ceremony because that's what they wanted. He'd thought. She had no siblings and his brother had moved to Alaska. His brother was a high-school teacher. He taught physics and in his spare time he made vodka. "Two hundred gallons a year," he used to tell the man every time they talked. They didn't talk much anymore. The man's brother had sent them a case of homemade vodka as a wedding present. It was somewhat thoughtless in a way the brother couldn't have known: alcohol was implicated in many of the woman's pen pals' deaths. The man didn't tell his new wife about the present and she never missed it. He asked his brother not to mention it. So his brother didn't come to their wedding.

But history was never gone. It was always popping up, recycling itself into the present.

One of his wife's pen pals was alive. She had been a friend in college and now she was in prison. They'd been sorority sisters. After a party in their sophomore year, the man's wife – although they did not meet for years, he knew the story well – had declared she would walk back to the sorority house. This had been the early nineties and Seattle was repudiating grunge, full of riot grrls and empowerment and defense classes; so mostly safe. The future letter-writer's friends decided to drive, and the letter-writer gave them a few pithy phrases and walked off. She arrived home safe (as she always did, even in her junior year abroad when she lived in Hui-San and did many things she never told anyone about). But her friends did not return. Her friend who was now in prison was the quieter of the three and decided she was best suited to drive. But as she was going around a long curve she drifted over the line into the next lane and ran her Ford Explorer right into a high-school student's Honda Accord. The student was returning from her job waitressing at a pizza restaurant. She was killed instantly, and the wife writes to her to this day. The dead student doesn't answer. The wife sends the letters to her friend in prison. Her friend was sentenced by a hanging judge so she'll be in prison for a while. Her friend reads the letters, and sometimes writes back to the wife.

His wife left him a note this morning that said, "The landscaper says they're going to lay down traps and see if they can catch whatever's leaving those tracks around the house." He had thought his footprints were clear.

*

He often dreamed of the ghosts, of the years lived and those missed. Then in the morning his wife would tell him about the same girls.

Since we're all always dying she also wrote letters to herself. Some of them she had mailed years ago and they would arrive when she wanted them to. When they used to live in the city she had sent postcards to the two of them here in this echoing new house. He hadn't believed her then.

She only writes to girls. She says that she hardly claims to understand men in life – and she stretches up and kisses him on the cheek – and after that...

She gives a roll of her shoulders that later, when he is walking around the house, he tries to replicate. When he can't quite get it he blames the weight of the antlers.

He never reads her letters. Once she starts writing she doesn't stop until she seals it up, puts it out for the postman to pick up the next day. Sometimes he's been tempted by the postcards but he cannot cross the line. She has never offered (but why would she?) and he cannot ask.

She writes to a girl she knew in high school. He watches football sometimes with the girl's brother. The world is smaller than he expects, sometimes. He loved the girl back then but everyone did. This was in the seventies, a different age. The girl was another car crash ghost. His wife didn't put return addresses on her letters because she didn't want the ghosts finding them. He didn't tell his wife this girl's ghost was passing her years quite happily in her brother's apartment.

He finds he is suddenly taken with inexplicable exhilaration. He is having a moment. He feels that the top of his head may have flown off. He is near to laughing, expects that if he looked up he would find that the antlers will have stuck to the ceiling. But he daren't look because his brain would spill out. He clenches his fists and looks at his stubby fingers going white. He is paler than the ghosts. And this calms him. As his fingers relax, the top of his head drifts slowly back down. The ghosts are colorful and he is not.

Later when he is walking around the house he is afraid of happiness taking him. What if the top of his head flies off? There is nothing to stop it getting away. He keeps his hands on his head while he walks around the house. The rut is getting deeper. If his hand were free he could point to it and say I made that. But he knows he won't. He is walking down the side of the house along the ornamental fence the neighbors put up. It is about twenty feet long.

Neither house has any pets. He has seen the grandchildren next door play around the fence so it serves the purpose of amusing them. He would like to take his chainsaw and cut it down. But he hasn't touched his chainsaw in years. He thinks he should be able to say he isn't even sure if he has a chainsaw but it's not true. He could list the contents of his garage. The troupe of gardening men take care of everything. He wonders if they would cut down or remove the fence. He wonders where they are from. At work there's a partner from Ecuador, maybe she could tell him. But he knows he will never ask the gardeners nor the partner. It is too late. He should have asked his wife where they were from years ago.

He feels as if his life is full of these moments when he realizes it is too late. Too ask. To do. To cut down. To be someone that he is not now. A ghost of his impossible present is raging toward the fence pulling it out stake by stake. He watches the ghost and knows that this is a terrible thing. Not pulling out the fence, not being stupidly angry, not doing anything else but letting this ghost out of himself. Ghosts see or smell or leech onto other ghosts. He knows there are some ghosts here but so far his wife does not. If he attracts more ghosts they will have to move, to run away again. She cannot live with all the ghosts that would come. But he cannot look away, cannot ignore the ghost and make it go away. This ghost is not another dead teenager. This is his own self. He likes the ghost's shirt. It is white like his but has a subtle stripe. He hates that he noticed. This ghost is stronger than he is. This ghost will take him over and push him out of his life. He must look away. He wrenches his gaze away. The path is in front of him. He must walk around the house. His long nights of walking will save him. He must tie the present into itself. He must, for his wife. For himself. He must make this the world he lives in and not let the ghost overpower him. He is crying.

Around the next corner he trips over a rainspout. He has never seen it before. His ghost is pushing him out. He closes his eyes and insists that the rainspout is not there. There is a plant here, he thinks. He damns himself for knowing nothing about his own garden, for stopping caring, removing himself from his own life. He can see the plant and the way it had been trained up the wall on some kind of wooden frame. Wisteria on a trellis. He could hear his wife talking about it as they stood just over there. He faced where they had been standing. His wife was solidly in his memory but he could not picture himself from the front. His parallel ghost comes around the corner. He is clean and tidy and has a tie on. The man was pleased to see that the ghost is wearing an ugly box-patterned sweater. The ghost was grinning in a horribly toothy manner and his ears were trembling. The man smiled. His wife would never go for a bucktoothed fool like that. He tipped over from the waist and tried to touch his toes. His feet were on the ground and the ground was worn down. This trough is the depth of his heart, his work. His ankles are level with the ground. This was something he had done, something he had to do.

He stood, put one foot in front of the other. His ghost was gesticulating and exploding. You have no power, he thought. I will not see you I will not write to you I will not give you a second thought. This was not the ghost of himself that he feared. This ghost had no strength. By not fearing this ghost he gave strength to the other ghosts. But he did not know what else to do.

He turned from the ghost, walked around the house. When he came back around, the ghost had disappeared.

It wasn't the first or last ghost of himself he'd seen. His favorite hadn't ever gotten old because he'd died young. Apparently he was a gigolo or courtesan or pirate or had died at a Halloween party. The man never knew. This ghost had appeared to him on his wedding night. The man really didn't want to see him there but the libertine ghost had been enjoying himself with the ghost of the man's wife and the horror of that and the hidden flask of vodka the man had partaken of had combined into a night of fucking and lovemaking that he felt he had never quite managed to rise to again. So he loved that ghost even if he insisted on his own life and not giving it over to the ghost.

He'd known other people who lived in the shadows of their own demons, real or imagined, but not a ghost of themselves. He missed his brother's vodka more than he missed his brother.

Another dead girl. A black girl who'd died a couple of years ago. He'd liked her even though they'd barely met. She was interning at one of the offices on his floor and they'd met at some kind of building maintenance meeting. She'd been taking notes and he'd passed her a note suggesting that she not bother. But he'd remembered being young and disconnected and knowing that he knew nothing and having to pay attention to everything. So he wasn't surprised when she gave the slightest shake of her head and kept on taking notes. He'd liked her compact, quick handwriting. He wished he had an assistant as smart. He thought she was pretty but she was so young that it did not go beyond that.

He met the intern in the building cafeteria. He had realized he'd seen the girl there before. She was usually in a group of four or five young women her own age. Sometimes she was on her own; she always had a paper or a magazine. Something to keep her busy and make her unavailable to the dirty old men like him. But when he saw her eating salad one cold February day he couldn't resist stopping by and talking to her.

She put her copy of the *Times* away and shuffled over on the curved bench enough to denote an invitation. He sat far from her and thought they both enjoyed talking with someone quite unlike themselves.

He saw her now and then and sometimes they ate together. Once or twice he took her out for a coffee – she liked her coffee unsweetened and without milk. He horrified her by telling her that she should enjoy it while she could because the only way he could drink it that way was if he had Rolaids with him.

His wife thought the intern was a stand-in for a daughter or a lover. But she laughed when she said it.

In May the intern told him her internship was over at the end of the month. He remembered to give her his card and told her if she was interested in joining the firm after college, or if there was anything he could do, to give him a ring. But a week or so before she left – after the office manager had sent around an email about the intern's departure and to come by for cake on Thursday afternoon – a week or so before that, she'd died.

He'd never found out how. He was surprised how upset he was. His wife told him again about her stand-in theory and he had said sure, maybe there was something in that. Both of them knew she didn't mean it. She was just talking, helping him fill the empty space until he got used to the girl's death. He thought about the girl a lot and realized that she had been alive to him, she'd encapsulated a universe in a way that he felt many of the people he knew didn't. He'd believed in her in a way he didn't believe in other people.

He didn't ask, but later he realized his wife had been writing her letters for years.

His wife has dark hair with a streak of white in it that leads from her temple back to her right ear. Sometimes when she colored her hair it took on the color until she next showered and it went back to white. She said she'd always had it and it always drew his hand. He loved the way it looked even though he knew it had nothing to do with her. It wasn't fancy or affectation. He knew she had not had it when they met. He did not know when it had appeared. Perhaps when she realized the ghosts were following her. It wasn't in her childhood pictures, but he had never carried out a forensic examination of her photographs to find its first appearance.

★

The antlers lasted until autumn. He was used to them by then. The dead girl hadn't been around for a couple of weeks. He'd been walking around the house at night and working away during the day. His wife had been planning a trip to see her sister's new baby and the dead girl appeared beside him and told him if he went he couldn't keep the antlers.

"The horned god has many aspects," the dead girl shouted over whatever she had playing on her earphones. It was a whisper, a shout. "If you go with your wife, the Hunter there might not remember – that's not the right word, but you know – remember that the Hunter here gave you the antlers. I'm just saying it probably wouldn't go well."

The husband stopped walking. He was deep in his trench. This was the first trip his wife had planned since they had moved into this bare mansion. The first trip since she had fled the ghosts that had taken over their last house. The house they had bought after years of saving and worked on every weekend for so long he would have lost many sets of antlers if he had had them then.

The dead girl is shouting something at him and he is scratching the antlers.

Their first house was so different from their first home: his apartment in the city which she had moved into and slowly made into a new thing: theirs. The ghosts were too busy in the city to notice her. It was only later when they bought their first house that the ghosts had realized how lovely, how tasty and sweet she could be for them. They followed her, buried into her habits, tried to eat of her life and he hadn't believed her until one day he saw them, too. So they left the house that they had spent so much time on but which never became a home. He had a short time when he thought the ghosts had been left behind.

He took off the antlers and laid them on the ground. He immediately missed them. He was so short. So base. So uninteresting; ghostlike. He had walked around his neighborhood and scraped the velvet off the antlers on all his neighbors trees. He had enjoyed watching them find his marks.

"Your loss, asshole," the dead girl shouted at him and picked up the antlers. She walked into the space beside and away from him.

He'd asked his wife about her letters once and she had said:

Long, long ago when the world was young and before there was paper or shopping malls or road rage there were the living and the dead and the sea and the sky. The dead had the sea and the living had the sky and land hadn't been invented yet.

When the bodies of the living wore out they would kiss one another, kiss on one cheek, kiss on the other, more kisses for the loved, the family – it all took a long time but they were in no hurry – and they would tidy up their lives and drop down to the sea and they would never be seen again.

One eternal morning the living decided they were tired of flying and that they would set down on the sea. There was no word for doing this, which was hilarious and exciting. None of the living had ever seen what happened to those that were tired and gave up the sky. The living gathered together and the first among them dropped to the sea. All followed. The first living ones to touch the sea died instantly. Those coming down from above saw the first people touch the sea and watched as their bodies went under. The living did not understand that those who had touched the sea had immediately joined the dead. They thought the first among them were flying through the water the way they all flew through the air. They could not see the dead coming up from the depths. They could not see the ghosts of the newly dead leaving their bodies, trying to fly above the water, trying to stop the living from joining them.

And the bodies of the living – there were thousands upon thousands of them – settled deep in the sea as they fell and piled up and up until there were so many the living could drop from the sky and stand upon the dead.

Then the living who stood upon the dead understood what had happened. And they wailed and ground their teeth and drove their elbows into one another's sides and bit one another and gouged their unhappiness upon their skins and they stopped others from going into the water. And most of the living flew back into the sky and vowed never to return, never to see water until they were ready to die. But some of the living did not leave. They stayed there and lived upon the bodies of the dead. And among those who stayed was an even smaller number who, when they touched the bodies that touched the water, could see the dead and the ghosts below. And since all that they stood on were the bodies, they could always see the ghosts. And the ghosts would see that they were being seen and the ghosts tried to follow those living that could see them.

And it has been the same ever since.

She was his wife. He believed in her in the same way he believed in dentists, hybrid cars, the logarithmic tables he had memorized as a boy.

He walked around the house and he walked under the plank he had placed over his trench so that they could still use the front door. He had removed the flagstone path when his walkway became too deep. He had walked around the house for a year. More. He had walked through winter and spring, down summer and autumn. He had walked through a presidency, a Super Bowl, and an Olympics. Through a promotion, through the antlers. His trench was as deep as he was tall.

The ghost he had hidden from his wife was there. The ghost of his wife – one he hadn't recognized she was so alien to him, the one with the three girls and the rolled-over SUV with no seatbelts – was there. He could feel the ghost of himself – the ghost of himself in this world – walking with him. Hundreds of himself walked behind him. He thought he might catch up with himself. But he could not walk fast enough. And he walked and walked around the house.

He was watching television and she was writing again. He was in his office battling their health insurance and she was writing again. It was her birthday and at the Tex-Mex place she liked, all her friends had their straws in a Meg's Massive Margarita and they were waiting for her before they could all drink and she was writing on the napkin. The dead girls were coming closer and she kept writing, hoping to keep them back.

He drove to work and he trailed a string of heartbreak and bad haircuts and torn-up Valentine's Day cards to draw away the ghosts but they had her scent and each night when he returned his wife looked a little older. She knew they were coming even if she could not see them yet.

She was being surrounded and knew it but didn't know it. He was building a wall in reverse, digging down with his life and energy and his walking night after night. She knew it was him but didn't know why. She'd talked to her gardening team and told them not to disturb his project. He knew she thought he was losing himself.

The ghosts thought they would get past him, they thought he was cutting away her privacy and letting them in. He let them come closer, let them follow him around and around and down and around the house. They twisted around him as he walked. They obsessed over the prints his bare feet left. They did not know that he was building a trap for them.

His wife was talking about Colorado and New Mexico. Places high and far away. Switzerland. She asked him about transfers and started watching his company's job boards. He did not tell her because even then he was not fully sure. He walked and drew the ghosts down into his dry moat and thought perhaps he and the house were becoming stronger.

He would not disappear. This was his wife. This was his life. This was his path around his house. His home. This was his city. His country. He had begun with the ghosts and he had made his way past them.

He climbed out of his trench. His clothes were muddy, his bare feet going numb and blue with cold. He looked back down and saw the roaring tornado of ghosts. He could see the letters his wife was writing next year and the year after, already arrived and whirling in around the ghosts. Being read and eaten and absorbed and loved. He was certain that he and his wife would not be leaving. They would live in this house for long years to come.

There were ghosts of himself and his wife in possible futures and some of them were better and some of them worse.

He walked back around the house and for the first time he walked clockwise. He went deep into the garden away from the house. All lights were on in the house and they lit his way. He picked up his shoes and socks from under the fir tree. He walked beside his trench, back around the house. He rang the front door bell. The door opened and his wife was waiting. She had a pen in one hand and with her other hard she took hold of his and they walked into their house.

Sea Air

Nina Kiriki Hoffman

Nina Kiriki Hoffman (tribute site: *www.ofearna.us/books/hoffman*.html) lives in Eugene, Oregon. She plays fiddle, and takes photographs. She has published more than 200 fantasy and science fiction stories since 1983, and ten novels, including *The Thread That Binds the Bones* (1993), *The Silent Strength of Stones* (1995), *A Red Heart of Memories* (1999), and *Catalyst* (2006). She writes in the tradition of Zenna Henderson, Alexander Key, Andre Norton, and to a certain extent, Ray Bradbury. Her fiction is optimistic, generous to her characters, and somewhat sentimental, often about finding your place in life and your community. In 2002, she was a guest of honor at Wiscon, the major feminist SF convention. Her guest of honor speech began: "Hi there. This is the first speech I've given since the eighth grade. Back then, every kid in my little prep school had to speak at an all-school assembly sometime during the year. What I did was stand in the middle of the stage and say, 'Here's something I prepared. I call it "Fun with a Tape Recorder."' I then snuck offstage and turned on the reel-to-reel tape recorder my dad had helped me bring to school and hook up to the P. A."

"Sea Air" was also published in *Elemental*. It is the tale of an adopted boy, when his family moves to the new town by the seaside, discovering his inner sea creature.

"IT'S LIKE Michael's allergic to seawater," Mom said. She offered Lizzie a plate of chocolate chip cookies, and Lizzie grabbed two.

"Shut up," Michael muttered.

For the eighth time in thirteen years, he and his adopted parents had moved into a new house in a new town. For the eighth time in thirteen years, Michael had to start life over, find new friends.

Mom didn't make it easy.

Lizzie lived in the house next door, but right now she was sitting on the couch in the new living room between Mom and Michael. Lizzie looked about sixteen, Michael's age. She had frizzy brown hair, yellow-brown eyes, and a wide, friendly smile; she wore a baggy brown sweatshirt, tight jeans, and duck shoes. The hem of one of her pantlegs had crept up. Michael saw she wore socks with animal tracks on them.

The moving van had unloaded everything the night before and left. Michael and his parents were so tired after driving to Random, on the Oregon coast, from central Idaho that they only unpacked enough things to sleep on last night. This morning, they'd walked to the beach, then come home and worked all morning to set up the house the way Mom had planned it back in Idaho with a graph paper layout of the house and little paper cut-outs of the furniture.

After Dad and Mom and Michael had unrolled the carpets, set up the furniture, and put things away, Lizzie had appeared on the front stoop, hands buried in her pockets, questions in her mouth. Dad had met Lizzie before he raced off to meet his local boss for a sales lunch.

Lizzie balanced a teacup and saucer on her knee. She smelled like vanilla. She snitched a third chocolate chip cookie from the plate Mom had set on the coffee table.

"It's funny, because Michael came from a coast town, which is about all we know about his life before we adopted him. We've never lived in a seaside town before," Mom continued. "I love the beach. But I took Michael there this morning, and he wouldn't go near the water."

Lizzie turned her gaze to him. "Why not?"

"I don't know. It just bothers me." Michael didn't mention the way his flesh crept, the strange shuddery feeling of not wanting even the wet breeze on his skin. The rolling rush of waves had terrified him. He had felt as though fingers of sea were seeking him.

"When he was little, he was like that about all water. When we first adopted him, it took both his father and me to get him into the bathtub, and he was only three years old."

"Shut up," Michael whispered under his breath. He loved Mom, but why did she have to tell everybody weird stuff about him before he'd had a chance to make his own first impressions?

"Don't worry," Mom said. "He bathes regularly now."

"I can tell," said Lizzie. She smiled at him.

"Mo-om," said Michael.

Mom smiled – the tender look that frustrated him because it made him feel like he couldn't get mad at her. She had done so much for him, how could he even think about being angry with her?

"Right," she said. "I'm talking too much. Lizzie, what's your favorite subject in school?"

"Mo-om," Michael muttered again.

"My favorite subject isn't at school," said Lizzie. "My uncle's a marine biologist, and sometimes I get to go out to sea with him. I want to be a marine biologist when I grow up. Hey, Mike, what do you like?"

Of all the dorky conversations to have with his mother in the room. But if his mother wasn't in the room, what would they end up talking about? Probably nothing. Michael was a master of the uncomfortable silence, even though he didn't want to be. "Music," he said.

"Oh? That's cool. I've been taking flute lessons, but I never practice. Do you listen to music, play it, or both?"

"Both." He hoped she wouldn't ask him about his favorite bands. He had a very small CD collection, all of them by people most kids his age had never heard of. He was picky about music. He earned the money to buy CDs by babysitting, mowing lawns, whatever work he could drum up from neighbors. He spent hours at the CD store listening to whatever was open, and only bought CDs when he liked all the tracks. He couldn't pinpoint why he liked the things he liked, which ranged from thirties blues albums to compilations of Celtic music in languages he didn't speak.

"What instrument do you play?" Lizzie asked.

"Just piano. Not very well."

Mom sighed. "We had a piano a couple years ago, but when we moved, we couldn't bring it with us. Michael's had to make do with singing and pennywhistles. Does the high school have piano practice rooms, Lizzie?"

"No, all the funds for the arts got cut." Lizzie sipped tea. "Hey. How about this, though? Mrs. Plank, two houses past mine, has a piano. She never plays, but she might let you practice on it. She's pretty nice unless you step on her flowers."

Michael looked at Mom. It had been so long since he'd played a piano he was afraid his hands had forgotten everything he knew.

"Okay," said Mom, "we'll bake some cookies and go visit. Do you know if she likes cookies, Liz?"

"It's never come up in conversation," said Lizzie. "She's not the type to invite people over. Mostly she just says, 'Lizzie, you have a well-behaved dog, not like some people I could name,' and 'Has the mailman come by yet?'"

"We can but try," Mom said. It was one of the ways they met new neighbors, at least in towns where they planned to stay for a while. Mom baked a big batch of cookies. They made up gift plates and dropped them off at nearby houses in the evening when people were home from work and school. It was a quick way to take the emotional temperature of a neighborhood.

Dad never came with them on these expeditions. Michael used to think this was because he wasn't interested, but lately, now that Michael was six feet tall, he noticed that doors didn't open as easily to him and Mom. Dad was a big man. Maybe Dad thought he would scare the neighbors. When Dad was home, he did all right with the neighbors, once Mom and Michael had made first contact and invited them over for back yard barbecues or card games or shared video rentals.

Michael had taught himself to slouch.

"How'd you find out about Mrs. Plank's piano?" Michael asked Lizzie. His fingers were already twitching.

"I saw it when I trick-or-treated at her house."

"We can but try," Mom said again. She watched Michael's fingers play inaudible scales on the couch cushions. "I didn't realize how much you missed it, hon. If this doesn't work, we'll find another way."

"Well," said Lizzie, "aside from not playing the piano, what do you do for fun?"

"Read," Michael said. Oh no. Way to brand himself as an utmost geek. He needed a save. "Walk around and look at things." Jeez, almost as dorky.

"Do you walk at night?"

"Sure."

"Don't do that here. Lots of people have big dogs here, and they let them loose at night."

"Aren't there any leash laws?" Mom asked.

Lizzie frowned. "Well, that's the thing. People are encouraged to let the dogs loose at night, because there's other things that come out at night." She sucked on her lower lip, then said, "Okay, we don't usually mention this so soon after you get here, but I like you guys, so I'm going to tell you right up front. Things come up through the gorse at night. They make noises. They do nasty things. Stay inside, okay? People disappear at night. If anybody asks, we say the riptides carried them away, but that's not what happens. We lose people here every year."

"Heavens," said Mom. "You're not pulling our leg, are you, Liz?"

"I'm not serious about much, but I'm serious about this. Michael, Mrs. Welty, don't leave the house after dark, unless it's to go to your car and drive someplace with lights around it, like the supermarket or a restaurant. Don't let Mr. Welty wander around after dark either, okay?"

"You went trick-or-treating," Michael said.

"Halloween's different. All the kids go out in big groups, and we make a lot of noise, and take dogs and grownups with weapons with us. We scare the Strangers off that night."

Michael and Mom exchanged glances.

Lizzie set her teacup on the coffee table and stood, dusting off her pants. "Ignore me if you want," she said in a flattened tone.

"No, wait, Lizzie," Michael said. He followed her to the front door. "Give us another chance. We're new. We don't know what's going on around here. Thanks for warning us."

Lizzie turned the front doorknob, paused with the door open. She stared at him without expression for what felt like ten minutes, then, finally, smiled. "Hey. I'll take you to the library. How about that?"

"That would be great."

Lizzie darted back and grabbed another handful of cookies. "Thanks, Mrs. Welty."

"You're welcome. Thank you for the introduction to the neighborhood. I'm going to bake now, kids. Michael, be home before five, okay?"

"Sure, Mom."

Michael left his bedroom window open a crack that night. He lay in the dark and listened to the pulse of the waves beating against the sand. It took him a long time to fall asleep. The waves' murmur terrified and thrilled him, the same way the smell of the salty air here had affected him when Dad turned the station wagon off the highway and into town. He had smelled and tasted the sea, and his heart speeded; his skin tingled, hairs rising, bumps goosing. Even now, two blocks from the ocean, sea sound, sea scent kept him awake.

Was there a voice under the surface of sound, whispering his name?

Dogs barked in the street outside. He turned over and put the pillow over his head. More barking in the distance, and then the sound of a chase.

A town where he and Mom couldn't go out after dark? One of the things they did to learn about new communities was to wander the streets in the dark and study uncurtained windows, talking over the lives they glimpsed. Living rooms with lots of pictures of family on the walls always gave Michael a strange lost feeling; he hadn't told Mom about that. They had a few pictures of the three of them on the wall at home, mostly taken when Michael was six, seven, eight. Nothing recent. Dad was gone so much, traveling his sales territory, signing up new accounts, servicing the old ones. He was so successful the company kept moving him into territories where other people had failed. In fact, he had already left on another trip, leaving Michael and Mom to unpack. They were used to that.

Once while she was talking to Dad on the phone, Mom had said it didn't matter if they moved with him, since he was never home, anyway. Then she had gasped and covered her mouth with her hand, glanced at Michael to see if he had heard. He pretended he was so engrossed in his comic book he hadn't, but it had haunted his mind ever since.

Only the three of them, together, more or less, everywhere they went. No pictures of Mom's or Dad's parents, siblings, cousins, aunts, uncles. Were Mom and Dad orphans too?

"Michael," a voice whispered at his window.

Michael sat up. Who –

"Michael."

It was hard to recognize a whisper. Who did he know in Random who wasn't already in the house with him? Only Lizzie, and a few people she had introduced him to. Lizzie said she never went out at night. Was that just a dodge to keep Mom from suspecting that Lizzie wanted to invite Michael out for a midnight walk?

"Lizzie?"

"Michael."

Michael pulled on his robe and crept to the window. "Lizzie?"

The window slid wide and a face peered at him over the sill.

In the semidarkness, he couldn't really see the face, but he smelled a wet, salt, fish smell, nothing like Lizzie's vanilla scent.

"No," whispered the face.

"Who are you?" Michael took two steps back, reached for a weapon. He couldn't find a thing. Most of his possessions were still in boxes. The floor was chill under his feet; a worm of cold twisted in his stomach. Something about the person, the face, the whispering voice, something was not right.

"A friend."

"Come back during the day if you're really my friend," Michael said. He darted forward and slammed the window shut, then ran out into the hall, slamming his bedroom door behind him.

His mother rushed out of her room. "What's the matter?"

"Something at my window," he said, his breathing ragged.

"Should we call the police?" She took his arm and tugged him toward the master bedroom.

"I don't know."

Mom dragged Michael into her room and shut and locked the door, then got the baseball bat from the floor beside her bed. Her breathing was harsh in the darkness. "Tell me," she said.

"It was a person, Mom. I left my window open a crack, and someone called me. Whispered my name. Mom...."

He felt her hand tremble on his arm. "All the doors are locked, right?" she asked.

He nodded. When Dad wasn't home, which was most nights, it was Michael's job to check every door and window before he and Mom went to bed, and he had never forgotten since the night they had a break-in, back when they were living in Los Angeles. Everything was so much scarier when

Dad wasn't home. Someone had come into their apartment, but Michael heard him, ran to Mom's room, where they locked themselves in the bathroom and screamed until one of the neighbors beat on the wall and another called the police. By the time they came out of the bathroom the intruder had fled. He had taken Mom's jewelry box, but he hadn't taken anything else.

The jewelry box was where Mom had kept the things that reminded her of her life before. Michael remembered playing with her "pretties" when he was a little kid. She had let him take one piece of jewelry out at a time and look at it. She had had a charm bracelet with tiny gold sea creatures on it, some of them as strange as monsters from outer space. His favorite of all the things she had had, gone now.

Ever since, Michael had been compulsive about checking doors and windows nightly, sometimes checking three or four times to make sure. On nights when he felt particularly restless, he had to get up after a while and check again. Tonight he remembered the particulars; it was always that way in a new house the first few times he made his rounds.

"The doors were all locked. My window was only open an inch," he said. "There was this voice."

"The voice of a person who knew your name?"

"Yes. He said "Michael, Michael." I asked if he was Lizzie, and he said no. He said he was a friend."

"Was it someone you met when you were out with Lizzie today? How did you know it was a man?"

"I'm not sure." He thought back to the day they had just had. Lizzie had taken him to the library, where they met her least favorite librarian, and then over to Bob's Burger Grill, where she said the high school kids went after school, and sometimes during school. She had introduced him to Bob, a genial bearded man who had welcomed him to the community and shook his hand so hard his fingers felt crushed. After he squished Michael's hand, Bob had introduced Michael to a few of the kids in the restaurant, most of whom had acted completely not interested.

Lizzie told Michael later that most of the kids their age were gone for the summer. Off for obligatory time with noncustodial parents, summer camp, visiting relatives, camping, Disneyland – everybody was trying to get in one last spree before September crashed down on them. Everybody still in town was some kind of loser.

Michael had carefully avoided looking at Lizzie when she said that. They were climbing onto their bikes, anyway, so he had an excuse to focus on something else. They rode half a block before she burst out laughing and nudged his shoulder. "You were supposed to give me this look," she said, "or make an L on your forehead, you know? You're no fun!"

"Oh, yes I am!" He surprised himself and her with how loudly he spoke. He had lived in too many different places, started over too many times. He knew these early impressions set in cement, locked around his feet; he'd be dragging them around with him the rest of the time he lived here, especially if they only stayed half a year. He wouldn't have time to change people's minds. "Well, okay, that's no way to prove it," he said, "so never mind. Give me another shot."

"Maybe," Lizzie said in a teasing voice. "Anyway, everybody at Bob's was in the Ick Clique today. I'd introduce you to some of my real friends, but they're all gone this weekend. Let's go to the beach."

"The beach," Michael muttered.

Lizzie, ahead of him, had glanced back. "Oh, yeah. Your mom said you don't like the beach, huh? We could just go to the park and look at the beach."

"Okay."

They rode on a pitted street between looming, dusty hedges of yellow-flowered scotch broom. She took him to a wayside where tourists' cars could pull over and people could look at the beach without going down to it. There were wonderful standing stones on Random Beach, many like giant black teeth sticking up out of the sand and the water, a rock with an arch in it that looked like a Star Trek prop for a dimensional portal, another flat rock a little way offshore covered with fat slug-shaped creatures Lizzie told him were sea lions.

Then, of course, there was the water.

He had thought he'd be all right, standing on the cliff above the sea, far out of the reach of waves. The gulls cried as they circled in the air above, or swooped down to search tourist garbage. The waves whooshed, foaming, to the shore, then pulled away again. People walked and ran on the sand below, some tossing things for dogs to chase. Lizzie had pushed past him and taken a path out along the tops of some rocks, but Michael stayed at the viewpoint and just watched the water, wondering why he was afraid of it.

A thud had tripped in his chest, a thump, then another, slow footprints of something walking through him. His sight wavered: the sun-shod surface of the water vanished, and beyond it he saw – curls and currents, abysses and clouds, depths and darkness and flying creatures, a whole hollow world outlined by sound pulses –

He rubbed his eyes furiously until he could open them and not see it.

"Lizzie!" he had yelled. "I'm going home!"

She had come back then, and they rode home.

He hadn't spoken to anyone but her at the wayside.

Nobody from their visit to Bob's would consider him a friend yet, right? He doubted anybody he had met there would even remember his name. Well, except maybe Bob. Bob had a great memory for names, Lizzie said. Was Bob the type to cruise around after dark and speak to people through barely open windows? Michael didn't think so, but he didn't even know the guy.

"I don't think it was anyone I met today," he told his mother.

She picked up her baseball bat. "You get the big flashlight. Let's go check it out."

He got the four-cell flashlight from her closet. They crept through the house in darkness, Michael going a little ahead of his mother. With her at his back, he wasn't so afraid, even though he knew that didn't make a lot of sense. Well, she had the baseball bat.

They eased open his bedroom door and waited, staring toward the pale square of curtained window beyond his bed. No sounds. No voice. They sneaked up to his window and looked out. Ambient light revealed that there was nothing outside but dark lawn and bushes.

Michael switched on the flashlight, opened the window, leaned out. Footprints patterned the soft dirt of the empty flowerbed below. He swept the beam over the dirt. Something was wrong with the footprints.

Mom leaned out the window beside him. "That's odd," she said.

"What is?" Michael focused the light on one clear print.

"The toes," said Mom. "They're – they're too long, and what's that between them?"

They stared at the ground. Michael moved the light, shifting the shadows, and the strangeness in the footprint vanished.

"We'll look at it tomorrow," Mom said. "For tonight, let's lock the window, and you spend the night in my room."

He lay on the floor in his parents' bedroom, zipped into his mummy bag, and stared at the ceiling. Mom had left one light on. She tossed and turned in the bed. They didn't speak. He wasn't sure whether she slept before dawn lightened the windows beyond her curtains, but he knew he didn't.

Morning came. They headed for different bathrooms, then went to his room again together.

When they opened the window to look out, the soil of the flowerbed had been swept clean.

★

"We could board up your window," Mom said as she buttered toast.

"I couldn't live in a room with boarded up windows." He always felt restless and panicky in enclosed spaces.

"Well, okay, put shutters on them. You could open those during the day."

"We could do what Lizzie says everybody else here does. Get a dog."

Mom sat at the table across from him. Michael ate a big bite of cereal. He knew he should have kept his mouth shut on that particular topic. Mom was giving him the thousand-yard stare she always unleashed when he mentioned something unforgivable. He had asked for a dog many times over the years. She had gotten tired of telling him that they moved too much.

Finally, Michael said, "Okay. How about a burglar alarm?"

"Stronger locks. Let's go to the hardware store and get stronger locks. I'll get you a baseball bat of your own, too. I guess the other thing would be that for now, you sleep in my room."

"Ouch," he said. His back hurt this morning. A hot shower had helped, but not enough.

"We could pick up an air mattress for you."

"What about talking to the police?"

"There's no evidence that anyone was ever here."

"We could ask them if there's peeping Toms."

Mom turned away, munched meditatively on a corner of toast. She never liked to talk to police. "How about we go to the Chowder House for lunch and talk to Gracie?" she said. Gracie was the restaurant manager. Mom had met Gracie when she and Dad drove over from Idaho to buy the house. "Gracie knows everything."

"Okay," Michael said.

Lizzie went with them to lunch. She said she was a chowder hound. Michael was glad she was still speaking to him after spending an afternoon with him.

"Gotta have the slumgullion," Lizzie said when a waitress named Dani had seated them at a picnic table by the window. All the tables at the Chowder House were picnic tables, with benches. They could seat at least twelve people. Often in the height of summer, strangers sat together, Lizzie said. She liked that part. She'd met people from Pittsburgh and Montreal and Florida. Maybe one of her hobbies was collecting out-of-towners, Michael thought.

"What's slumgullion?" Mom asked.

"Chowder with a bunch of shrimp thrown in."

Michael ordered a cheeseburger and fries when Dani came back. Mom and Lizzie ordered slumgullion and garlic toast.

"Come on, Michael, gotta taste it," Lizzie said, holding out a spoonful of her chowder to him.

"Michael doesn't care for seafood," said Mom.

"Sure, has he ever tried it? Are you one of those guys who looks at something and says, 'Never had it, don't like it'?"

He grinned at her because he knew he had said that.

"Open your mouth."

His insides squirmed at the thought of sharing a spoon with her. On the other hand, she was a girl he liked, and maybe her willingness to share her spoon was a sign she liked him back. He opened his mouth and accepted the spoon.

The dense white flavor burst across his tongue: cream and potato and melted butter, but more than that, the chewy, salty meat of the clams, the slightly squeaky texture of the shrimp, and something else, something primal that made him gasp after he had swallowed. He wanted more. He felt as though he had found the One True Food. He grabbed Lizzie's bowl and drank from it, emptied it in rapid swallows, set it down and licked the last of the chowder from his lips.

"Michael!" Mom said. Lizzie stared at him, wide-eyed.

The flavor opened something inside him, a pulsing feeling in his center that reached outward to his skin, a second heartbeat that pumped power through him. After a moment it subsided. He shook his head. "No," he said. Then, "Oh, God. I'm sorry, Lizzie. You were right, I never had that before. I didn't know how much I'd like it. I'm sorry. You want the rest of my burger?"

"I can order more," she said, her voice doubtful. "You want more?"

"I don't think I better." It was too intense. Plus, what had that weird reaction been? A heart attack? The roaring appetite for more scared him. He had to ignore it, the way he ignored other things.

He took a bite of cheeseburger to chase the chowder taste out of his mouth, and the world settled back to normal.

Lizzie ordered another bowl of slumgullion but didn't offer him any. He tried not to smell it from across the table. His stomach wasn't hungry, but something in him was.

They had reached the crumbs-and-cold-salty-ends-of-fries stage of their meal when Gracie slid onto the bench beside Mom. "Howdy, Caroline. How you doing?"

"I'm glad you asked," said Mom. "We were wondering about something."

"Yeah? What?"

"Do you get a lot of peeping Toms in this town? Liz warned us about this yesterday, but we weren't sure. Someone came right up to Michael's window last night and spoke to him."

Gracie and Lizzie flinched.

"I thought peeping Toms were only interested in watching women," Mom went on. "But Michael's light was already out when this one approached the house. So watching doesn't seem to be the motive. What did it say to you, Michael?"

"It said my name, and that it was a friend."

"It left bare footprints in the flowerbed, but when we went back to look this morning, they were gone. Is this a common occurrence around here?"

"It spoke to you?" Gracie asked after a moment of uneasy silence.

"Yeah," said Michael.

"They don't usually talk."

"What do they usually do?" Mom asked.

"They hiss until you run for a shotgun, and then they slip off. If you go outside to chase them, though...."

"What?" asked Mom. "Michael and I are often alone in the house, and we need to know how to protect ourselves."

"Don't ever leave the house at night," Gracie said. "They can't hurt you if you don't go out to them."

"Who are they, Gracie?"

"The Strangers."

"The Strangers," Mom repeated. "What's that supposed to mean?"

"People disappear every year," Gracie said. She glanced around, as if looking for listeners. "We blame the tide. It's usually the newcomers who vanish. We try to warn everybody, but most don't take us serious."

"What are the Strangers?" asked Mom.

"Don't rightly know," said Gracie. "Anybody who really knows is gone. Been a plague on the town for ages. One came to my window when I was a girl. Thought it was my boyfriend, and almost went outside, but glory be, my mother stopped me. They haven't come by my house in twenty years. They always know when someone new moves in, though."

"So you have this conversation a lot?"

"Try to," said Gracie.

"Does anybody ever do anything about these Strangers?"

"Not anymore. Had a sheriff back in the seventies who tried to ambush 'em. Set up traps, with guns and dogs and floodlights. They never came, no matter where he set up. Always knew somehow. Minute he moved the trap away from a newly occupied house, they'd show up and hiss at people if they left a window open, even a crack."

"As long as we stay in the house, we're safe?"

"Far as I know," Gracie said.

"How about yard lights?" Michael asked. "Motion detectors?"

Gracie shrugged. "Couldn't hurt. But nobody I've ever talked to has caught a clear sight of them, even with good lights. They move like shadows."

"Nobody knows what they are? Nobody? And you just go on living here?" Mom asked.

Gracie shrugged. "Whatcha gonna do? We know how to deal. So there are Strangers around and they hiss at you. Occasionally a Chihuahua or a cat disappears. We still got the beach and the tourist trade and the balmy weather. And the threat of the Strangers cuts way down on petty crimes; burglars don't go out at night around here. Now you know, and you can be safe here, too. All right?"

Mom beat her fingers in a gallop on the tabletop, staring at the bucket of saltines on the table. Her mouth firmed. "I guess," she said. "But we're getting those lights anyway."

"Don't sleep with the windows open," Lizzie told Michael.

It wasn't a hiss, he thought, but he didn't say anything.

At the hardware store, he bought some Plaster of Paris and three-penny nails. Together he and his mother bought fancy new yard lights with motion detectors to turn them on. They picked up an inflatable bed and a footpump, too. Lizzie showed them where the baseball bats were, and Mom bought a nice heavy aluminum one so Michael would be armed too. "But you won't be able to hit them," Lizzie said. "Nobody ever has."

"What do they want?"

Lizzie shook her head. "Just treat it like bad weather you won't go out in. Shadow weather. That's all. We have the day, and that's enough."

Back home, Michael and Mom rigged the lights and the motion detectors. They inflated the new bed, and Michael lay on it, bounced on it, wondered if he could sleep on it. Better than the floor, anyway.

Michael took his bag of supplies, went into his room, and threw the window all the way open. It was still afternoon; he was safe enough. Cool salty air blew in, ruffling the curtains and fluttering the edges of the comic books on his desk. Outside, sunlight shone, bright and cold. A bird he didn't recognize called a sharp sweep of notes.

Lizzie had followed him into his room.

"It spoke to you?" she muttered. "Never heard of that before."

He set the jar of nails on the windowsill and went to get the hammer. Maybe if he nailed the window so it couldn't open more than an inch – sound could travel in and out of his room, but the thing couldn't come in after him.

"It said it was a friend?" Lizzie asked.

"I thought maybe it was you."

"That's crazy. I don't go out after dark."

He slid the window almost shut and positioned the nails on the sill above it. He wasn't ready to make the change yet, though. It was still broad daylight. He put the nails back in the jar. "Except on Halloween."

"Right."

"But they never go in houses."

Lizzie came and stared at the small dimples he had pressed into the paint of the windowsill with the tips of the nails, marking the places he planned to hammer them into later. "It's better if the window's closed all the way."

"I want to hear what it has to say."

"You don't."

"How do you know, if they've never talked to people before?"

"What if they have? What if they talked to the people who went outside at night and never came home? What if that happens to you? I don't want that to happen to you." She paced around the room, picked up one of the superhero comics from his desk, put it down. "See," she said, "I want you to be my neighbor. The last people who lived here were awful. I was so glad when they moved away. Then when I saw you guys moving in yesterday – I thought...." She paced between the door, the desk, and the bed, avoiding the stacks of boxes. She kept her gaze directed at the rag rug on the floor. "Okay, you know, the other kids think I'm weird. You know?"

"Why?"

"Well, because I *am* weird. I like school. I read more than they do. I hate video games. I don't like shopping. I don't wear makeup. I don't have a cell phone. I like to dissect weird, smelly things I find on the beach." She paused, watched him, anxious. "Don't you think that's weird?"

"Yeah. So what?"

Some of the tension left her shoulders. "See. That's what I was hoping for. You're a little peculiar yourself, so I thought maybe we could get along. But if you start obsessing about the Strangers – I might lose you before I even find you." She turned her back on him. "God. I'm sorry to be so lame."

"What's lame about that?"

"I'm pretty sure I'm not supposed to talk about anything substantial until we've known each other for weeks and weeks."

"It's all right." Michael opened a box marked "Electronics" and rooted through stray electric cords and adapters and various small devices, some of them broken, until he came up with his handheld, voice-activated cassette recorder. There was a cassette in it already. He rewound it a little and listened, realized the last thing he had taped was an anime theme song from TV, and it was fuzzy and tinny. But the batteries were still good, and there was still half the tape to go. "I want to find out what it wants. I'll try to tape it tonight. It might not leave footprints, but maybe I can catch its voice."

"Okay," Lizzie said, her voice shaking a little. "If you can be scientific about it. But don't let it – hypnotize you."

He stared down at the tape recorder. "I want proof that it was even here." He dug the sack of plaster of Paris out of the hardware store bag and turned it to read the instructions. "If there is a footprint after it leaves, I want to make a cast before it comes back to wipe it away."

"Don't. You'd have to go outside at night to do it. Don't go outside like a walking all-you-can-eat buffet."

"Do you really think they're eating people? Did anybody ever find body parts left over?"

"No!" she cried. Then, "No," a little less certainly. "I don't know," she said at last. She paced faster, then glanced at him. "When I was eight, my best friend was this girl, Beth, who used to live in this house. That was before the horrible neighbors came. Her family wasn't local. We told them about the Strangers right after they moved here, but I could tell they didn't believe us. But nothing happened for a couple years, except Beth was my friend."

He watched her jitter across the room. She said, "She was just the greatest girl. Fearless. She ran everywhere. It was hard to keep up with her. She was excited about everything. When I was with her, I'd get all excited, too. She loved the beach. We went every day when the tide was out. She had books about sea life, and she taught me the names of things in tidepools. And then – well, she wanted to go to the beach at night, to see the phosphorescence she read about, where you stamp sand and it lights up. I kept telling her not to. But she didn't believe me."

Lizzie stopped, placed her hands flat on the window glass, her brows deeply furrowed. "I'm going to be a scientist. Then I'll figure out how to catch a Stranger. I'll study it and find out...what really happened to Beth."

Mom knocked on the open door. "Hey. Another batch of cookies is ready. I need some tasters to make sure they're safe. Any volunteers?"

Michael set the tape recorder on the windowsill and followed Lizzie to the kitchen.

There was just enough daylight to take the plates of cookies around to the neighbors' houses. Lizzie went with them, another new experience for Michael, already knowing someone who lived here. Mom and Michael met Lizzie's parents: Lizzie's mother was short and wide, with the same frizzy brown hair and tawny brown eyes Lizzie had, and her father was tall, wispy, and washed-out looking, with pale blue eyes and thin, blond-gray hair.

Lizzie's mother smiled up at Michael. "Oh my," she said, her low, pleasant voice flavored with the honey tones of the south. "Now I see why Lizzie's been gone so much."

"Mo-om," said Lizzie in the same tone of voice Michael had used on his mother the day before.

"Aw, honey." Lizzie's mother patted Lizzie's shoulder. Michael couldn't help smiling back at her, feeling a strange confusion inside at what she seemed to be saying: Lizzie was interested in him, and Lizzie's mother didn't mind.

"I'm Caroline, and this is my son, Michael," Mom said. "I'm afraid my husband Dan is gone. He travels a lot on business."

"I'm Rosie, and this is Wagner. Welcome to the neighborhood. Don't let Lizzie make a nuisance of herself. Send her on home if she's irritating you."

"On the contrary," said Mom. "She's terrific. It's like having a native guide."

"Mama, look, Caroline made cookies for you. They're great."

"You're a baker!" said Rosie. "Something we have in common! Well, Caroline, I'm so glad you and Michael are here now." Rosie peeled the Handi-Wrap off the plate of cookies, offered them to Wagner, who took one, bit it, and grinned. "What a sweet way to say hello. I see you have other deliveries to make, though, so don't let us keep you. Stop by afterward for tea if you like."

"Or tomorrow," said Wagner. "Dark's coming on."

"Or tomorrow," Rosie repeated. "Lizzie will give you our phone number. Let's make a date."

"Thank you, I will."

They trooped round to every house on their block. Lizzie already knew everyone, and introduced them, but rushed them, too. They lingered only at Mrs. Plank's house, where Lizzie broached the subject of the piano almost before the introductions.

Mrs. Plank, gray-haired and stern-looking, pursed her lips and studied Michael. She nodded decisively. "Come in and give it a whirl, boy," she said, gesturing him in, then leading them all to the front parlor, a room with comfortable-looking couches, tall lamps over the armchairs, a futuristic fifties coffee table in aluminum and glass, and a baby grand piano painted white.

Michael checked with her again, and she nodded. He sat down on the piano bench and lifted the key cover, rested his fingers on the keys. "It's been two years," he said.

"I won't expect virtuosity, then."

He stared into her gray eyes, then looked down and let his fingers go. Chopin emerged, startling him: a waltz. He didn't remember practicing it, but there it was, in his hands' memory if not his mind's; he played through to the end without stumbling, took a deep breath, let it out, and met Mrs. Plank's gaze again.

She nodded. "Come by between three and four on weekday afternoons if you're so inclined."

He stood up. "Thank you."

"That's all right. Couldn't have stood it if you were a rank beginner, but I can put up with a lot of Chopin."

By the time they'd reached the final house across the street, the sun was streaking the clouds with rose and amber. The young couple greeted them, grabbed the cookies, and slammed the door almost in their faces.

"Yeah," Lizzie said, "better get home."

She separated from them in the street and dashed to her front door. Michael and Mom, infected by everyone's urgency, rushed home and locked themselves into the house.

A breeze was coming from Michael's room; he'd left the window wide. He went in and shut it almost all the way, then hammered the big nails into the sill so the window wouldn't open more than an inch, but he only tapped them in a half an inch so he could pry them out again tomorrow. He grabbed the cassette recorder, said, "Test. It's the night of August 26th in Random, and I'm maybe expecting company tonight. Anything further will be the voice of a Stranger, with any luck." He tossed the recorder on his bed and met Mom in the kitchen, where they put together dinner and verbally dissected their new neighbors.

"Despite the weird night stuff," Mom said, "I feel like this is the best neighborhood we've lived in for a long time."

"Me, too."

They spent the evening unpacking boxes in the living room and setting up the bookshelves in the hall. Mom made up the inflated bed on the floor in the master bedroom. "Brush your teeth and check the locks," she said. "I'm going to turn the lights out in about half an hour."

Another thing he didn't like about sharing a room. In his own room, he could read himself into exhausted sleep. "Can you leave a night light on for me? I have something to do first," he said.

"What?"

Should he tell her? She'd forbid him to try to tape the Strangers, he was pretty sure. It might be dangerous – though how it could be, when he had nailed the window shut, he wasn't sure. She wouldn't want to take chances even in the name of science and detection. "Just something."

She narrowed her eyes. "Leave the bedroom doors open."

He went through the house and checked every door and window to make sure they were closed tight and locked. He checked the stove: all the burners were off. Then he slipped into his bedroom, leaving the door ajar and the lights off, grabbed the little tape recorder, and sat on the rug by his bed, a couple feet from the window. He had left the curtains open. Cool, damp, salty air flowed in through the crack.

Time inched by. The curtains fluttered as a damp breeze played with them. Outside was faintly lit by an orange street light. What if the Strangers didn't come? What if it was all some big hoax, some weird way to welcome newcomers to town, scare the crap out of them and laugh later? Quite a collaboration, though, with Gracie in on it, and Lizzie, and everybody on the block who had hesitated to answer their knock tonight, then ducked back into their houses a little too quickly for politeness.

"Michael."

The silhouette of a head showed in the window against the copper-edged night. Michael startled, then pressed the Record button on the tape recorder.

"What?" he said in a low voice.

"Michael." It was a whisper. Maybe it was too faint for his recorder to pick up.

"What?"

"Come here."

"I don't think that's a good idea. People have been telling us about you."

"What did they say?"

Michael wished it would speak with a voice instead of a whisper. He couldn't tell if it was male or female.

"They said you're Strangers and you lure people to their deaths."

The shadow laughed. It turned sideways. Its profile was strange. Something spiky lay along the top of its head.

It turned back. "Sometimes we do," it said.

"What do you want with me? I don't want to go to my death."

"We want you to come home."

"What?"

"Come home, Michael. You've been so long away."

Cold crept through his gut, arrowed up his spine.

"We lost you long ago. We couldn't reclaim you until now. Come home, Michael."

"What are you saying?" Michael whispered. He crept closer to the window.

"Come outside and we will show you." Then it hissed something, louder than its whisper, but not a simple hiss, something that divided into syllables and tones. Galvanized, Michael straightened. A hiss, but words, and he could almost translate –

Another hiss, a stroke, a caress. His name, but not Michael.

"Come back to us," whispered the voice, followed by the hiss Michael almost recognized.

"Michael!" Mom's voice was a yell from his doorway.

Mom switched on the light, and Michael dropped the tape recorder. Something pale, with spots of green glow where eyes should be, stared in through the window at them; then it was gone.

He rewound the tape recorder at the kitchen table while Mom made cocoa.

There was a lot of hissing silence on the tape, interrupted by his own voice, saying, "What?" "What?" "I don't think that's a good idea...."

"How could you?" Mom asked. "What were you thinking?"

"I wanted to find out what it wants."

"Why?" She brought filled mugs to the table, set one in front of him.

"What are you saying?" Michael's voice said from the tape recorder. A murmur that he could almost hear, and then a burst of hissing that was definitely loud enough to record –

"Is that its voice?" Mom asked.

"Shh!" Michael rewound and listened to the hisses again. Rewound, listened again. Again.

He pressed the stop button and sat with his hand on the tape recorder.

"What is it?" Mom asked.

The time and the chance for change has come again at last. Come back to us, Ssskzz. Come home.

Michael shook his head.

"That's it, isn't it? That hissing? Gracie was right. When I turned on the light and saw that face, oh my God, Michael, oh, my God, and you were talking to it?" The resurgence of her hysteria swept over them both. She had babbled like this just after she had looked into his room; it had taken him fifteen minutes to calm her. "We can't stay here. We can't stay here. No matter how nice the neighbors are, we can't stay here. It's a good thing we didn't finish unpacking. I'll get a U-Haul tomorrow morning and we'll head inland. We could go back to Idaho. Things like this never happened there, and our house hasn't sold yet...."

"Mom," Michael said.

She took three gulps of cocoa and a few deep breaths. "I'm going to call your father." She went to the phone, stared at the itinerary Dan had printed out and taped on the wall before he left on his trip, and dialed. "Daniel Welty's room, please.... Hello? Who is this? What? What? Is Dan there? He is? Tell him it's his wife on the phone, and I don't care what kind of meeting he's in, I need to talk to him right now." She held the phone away from her ear and muttered, "Sales associate, my ass."

Michael turned down the volume on the recorder, rewound it, and played it again, holding it up to his ear. There were nuances in the words that a simple translation couldn't catch, a strain of loss, a thread of opportunity, a breath of hope and longing, a whisper of welcome.

"Don't even bother trying to explain, Dan. I don't care what bimbo you're with. Michael and I are in a crisis here. We can't stay in Random. We're moving tomorrow morning. What? No. Why does everything have to be about you?"

Michael stood up and eased out of the room. His mother's back was to him; he was sure she didn't notice he was gone. He went to the front door and slid the chain sideways, eased it off, then opened the deadbolt. He clicked up the pushbutton lock on the doorknob and stood, his hand wrapped around the doorknob, and waited.

How could he leave her? Dad had been leaving Mom more and more, in increments, leaving them both for longer trips, with shorter visits in between, moving them around like knights on a chessboard, then leaving them behind. Mom and Michael depended on each other. He couldn't leave her.

He had to find out what the Stranger had been talking about. Did it really know who he was, where he came from? Could it tell him? He had to –

The doorknob turned in his hand. He eased the front door open and stepped out onto the porch.

But what about Gracie, and Lizzie, and all the new neighbors? What about Mrs. Plank, and permission to play the piano? What about a whole town that knew it had strange neighbors, and worked around them? What if the Strangers really ate people, and everything it said had been designed to lure him out of the house and into the open air, where it could net him, gut him, take his fillets home for its children to snack on?

What about Mom?

It stood to his left before he noticed its approach, a tall, shadowed figure that smelled strongly of fish and brine and dripped on the boards of the porch.

"Wait," he said. "I just want to talk."

"We want to free you," it whispered.

"From what?"

"From the chains of this limited existence. You've suffered enough."

"What do you mean? I'm not suffering."

"Aren't you? Trapped in this thin atmosphere that can't even support you? Glued feet downward to this dirt? Deaf to the feel of sounds? Come home, where every breath is a taste and every movement a touch. Come home. Your family longs for you."

"I can't leave Mom. I don't even know you. Everyone here says you hurt people. How can I trust you?"

"Look in your hearts. Walk with us, Michael, and we will teach you how to fly."

"Michael," said another. He glanced over and saw a second shadow. Three more materialized at the foot of the front porch stairs. They all peered up at him, slender forms with wrong-shaped heads. He felt it, then, the beat of a second heart in his chest, the thud of another system inside. It started slowly, but it accelerated as he stood among them.

"Michael!" Mom screamed from inside the house. "Michael! Where are you? Michael!" She flung open the door, letting house light fan across the creatures, and then she screamed, a loud, high, mindless shriek, heavy with woe.

"Come. Come quickly," said the one beside him, as the others melted into the darkness.

"No," Michael said.

It touched his left hand, and its wet touch burned, seared him like magnified sunlight. The burning spread across the back of his hand, sank down into his flesh all the way to the bones. The pain was excruciating; tears spilled from his eyes to cool on his cheek.

The creature vanished. The pain faded too.

"Mom." Michael turned and pushed his mother back into the house, shut the door behind them.

"Michael." She clung to him and sobbed.

He held her with his right arm. "Come on, Mom. Come on." He walked her back to the kitchen, where the phone's handset hung from the wall, a voice still squawking from it.

Michael eased his mother into a chair and picked up the phone. "What is it?" cried his father's voice. "What's going on? Was that a scream? Caroline, are you all right?"

"Dad, I'm hanging up now," Michael said.

"No, wait! Wait, Michael! What's going on there? What's wrong with your mother?"

Michael cradled the handset and sat down in a chair facing his mother's. He took her hands. Her breath hitched. Her face was pale, and her hands trembled in his grasp. She stared down at their hands, snatched her right hand out of his grasp. He looked down.

His left hand had stopped burning, but it had changed. The skin had bleached from tan to shiny gray-blue, and its texture had gone from calloused, with hairs on the backs of his biggest knuckles, to smooth, almost rubbery. Worst was what stretched between his fingers: drooping flaps of skin. He spread his fingers and watched the flaps tighten. His hand looked like an abbreviated bat wing; even his fingernails had changed, darkened and hardened into claws.

He gasped and shook his hand as though he could shed the change like a glove.

His mother had covered her face with her free hand, but she grasped his normal hand hard in her other hand. She was still crying. She straightened, lowered her concealing hand, caught a deep breath, hiccuped her way through a brief flurry of sobs, then rose from the chair and pulled him to the sink. "Maybe it'll wash off," she said. She gripped his altered hand and thrust it under a stream of warm tap water.

The flow of water across the new skin was strange and exciting. Its touch mesmerized him; he could feel the flutter of current, sense the braided pulses of it. He spread his fingers, and the soft water stroked across the webs between. He knew if he cupped his hand a certain way so that water would push on it, it would carry him –

Mom turned his hand under the water, scrubbed at it with dish soap and the soft side of a sponge. It didn't change. Gently he pulled his hand out of her grip and turned off the faucet, went to the cupboard, grabbed a glass, filled it with water, and handed it to her. She blinked tears, then drank half the glass. She offered him the rest. He took it in his good hand and drank, felt his own bumpy breathing grow steady again.

"Should we go to the hospital?" she asked him.

He hid his new hand behind his back, then sighed, pulled it forward, and stared down at it. He turned it so he could study the palm, spread his fingers. A few creases defined where it could bend, but the intricate whorls of his identity had been erased. He closed it into a fist. The extra skin made his fist into a new kind of gesture, bulbous, with pale pleats separating the fingers, not a hitting hammer but something else. Mom ran her fingertips over the outside of it, stroked the folds of new skin. He moaned with delight, and she stopped, startled, stared at him.

He hid the new hand behind his back again.

"Does it hurt?" she asked.

"Not anymore. Mom – the hospital – I don't know. I don't think it's that kind of injury."

The phone rang.

They stared at each other.

She swallowed. "Probably Dan," she said. "What do we tell him?"

His stomach churned. Had Dad really been with some woman when Mom called? What did it mean? Maybe it was innocent. It sounded like Dad had said it was. But he was gone so much. Family meant Mom and Michael now.

"It's up to us," he muttered.

Mom picked up the phone. "Hi," she said. "Oh! Hi. It's Rosie, Liz's mom," she told Michael, then spoke to the phone. "No, we're all right." She listened, covered the phone's pickup with her hand, spoke to Michael. "They heard me scream, but they couldn't come over. They tried to call, but the line was busy." She listened, her gaze on the ground. "Yes," she said. "They were here."

She listened. "Yes. Well, it's complicated. We don't understand it ourselves yet." She touched Michael's new hand, cupped her hand around it. "Maybe. We don't know. Yeah, thanks for calling. I appreciate it. Thanks. We'll talk to you tomorrow." She let go of Michael's hand, fetched the shopping list with its pencil on a string, and wrote something down. "Thanks, Rosie. Good night." She hung up.

They sat in silence side by side at the table. At last Mom sighed. "We never knew where you came from."

"You always said a coast town."

"Yeah. We didn't go through regular channels to get you. Dan and I had been trying for years to have a baby of our own, but we couldn't, even with medical help. One night one of Dan's friends came over. Uncle Mike, remember? He'd just got home from a sales trip. He had you with him. You were so solemn and quiet, and you had such big eyes. You were the most beautiful little boy. Mike said you were his nephew and your parents were dead, but he couldn't keep you, and he knew how much Dan and I wanted a baby. I just said yes, yes, yes, and you were ours. Dan handled the paper-work." She looked toward the stove, then shook her head. "Mike said you were born in Seaside. I always figured there was something suspicious in how he got you, but I didn't want to know. I wanted to keep you. But I was always afraid somebody would come after us and take you back. That's why I haven't minded moving so often. Guess our luck ran out this time."

She rested her hand on the back of his new hand. "How did this happen?"

"It touched me. It was wet. It burned."

"When they were hissing at you, could you really hear words in it?"

"Hissing?"

"Hissing. I was screaming, and I – but one of them made these hissing, clacking sounds before they all – and you answered."

"Hissing." He reached for the tape recorder. He rewound it and played the first thing the Stranger had said that he understood. *Come home.* "I do understand it." Had his whole conversation on the porch been in this language?

"Those are your people," Mom said, her voice incredulous. She laughed. And then she let out a little sob, and rubbed her eyes.

"Mom." He wrapped his right arm around her shoulders, hugged her.

She struggled, then subsided. "I'm so tired."

"Me too."

Michael changed into pajamas in the bathroom. He studied his new hand. The change in his skin had traveled past his wrist, raggedly up his forearm; it was not as though a circle delineated one part of him from another. He ran water into the sink and flapped the new hand around in it. He felt vectors, movement, change, powers. Once both his hands were like this, he would be able to –

He drained the water quickly, brushed his teeth, slipped under the blankets on the air mattress in Mom's room. She turned out the light. "Please," she whispered in the darkness. "Don't leave without saying good-bye."

He thought about sneaking off to his room to talk to the Strangers, but eventually he slept instead.

When he opened his eyes, Mom was sitting near the mattress, hugging her knees and watching him. The curtains were open, and morning light slanted across the floor behind her, touched her graying hair and a small patch of her cheek and brow. She smiled when she saw he was awake.

"What are you doing?" he asked.

"It's a mother thing. How's your hand?"

He slid his left hand out from under the blankets, and they both studied it. It was still changed. He sat up, using both hands to balance. Together, they supported him. He glanced at Mom. Her face wore a mixture of sad and worried and tired.

"What do you want for breakfast?" she asked.

Usually she let him get his own breakfast. She only asked on special occasions, like on the birthday they'd chosen for him.

"Pancakes."

She stood. "Do you even have a swimsuit?"

He couldn't follow her mental jumps. "No." Open water had always terrified him.

"Guess you won't need one. I don't think they were dressed." She left the bedroom, and he got up, wondering. The new hand worked as well as the other one, with only a few minor awkwardnesses when he snagged his webs on things.

In the kitchen, she set a plate of pancakes in front of him, and he grabbed his knife and fork, then stared at the new hand. The fork didn't feel natural in it. He switched the fork to his right hand and used it to cut, abandoning the knife. He tried pouring syrup with his left hand, and managed to get most of it on the plate. Mom watched behind a blank face.

Lizzie knocked at the kitchen door when they were halfway through their first plates of pancakes. She stared in at them. Michael hid his hand in his lap as Mom got up to let Lizzie in.

"What happened last night? Are you all right?" Lizzie asked as she came inside. "Mama said you were okay, but I saw the Strangers on your porch.

What happened? You're still here. Oh, God."

"Where do the Strangers come from, Liz?" asked Mom.

"The sea."

Mom's shoulders sagged. "Yesterday, you said the gorse."

"They come out of the water and hide in the gorse. That's what everybody says."

Mom sighed.

"What were they doing on your front porch last night? I've never seen so many in one place. We heard you scream."

"Do you want some breakfast, Liz?" Mom asked.

"I want some answers."

"Ask Michael. I have to go figure out where I packed the camera." She left.

Lizzie pulled out a chair and sat down beside him. "Hey," she said. "Come on. Tell me. What happened?"

"Mom's been weird ever since we woke up. I have to find out what's wrong with her." He pushed his chair back and stood up.

"Michael." Lizzie grabbed his wrist, then shrieked and released it. Then she grabbed it again, gripped it tight, pulled the new hand toward her, stared wide-eyed at the changes. "Michael!" she cried.

His throat closed. He couldn't breathe. He felt a ghostly fluttering on the sides of his neck, and then his throat unblocked, and he said, "I understand the Strangers. They talked to me, and I understood them. Mom couldn't. She thinks they're my real parents."

"What?" Lizzie stroked the back of his hand, uncurled his fingers, felt the web between them. "Your hand wasn't like this yesterday, was it? I would have noticed."

"One of them touched it, and that happened. But maybe that's what happens to anybody they touch." He wanted to pull away from Lizzie and go after Mom. Mom thought the Strangers were his real family. Mom thought – Mom assumed he was leaving with them. How could she think that? She was the one who had raised him. She was the person he loved best in all the world.

"I found it," Mom said. She raised the Polaroid. "Smile."

"Mom."

She snapped a picture, and the camera's motor raced as it spat it out. "Gotta try again, you weren't smiling. I know you hate having your picture taken, Michael, but won't you let me anyway, this time?"

"Sure." Heaviness sat in his chest, a hot, sour lump. He summoned up a smile for her. The camera flashed, leaving red ghosts across his vision. She dropped the pictures on the table and came to put her arms around him. He felt the silent sobs jerking through her.

"What makes you so sure I'm leaving with them?" he asked.

She shook her head against his chest. She took a deep breath, straightened, stepped away from him. "Orange juice?"

Lizzie still held his new hand. She stood uncertainly beside him, then put her own hand palm to palm with his. He could taste her skin with his hand, sense the blood flowing beneath its surface. There was a scent he didn't sense with his nose, something that meant Lizzie, everything about her; it came in through his palm, his fingers. How could that be? He felt like he would know her with his eyes closed now, just from a touch. Heat brushed his face. She wasn't running away in horror because of his deformity. He curled his fingers around her hand, and she clasped his. Then she let him go.

Mom studied the two Polaroids, then showed them to him. He grimaced. He hated pictures of himself; he always looked dorky and weird, not the way he imagined himself. In the first picture he looked irritated, his mouth halfway toward a word. Lizzie, beside him, was arrested mid-rise, and she, too, wore an expression between one emotion and the next.

In the second picture, he smiled too wide, and Lizzie stood beside him, holding onto his hand, smiling, too, a very fake smile that tried too hard and looked like a smirk.

"I'm such a lousy photographer," Mom said. "It's a curse. Liz, are you any good at this?"

"Actually, yeah." Lizzie picked up the camera. "The light's awful in here. Let's go outside."

They followed her out into the morning. It was a cool, sunny day, the sky high blue with hurrying clouds, the breeze damp and salt. "Stand together," said Lizzie. "Move sideways a little so the door isn't behind you. Yeah, that's good. The siding makes a better background, less distracting. Michael, do you want to show your hand?"

A peculiar heat pierced his chest. He shuddered, then shook his head. "Why not?" he said. He rested the new hand on his shirt below his collarbone, spread the fingers so the webs stretched. Mom stood to his right, the top of her head about level with his nose. When had she gotten so short? She leaned her shoulder against his right arm.

"Both of you, relax. Smile like you're thinking about your favorite dessert. That's good. Hold it. Hold it." Lizzie pressed the button, and the camera stuck out a picture like a tongue. "Okay. Another one just to make sure?

Lean a little toward each other, relax, just smile." Michael put his arm around Mom's shoulders, hugged her to him. She reached across, rested her hand on his chest beside the new hand, her little finger overlapping his little finger. He felt heat behind his eyes, a tightening in his throat. "Good. In fact, that's great, you guys. Smile just a touch more. Hold it." The motor raced.

He and Mom sighed simultaneous sighs. Michael's shoulders sagged. Lizzie snapped the camera again without warning. "Well, that ought to do it – at least one of them will be good," she said.

"Thanks, Liz."

They went inside. Lizzie put the pictures, with their green-gray-blue windows of mystery, side by side on the table, away from the food. Michael picked up his fork, stared at his pancakes, now soggy with syrup, and set the fork down again.

"Do you want more?" Mom stood by the stove, one hand around the handle of the batter pitcher, the other ready to move the frying pan back over the heat.

Michael shook his head.

"Is it time?" she asked.

"Time for what?"

"Time to go to the beach."

"Mom."

She rubbed her eye with her knuckle. "You know that's coming."

"I don't."

"You can't – " She pointed to his new hand. "I love you."

"I know, Mom."

"If that's who you really are – "

"I don't even know those guys."

"Something in you does."

He stood up, a rage of confusion inside, and slammed out of the kitchen in search of his jacket. When he found it – saw the little heart pin on the left side that Debbie, a girl he knew in school in Idaho, had pinned on his jacket when they'd gone to some dance last year – he was so angry he turned around, grabbed his dictionary, and threw it on the floor. It made a satisfying thud, so he did it again.

Did she *want* to get rid of him?

He sank down onto the bed and dropped his head into his hands. The left hand tasted the salt of his tears; there was a burning in his wrist, and he dropped his hand to look, watched the blue-gray slickness of the new skin spread half an inch up his forearm.

Inside him, a door closed. This change was coming, and he couldn't stop it or reverse it, at least not with anything he knew now.

Michael shrugged into his jacket, zipped it closed, and buried the new hand in his pocket. Mom hadn't come because he threw a book. Wasn't she even going to fight to keep him?

He went to the kitchen, found breakfast cleared from the table and Mom and Lizzie finishing dishes. Mom turned a pale face to him, then left the room, came back with her jacket and knit hat on. The beach had been windy yesterday and probably would be again today.

"I need my jacket too," Lizzie said, and then, "Is it okay if I come?"

"I – " said Mom. She looked at Michael.

He turned away, then said in a low, rough voice to Lizzie, "If I don't come back from this, Mom's going to need friends."

Lizzie nodded and ran out the back door.

Michael looked at the pictures on the table. All three of the ones Lizzie had taken were good. He saw a smile on his face he had never seen even in a mirror, tender as he stared down at his mother, who faced the camera with a sad smile, her hand touching his new, strange hand on his chest. His face looked innocent of the knowledge that the world as he knew it was about to end.

He glanced at Mom, smiled, and she smiled back. "I love you no matter what," she said.

"I know. I love you, too."

"Oh, good."

"Will you be all right?"

"Yes. I'll manage. I always do. Maybe you can visit."

"Dad," he said, and that was when she cried.

The sobs were great, gulping ones, the cries of someone who had lost everything in some kind of natural disaster. She wailed, and he didn't know what to do. Finally he hugged her, wishing she would stop it, this disturbing, wordless noise that grated on his heart. She clutched at his jacket. A little while later, she stopped, sucked in breaths, muttered something, pushed away from him, went to the sink, and drank a glass of water. She was rinsing her face by the time Lizzie came back, dressed for wind.

"Well," Mom said, "I'll slap your father around and see what happens. I'll find out whether he's really leaving me. I'm not sure what I want right now. A job, anyway. I checked the local paper. There were some possibilities in the want ads. I have a good feeling about this town."

"We'll take care of you," Lizzie said.

Mom smiled at her.

The beach was two blocks away, two blocks past other weathered houses, hunched trees shaped into waves by prevailing winds off the ocean, cars rusting from the salt air. As they walked, the wave sound grew louder. They reached the stairs down to the beach, and Michael stood at the top against the endless push of the wind and looked out over blue-gray motion and standing stones like the Earth's teeth rising from the sand and water. Was this really home?

Wind carried sand in low, scudding sheets before dropping it.

Lizzie clattered down the stairs, and Mom followed. Michael went down after them. At the base of the cliff, they sat on a drift log tossed high by a winter storm. Michael unlaced his tennis shoes and socks and hid them behind the log.

Seawater. He'd been wary of it for as long as he could remember, and even before, according to Mom. He still felt the shadow of terror at the thought that it was only feet away from him. He stood and drew in deep breaths until his heart slowed. Beside him, Mom took his plain hand and squeezed it.

"Ready?" she asked.

"Almost." He took three more breaths.

Lizzie looked up and down the beach, nodded, led the way left. "There's a cove this way that's closed off when the tide's high, but we should be able to get to it now. Not that many people go there."

They followed her along the beach. Gulls cried above them.

At last they came to a stretch of sand without many lines of footprints across it. Lizzie led them up over a spine of dark rock that stretched from the cliff to the water, and then they were in a cup-shaped cove, protected from the wind.

Mom still gripped his hand.

The three of them walked to the edge of the dry sand. Michael let go of Mom's hand and knelt, new fingers and palm against the wet sand. He felt the scorch of change rise up his arm.

He looked over his shoulder at Mom, who smiled at him. He touched his right hand to the wet sand. At the kiss of salty water, change attacked his palm and flared over his skin.

Water swamped his clothes, icy and aggressive and burning. He struggled out of them. Change twisted and worked through him.

The wave rushed out, beaching him on sliding sand in a haze of burning pain. Mom, her jeans wet to the knees, stared down at him, mouth open, eyes wide. Lizzie screamed and ran up the beach.

Mom dropped to her knees beside him. She closed her mouth and blinked three times, then reached toward his chest.

He lifted what had been his right hand.

Mom set her hand on his chest. He felt his second heartbeat pulse under her palm. "How do you feel?" she asked.

"How do I look?" he asked, but what came out of his mouth was a string of clicks and hisses.

She blinked rapidly, licked her lips.

He touched her cheek. She said, "Your eyes are golden now."

Something hissed behind him. He turned. There was nothing opaque about the ocean now: shafts of light plunged down into it, showed him the others, floating just offshore.

He struggled to his feet. Already that felt like a huge, uncomfortable effort, something his body wasn't made to do. He held out a hand to Mom, who took it. He hauled her up and wrapped his arms around her.

She hugged him, pressed her head against his chest.

"Love you," she whispered.

"Love you," he said, but it came out hissing. She smiled as though she understood and stepped away from him. A wave came up and he fell into it, grateful, and let it carry him out to where the others waited. The sea spoke along his sides and over his chest and belly, against his soles, under his palms. All around him spread a swaying world of light and distance, mixing with sand below and sky above, the standing rocks off shore like slices of mountains cut off at top and bottom, windings of seaweed beyond, and small living creatures flying toward him and away.

The others came to him.

He followed them out past the place where waves gathered and broke, out where the bottom dropped, deeper, where light grew dim. The others traveled around him, some darting close to brush along him, others teasing, sending patterns through the flow of water. Clicks and chunks and hisses flowed around him, and tastes filtered through his mouth, most of them unknown but somehow communicating. Joy thrummed in his chest.

A brief thought of something left behind, an image of sunlight on a face, a fading trace of longing and sadness. One of the others nudged his shoulder, and it was gone.

I'll Give You My Word

Diana Wynne Jones

Diana Wynne Jones (*www.leemac.freeserve.co.uk*) lives in Bristol, England. She has been writing fantasy novels for decades, most of them published for young adults or children. Her excellent novels include *Charmed Life* (1977), *The Magicians of Caprona* (1980), *Witch Week* (1982), the award-winning *Archer's Goon* (1984), *Fire and Hemlock* (1985), *Howl's Moving Castle* (1986; adapted for the Miyazaki film of the same name), *The Lives of Christopher Chant* (1988), *Dark Lord of Derkholm* (1998), *Year of the Griffin* (2000), *The Merlin Conspiracy* (2003), and her most recent novel, *Conrad's Fate* (2005). She is also the author of the insightful and very funny *Tough Guide to Fantasyland* (1996), a non-fiction book on the clichés of fantasy fiction, and of a number of collections of short fiction. In an interview with Judith Ridge, Jones discussed her child protagonists and their search for self: "In the wild, we'd be the only person that we wouldn't recognize, if you think about it. And I feel that, you know, it's terribly important to build up to children this notion that it's OK, that you are a person, and you will find [yourself]...one of the things is that all fantasy it seems to me works the way your brain basically works. This is perhaps a startling concept, but I think it's true. Your brain, when it's working on a problem, says 'what if, what if, what if?' Fantasy is just an extension of 'what if?' And if you think about it, your brain is aimed to come out with a satisfactory solution jubilantly, and you want really to point children in that direction and say 'there is a solution,' and you should be happy, and you should be hopeful. It's pointing people in the right way, and trying for sanity."

"I'll Give You my Word" appeared in the excellent original anthology *Firebirds Rising*, edited by Sharyn November, another of the very best anthologies of the year.

PEOPLE WERE ALWAYS asking Jethro, "How do you *manage* with a brother like yours?"

Jethro mostly smiled and answered, "No problem. He makes me laugh."

This was not really a lie. Jethro used to laugh a lot in the days when he and Jeremy shared a bedroom and Jeremy used to kneel up in his bunk-bed every morning, rocking from side to side and singing – to a tune he had made up himself – "Computers, computers. Caramel custard computers." He sang until Dad banged on the wall and shouted that it was only *dawn*, for goodness' sake, and would Jeremy just *shut up!* At this Jeremy would turn his very knowing big blue eyes toward Jethro, a small smile would flit across his mouth, and he would sing in a whisper, "Collapsed cardinal caramel custard computers!" Jeremy had a way of making his face into a solemn egg-shape and staring crazily into the space between Jethro's head and the win-

dow while he uttered, "Sweet cervical béchamel with empirical gladiolus."
This never failed to send Jethro off into squeals of laughter. And their father
banged on the walls again.

But Jethro's problem was that he was a worrier. In those days he worried
that he would stop breathing in the night or that he would prick himself in
his sleep and lose all the blood in his body, so that it was always a relief to be
woken by Jeremy's singing. When eventually their father Graeme got so sick
of the singing that he cleared out the box room at the end of the passage and
their mother Annabelle made it into a bedroom for Jeremy, Jethro started to
worry about Jeremy too. Jeremy took to wandering round the house then,
saying things. "Ponderous plenipotential cardomum," he would say. "In
sacks." And after a bit, "Sententious purple coriander."

"Does that come in sacks too?" Jethro asked him.

"No," Jeremy said. "In suitcases."

"What does plenipotential mean?" Jethro asked. "Or sententious?"

Jeremy just made his face egg-shaped and stared crazily over Jethro's
head. At first Jethro thought that Jeremy was simply inventing these words
and he worried that his brother was mad. But then it occurred to Jethro to
look up these words in one of the many dictionaries in their house, and he
found they were real. *Plenipotential* meant *possessing full power and authority* and
sententious meant *tending to indulge in pompous moralizing.* And it was the same
with all the other words Jeremy kept coming up with: they were always in
one dictionary or another, although Jethro was fairly sure Jeremy had no idea
what any of the words meant. He began worrying about how they got into
Jeremy's head.

Their house was full of dictionaries. Graeme and Annabelle's main work
was running an agency called Occult Security, which protected clients of
all kinds from magical dangers, exorcised haunts and cleansed evil from
houses; but this agency did not pay very well and there were long intervals
between commissions. So when they were not getting rid of malign spirits or
clearing out gremlins from factories, they both did other things. Annabelle
wrote little books called Hall's Guides to Witchcraft and Graeme feverishly
composed crossword puzzles for several newspapers. There were three computers in the house, one devoted to Occult Security, one on which Annabelle
pattered away, frowning and murmuring, "Now is that strictly shamanism,
or should it go under folk magic?" and a third full of hundreds of black and
white square patterns and lists of words. Graeme was usually to be found in
front of this one, irritably tapping a very sharp pencil and muttering, "I want
something Q something something K here and I'm not sure there is a word."

Then he would reach for one of the wall of dictionaries behind his desk.

Jethro began to suspect that these dictionaries – or maybe the computers or the crosswords – were leaking into his brother's brain.

Meanwhile Jeremy was marching round the house chanting, "Borborygmata, borborygmata!"

Jethro looked this one up too and found that it meant *rumblings of the stomach*. "Mum," he said. "Dad, I think this is serious."

Graeme shook his head and laughed. "You'd think he had a direct line to a dictionary somewhere."

"Yes," said Jethro, "but *how*?"

"You worry too much, my love," Annabelle said. "He probably only wants his lunch. I'd better stop this and find him some food."

"But it's not *natural*!" Jethro said. "And he doesn't know what any of his words *mean*. *Ask* him!"

Graeme bent down to Jeremy and said, "Jeremy, old son, have you any idea what *borborygmata* means?"

Jeremy went egg-shaped and angelical and answered, "Avocado pears."

"That's just your favourite food, old son," Graeme explained. "It means tummy rumblings."

"I know," Jeremy said, looking crazily over Graeme's right shoulder. "With pendulous polyps."

"You see!" said Jethro. "He can't go on like this! What happens when he starts school?"

"I think school will cure him," Annabelle said. "You have to remember we're a rather special household here. When Jeremy discovers that none of the other children talk like he does, he'll stop doing it – you'll see."

Jethro had nothing like Mum's faith in this. The week before Jeremy started school, Jethro took his brother outside and tried to explain to him that school was very different from home. "You have to speak normally there," he said, "or everyone will laugh at you."

Jeremy nodded placidly. "You laugh at me."

"No, *not* like I laugh at you," Jethro said. "I mean they'll *jeer*. Some of them may hit you for being peculiar."

"Cacophonous incredulity," Jeremy retorted. "Turnip fondue." And then went back indoors. Jethro sighed.

He worried a lot about Jeremy when school actually started. Jeremy was put in Miss Heathersay's class. Miss Heathersay was known to be a really nice, understanding teacher. If anyone could deal with Jeremy, Jethro hoped it was Miss Heathersay. He watched anxiously that afternoon as Jeremy came out with the rest of the class, ready to go home. Jeremy sauntered out, serene and angelic, as if nothing at all had happened to disturb him, and smiled blindingly when he saw Jethro. Jethro noticed that a crowd of other little kids followed after Jeremy, looking awed and maybe even respectful.

"What happened?" Jethro asked. "Did you talk normally?"

"Replenishment," Jeremy replied. "Hirsute haplography."

Whatever that meant, it was all Jeremy would say. Jethro never did manage to find out how his brother got on in Miss Heathersay's class, except that it seemed perfectly peaceful there. No one complained. Nobody seemed inclined to bully Jeremy. All that happened was that more and more people came up to Jethro and asked, "How do you *manage* with a brother like that?" Jethro got very used to answering, "No problem. He makes me laugh." Which was only half a lie, because Jethro *did* laugh at Jeremy even while he worried about him more than ever.

All through the summer holidays that followed Jeremy's first school year, Jethro laughed and worried. Annabelle and Graeme were very busy sitting over the Occult computer, trying to solve the problem of a lady Town Councillor who kept hearing voices, and whether it was because that computer was leaking or for some other reason, Jeremy came up with a new set of strange words every half hour or so.

"Impermanent epistemological urethra," he remarked to Jethro in exactly the same tone of voice ordinary people would say, "Nice day, isn't it?" At Jethro's worried stare, the knowing look came into Jeremy's round blue eyes and he added, "Febrile potlatch, don't you think?"

Jethro's worry turned to giggles as he looked these words up in several dictionaries. *Urethra* meant *the canal that in most mammals carries urine from the bladder out of the body.* He told Jeremy it did and Jeremy answered, "Obloquy," with a cheerful smile.

"Do go and laugh somewhere else, you two," Annabelle implored them. She and Graeme were leaning over a recording they had managed to make of the Town Councillor's voices. It was faint and far off and ghostly.

"These are real," Graeme said. "Mrs. Callaghan is certainly not imagining them."

"And she's not going mad either," Annabelle agreed. "I'm so glad for her, Graeme."

"No, they're being broadcast to her somehow," said Graeme. "Someone's playing a very unkind psychic trick on the poor lady. Now, how do we make life bearable for her while we track down who's doing it?"

"Earplugs?" Jethro suggested, on his way to the dictionary to find out what *obloquy* meant.

"Now that's a very good idea," Graeme said. He pointed his beautifully sharpened pencil at Jethro in the way that meant "Congratulations!" – which was almost exactly the opposite of *obloquy*, Jethro discovered. "Occult earplugs," Graeme said. "How do we go about making some, Annabelle?" He and Annabelle began tapping keys and bringing up diagrams.

"Scrutinizing congenial tinnitus," Jeremy remarked, coming in to look at the diagrams. "Pending conglomerate haruspication."

"Shut up, Jeremy! Go away!" both his parents commanded.

"Toads," Jeremy said disgustedly, "implicated in paradigms of exponential frogspawn."

He went away, and Jethro pulled down the dictionary again. But Jeremy kept coming back while his parents were doing delicate wiring on two deaf-aids and leaning between them to make remarks such as, "Subaverage nucleosis," or, "Tendentious bromoids."

At last Graeme said, "Jeremy, we are very busy with something very small and delicate that we have to get right. If you don't want your neck wrung, go *away!*"

"Halitosis," Jeremy said. "You never have time for *me.*"

"Play with him, Jethro," Annabelle said, "and I'll double your pocket money."

"But he's so boring," Jethro objected. "He only knows Snap."

"So teach him a new game," Graeme said "Just get out, the pair of you."

Jethro gloomily took Jeremy away and tried to teach him to keep goal in football. It was no good. Jeremy always dived the wrong way like a goalkeeper missing a penalty and the football kept going over into the road. But Jethro had to keep playing with Jeremy, all that summer, because Graeme and Annabelle soon grew busier yet. While they were still trying to trace the person who was broadcasting Mrs. Callaghan's voices, trekking out at night with earphones and backpacks of equipment, Mrs. Callaghan was wearing the deaf-aids. These earplugs cut out the broadcast so effectively that Mrs. Callaghan became convinced that Occult Security had already solved her problem. She recommended Graeme and Annabelle to everyone else on the Council. The consequence was that the Lord Mayor ordered psychic protection around the Council Building, several Councillors requested their homes made safe against occult invasion, and – while Annabelle began worrying that she was not going to meet her deadline with her latest Guide to

Witchcraft – Jack Smith, the local Member of Parliament, came to visit them in person.

"Elephantiasis," Jeremy said. Jack Smith was indeed rather fat.

Jack Smith was convinced that he was being persecuted by a coven of witches. "It's hard to explain – it's so nebulous," he said, rubbing his fat hands nervously together. "Most nights I wake up with a jump, thinking I've been hearing horrible strident laughter, and then I can't get to sleep again. Or I become quite sure someone is walking softly about in the house, when I know I'm the only person there. And if I have an important speech, or an urgent journey to make, I'm sure to get ill in some way. It happens too often to be an accident. By now I feel quite awful, and I'm getting a name for being a shirker too. The Party Chairman has said hard words to me – and all the time I feel as if something malevolent is watching me and sniggering at my misfortunes."

"It sounds more like a curse," Annabelle said. "What makes you think it's witches?"

"Stridently nebulous," Jeremy explained to her. "Perforated herrings."

Jack Smith shot him an astonished look. Graeme sighed. "Jethro," he said, "take your brother away and teach him another game, or I won't answer for the consequences."

"I've taught him everything I can think of," Jethro said sulkily. "I've even invented – Oh, all right," he said hastily as his father started to get up. "But don't blame me if we break something."

So they played cricket and Jeremy somehow bowled a ball backwards and broke the kitchen window. Jethro protested that it was not his fault. "I was only acting under orders," he said.

"Follow your orders out in the park next time," Annabelle told him, "or I might be tempted to use an unkind spell on you. Look at this mess! My saucepans all full of glass!"

"With you two about, who needs witches?" Graeme grumbled, fetching the broom. "As if we haven't enough to do with Jack Smith's coven."

By the end of that summer, Graeme and Annabelle were still nowhere near discovering Jack Smith's witches. "They're coming in out of the astral plane, obviously," they kept telling each other anxiously. "We have to protect him there, as well as physically."

"I suspect they're the same lot as Mrs. Callaghan's," the other would reply. "We have to locate that coven and close it down."

But the witches proved to be very well hidden indeed. Graeme filled and surrounded Jack Smith's house with every detection device he could think of, with tracers on each device to lead him to the coven. And no tracers led anywhere. Not one sniff or sound of a witch could be detected. In the end, he simply enfolded Jack Smith himself with a hundred different protections and went on looking. Jack Smith arrived, rubbing his hands and smiling, saying he felt much better now. "My dear fellow," he said to Graeme, "the two of you are like hounds. Never let go of a scent, do you?"

"We don't like to leave a thing like this unsolved," Graeme said. "Neither of us do. But you don't need to go on paying us. It's something we both feel we have to do."

"My dear fellow," Jack Smith said. "My dear lady."

Things were to this stage when the boys started school again. Jethro was now in the top class, the last one before he moved up into the senior school. Every lesson seemed to start with, "You'll be in trouble in Seniors if you don't learn this *now*," or, "Everyone in Seniors has to know this before they begin." To a worrier like Jethro this was seriously alarming. He lay awake at night worrying about the way he was going to arrive to Seniors knowing nothing and be punished for it. And as if this was not enough, Jeremy was put in Miss Blythe's class.

Miss Blythe was notoriously strict. People made rude drawings of her in her tight purple sweater and big round glasses. She had a beaky nose and thin black hair that frizzed out around her angry owl-face. All the best drawings did her as an owl with thick legs and clumpy shoes and these often looked very like Miss Blythe indeed. In Miss Blythe's class no one was allowed to talk or fool about, and they had to form up in lines before they did anything. Miss Blythe called the ones who never talked or played and who formed up in lines quickest her little flowers. The best ones were called her little daisies. You could always tell someone who had been in Miss Blythe's class by their subdued, frightened look and by the way they sat with their hands primly folded and their feet side by side. It was said they were trying to be daisies. Jethro could not imagine Jeremy being made into a daisy. He worried about that almost as much as he worried about Seniors.

For a fortnight nothing much seemed to happen. Then, one lunchtime, Jethro stood in the playground and watched Miss Blythe's class come outside, walking in a line as usual. As usual, Jeremy was about halfway along the line, looking more than usually egg-shaped and angelic. Jethro paused long enough to see that Jeremy was there and turned away to his friends, who were worrying about Seniors too.

The next moment, Jeremy came charging out of the line straight towards Jethro. He flung both arms round Jethro and butted his face into Jethro's chest.

"Hey!" Jethro said. "What's up with you?"

Jeremy said nothing. He just butted harder. People began gathering round to stare.

"Now, look – " Jethro was beginning, when Miss Blythe came shooting out of the school and advanced on Jethro and Jeremy with big strides.

"Jeremy Hall, "Miss Blythe said, "did I or did I not order you to stay behind and wash your mouth out with soap?"

Jeremy just clutched Jethro harder. Jethro realised he was supposed to protect Jeremy, although he was not sure how. He looked up at Miss Blythe. She was even more like the rude drawings than he had known. She glared like an angry owl.

"Jeremy Hall," said Miss Blythe, "let go at once and look at me!"

Jethro, feeling distinctly brave, said, "What has my brother done wrong?"

"Disobeyed me," snapped Miss Blythe. "Went out with the others when I told him not to, and now he's behaving like a baby! After he said such things!"

Jeremy turned his head sideways. He said, "I only said words."

"Don't you contradict me!" Miss Blythe said. "Indoors at once! Now!"

"Shan't," said Jeremy, and he added, "Hendiadys."

Miss Blythe gasped. "What did you call me?"

Jeremy repeated it. "Hendiadys."

At this Miss Blythe made a noise somewhere between a growl and a scream and seized hold of Jeremy's arm. "For this," she said, "you are going to come with me to the Headmaster this instant, my boy. Come along." She pulled, irresistibly. Jeremy was forced to go where she pulled. But, since he refused to let go of Jethro, Jethro was forced to go too. Like this, watched by nearly the entire school, Jethro shuffled with Jeremy's head in his stomach, into the school, along a corridor and to the door of the Headmaster's study. MR. GARDNER, said the notice on this door. HEADMASTER.

Miss Blythe gave the notice an angry bang, flung the door open and dragged both boys inside. Mr. Gardner looked up with a jump from his egg sandwich. Jethro could see he did not like being disturbed in the middle of his lunch. "What is this about?" he said.

"Mr. Gardner," said Miss Blythe, "I demand that you expel this boy from the school at once!"

"Which one?" Mr. Gardner asked. "There are two of them, Miss Blythe."

Miss Blythe looked down and was clearly surprised to find she had brought Jethro along as well. "The small one of course," she said. "Jeremy Hall. He does nothing but make trouble."

Mr. Gardner looked at Jeremy. Jeremy turned his face out of Jethro's stomach to give Mr. Gardner an abnormally egg-shaped and angelic look. Mr. Gardner gave the look a strong scrutiny and did not, to Jethro's alarm, seem to be convinced by it. "He's not a troublemaker, sir," Jethro said. "Honestly. He's just strange."

Mr. Gardner looked at Jethro then. "And why are *you* here?" he said.

Jethro began rather to feel like a lawyer called in when the police have just arrested a criminal. "He's my brother, sir," he said.

"Can't he speak for himself, then?" Mr. Gardner asked.

"Speak? I should just think he can speak," Miss Blythe burst out. "Do you know what this child has just called me, Mr. Gardner? Hendiadys, Mr. Gardner. He said it twice too! Hendiadys."

A strange look came over Mr. Gardner's face. "And what, exactly, Miss Blythe," he asked, "do you take 'hendiadys' to mean?"

"Some sort of bird, I imagine," Miss Blythe said. "It was an obvious insult anyway."

Jethro, feeling more like a lawyer than ever, cut in hastily, "My cli – er – brother – er, Jeremy never knows what any of his words mean, sir."

"Really?" said Mr. Gardner. "Well, Jeremy, what *does* 'hendiadys' mean?"

Jeremy's eyes went round and gazed over Mr. Gardner's shoulder. He contrived to look sweetly baffled. "Mouse eggs?" he suggested.

"Jethro," said Mr. Gardner. "Your turn to guess now."

"I – er – think it could be a kind of crocodile," Jethro guessed. He tried to ignore the venomous glare he got from Miss Blythe.

"Do you indeed?" Mr. Gardner turned and picked up the dictionary lying beside his lunch. "Let's see what the truth of the matter is," he said, turning pages with an expert whip-whip-whip. "Oh yes. Here we are. 'Hendiadys, *noun*, a rhetorical device by which two nouns joined by a conjunction, usually *and*, are used instead of a noun and a modifier, as in *to run with fear and haste* instead of *to run with fearful haste*.' Did you know that?" he asked Jeremy.

Jeremy looked stunned and shook his head.

"Neither did I," admitted Mr. Gardner. "But it isn't a kind of crocodile, is it? Miss Blythe, I fail to see that a rhetorical device by which two nouns et cetera can possibly be any form of insult, quite honestly. I suspect we have a personality clash here. Jethro, take your brother home. You can have the afternoon off. Jeremy, you are suspended from school for half a day while Miss Blythe and I talk this matter over. Off you go."

They went, thankfully scooting under Miss Blythe's purple arm. Before they reached the door, Miss Blythe was slapping her hand down on Mr. Gardner's desk and saying, "I don't care what that word means, it was intended as an insult! That child is nothing but trouble. I ask them all to say what flower they're going to be, and what does he say?"

"I said I'd be Rhus radicans," Jeremy said when they were outside. "That's a flower. She made me stand out in front all morning. I don't like her."

"I don't blame you. She's a hag," said Jethro. "What do we tell Mum and Dad?"

As it happened, they did not have to tell their parents anything. They arrived home to a scene of excitement. A lady called Pippa from Annabelle's publisher was there with a briefcase stuffed with letters, contracts, forms and maps. It seemed that Hall's Guides to Witchcraft had become so popular that Pippa was arranging for Annabelle to go on a world tour to covens and magic circles as far away as Australia to promote the latest Guide. She was to go in three weeks' time, in order to be in New York for a Hallowe'en book-signing, and Pippa was to go with her. Such was the excitement that Jethro nearly forgot to look up Rhus radicans. When he did, he found it was poison ivy. Hm, he thought. Perhaps Jeremy does know what his words mean, after all. He thought it was lucky he had not discovered this before they were hauled in front of Mr. Gardner.

Altogether he felt a fierce mixture of relief and worry: relief that neither of his parents had asked why he and Jeremy were home so early, worry that Jeremy was in bad trouble; relief that something nice had happened for a change, worry because Mum had never been away so far or for so long before; relief that his father was taking the plan on the whole quite well –

"Of course I can manage," Graeme was saying, a touch irritably. "I've no wish to stand in your way, and Jethro is pretty sensible these days." This brought on Jethro's worry again as he realised he would have to look after Dad and Jeremy while Annabelle was away. "But," Graeme continued, "if we haven't located this coven before you leave, I can always go on looking by myself. You go and enjoy yourself. Don't mind me."

While Jethro was trying to decide whether this meant he could feel relieved, Annabelle said to him, "Don't look so worried, love. I'll be back by Christmas."

"Hirsute intropic ampoules," Jeremy said gloomily.

Did Jeremy know what this meant? Jethro wondered. Worry came out on top. And there was always Seniors to worry about as well.

They went back to school next day to discover that Jeremy had been transferred from Miss Blythe's to the parallel class taught by Mr. Anderson. Mr. Anderson was young and jolly. When Jethro had been in Mr. Anderson's class, he remembered, Mr. Anderson's favourite saying had been "Let's have fun looking this up together, shall we?" He wondered if this would suit Jeremy. Or not.

Anyway, Jeremy did not complain. Nor, more importantly, did Mr. Anderson. Life rolled on quite peacefully for three weeks, until Annabelle departed for the airport in a flurry of schedules, maps and lecture notes. The house felt amazingly quiet and rather sombre almost at once. Jeremy went round saying "Calisthenic ketchup" in a small dire voice and sighing deeply. Both of them missed Annabelle badly.

Graeme tried to make it up to them. He put in a real effort for a while. He took them to the cinema and the zoo and he provided pizza and ice cream for every meal until, after a week or so, even Jeremy began to get tired of pizza. "Dad," Jethro said, worrying about it, "this kind of diet is bad for you. We'll all be overweight."

"Yes, but you know I can't cook," Graeme said. "I'm much too busy with this witch hunt to spend time in the kitchen. Bear with me. It's only till Christmas."

"That's two months, Dad," Jethro said.

"Proverbial bouillabaisse," Jeremy said, and sighed deeply.

The next day they had a cook. She was a large quiet lady called Mrs. Gladd who came silently in while the boys were having breakfast. Graeme seemed as surprised as they were to see her. "I don't do dishes," she said, putting on an overall covered with sunflowers. "Or," she added, tying the belt, "beds or cleaning. You might want to get someone else for that."

Mrs. Gladd was still there when the two of them came home from school, cooking something at the stove which smelt almost heavenly. The kitchen table was spread with cakes, jam tarts and sticky buns.

"Herbacious anthracite," Jeremy said, sniffing deeply. "Hagiography," he added, nodding appreciatively at the table.

Mrs. Gladd just shrugged. "Eat up," she said.

They did so. Everything was superb. It almost made up for the fact that Mrs. Gladd was living in and had to have Jethro's room, while Jethro moved in with Jeremy in the little room down the corridor. Graeme had to break off his witch hunt in order to heave beds about – Jethro spent several uncomfortable nights because his father had somehow twisted Jethro's duvet inside its cover. It was like sleeping under a knotted sheep. And Jethro didn't do beds any more than Mrs. Gladd did. Even with Jeremy trying to help him he only succeeded in giving the duvet a second twist, so that he now seemed to be sleeping under a rather large python.

But this was straightened out by the end of that week when Rosie, Josephine and Kate arrived, Rosie to wash up the stacks of plates and pans in the kitchen, and Josephine and Kate to make beds and clean the house. Consequently, when Annabelle phoned from Los Angeles that Sunday, Jethro and Graeme were able to assure her that they were doing splendidly. Jeremy said, "Curdled phlogiston," which may or may not have meant the same thing.

On the Monday, however, Josephine and Kate said the work was too heavy for just the two of them and were joined by Gertie, Iris, Delphine, and Doreen. As Jethro and Jeremy left for school, all six ladies were hard at work mopping floors from steaming buckets. Graeme had turned all the computers off and was composing crosswords instead. Jethro spared a worry about how Graeme was going to tell which lady was which. Nearly all of them had blonde hairdos and smart jeans. Iris, Doreen, and Josephine wore pink sweaters and two of the others had glasses, but they were otherwise hard to tell apart. All were slim and very talkative. The house rang with happy chatter, the clanking of buckets and the drone of vacuum cleaners.

Jethro could only spare a few seconds for Graeme's problems, however. This week there were going to be Tests on All Subjects, and if you had bad results, your life was going to be not worth living in Seniors. He was far too nervous to think much about anything else.

On Tuesday, three terrifying tests later, Jethro came home trying to forget the tests by wondering what cakes and fat buns Mrs. Gladd had made today for tea. He found their car out on the drive in a puddle of water, surrounded by three ladies with cloths tied round their heads. Two had large sponges and the third had a hose. They were shrieking with laughter because one of them had just had her shoes hosed by mistake. Jethro thought at first this one was Rosie and that the others were probably Katie and Iris, but when he looked closely, he saw they were three quite new ladies.

"Perspicuous colonization," Jeremy remarked to him.

Jethro took him along to find Graeme. Graeme's study was knee-deep in sleeping bags. Graeme himself, already noticeably plumper from Mrs. Gladd's cooking, was sitting at a new table in the corner of the kitchen. Crossword patterns and dictionaries were heaped on the table, but Graeme was busy eating a large sticky bun. Someone had provided him with new, wider jeans and a wide bland sweater. He hardly looked like Dad any more.

"Dad, who are the new ones washing the car?" Jethro asked.

Graeme smiled, again quite unlike himself. "Two Kylies and a Tracy," he said. "They do the outside work, garden, wash the windows, all that. Aren't we lucky?"

"Troglodytic contralto," Jeremy said.

"Yes, but," Jethro said, eyeing the sheets of half-made crosswords, "can you get on with your witch hunt with all these people about?"

"Not at the moment," Graeme admitted. "But it's only temporary – only till Christmas – after all."

But *was* it only temporary? If Jethro had had any worry to spare from the tests, he thought he would have been quite worried about this. There were ten new chairs round the kitchen table – which seemed much bigger than it ought to be, somehow – and here Mrs. Gladd served succulent meals for fourteen. Jethro ate with his head down, avoiding elbows, and his hearing filled with screams of laughter at jokes he didn't understand. All eleven ladies seemed to be living here now, not only Mrs. Gladd. There were sleeping bags everywhere, in the airing cupboard, behind the sofa and bundled to the sides of the upstairs corridor. On Friday, when Jethro had done a test on everything possible from spelling to cookery, the ladies turned the living room and Graeme's study into hairdressing salons and did one another's hair. The booming of vacuum cleaners was replaced by the roaring of hair dryers. The house filled with strong perfumes.

Almost the only place that was empty of ladies was Annabelle's deserted study. Jethro took to sitting there beside Mum's blank turned-off computer, worrying about the results of the tests and wishing he knew the password to get into that computer. He thought he might feel better if he could read some of the things Annabelle had been writing before she left. But when Annabelle rang that Sunday from Sydney in Australia, Jethro had not the heart to tell her about the tests or the ladies either. He was sure he had failed all the tests and there was nothing he could do about the ladies. Graeme, beaming all over his newly plump face, said they were getting along marvellously. Jeremy said, "Hypno-therapeutic distilled amnesia. In blue bottles." At which Mum laughed and said, "Oh *really*, Jeremy!"

Jethro came home from school the next day in a worse worry than ever. None of the results of the tests were ready. Every teacher he asked told him to be patient: it took time to mark them all, they said. He made for Annabelle's study, tripping over sleeping bags on the way, longing for some peace and quiet to worry in, only to find Jeremy in there. Jeremy was sitting at the computer, playing a computer game.

"How did you find the password?" Jethro demanded.

Jeremy turned to him, angelically egg-shaped. "Imperfect clandestine logistics," he said.

Jethro stumped away to consult a dictionary, which was not easy. Mrs. Gladd pushed him aside when he tried to reach the one in the kitchen, and Delphine and Rosie said, "Not in here, please!" when he tried Dad's study. When he took down one of the dictionaries in the living room, Josephine moved the small table away in order to do her toenails on it and he was forced to spread the heavy book out on the floor. The sofa was filled with Tracy, one of the Kylies and Josephine, who were all laughing about something. Jethro had to push away a heap of sleeping bags to make room for the dictionary, from which he discovered that logistics meant the science of moving, supplying and maintaining of military forces in the field. It had nothing to do with logging on, as Jethro had supposed. He went back to Annabelle's study. "I want to use the computer after you," he told Jeremy. "Or it's not fair."

"Fulminating lohan," Jeremy said.

Jethro tried to do without a dictionary, this time by going and asking Graeme what lohan meant. But Graeme simply crouched at his corner table and tapped with his pencil. "Don't bother me now," he said. "I have to find a proper clue for stethoscope."

Sighing, Jethro collected all the dictionaries the ladies would let him get near and took them up to the little room he was forced to share with Jeremy. It was really annoying, he thought, turning pages, the way he and Jeremy and Graeme were getting pushed away into the corners of their own house. The ladies seemed to feel it belonged to them now. A lohan, he discovered, was a rather good Buddhist – something he himself would never be, Jethro knew. He was too worried about those tests. He sat on his bed and worried.

It was an awful week. None of the tests got marked and Jethro began to fear that he was not going to be allowed to go to Seniors. When he got home, the house was always full of vacuum cleaners and shrieks of laughter, and however early he arrived, Jeremy had somehow managed to get to Mum's computer before Jethro did. He tried complaining to Graeme, but Graeme simply tapped his pencil on his teeth and said, "I can't find a decent clue for stethoscope." After five days of this, Jethro said to Jeremy, "Dad isn't listening to a word I say."

Jeremy astonished him by saying, "Yes, I know," before turning back to his game.

"No long words?" Jethro asked.

"Not yet," Jeremy said, and killed a swathe of aliens with one burst of gunfire.

"Supper! Hurry up!" Mrs. Gladd called from the kitchen.

Jeremy left the computer running, and as they both went down to the kitchen, Jethro was determined to get back to that computer before Jeremy did or die in the attempt.

Supper seemed to be over very quickly. Graeme went straight to his corner then. Jethro and Jeremy edged through the bustle of clearing up, each with an eye on the other, each ready to make a dash for the computer as soon as the other did. They had only just reached the door when someone rang the doorbell at the front door. Josephine and one of the Kylies pushed them aside, right up against Graeme's table, rushing to answer it.

Jeremy looked at Jethro. "Penultimate epiphany," he said. They stayed to see who it was.

It was Miss Blythe. She came striding in, all owl face and purple bosom, and rapped on the kitchen table. "Everybody gather round," she said. As Mrs. Gladd turned from the fridge and Kate from the sink and the nine other ladies came back into the kitchen, most of them carrying hair dryers, Jethro had one of those horrible moments when you realise you have been worrying about quite the wrong thing. He had spent all the last fortnight worrying about tests at school, when he should have been looking at what was going on in his own house. He stared at Miss Blythe, feeling empty.

"Now, my flowers," Miss Blythe said, when everyone was gathered by the table, "most of you have been here a full two weeks. I want full reports on progress made and objectives achieved. Mrs. Gladd?"

"The way to a man's heart is through his stomach," Mrs. Gladd said. "I've cooked up three spells daily and four at weekends. All three of them should be well under by now."

"So I see," Miss Blythe said. Her glasses flashed towards Graeme sitting chewing his pencil in his corner, and then travelled quickly, with evident dislike, across Jethro and Jeremy. "Well done," she said. "Kylie, Kylie and Tracy?"

One of the car-cleaners, the one who wore glasses, said, "We've made absolutely sure that none of their neighbours even see us, Miss Blythe, and we've stopped all communication from outside."

"So have we," said Rosie, stroking her blond hairdo. "Not a soul has been able to consult Occult Security since we came here. The only phone calls we allow in are from Mrs. Hall."

"We're working on making everyone forget the Halls exist," Josephine added. She giggled. "Mr. Hall's forgotten already."

They all looked over at Graeme, who frowned at his crossword and did not seem to notice.

"Good," said Miss Blythe. "Occult Security isn't going to bother us any more then – none of them are going to bother us much longer. We'll be able to sell this house soon. Have you worked out how much we'll get for it?"

"We priced it up," Kate said. "A quarter of a million seems about right."

A very satisfied expression came across Miss Blythe's face at this. "Then we're in business," she said, "except for one little matter." Her satisfaction faded rather. "Have any of you worked out what we do about getting rid of Mrs. Hall? Coven Head will be here any minute, and he'll want to know what we're doing about her."

Mrs. Gladd said, "She's leaving Australia later today and flying to Rome."

"Lots of nice deep ocean on the way," said Doreen.

Iris added, "What say we simply bring the plane down while it's over the water?"

Miss Blythe nodded. "Yes, that should do it. It sounds like the neatest way. You can start setting that spell up as soon as Coven Head gets here."

The doorbell rang again.

"Here he is now," Miss Blythe said. "One of you let him in."

As Josephine scudded away to the front door, Jethro stood next to Jeremy thinking, What are we going to do? They're behaving as if we don't exist. Do we exist any more?

Just as if thinking that was a signal, Miss Blythe's big owl spectacles turned Jethro's way. She pursed her lips irritably as if he were something offensive like a very dirty sock someone had dropped on the floor. Then she turned with an effusive smile as Josephine ushered Jack Smith into the kitchen. "Oh, Coven Head," she said. "Good to see you!"

Jack Smith was fatter and more tightly packed into his expensive suit than ever. He beamed round at the ladies and nodded happily at Graeme in his corner. "Good, good, all going to plan, I see," he said. Looking very humorous, he reached into his waistcoat and then into his pockets and fetched out hundreds of charms, protections and wires, which he threw into a heap on the table. "No need to carry these silly things about any more," he said, tossing a couple of batteries on to the heap. "I see the Hall family is pretty well obliterated."

"Not quite," Miss Blythe said, pointing at Jethro and Jeremy. "Those two don't seem to me to be quite under yet."

"Oh, we'll soon settle that." Jack Smith rubbed his hands together and came to stand over Jethro and Jeremy, smiling down at them, exuding such good cheer that he could have been Santa Claus in a dark suit. "Boys," he said, "this is very important. I need you both to give me your solemn word that you will never, ever say one thing about any of us here – about me, or Miss Blythe, or any of these charming ladies. You." He beamed at Jethro. "Give me your word. Now."

Jethro felt some sort of huge numbness spreading his brain out, squashing it flat, combing away all feelings until there was nearly nothing but a blank white space where all his thoughts usually were. Almost the only thing left was frantic worry. This is *awful!* he thought. If I give him my word I shall be like this for *ever!*

"I'll give you my word," Jeremy said from beside Jethro. He stared up towards Jack Smith, past Jack Smith and into empty space deep beyond Jack Smith, and his face was more egg-shaped and angelic than Jethro had ever seen it before. "I'll give you my word," Jeremy said, "and my word is FLOCCIPAUCINIHILIPILIFICATION!"

Jethro suddenly felt much better. Jack Smith said, "*What?*"

"Take no notice," said Miss Blythe. "He's a naughty little boy. He's always doing this."

"All right," Jack Smith agreed. "Forget the kids. Fill me in. What have we decided to do about dispensing with Annabelle Hall?"

"Bring down her plane between Australia and Italy," Miss Blythe told him. "Over the sea if we can. Does that seem good to you?"

Jack Smith said, "Perfect. Let's get on and set the spell then." He strode over to the table and sat himself in the chair next to the sink, rubbing his hands together gladly. Miss Blythe and the other ladies hurried to pull out chairs and sit round the table too. Amid the squawking of chair legs on floor, Jethro bent down to his brother and whispered, "What does floccipaucini-hilipilification mean?"

Jeremy shrugged, egg-shaped and innocent. "I don't know."

Jethro snatched a look at everyone sitting at the table and staring respectfully at Jack Smith and whirled round to Graeme, smiling vaguely at his table just behind them. "Dad!" he said urgently. "Dad, what does floccipaucini-hilipilification mean?"

"Eh?" Graeme said. "Floccipaucinihilipilification? Supposed to be the longest word in the language. It means – " Jethro held his breath and watched the smile drain from his father's face into the pinched, grumpy and attentive look he was much more used to. "It means, Jethro, *the act of regarding something as worthless*," Graeme said. Now he looked almost his usual self. He seemed to have gone thinner, with lines where he had smooth fat cheeks before. He stared silently at the twelve ladies seated at the table and at Jack Smith sitting by the sink, facing them. "My God!" he said. "A full coven! What are they doing?"

"Casting a spell to make Mum's plane crash," Jethro said.

"Right," said Graeme. None of the coven had even noticed him. He leapt up from his corner and went with long, noiseless steps, through the kitchen doorway and round into his study, where he kicked aside three sleeping bags and dived into the chair in front of his Occult Security computer. "Exorcism programme," he muttered as the machine hummed and flickered, "spell cancer, expulsion of alien magics programmes, all of them I think, block and destroy magics...what else am I going to need?"

Jeremy's voice rose up from the kitchen. "Wanton aquamarine steroids. Epigrammatic yellow persiflage with semiotic substitution."

"Oh yes, personal protection for both you boys," Graeme said. "Go and get Jeremy out of there, Jethro!" The exorcism programme came up and he began stabbing at keys, furiously and at speed.

Hendiadys! Jethro thought. Instead of *with furious speed*. He sped back to the kitchen to find everyone sitting in a fixed, spell-making, concentrating silence, except for Jeremy. Jeremy was marching up and down beside the cooker, chanting. "Haloes and holograms, ubiquitous embargoes, zygotes and rhizomes in the diachronic ciabatta." Miss Blythe kept turning her spectacles towards him venomously, but she did not seem to be able to interrupt the spell-making in order to stop Jeremy.

Jethro seized his arm. "Come away. It's dangerous!"

"No, I've got to stay. *Gladiolus!*" Jeremy shrieked, bracing both feet. "*Rosacea!* Dahlias and debutante begonias. Recycled stringent peonies. Pockmarked pineapples, tormented turnips, artichokes with acne. Let *go*, Jethro! Cuneiform cauliflowers. It's *working!*"

Right in front of Jethro, Mrs. Gladd shrank to nothing in her chair. Where she had been sitting there was now a fat clod of earth with a small spiked shoot sticking out of it.

"*See!*" Jeremy shouted. Rosie winked out downwards as he yelled, into a smaller clod with two green leaves glimmering on top of it. "Monocotyledenous, dicotyledenous, myrtle and *twitch!*"

Almost at once – blink, blink, blink – Kate, Doreen, Josephine and both Kylies shrank likewise and became clumps of earth with tiny seedlings growing in them. Though Jethro had no doubt that Graeme's programmes were now running, he was also equally sure that Jeremy was somehow directing what these programmes did. Blink, blink, blink, all round the table. Gertie, Iris, Delphine and Tracy shrank into seedlings too, until only Jack Smith and Miss Blythe were left. Jack Smith was staring around in bewilderment, but Miss Blythe flopped forward with her face in her hands, looking tired and defeated.

"It's Miss Blythe's magic, see," Jeremy explained out of the corner of his mouth, and turned back to shriek at Jack Smith, "*Defenestration!*"

Jack Smith sailed up out of his chair and hurtled backwards towards the window.

"*Oleaginous* defenestration, I meant," Jeremy said quickly, just as Jack Smith's fat back met the glass.

Jethro watched, fascinated, as the glass went soft and stretched like elastic to let Jack Smith shoot through into the flower bed outside. Then it snapped back into unbroken glass again. Through it, Jethro watched Jack Smith pick himself up and shamble off, looking puzzled, to the big car parked in their driveway.

"You appalling little boy!" Miss Blythe said faintly. "How did you know all my girls were flowers from my garden? And just look at what you've done to that poor dear man, Jack Smith! He was going to be Prime Minister with our coven for a Cabinet."

"Questionable offal," Jeremy retorted. "*You* were going to kill my mum."

"Well, we had to neutralise your parents," Miss Blythe said, in a tired, reasonable way, "or they would have spoilt all his plans, poor man. They are far too good at their job."

Jethro felt he had had enough of Miss Blythe. He went up to her and took hold of her by one purple arm. "The front door's this way," he said. "You'd better go now."

Graeme's programmes were obviously running sweetly by then. Miss Blythe stood up quite meekly and let Jethro lead her out of the kitchen and through the hall. "He was going to let me be his private secretary," she said sadly as they went.

Jethro felt the school could probably do without Miss Blythe too. "Why don't you give up teaching and be his secretary anyway?" he suggested, opening the front door and giving her a push.

"What a good idea!" Miss Blythe exclaimed. "I think I will." She turned round on the doorstep. "Jethro Hall, you're a very understanding boy."

Jethro shut the door on her, wondering if he really wanted to be called understanding by someone like Miss Blythe, and scooted to Graeme's study to check on his father.

Graeme, looking lean and irritable and entirely his usual self, was bending over the computer, where programme after programme was racing downwards on the screen. "I don't know which flight your mother's going to be on," he told Jethro. "I'm having to put protection round every plane that comes into Rome for the next twenty-four hours. Go and shut Jeremy up. He's distracting me."

In the kitchen, Jeremy was still chanting words, although they now seemed to have become a song of triumph. "Highly benevolent botulism," he howled as Jethro came in. "Crusading gumbo extirpated by chocolate pelmanism. Transcendent aureate thaumaturgy!" Jeremy's eyes blazed and his cheeks were flushed. He had worked himself into quite a state.

"Stop it!" Jethro told him. "It's over now."

"Creosote," Jeremy said, the way other people might use a swear word. "Ginseng. Garibaldi biscuits." His cheeks faded to a normal colour and he looked humorously up at Jethro. "I've never done real magic before," he said. "Has Dad made Mum's plane safe?"

"He's just fixing it now, " said Jethro. "What do we do with all these seedlings? Throw them away?"

"No, plant them of course," Jeremy said. "Tomorrow."

So, when Annabelle rang up from Rome the next day, after Graeme had said as usual that they were all fine, Jethro took the phone and told her that he and Jeremy had been gardening. Then Jeremy snatched the phone to say, "And we got rid of those witches for you. They weren't attacking Jack Smith because they didn't exist really."

"Oh good!" Annabelle said. "And I want to tell you that Pippa and I have had enough. There was no one at all at the signing this morning. We're going to cancel the rest of the tour and fly home tomorrow." She stopped in a surprised way. "What's this, Jeremy? No more of your big words?"

"No," said Jeremy. "I've used them all up."

Jethro let his breath out in a long, gentle sigh. There was nothing to worry about any more. He was not even worried about the tests, he found. What was done was done.

Graeme wrestled the phone from Jeremy's fist. "Give me your flight number," he said. "I'll put protection round it, just in case."

"If you feel you need to," Annabelle said. "It might make Pippa feel better. She turns out to be terrified of flying."

AUTHOR'S NOTE

This story started with my love of dictionaries, not just for being full of words, and I love words, but because of the wildly different words that occur side by side in them. You find shire horse next to shoestring and cutwater beside cynical. My grandson Thomas loves words too, the more preposterous the better. I was trying to teach him "borborygmata" when I got the idea. He was delighted with the word, particularly when he discovered it meant your tummy rumbling, but he couldn't say it. The nearest he got was "babagatama," which ought to be a word anyway. But the main character in the story is in fact another of my grandsons, Gabriel, who spends much of his time away in a distant part of his own head. Then he comes back and tells you something extraordinary. I suspect him of having uncanny powers. This worries his brother, who is Jethro in the story, and a worrier.

Bea and Her Bird Brother

Gene Wolfe

Gene Wolfe is the only writer with two stories in this book (see "Build-A-Bear," the first story in the book), and at least two others could with justice have been included, "Six from Atlantis" and "Sob in the Silence." He has several more new stories forthcoming in 2007, and his next novel, *Pirate Freedom*. He tells us he is working on a horror novel now, an idea that demanded his attention. Soon he will be due for another story collection. In an interview with Neil Gaiman, Wolfe made a remark which goes to the heart of his approach to writing, "It's always hard to get information across in the way it should be gotten across...because the way information is conveyed is generally more important than the information itself."

"Bea and Her Bird Brother" appeared in *The Magazine of Fantasy & Science Fiction*, and was included in his chapbook *Strange Birds* (2006), a collaboration with artist Lisa Snellings-Clark. At her father's deathbed, a woman discovers that she has another brother, a twin brother, and her twin brother has wings. She is compelled to face the fantastic. And there's a lot more to it than that, since this is, after all, a Gene Wolfe story.

"YOU JUST MISSED your brother," the nurse said.

Bea glanced at her watch. "He can't have stayed long." It was six; visiting hours were six to eight.

"He wasn't supposed to be in there," the nurse said. "I didn't see him until he left."

Bea signed the screen and went to the elevator. It was smooth and silent – remarkably so, she thought, for a hospital built in the nineteen-twenties.

The corridor looked clean, though she knew the boy-high dark green and the tousled-hair-to-ceiling light green had been chosen to hide dirt. Before she was born these walls had been white and immaculately clean and these halls had smelled of disinfectant instead of room deodorant.

Things didn't always get better. Sometimes they got worse. Dad would go. Soon. Very soon. Go, and never come back to her.

"Hello, Dad." She gave the old man in the bed her best and brightest. "How are you feeling today?"

"Light." His voice was thin but melodious, as if some tiny person in his throat were playing a flute. Old men were not supposed to have voices like that. For the first time it occurred to her that no one enforced such things.

"Sit down, Bea. I can't see you."

She sat, the hospital chair so low, and the hospital bed so high, that their faces were nearly at a level. "Did Benjy come? One of the nurses said he had."

"Him?" The fluting little voice was not contemptuous, only tired. "He won't come. Never."

His eyes turned toward her, moving more slowly than other eyes. Their whites were yellow. "You're sitting. That's good. I've got to tell you about the bird people."

Bird watchers, she thought.

"The Big Folks didn't like us, Bea. Spread poison to wipe us out. Me and Annie, we run. Maybe others run, too. I don't know. Only there wasn't any with us. It was just me and Annie for...I don't know. It seems long sometimes, when I think back. Only...."

"Who was Annie, Dad?"

"Maybe it was only a day or two. Maybe three before they got her. After I buried her, I just kept going deeper in to get away from them, Bea. Oh, I knew where a gate was. I just didn't want to go back. Back to what? That was the question. That was always it. Ugly buildings on ugly streets and work I hated. That was what it was to me, and I knew it and didn't want it."

"But, Dad...."

"You won't ever understand why I stayed, because you won't ever see it. Flowers bigger than I am, and smell so sweet it got you drunk. Cold springs to drink of, and hot springs. Some so hot you had to walk a mile down to wash. Trees up to the sky, and people with wings living in them."

"Bird people, Dad? Is that what you meant?"

"I could climb those trees, Bea, or some of them. The ones with rough bark, you know. Climb way high up. Only I didn't have wings. I'd watch, every day. At night, when I'd found a little hollow or something way high up, I'd dream about it – how I'd wake up with wings and go flying from tree to tree and sometimes way up to the tops of the tallest, up where the air was thin and cold. I'd wake up, and for a minute or two I'd think it was real and feel for my wings and try to move 'em." The old man in the bed chuckled, a ringing of wooden chimes very far away. "I'd cry then, sometimes, Bea. Bawl like a baby. You'd have been shamed of me."

"I'd never be ashamed of you, Dad."

"I said the day would never come when I decided to go back, only I was wrong. I got to missing certain things and forgetting certain others, and decided I'd had enough. I'd learned the language, you see, or bits of it, only I'd never be one of them. And I knew it. I told myself they weren't my kind

– which was the truth – and it would be better for me to get back to my own people. Which wasn't."

"Are we so bad?"

"Not you, Bea. Off I went. It was slow, you see. If I'd had wings, I could have done it in an hour. Only I didn't, and that was the whole trouble. I had to walk, and ground was the most dangerous place. The higher you got, the safer you were. How it always was there. So I'd go from limb to limb when I could. Sometimes they touched, and I could step over. Sometimes I had to jump, and that was risky. Sometimes there was nothing close enough. I'd have to go down to the ground, a long climb down and a long climb back up. Scared, too. Scared every minute I was on the ground, and every minute when I was just down low."

Bea smoothed her skirt over her knees, as she always did when she was thoughtful. "There are things...certain things I recall from childhood, Dad. The dog that mauled Benjy when we were little.... You were never scared, never scared of anything or anybody, and everybody knew it. All the kids. All the neighbors."

Dry and remote, the chuckle returned. "After being there? No. No, I wasn't. I'd got away from things that would've eaten that little doggie for a snack. You hid, too, once. Remember that?"

"When I was little, Dad?" For the first time, Bea really saw the hospital room, all taupe and pastel green, save for the bouquet she had sent from the office. "Sure. Lots of times. Behind the couch, mostly. Under the dining room table. Even in the clothes hamper."

"Further back."

She smoothed her skirt again. "Well, it was – "

"Not that time. Go back further."

"You didn't even let me say it, Dad."

"You hadn't gone far enough. Your eyes told me. Further. The first time you ever hid. The very first."

"But – "

"Back. Go back now. I'm not going to be around much longer, Bea."

She shut her eyes, and something horrible stalked the dark, strewing its sharp stench on the sweet, moist air.

"There! That's it. Where are you?"

"In the leaves." She heard her own voice, and had no idea what it was talking about. "Big leaves, Dad...." Her eyes opened. "They can't have been as big as that."

"You remembered." He was trying to smile, this though Death (invisible, ever-present) blew each flickering smile away. "Wanted to see if you could. I found your ma, Bea. Found her on the ground one day when I was trying to get back here. She'd hurt her wing. Hit a limb or something. She was never sure what. Not Elsie. This isn't Elsie."

"My real mother."

"That's right, Bea. Your real mother. I called her Ava, even if it wasn't her name. I couldn't sing the real one, so Ava's what I called her."

"You and Mom always said I was adopted." The flowers should have perfumed the room, but for some reason they did not. There was only odor of the spray.

"It was true in a way, Bea. Elsie adopted you, and when Benjy came she treated you – "

Bea shook her head. "She's gone, Dad. Don't get me started on how she treated me. The woman's name was Ava?"

"No…not really. It was just what I called her. I couldn't sing her real name. Didn't I say? She'd hurt her wing, the one over on the right side. It wasn't cut off or anything, but she couldn't fold it right, and she couldn't fly. She used to lay it over us both when we slept."

Bea would have objected, but something inside seemed to be choking her.

"She's ready to die when I found her. She hadn't been getting a thing to eat. I climbed, and ate some myself, and carried some down to her." The old man's eyes closed.

"Dad?"

"Just remembering, Bea. I'm not ready to go yet, and I won't go till I am." He fell silent, breathing deeply.

She waited, and at last he said, "I had to beg her to eat. I put it in her mouth and begged her to chew. All sign language, you know. I couldn't sing it at all then, and I never did sing it well. Not half what they did. But I got her to eat, and she felt a little better afterward, a little stronger, and I got her to climb up a ways. Not far, but we were off the ground, and that was safer."

Bea nodded, wondering whether he had always been – like this. Was this what he had been hiding so long, this irrationality?

"Pretty soon we climbed way, way up, the two of us. We built a nest up there – a better one than the flying ones did, because I knew more about building. I had more patience, too. By then I knew she was going to lay. She'd told me, part by signs. But part by song, because I'd got to where I could understand a little, and even sing back a bit myself. It always made her laugh, but I didn't mind."

"Elsie used to laugh at you, too," Bea said. "That was the only time I felt sorry for you. You were so good, so competent. But you'd try to explain baseball to her, and you never seemed to understand that she didn't want to know."

"I never did understand people who don't want to know, Bea." The distant flute was humble now, apologetic for a fault found only in the instruments of music. "Now, well, maybe you don't want to know this. About Ava and me. But it's about you, too, so you ought to."

"And it's been tearing you up for years, keeping it in." Bea sighed, and wondered whether her flowers were starting to droop, just as she was. "So go on. Please go on. I want to know." How long would the knowledge that her father had died insane tear her up?

"She laid, and it was two eggs like I knew it would be. When the women laid, it was always two. I asked about it one time and she showed me her breasts – one child for each nipple is what she said, and I still think it makes more sense than what we do."

For the rest of her life, probably.

"The eggs are pretty. Not just white or brown like hens' eggs. Big blue eggs with white and gold speckles. The way they usually do is for the woman to warm them while the man gets something to eat, and him to while she does. But I was better at finding food than Ava was, and a better climber, so I'd get enough for us both and bring it back to the nest, and we'd eat it there together."

Trying to be brave, Bea nodded. "That's nice."

"It was. It sure was. I think back, and...."

She did not know what to say.

"And I wish all over again that they'd never ended. Well, they did. Not because Ava died – she didn't, not then – but because her eggs hatched. It's just about always a boy and a girl. Have I said that?"

"No, Dad. Not till now."

"Not always, but nearly. That's what it was for us. The girl...."

"Oh, Dad!" She squeezed his hand.

"The boy had wings. At first I thought he wasn't mine. He was just a little bit of a thing. You both were. Preemies, the doctors would've called you. You could nurse, though, and you got bigger every day. When he was bigger, I could see he was mine after all. It was the same face I'd had, the face I'd seen in pictures my mother took, and he had my eye color."

"Bright blue."

"That's right. Their eyes are dark, or Ava's were."

"Like mine, Dad?"

"That's right. Just like yours, because it was you, Bea. You were that girl. I know you don't remember, but you were, and you didn't have any more wings than I did. Ava pretended she was happy with it, when it tore her up something awful. I could see the hurt under the smiles, and it just broke my heart."

"Benjy doesn't have wings, Dad." She tried to make her voice and words as gentle as she could. "I've seen him with his shirt off, seen him like that a lot of times, and he doesn't."

"'Course not, Bea." The old man in the bed sounded a trifle impatient. "Benjy's Elsie's. Elsie's and mine. This's your full brother."

"My full brother?" She almost felt that she and her father were conversing in a dream.

"What I just said." The old man's eyes shut, one and then – perhaps five seconds after it – the other. She took his hand, warming it between her own and listening to his rasping breaths. Half an hour later, when she had nerved herself to speak, there was no reply.

She was still holding that hand when Raeburn came in with little Megan. Raeburn said, "How is he, honey?"

She sighed, and Raeburn repeated his question a trifle more loudly, this time without honey.

"He's gone," Bea whispered.

Raeburn looked at Megan, then back to Bea.

She sighed again. "She has to learn, and this is the lesson time. Megan, do you remember the toad you found in our yard?"

"All stiff." Megan nodded, her guarantee of her own truthfulness.

"Well, what happened to that toad has happened to Granddad. Come take his hand. He won't hurt you."

"He never done." The old man's cold hand was three times the size of Megan's warm and chubby ones.

"That's right," Bea said. "He never has and he never will. He's with the angels, darling, where he can tell God what a good girl you are."

Megan nodded again.

That night Bea – younger than Megan again – hid among leaves once more. Something huge paced the limb; footfalls more silent than sighs thundered over her mother's screams. Soon, very soon, it would find her.

She woke.

Raeburn was getting out of bed and searching for his slippers when she said, "Mama's dead."

He hugged her, and his voice was as gentle as it ever became. "It's Ace, honey." And then, feeling she did not understand. "It's your dad, Bea. Asa's passed on."

"And now," the funeral director intoned, "you may pass the coffin one by one to pay your final respects."

He was short and pudgy, with a bald head that looked like the old paint in the kitchen.

"One at a time, please, and we'll begin with the front row on this side."

She rose.

The thing in the coffin might have been a badly made waxwork of her father. My father, she wanted to say, was full of life. My father was a fighter, a man even Elsie's carping and dirt could not pull down.

A man who might have been telling the truth, even when Death stood beside his bed and his mind was clearly gone. A man who might really have been my father, though God knows Elsie was never my mother.

She turned away to go back to her seat. Somebody sat alone in the last row of the room of repose. Benjy? He did not look like Benjy, and certainly that big black coat – buttoned up indoors on this mild autumn day – did not look like something Benjy would wear anyplace.

She walked toward him, Raeburn and Megan momentarily forgotten. He rose at once, and her soft, "Please?" did nothing to slow his retreat.

He was tall, and clearly vigorous. Though he did not run and she trotted, she was handicapped by three-inch heels and gained only slowly. She was still ten strides behind, still pleading with him, when he turned onto a nameless suburban street. By the time she reached it he was gone, though the black raincoat he had worn lay empty on the sidewalk, half covering a pair of black shoes.

Moved by a premonition akin to dread, she looked up.

A bird of condor size threshed the air with eight-foot wings. When a puff of wind shook the treetops, it rose like a kite, trailing a swallow tail that might....

That could have been legs.

Someone saw Bea fall to her knees, watched her pound the concrete with futile fists as she wept and screamed, and called the police. Hours afterward, Raeburn was able to explain to a sympathetic sergeant that her father's funeral had been that day.

The Bonny Boy

Ian R. MacLeod

Ian R. MacLeod (*www.ianrmacleod.com*) lives in Sutton Coldfield in the Midlands, England. He has published more than thirty stories since his first, in 1990, and four novels to date. His next novel, *Song of Time*, is forthcoming in 2008. He has appeared
in one or more best of the year collections nearly every year since his first story was
selected by three of them. The dark, Dickensian, richly detailed factory setting of
his early story, "The Giving Mouth," was apparently influential upon, for instance,
Michael Swanwick in the origination of his Iron Dragon fantasy world, and MacLeod
has remained more influential than popular throughout his career. He is generally
regarded as one of the finest prose stylists working in genre fantasy and SF. His story
collections are *Voyages by Starlight* (1996), *Breathmoss and Other Exhalations* (2004), and
Past Magic (2006). He is a non-religious writer who writes about religious faith. In an
interview posted on his web site, he says: "I'm an intellectual atheist who, emotion-
ally, is always looking for God. The explanations religion offers of the way the universe is are both so rich and so flawed that they also make for a fascinating subject
to dramatise. I would also place science in a similar category. People who don't have
religious belief do tend to cling to it with almost equal fanaticism."

"The Bonny Boy" was published in *Past Magic*. It is a piece not used in MacLeod's
novel, *The House of Storms* (2005). It is a marvelously detailed fantasy about a very
unusual adoption agency in a fantastic version of Victorian England, on a day when
something unique happens. Part of the enduring appeal of fantasy is a reading experience rich in otherness, an experience that this story certainly provides.

"IT'S THEM. It's got to be..."

Mistress Pattison peered around the curtains of her bedroom window at
the top of the carriage, which was proceeding above the garden wall. She
glanced back at her husband, who was still fiddling with his boots in his
night-gown.

"Get a move on Neville!" She gave a shudder. "Sweet Elder. The whole
idea gives me the creeps."

"It might just be – "

"No one comes this far along the street, least of all this time of a morning."

The carriage had stopped and was just visible beyond the wrought iron
gate. A door shone as it opened and first one, and then a second, figure
emerged.

"There's two of them!"

"What did you expect, Nell?" Giving up with his boots, and vigorously scratching his thick grey hair, Master Pattison shuffled towards the bedroom door, where hung the old coat that he used as his dressing gown.

"You can't go down like that."

Dimly, a bell rang.

"Then you answer. The girls'll hear – and you're still dressed."

"They'll hear nothing. I put plenty in last night's tea." Mistress Pattison, a picture of exasperation in her stained apron and matron's cap, dragged the night-shirt off her husband's head, found him trousers and a shirt, and, between further peeks around the curtain and some confusion over his booted but sockless feet, crammed him into an approximation of his usual daywear.

"What time is it anyway? I'm sure they're early."

"Does it matter?" She attempted to comb his hair before he scratched it again. "Now get!"

Master Pattison made his slow way down the stairs. He glanced up at the bell in the front hall and the long mechanism which ran from it to the gate. It hadn't rung again. It was as if they weren't really there, which was what he was hoping. Between yawns, he breathed the spell which caused the door to unclick its lock and swing open. The air outside was misty and cold as his boots scraped the paving which ran between dried heaps of last summer's lavender and sallow. The shapes were there beyond the spiderwebbed gate. Two of them, just as Nell had said.

"Master Pattison?"

The voice came as he fiddled with the freezing padlock on the gate.

He heard himself give a laugh. "S'pose that's me."

"And we're expected?"

No, he thought. They were wearing grey-green cloaks and their faces, he was glad to note, were entirely invisible inside the gloom of hoods. Not things like you. Not – But he couldn't think the word. Shouldn't think anything. The gate finally gave, and he stepped back, and a stray bit of Nell's voice reminded him of its need of oiling as it gave a tooth-aching screech, and they entered. Two of them. The changelings.

The parlour of St. Alphages Refuge for Distressed Guildswomen – which its occupants and the people of Bristol called Alfies – was an important but little-used room. It always seemed to Master Pattison that the short interludes of its occupation had soaked a needy solemnity into the velvet of its curtains and cold gleam of the firegrate. The pictures on the walls were of patrons, children, smiling families, lists of donations and letters of gratitude, all of them resolutely jolly. But it was like the sun on this grey April morning; you knew that warmth was somewhere, but not here. The mistresses of the great and high guilds who came to sit here – for the girls who dwelt at Alfies were never admitted – were almost always impossibly nervous, and there was a wanting in their eyes which had nothing to do with rank or age. If he was entirely honest, which wasn't a luxury he regularly permitted himself, Master Pattison felt even more excluded from the life he was living on these occasions than he did in the generally happy bustle of day-to-day at Alfies. Both he and Mistress Pattison were members of the Matrons' Guild, which was resolutely feminine in most of the thousands of its affiliations and members. The fact was, he much preferred the company of women to men. But to be here in the parlour which felt cold even when they did manage to get a fire going, and to witness the exchange of lives upon which Alfies was founded, always left him brooding.

Over the years, there had been tears and wild threats and offers of amounts of money so huge that only the sternness of their guild prevented them from accepting. Each exchange was unique, but there was something beneath, a steely template locked into the air of this room, which was always the same. Invariably, it was at some odd hour, which was dictated both by the guild-smistresses' need for secrecy and the unpredictable circumstances of birth. Most of the clients arrived without husbands or companions. Many came padded as if they were heavy with child, shuffling through the front hallway with a ponderousness which, after months of pretence, made a good likeness of Alfies' genuine occupants. Some, the wealthiest or most driven, had swallowed potions and performed conjurations which truly caused the swellings and symptoms of pregnancy. But, even for those few women who were prepared to openly admit that they were adopting an infant from Alfies, and the custodians of the orphanages who collected those who were deformed or unfortunately coloured, all impression of frankness and honesty tended to fade once they were inside this parlour. Always, the house was unnaturally quiet, for Nell made sure she'd put a bit extra in the girls' tea. Always, the Pattisons were tired after attending the labour. Often, although the girls signed up to this exchange as an essential part of the conditions of their admittance, there had been what Nell called awkward scenes. From there, to the calm of this moment, was like switching worlds.

Even though these visitors were changelings, Master Pattison still found himself trapped in the usual ritual. Should he offer refreshment, which was nearly always refused? Should he comment on the weather to set them at their ease? They sat down – yes, they used chairs – and Master Pattison found

himself alone with his guests, just as he always did, whilst he waited for Nell
to collect the baby from the alcove just off their bedroom, which was set well
away from the sounds of the rest of the house even though (for Nell had gifts
of the Matrons' Guild to which he was not privy) the infants invariably slept
blissfully.

The creatures were still in their cloaks, those raised hoods, which were
of a greenish shade similar to this room's shadows. Master Pattison was,
he realised, standing at his normal spot beside the fireplace. This was, after
all, just another moment in the parlour's thinly protracted history. His eyes,
though, were drawn irresistibly towards the hand which now snaked out
from the sleeve of the nearest changeling's cloak, curling far whiter than the
lace cover of the armrest on which it lay. Then it moved, and he started, seeing nails as black as the hand was pale play along the stitching with a gesture
which, had the thing been human, might have been taken for impatience.

But what did he know? Never before in his life, Master Pattison realised,
had he ever seen a changeling. Yet the thought came as a surprise to him.
Somehow, they were always there from your earliest age. Tales mothers used
to frighten their misbehaving children. A particular flap of shadow which
had seemed to lie, on winter nights as he looked out from his window for
fear of not looking, behind the dolly tub and the empty lines of washing.
Then had come the Day of Testing, when he and his elder sister were lined
outside the trollman's caravan with all the rest of the local offspring. An
odd moment alone inside that wheeled shed, which smelled of pipesmoke
and sour bedlinen, as the trollman dripped your left wrist with some glowing stuff, which Master Pattison had never seen before in his life, but which
even the most idiot child knew was called aether. And there you were. Your
whole arm smarting and this blazing scab which would never really heal. It
was called the Mark of the Elder, and some of the high guildswomen they'd
had in this parlour ornamented it with cleverly constructed bracelets, but for
the rest of the world it was soon tide-rimed with dirt and everyday life. But
your Mark was never quite forgotten. It proved, as long as it didn't fade and
you were careful and worshipped the Elder and did all the things your guild
expected of you and none of the things it didn't, that you weren't a troll, a
changeling.

Master Pattison couldn't help thinking as he leaned his left elbow on the
cold mantelpiece in an attitude far beyond relaxation and began, unconsciously, to finger the gritty lump this pulled-up sleeve had revealed, that
changelings had done something morally wrong to become that way. Whatever – for he could still see nothing but a slight dimming of the shade inside

the nearest one's hood – whatever that way was. For changing could happen
to anyone. That was the thing to remember. They had all once been guildsmen just as he was now until some accident or poorly tuned spell tipped their
souls into whatever lay on normality's other side. And they were all different,
he knew that as well; as different as the many workings of aether. There had
once been long names and severe methods of study for these differences.
Back in Ages less civilised than this one, changelings had been burnt, or
chained and imprisoned and dragged around like familiars or drays under
the auspices of the now greatly shrivelled Gatherers' Guild. Now, though,
such practices were frowned upon. Although there were rumours of changelings in attics, glimpses of covens on windy nights on Polden Hills, they now
mostly dwelt at a place called Einfell, which lay not so very far from Bristol, although Master Pattison had never had cause to visit it and sincerely
hoped that he never would. The changelings, the trolls, the hobgoblins – all
the words he knew he shouldn't be thinking – took care of their own. And
the guilds – the guilds conspired forgetfully to allow them to dwell unmo-
lested because it dealt with the problem and was mostly in their interest. But
what went on inside Einfell's walls, which Master Pattison had heard were
of mile-high brick, or of glass, or of engine ice, or solid darkness, or all of
those things, remained a mystery to far greater guildsmen than him.

"She shouldn't be long..." He jerked his right hand, which he saw had
been picking at his Mark so hard that there was blood over his fingertips,
away from his wrist and wiped it down his trousers where he hoped the stain
wouldn't show.

"We're in no hurry. I understand how you must feel. This is a strange
moment for us as well." A lisp to the voice, and the trace of a more east-
erly accent. Otherwise, once Master Pattison had run the phrases around his
head enough times to squeeze the sense out of them, it sounded ordinary
enough. His eyes travelled towards the second creature sitting closer to the
bay window in the morning's slowly gaining light. The shape it formed in
the chair was approximately human, but there was a lumpiness to the fall of
its cloak suggestive of scales.

"You should call me Silus, by the way." The lisp was more obviously pronounced around the name. "My colleague here is Ida. We have brought proof
of identity. If you think that is necessary."

"No," Master Pattison shook his head and the room revolved. "I don't
think that will be..."

Here, at last, were Nell's footsteps on the back stairs. The parlour's further door creaked open and Mistress Pattison emerged carrying what looked

like a trailing bundle of fresh sheets. Babies were such tiny things, really, to beset the world, in their growth and multiplication, with everything which filled the city which lay beyond.

Ahhhh... The sound swept through Master Pattison; a still wind. Then the changelings were up, just as the clients always stood at this moment, sighing across the carpet towards Mistress Pattison. "...So beautiful." Now, there was definitely a voice, although the movement across the room had caused the hood of the one called Silus to slip back a little and both of its terrible white hands were extended. Master Pattison thought that Nell, who'd put on a fresh apron as well as collecting the baby, did extraordinarily well not to back away.

"It's a boy," she said with scarcely a quaver. "He hasn't got a name. We always leave that up to the...the new family."

"May I take him?"

This time she did hesitate. But to resist might have involved some sort of contact with the creature which loomed in front of her, so she let go, and the child seemed almost to fall between them in its drooping blankets. Then he was lifted and ahhh...that same soundless phrase, which felt to Master Pattison like a distillation of all the parlour's quiet longing, swept through him again.

The changeling which was holding the baby settled back down in its chair. The other one crouched, with a rustling sound, beside it.

"I would never have thought," the seated one called Silus murmured, its voice so quiet now that the lisp was almost all there was, "that I would live to feel this again." It leaned over the baby. All pretence of the hood was gone now, and its head was as white as its hands, and the bones of the skull were oddly planed. The lips were indrawn, a mere gash, with no nose to speak of, and the eyes were like globes of moonivy; faintly glowing – entirely grey. "I used to be a guildsman, you know. I used to have a family. The monstrous thing about us – and I know that's how you feel – is that *we're not monsters at all. I remember the fevered nights, that sense of a burden you would carry until the world decided to end. Scents like honey and the song of blackbirds. The sheer, inexplicable hope for everything you were and could never be... And it's gone now and it's here again and yet everything is different and I'm pulled by the ache of this room...I should never...*

The baby, awake now, gazed up at the changeling, and, as much as newborns can feel or see anything, seemed confident and unafraid. The changeling's words had rung in Master Pattison's head; they rang there still. The other creature called Ida – the one crouching and rustling, and whose face was still hidden – reached out with pinecone fingers that the baby, as he mewled faintly and stretched an arm above his nest of blankets, enclosed in a minute ivory grip. That feeling came flooding over Master Pattison again. Too deep for words, wyrebright and flood-dark, it slowed his heart. Ida, he remembered, as he studied the scene before him, this triptych, was a woman's name.

"There'll be a few forms." Nell unlocked the bureau in the corner and extracted the necessary quadruplicate sheets and stamped them and gave them a drying wave.

"There would be forms, wouldn't there?"

Nell, who'd never been much of a one for irony, clipped them to a board and presented them to the seated changeling with an uncapped fountain pen. "You'll need to sign here and here and also tick these boxes but you must leave that part blank – and also sign and date these and initial here but not here."

The changeling freed a hand from beneath the baby and took the pen. It studied each clause with the air of one who had done such things many times before. Its breath gave a hissing sigh, and Master Pattison saw, entirely unwilled, the barred windows of a fine, sunlit office, files piled upon a fine leather desk; heard, even, the buzzing, itchy hum of some vast kind of industry. Then the vision was gone and the changeling had completed all the papers and Nell was blotting them.

"I once used to wonder," he thought he heard it say, "what would happen to the world if we didn't bother with all of this paper and ink. Would it cease turning? Would we learn to love or hate each other a little more or less?"

But Nell was too busy sorting the sheets to notice, and Master Pattison was no longer sure if what he'd heard had really been said. *This is what it's like,* he thought, *to be with these creatures. All the ordinary things of life start to unravel. It's why they can't live with us. It's why people so fear them...*

"Well." Closing the bureau, Nell gave her usual brisk smile. She really was managing this most extraordinarily well. "That's everything we need from you."

The changelings rustled, stood up. The baby mewed. Outside, down in Bristol, the morning's first shift sirens started howling. Sometimes, the guildsmistresses asked to have a baby stripped. They would count fingers and toes and prod ribs and scan every crinkle and crease as if they were buying a goose for Christmas. Then there was all the talk about wetnurses and the boiling of nappies. But none of that seemed relevant today.

The changelings moved out into the hallway, and the parlour, even though its door remained ajar, seemed to snap shut behind them so tightly that Master Pattison wondered if things would ever be quite the same in there again. All the other exchanges now seemed like rehearsals for this one. Ahead lay – but the future, despite the orderliness of the vaguely contented life he and Nell lived here at Alfies, suddenly seemed strange and harsh and dim.

"I know you won't quite believe this," the pale changeling called Silus said as it stood with the other beside the front door and Master Pattison, his hand eagerly on its handle, found himself close enough to be breathing the scent of the baby boy, which was of tallow and berries and new dough. "But this wasn't of our willing."

"Oh, that's all right." As if such things happened all the time, and eager to be rid of them before the girls began to stir, Nell gave a magnanimous wave. "Our instructions for this exchange came from very, very high. So high that we don't even quite know – "

"And I know that you'll worry, when we leave you, and if you have any human hearts within you at all, that you've done something terrible, and that orders from on high and forms in quadruplicate are never enough – "

" – It doesn't – "

" – and perhaps that may be true, although we're all old and wise enough not to believe in things glimpsed through windows and stupid childhood tales. But we must all bow and bend to the ways of the Guilds – even us..." No word actually followed.

Master Pattison heard, felt, his hand opening the front door, and birdsong, all the stirrings of Bristol, flowed in. The baby, shocked by this strange new sense, tensed within his blankets. The face of the changeling which hadn't spoken and was called Ida was half-visible now, and seemed to be made of crumbling charcoal. Something, the impossibility of a smile, twisted on the other's lipless mouth.

"Day after day, year on year," it said, "England seems becalmed. These Ages of ours seem incapable of ever ending. Then, suddenly a storm sweeps in from nowhere and bears everything away. Perhaps, when all of that has passed, any of us who remain will be fit to do the judging."

"Well..." Nell, who was certainly unused to clients launching into odd philosophies at the end of an exchange, made a vague gesture.

Then the changeling raised its hood, and Master Pattison gave a small inward cheer as it and its companion turned to go. Then it paused. There was a silvered flash of cataract eyes.

"And the girl, the mother?"

On firmer ground again, Nell shook her head. "She'll go away from here. She doesn't matter."

The changeling chuckled. It was the most human sound it had made. "I think you may be wrong."

They turned and left.

Ghost Mission

L. E. Modesitt, Jr.

L. E. Modesitt, Jr. (*www.travelinlibrarian.info/recluce*) lives in Cedar City, Utah. Initially established as a science fiction writer in *Analog* in the 1970s, and then with a number of SF novels in the 1980s, he began to focus a significant part of his writing at the start of the 1990s on fantasy, launching the famous world of Recluce. The Recluce combine the manner of fantasy written with many of the rationalist attitudes of SF. This is the way Poul Anderson and Gordon R. Dickson wrote fantasy. In *The Magic of Recluce* (1991), the novel that introduced the world and the magical system that operates there, a magical battle occurs that includes attack via the weather. The battle is won but the disruption in weather alters the climate and the economy for years. There is also a love story embedded in most of the Recluce books, and indeed in most of Modesitt's novels. He is a romantic. He is also one of the most successful fantasy and science fiction writers of the last couple of decades, with over forty novels in print. He has two novels coming out in 2007: *The Elysium Commission* and *The Natural Order Master: A New Recluce Novel*. He worked for seventeen years in the belly of the beast that is Washington, DC, and this has influenced the way he writes about political intrigue: "The way Washington works is not the way people really want to think of Washington working. For example, you see movies like *No Way Out*, you see all these Washington films – people are dying all over the place. In the whole time I worked in Washington, I don't know of a single death that was caused by somebody else. Washington doesn't work that way. Washington is too cruel to kill anybody outright. Now, the number of suicides – that's another question.... They will destroy your life, and they will destroy your family, but they won't kill you. They leave that up to you." During his time in DC, he was the Director of Legislation and Congressional Relations for the EPA and also a staff director for a US Congressman.

"Ghost Mission" was published in the original anthology, *Slipstreams*, edited by Martin H. Greenberg and John Helfers. It is an independent story set in the world of his alternate-universe science-fantasy trilogy introduced in *Of Tangible Ghosts* (1994), a vaguely contemporary world in which ghosts exist and can interact with the living. It is an interesting comparison to the Michael Moorcock story, another fated hero story.

AFTER SUNSET ON WEDNESDAY, I found myself standing outside the Sherratt Inn, one hand on the small pack attached to my belt and concealed by the dark gray windbreaker. I took a deep breath, lifting my hand carefully away from the pack. I didn't want to touch it again any sooner than I had to.

The air was cold and still, the acridness of burning coal confined by a winter inversion, but even that smelled wonderful. I'd enjoy it while I could, for all would change, change utterly. I gathered myself together, pushing away the burning that ran along all my nerves and the thought of how little time I had, and stretched my legs, turning toward the Relief Society House. Four blocks later, I could see it, an imposing structure on the south side of the park, almost directly across from the Tabernacle. Covering the re-dedication was the assignment for Thursday, not that it mattered to me, except for the conditioning. Tonight was what counted.

The sky to the west glowed faint orange from the last rays of the sun striking the particulates emitted from the iron works. The massive power plant in the flats to the north of the iron works didn't emit anything. In a convoluted but direct sense, that special high-tech power plant, surrounded by more security than the Saint air base farther to the northwest, was why I was in Iron Mission.

When I reached the rear of the Relief Society House, I waited in the shadows on the far side of the back gate, my breath steaming in the chill and still winter air. The dark gray windbreaker and gray slacks let me blend into the indistinctness of late twilight. By moving my head just slightly, I could see the door to the Relief Society kitchen. Before long, the scullery maids would be bringing out the refuse from the evening meal served to the disfavored wives – that was the semi-official term for unpropertied wives who had either lost their beauty or been unable to provide sons and who had been discarded.

The first scullery girl was short and squat. Her eyes darted from side to side. She wasn't the one. I eased farther back into the shadows. After she dumped her load from her basket into the squarish brown dumpster, she walked hurriedly back along the stone walk to the rear door of the Relief Society kitchen. There was silence for a long time then, and in the stillness I was far more aware of the nerve-burning sensation, psychosomatic as it was, that nagged at me.

I didn't like the thought of having to enter the servants' quarters to find the scullery girl I needed, but I could...and would, if I had to. Intelligence had confirmed she was there, but zombies had no legal rights in Deseret – not that they had many in the Republic – and the Spazi wasn't about to waste assets to recover an operative with blown cover and a memory they believed worthless – if not lost entirely. The Federal Security Agency believed otherwise, but the FSA had no official jurisdiction outside Columbia.

Finally, the door opened again. But it closed, and no one came out.

I kept waiting. A good fifteen minutes passed before the kitchen door swung wide, and light cascaded on the stone walk. A tall and slender figure carrying a large basket stepped out onto the walk. The door closed. The scullery girl's steps carried her toward the refuse dumpster. They were the mechanical steps of a zombie. She was the target, and I eased around the brick pillar of the gate.

She lifted the basket and dumped the contents into the open dumpster.

"Charity?" I said softly, looking up to meet her eyes.

"Yes, sir?" Her voice was flat, or almost so. In the deepening darkness, standing behind the twilight-darkened red stone of the Relief Society House, her brown cap, dark gray ankle-length frock, and grayer jacket made her seem almost invisible.

I couldn't see the color of her eyes, and it was probably better that way.

"I've come to take you to the General Authority, Charity. You're to come with me."

"Sister Barrow told me to come right back."

"You must always obey a brother over a sister. Come with me."

She didn't argue. No female, zombie or otherwise, would have dared to contest a man in Deseret, even one much shorter. Besides, we were headed to one of the General Authorities. Zombies do know when you're telling the truth. That, too, is a terrible beauty.

We walked over to Third South and took it west along the south side of the university – Joseph Smith University – and then up the curving road onto Leigh Hill, wide enough for an ox to turn with a wagon in tow, as were all the main streets in Deseret, although the oxen had long since been replaced by steamers and steam-lorries.

It was close to pitch-dark when we reached the high stone wall on the south side of the estate – and the maintenance gate that was our immediate destination. It took me a good three minutes to open the lock, even with the picks and my training. I gave the hinges liberal doses of the special lubricant before I opened the gate and stepped through the stone archway. It did not squeak. After closing the gate, but not locking it, I led Charity a good ten yards along the gravel path before turning uphill. We stopped in the darkness.

"Stay here. Say nothing." I kept the words to Charity simple and low.

She stood, mute, beside the pinon pine and just forward of the wall between the upper and lower gardens. Her gray garments blended against the dressed stones of the wall.

As I eased along the wall, I knew I wouldn't have much time – just the one night. My borrowed body wouldn't take more, especially if I had to call up full hysterical boost – what once had been thought to be a property just of berserkers – and even a zombie's absence would be noted before long. My palms were damp inside the black leather gloves.

After another twenty yards, I could see the target – a ghost who stood alone in the shadow of a juniper just a few yards downhill and east of the wall. On both sides of that darkness the reflected light of the full moon flooded down. I wouldn't even have noticed the ghost if I hadn't been looking specifically for her. I remained in the shadow of the wall, moving across the frozen grass, knowing that I had left footprints. From what I could tell, no one else had walked the lower garden recently, not since it had frosted, but the prints would either melt with the next day's sun or be covered by the next snowfall.

Absolem had said there was a ghost in the older section of the garden, and one not seen before six months previous. That late June had been when Verial had vanished, not that I'd known it then, leaving but a zombie behind, found sitting on a bench in the Bishop's Park of Iron Mission. That was the official report filed with the Iron Mission police. Where there was a zombie, there should have been a ghost, but one was never reported.

Everyone in the FSA was hoping that the ghost in the garden was the one I sought. But why had the Saints zombied Verial in the lower garden – if indeed the ghost was Verial? It didn't make sense, unless they thought her ghost would fade into oblivion before being discovered and that no outsider would see her there.

I kept moving, slowly, deliberately, until I finally stood in the patch of shadow closest to that where the ghost hovered, concealed from the mansion uphill and to the west by the upper garden, and by the wall in whose moonlight-created shade I stood. She'd been young when she died. Had she been beautiful? Verial had been, especially to me, but with ghosts, it's hard to tell, because so much of beauty is vitality, and most of that vanishes when the body dies – or when spirit and body are separated.

What was I doing? Certainly, I was trespassing by sneaking around the walled hillside gardens of Heber Cannon, but trespassing would be the least of my sins were I to be discovered on the private grounds of one of the General Authorities of Deseret. My alter-ego's cover as a journalist for Republic Press International might be jeopardized, not to mention both our lives, such as mine was. Building that journalistic cover had been difficult enough, especially with the assignments in occupied France. Deseret was nominally neutral, but few foreign reporters were allowed into Deseret, and only those deemed either harmless or helpful in some way.

My alter ego had come the first time to cover the second Salt Palace Concert of Llysette duBois and Daniel Perkins. With her kidnapping and her husband's heroics, no one had ever remembered the small and slightly lisping reporter from West Kansas. So when she'd been asked to sing for the re-dedication of the renovated Iron Mission Tabernacle before her final Deseret concert in St. George, his visa to cover her tour was accepted without objection.

I eased closer to the ghost, careful to remain in the shadows. My breath steamed, appearing almost more solid than the figure of the ghost. She did not breathe, although her chest seemed to rise and fall under the filmy and bare-shouldered gown that was so unlike anything a woman of Deseret would have worn. I frowned. Was this the right ghost? Verial had been a mistress of disguise, and never would have worn something so inappropriate. At least, not without a good reason.

"Verial?" I whispered.

The reply was much as I had expected, typical of a ghost who'd been surprised and fully aware when killed – or one who'd been zombied.

She turned to me and cocked her head – that was one of the mannerisms in the file, although I'd known it far earlier. Then she spoke, if a faint whisper in one's thoughts could be considered a voice.

First dew that gives the grass its sheen,
then for the frost that coats the green...

Had I heard a door creak? Steps on stone? Much as I disliked it, because it shortened the time I had, I concentrated, bringing up full sensory intensity. I had to hold onto myself to keep from staggering. Every nerve tingled with edged flame, and the steps on the stone walk in the upper garden sounded like distant thunder. No one else would have heard them at all.

"Who was the prince who loved you?" I asked, quietly, pressing the question toward the ghost.

The hint of a smile crossed her face before I heard the words in my own thoughts.

My prince had proffered love in words so meet
that seraph birds alone could sing that sweet...

That didn't tell me enough. It hinted that the ghost was Verial, because Prince Mykail had fallen for her – before the Cheka had warned him off, if after she had gotten what she had been tasked to obtain. I don't know that she had fallen for him. She'd always kept her feelings to herself. Good agents do. That was why I'd never been a good agent. Now, there was no one other than me available to recover Verial, if it could be done at all. The FSA only had a handful of agents, and that was a handful more than the Security Act allowed. No one else had been available, not without jeopardizing other priorities. And it didn't hurt that I cared about her. I always had, and that had been my undoing. FSA had nothing to lose. I had everything to lose, one way or another, and little enough to gain – except a final measure of self-respect.

The psych-scientists had said I should try indirect prompts first, but I was running out of time, and I couldn't ignore the two men descending through the upper garden to the gate in the wall to the lower garden.

"Why did you leave physics for the Spazi?" I asked hurriedly.

As humans, rules of law we'll change,
as time and fate shift what we know,
but nature's laws, fixed fermions,
endure unchanged, forever so.

The rhyme made sense, and would have made more sense had I been able to identify the poet – or poetess. Only a handful of ghosts could communicate, and always by rhymed words, usually of a favorite poet. Still, the use of the term fermion was a favorable indication that the ghost I was dealing with was Verial. She had been a brilliant grad student in the physics of materials engineering when she'd been recruited.

The gate from the upper garden creaked as it opened.

"What is the formulaic basis of fossil-fueled MHD?" The question was nonsensical, but the terms weren't and were calculated to get a response.

The enigmatic smile of the ghost vanished. She almost did as well, wavering for a moment in the deep shadows. Then, her intensity re-doubled, her features clearer. In one hand was the shawl that had surely covered her shoulders before it had been ripped away, most certainly after she had been zombied.

I was certain now that she was Verial, but I had so little time, in more ways than one.

Two figures – they had to be men – walked unhurried through the stone archway to the lower garden.

I eased back along the stone wall, as quickly as I could. With each step, the crackling of the frozen grass threatened to engulf me, and with each step, the knives of sound pierced my eardrums. I kept moving, then froze. Three Saint security types waited outside the gate. Not Danites, not police, but security, in the black and brown they wore when they wanted to be noticed.

The footsteps from higher in the garden were louder, thunder drawing ever closer to the ghost by the juniper – and me.

"This way…" I whispered to Charity. "Follow me."

She did not move. I took her hand and led her back toward the juniper and the ghost, staying in the shadows.

"Take two steps forward and wait until I speak again." I couldn't tell her to stand behind the ghost, although that was where I wanted her, because zombies cannot perceive ghosts.

Charity took the two steps, standing immobile just behind the ghost.

In turn, the ghost that I hoped was, and wanted to be, Verial glowed brighter.

The two men slowed as they neared the juniper. Verial's sudden brightness almost obscured the zombie, as I had planned.

"She is still there. Nothing has happened." Those words came from the younger and taller man.

"Footsteps," said the older and broader figure. "There in the frost on the grass." His deep voice boomed in my ears, even though I was crouched against the wall, at an angle where the juniper most obscured their view of me – hardly enough if they actually were looking.

"More like a child's."

"Or a woman's. I told you there would be an agent using duBois as cover."

"Her husband is with her. He has been the whole time."

"This time, he is a decoy. They want us to watch him."

"Your ghost was still here, Father. She was beautiful."

"She was nothing of the sort. She was brilliant, and slightly attractive. More important, she was a typical Columbian woman – hard and calculating – a perfect spy beneath that persona. She almost got away with it, too... because of my own son. She was not my ghost. She only wanted you to think that." The snort that followed was deep and rumbled in my ears. Verial had never been anyone's, and Heber was right. She had been hard and calculating. I'd known that. It didn't change anything.

"She was just using me to get to you, Father. I told you that. That was why she was here... "

"And you let her?"

"How was I – "

"Enough, Jared... Enough. The trap is set. Before long, we'll know."

Heber Cannon was right. The trap was set. In fact, several traps were set... and a net. Could I avoid theirs and spring mine?

I eased the projector from inside the windbreaker, easing open the wide film antenna. I made sure the projector was not pointed anywhere near me or toward any energy-reflective surface – and that I was shielded behind the antenna that was both transmitter and collector.

The ghost spoke to them, not to me.

What you did in faithless need,

in time, no one will heed…

The irony of those words almost paralyzed me, because they could have applied to Verial when she'd left me to the Cheka.

"Silence, hussy." Heber's words rattled my skull.

I stepped to the side and aimed the projector toward the ghost and Charity. I wasn't sure I wanted it to work, but the conditioning held, and I pressed the activating stud. Energy flared from the projector, returned, and was re-projected, far too fast for anyone to see.

The ghost vanished. Charity's face went from immobile to angry in that microsecond before she moved – not toward Heber, but toward Jared.

I knew the moves she used. Jared didn't. His throat was crushed, and his nose broken in less than a second. He grasped at his throat, flailing.

I had already dropped the projector and was moving far faster than any man should, especially one so small and slight.

Heber Cannon gaped for a second, then reached for the sidearm he always carried. "You killed him." He looked as though he were about to yell for the security types. Yet he hesitated, still arrogant, his eyes looking at a woman and a man not much larger than a pre-pubescent boy.

Knowing about the sidearm, I was already moving. My knife was quicker than he was. That was to be expected from an agent under conditioned hysterical boost. For a moment, he looked down, stupidly, at the blood welling out over his waistcoat and overcoat, his mouth moving silently, with only gurgling sounds, unsurprisingly, since I'd slit his throat first, deeply.

"You had a choice, Heber," I said quietly, not that he'd be likely to hold the thought before he died. "You chose to protect a corrupt and evil son." Was I any better? Probably not, but that wasn't the question. It never had been.

I could sense the life leaking out of both of them. Where there had been one ghost by the juniper, now there would be two, both different from the first. The conflict had been quick, and almost silent – quiet enough that the Saint security men still stood by the lower south gate, waiting for a signal from Heber Cannon.

"Jared brought me down here," murmured Verial. "He said he wanted a picture of me in the garden. One that could be made into a portrait. I should have known better."

"Heber was probably watching." I bent and scooped up the projector before rummaging through Heber's waistcoat and jacket pockets. In a moment, I came up with a set of keys.

"Now what?" asked Verial in the lowest of voices, knowing that I would hear.

"We walk up the way they came and out the west gate. Then we'll walk to the safe house. In this case, it's the Republic consulate. The Saints may know that, but they won't violate it for a youth and a woman."

"You have a key to the gate?"

"Heber's keys here will do." I held them up. "We should go." The keys would be faster than picking the lock – if they were the right ones.

I followed the footprints in the grass back through the gardens until I could see the north gate to the upper garden. Then I took the graveled path to the gate. The third key I tried fit the lock to the outer gate, the one on First South. I locked the gate behind us, then tossed the keys back over the gate.

We walked in the shadow of the wall until we reached Ridge Lane, where we turned south until we got to Third South.

"Do I know you? You seem familiar," she finally said.

I didn't want to answer that question. Not in the slightest. "Do you have the plans? Can you recall what you learned?" I hated to ask, but I wanted to know if what I faced would be for something.

"What are you talking about?"

"You're Verial. The code is absolem green, and the plans are for the proprietary and secret technology to the magnetohydrodynamic power plant here. I wouldn't know one end of an engineering spec from the other, but once the Spazi wrote you off, FSA decided on an experimental effort to reclaim you. Call it a terrible beauty being born." That could have referred to the way I had been used or Verial had been reclaimed – or the theft of the power plant technology.

"I should be grateful?"

I recalled that tone of voice all too well.

"No. You never were. You don't have to tell me. I have no need to know. I just was the tool able to get you back. I wondered if it was worth the cost."

"Don't speak of costs."

"I won't." I kept walking along the shaded side of Third South.

"They'll be glad you succeeded. That's all I'll say."

That was about what I'd expected.

"You never answered my question about whether I should know you."

"I couldn't say, not in a way that would make sense in the present tense."

"Don't mouth rhymes at me. I recall enough that I'd prefer not to hear another line of verse."

I ignored her request and quoted Yeats, in my own fashion.

> *"Being high and solitary and most stern,*
> *Why, what could you have done, being what you are?*
> *Was there another Troy for you to burn?"*

"Alexander? You're not Alexander."

Again, I misquoted.

> *"You could have warned me, but I was young,*
> *And we spoke a different tongue."*

"You knew the risks. Still... how – ?"

> *"Birth-hour and death-hour meet...*
> *I dance on other's deathless feet..."*

She was silent. What else could she have said?

We walked eastward in the darkness, down Leigh Hill and along Third South, still on the dark side. Behind us, sirens rose. The security types had found bodies, and perhaps ghosts. They would find little else, besides the footprints that looked to be those of a woman and a boy and Heber Cannon's keys beside a gate.

Neither of us said another word until we approached the heavy wrought-iron gates of the small estate on the east side of Iron Mission, set on the north side of Coal Creek. I could see the Republic Marines manning the gatehouse. They were expecting us.

"You wrote and memorized your own poetry, didn't you?" I asked.

"Yes."

"Because you thought they would find you out?"

"No. It was the logical thing to do, whatever might happen. Sommersby knew from my first assignment."

"She would have." I didn't really want to escort her through the gates. I did anyway, after the Marines opened the gates. They closed them behind us.

When she stood at last in the archway of the front door to the Republic consulate, the two guards flanking her, she turned, and all three looked down at me. I handed her the knife and the now-useless projector. The single-use film antenna had destroyed itself in accomplishing its task. "Dispose of them. You know how and why."

She would, but only to protect herself. As always.

"What happens to you now?" she asked.

I just smiled and shook my head.

I left her there, as once she had left me. She had not changed, and tomorrow the man whose body I held so briefly would cover a rededication concert, sore and bruised, but his nerves would not burn. He would doubtless wonder what had happened in the hours that he had lost – and I would become, at last, what lay beyond ghost and zombie.

I walked toward the darkness of oblivion, out of my own nerve-jangled, gong-tormented sea, toward my freedom from what never could have been. In some ways, I pitied Verial – now. I had repaid her in the only way possible. My fingers moved toward the waistpack under the windbreaker.

The Christmas Witch

M. Rickert

Mary Rickert (*www.ideomancer.com/ft/Rickert/Rickert.htm*) lives in Cedarburg, Wisconsin. Her short fiction has appeared often in recent years in *The Magazine of Fantasy & Science Fiction*, and in both our *Year's Best SF* and *Year's Best Fantasy* volumes. She said in an interview, "My stories are not factual but the factual existence is not the only one and they are, really, a truer record of my soul than a photograph or a journal could ever be." We see her fantasy as somewhere in the range of Kit Reed's and Shirley Jackson's work, literary as well as fantastic. She is probably the best new short fiction writer to enter the fantasy field since Kelly Link. Her first collection, *Map of Dreams*, was released in 2006 to very favorable reviews, and she received the Crawford/IAFA Award for best first fantasy book for it. We said earlier that the Peter S. Beagle collection is the best of the year, but some mornings we feel that *Map of Dreams* is the best. It is astonishingly good. In a letter to Chris Barzak, quoted in the introduction to Rickert's collection, she described a story she had written as a child: "I was young, and basically fairly unpopular and a skinny, cross-eyed girl with cat-eye glasses and I wrote this story that I decided to perform for the class as a monologue. So the whole thing is about how nobody likes me or plays with me and I don't know why, and how alone I am, and how I try to fit in. The last line is something like, 'Then she turned and walked away dragging her tail behind her.'"

"Christmas Witch" was published in *The Magazine of Fantasy & Science Fiction*, a magazine notable throughout its history for its powerful fantasy stories by women. It is a story that reminds us of some of the work of Robert Aickman, who is identified with both fantasy and science fiction, about kids who collect bones for magical reasons in a contemporary Massachusetts town that once executed a witch, a little girl in touch with the supernatural who is sadly disturbed by the murder of her mother and unable to communicate her feelings adequately, and (ironically) about child abuse and about death. It is an interesting contrast to the Greg van Eekhout story, earlier in this book.

THE CHILDREN OF STONE collect bones, following cats through twisted narrow streets, chasing them away from tiny birds, dead gray mice (with sweet round ears, pink inside like seashells), and fish washed on rocky shore. The children show each other their bone collections, tiny white femurs, infinitesimal wings, jawbones with small teeth intact. Occasionally, parents find these things; they scold the little hoarder, or encourage the practice by setting up a science table. It's a stage children go through, they assume, this fascination with structure, this cold approach to death. The parents do not

discuss it with each other, except in passing. ("Oh yes, the skeleton stage.")
The parents do not know, they do not guess that once the found bones are
tossed out or put on display, the children begin to collect again. They collect
in earnest.

Rachel Boyle has begun collecting bones, though her father doesn't know
about it, of course. Her mother, being dead, might know. Rachel can't figure
that part out. Her mother is not a ghost, the Grandma told her, but a spirit.
The Grandma lives far away, in Milwaukee. Rachel didn't even remember her
when she came for the funeral. "You remember me, honey, don't you?" she
asked and Rachel's father said, "Of course she remembers you." Rachel went
in the backyard where she tore flowers while her father and the Grandma sat
at the kitchen table and cried. After the Grandma left, Rachel and her father
moved to Stone.

Rachel doesn't get off the school bus at her house, because her father
is still at work. She gets off at Peter Williamson's house. The first time she
found Peter with his bone collection spread out before him on the bedroom
floor she thought it was gross. But the second time she sat across from him
and asked him what they were for.

Peter shrugged. "You know," he said.

Rachel shook her head.

"Didn't they teach you anything in Boston? They're for Wilmot Redd, the
witch. You know. A long time ago. An old lady. She lived right here in Stone.
They hung her. There's a sign about her on Old Burial Hill but she's not buried there. No one knows where she ended up."

That's when Rachel began collecting bones. She stored them in her sock
drawer, she stored them under her bed, she had several in her jewelry box,
and two chicken legs buried in the flowerpot from her mother's funeral. The
flowers were dead, but it didn't matter, she wouldn't let her father throw
them out.

For Halloween, Rachel wants to be dead but her father says she can't be.
"How about a witch?" he says. "Or a princess?"

"Peter's going to be dead," she says. "He'll have a knife going right
through the top of his head, and blood dripping down his face."

"How about a cat? You can have a long tail and whiskers."

"Mariel is going to be a pilgrim."

"You can be a pilgrim."

"Pilgrims are dead! Jeez, Dad, didn't they teach you anything in Boston?"

"Don't talk to me like that."

Rachel sighs, "Okay, I'll be a witch."

"Fine, we'll paint your face green and you can wear a wig."

"Not that kind of witch."

Her father turns out the light and kisses her on the forehead before he leaves her alone in the dark. All of a sudden Rachel is scared. She thinks of calling her father. Instead, she counts to fifty before she pulls back the covers and sneaks around in the dark of her room, gathering the bones, which she pieces together into a sort of puzzle shape of a funny little creature, right on top of her bed. She uses a skull, and a long bone that might be from a fish, the small shape of a mouse paw, and a couple of chicken legs. She sucks her thumb while she waits for it to do the silly dance again.

On Tuesday, Mrs. Williamson has a doctor's appointment. Rachel still gets off the bus with Peter. They still go to his house. There, the babysitter waits for them. Her name is Melinda. She has long blonde hair, a pierced navel, pierced tongue, ears pierced all the way around the edge, and rings on every finger. She wraps her arms around Peter and wrestles him to the floor. He screams but he is smiling. After a while she lets go and turns to Rachel.

Rachel wishes Melinda would wrap her arms around her, but she doesn't. "My name's Melinda," she says. Rachel nods. Her father already told her. He wouldn't let her be watched by a stranger. "Who wants popcorn?" Melinda says and races Peter into the kitchen. Rachel follows even though she doesn't really like popcorn.

Peter tells Melinda about his plans for Halloween. He tells her about the knife through his head while the oil heats up in the pan. Melinda tosses in a kernel. Peter runs out of the room.

"What are you going to be?" Melinda asks but before Rachel can answer, Peter is back in the kitchen, the knife in his head, blood dripping around the eyes. Melinda says, "Oh gross, that's so great, it looks really gross." The kernel pops. Melinda pours more kernels into the pan and then slaps the lid on. "Hey, dead man," she says, "how about getting the butter?"

Peter gets a stick of butter out of the refrigerator. He places it on the cutting board. He takes a sharp knife out of the silverware drawer. Popcorn steam fills the kitchen. Rachel feels sleepy, sitting at the island. She leans her head into her hand; her eyes droop. Peter makes a weird sound and drops the knife on the counter. Blood trickles from his finger and over the butter. Melinda sets the pan on a cold burner, turns off the stove, and wraps Peter's finger in a paper towel. Rachel isn't positive but she thinks Peter is crying beneath his mask.

"It's okay," Melinda says. "It's just a little cut." She steers Peter through the kitchen toward the bathroom. Rachel looks at the blood on the butter; one long red drop drips down the side. She stares at the kitchen window, foggy with steam. For a second she thinks someone is standing out there, watching, but no one is. Peter and Melinda come back into the kitchen. Peter no longer has the knife through his head. His hair is stuck up funny, his face, pink, and he has a band-aid on his finger. He sits at the island beside Rachel but doesn't look at her. Melinda slices the bloody end of butter and tosses it into the trash. She cuts a chunk off, places it in a glass bowl and sticks it in the microwave. "So, what are you going to be for Halloween?"

"Wilmot Redd," Rachel says.

"You can't," says Melinda.

"Don't you know anything?" Peter asks.

"Be nice, Peter." Melinda pours the popcorn into a big purple bowl and drips melted butter over it. "You can't be Wilmot Redd."

"Why not?"

Melinda puts ice in three glasses and fills them with Dr. Pepper. She sits down at the island, across from Peter and Rachel. "If I tell you, you can't tell your dad."

Rachel has heard about secrets like this. When a grownup tells you not to tell your parents something, it is a bad secret. Rachel is thrilled to be told one. "I won't," she says.

"Okay, I know you think witches wear pointy black hats and act like the bad witch in The Wizard of Oz but they don't. Witches are just regular people and they look and dress like everyone else. Stone is full of witches. I can't tell you who all is a witch, but you would be surprised. Who knows? Maybe you'll grow up to be a witch yourself. All that stuff about witches is a lie. People have been lying about witches for a very long time. And that's what happened to Wilmot Redd. Maybe she wasn't even a witch at all, but one thing for sure she wasn't an evil witch. That's the part that's made up about witches and that's what they made up about her, and that's how come she wound up dead. You can't dress up as Wilmot Redd. We just don't make fun of her in Stone. Even though it happened a long time ago, most people here still feel really bad about it. Most people think she was just an old woman who was into herbs and shit, don't tell your dad I said 'shit' either, all right? Making fun of Wilmot Redd is like saying you think witches should be hung. You don't think that do you? All right then, so don't dress up as Wilmot Redd. You can go as a made-up witch, but leave poor Wilmot Redd out of it. No one even knows what happened to her, I mean after she died. That's how much she didn't matter. They threw her body off a cliff somewhere. No one even knows where her bones ended up. They could be anywhere."

"Do you collect bones?" Rachel asks and Peter kicks her.

"Why would I do that?" Melinda says. "You have some weird ideas, kid."

Witches everywhere. Teacher witches, mommy and daddy witches, policeman witches too, boy witches and girl witches, smiling witches, laughing witches, bus driver witches. Who is not a witch in Stone? Rachel isn't, she knows that for sure.

Rachel makes special requests for chicken "with the bones," she says, and she eats too much, giving herself a stomachache.

"How many bones do you need?" her father asks, because Rachel has told him she needs them for a school project.

"I don't know," she says. "Jack just keeps saying I need more."

"Jack sounds kind of bossy," her father says.

Rachel nods. "Yeah, but he's funny too."

Finally, Halloween arrives. Rachel goes to school dressed as a made-up witch. She notices that there are several of them on the bus and the playground. They start the morning with doughnuts and apple cider and then they do math with questions like two pumpkins plus one pumpkin equals how many pumpkins.

Rachel raises her hand and the lady at the front of the room who says she is Miss Engstrom, their teacher, but who doesn't look anything like her, says, "Yes, Rachel?"

"How many bones does it take to make a body?"

"That's a very good question," the lady says. She's wearing a long purple robe and she has black hair that keeps sliding around funny on her head. "I'll look that up for you, Rachel, but in the meantime, can you answer my question? You have two pumpkins and then your mother goes to the store and comes home with one more pumpkin, how many pumpkins do you have?"

"Her mother is dead," a skeleton in the back of the room says.

"I don't care," says Rachel.

"I mean your father," the lady says. "I meant to say your father goes to the store."

But Rachel just sits there and the lady calls on someone else.

They get an extra long recess. Cindi Becker tears her princess dress on the swing and cries way louder than Peter cried when he cut his finger. Somebody dressed all in black, with a black hood, won't speak to anyone but walks slowly through the playground, stopping occasionally to point a black-gloved finger at one of the children. When one of the kindergartners gets pointed at, he runs, screaming, back to his teacher, who is dressed up as a pirate.

Rachel finds Peter with the knife in his head and says, "Don't tell, but I'm still going to be Wilmot Redd tonight." The boy turns to her, but doesn't say anything at all, just walks away. After a while, Rachel realizes that there are three boys on the playground with knives in their heads, and she isn't sure if the one she spoke to was Peter.

They don't have the party until late in the afternoon. The lady who says she is Miss Engstrom turns off the lights and closes the drapes.

Rachel raises her hand. The lady nods at her.

"When my mom went to the store a bad man shot her – "

The lady waves her arms, as if trying to put out a fire, the purple sleeves dangling from her wrists. "Rachel, Rachel," she says. "I'm so sorry about your mother. I should have said your father went to the store. I'm really sorry. Maybe I should tell a story about witches."

"My mother is not a witch," Rachel says.

"No, no of course she's not a witch. Let's play charades!"

Rachel sits at her desk. She is a good girl for the most part. But she has learned that even without her face painted, she can pretend to be listening when she isn't. Nobody notices that she isn't playing their stupid game. Later, when she is going to the bus, the figure all dressed in black points at her. She feels the way the kindergartner must have felt. She feels like crying. But she doesn't cry.

She gets off the bus at Peter Williamson's house with Peter who acts crazy, screaming for no reason, letting the door slam right in her face. I hate you, Peter, she thinks, and is surprised to discover that nothing bad happens to her for having this thought. But when she opens the door, Melinda is standing there, next to Peter who still has the knife in his head. "Don't you understand? You can't dress up as Wilmot Redd."

"Where's Mrs. Williamson?" Rachel asks.

"She had to go to the doctor's. Did you hear me?"

"I'm not," Rachel says, walking past Melinda. "Can't you see I'm just a made-up witch?"

"Is that what you're wearing tonight?"

Rachel nods.

"Who wants popcorn?" Melinda says. Rachel sticks her tongue out at Peter. He just stands there, with the knife in his head.

"Hey, aren't you guys hungry?" Melinda calls from the kitchen.

Peter runs, screaming, past Rachel. She walks in the other direction, to Peter's room. She knows where he keeps his collection, in his bottom drawer. Peter hasn't said anything about it, maybe he hasn't noticed, but Rachel has been stealing bones from him for some time now. Today she takes a handful. She doesn't have any pockets so she drops the bones into her Halloween treat bag from school. She is careful not to set the bag down. She is still carrying it when her father comes to get her.

They walk home together, through the crooked streets of Stone. The sky is turning gray. Ghosts and witches dangle from porches and crooked trees behind picket fences. Pumpkins grin blackly at her.

Rachel's father says that after dinner Melinda is coming over.

"She just wants to see what kind of witch I am," Rachel says.

Her father smiles, "Yes, I'm sure you're right. Also, I asked her if she could stay and pass out treats while I go with you. That way no one will play a trick on us."

"Melinda might," Rachel says, but her father just laughs, as if she were being funny.

When they get home, Rachel goes into her bedroom while her father makes dinner. He's making macaroni and cheese, her favorite, though tonight, the thought of it makes her strangely queasy. Rachel begins to gather the bones from all the various hiding places, the box under her bed, the sock drawer. She puts them in a pillowcase. When her father calls her for dinner, she shoves the pillowcase under her bed.

In the kitchen, a man stands next to the stove with a knife in his head. Rachel screams, and her father tears off the mask. He tells her he's sorry. "See," he lifts the mask up by the knife. "It's just something I bought at the drugstore. I thought it would be funny."

Rachel tries to eat but she doesn't have much of an appetite. She picks at the yellow noodles until the doorbell rings. Her father answers it and comes back with Melinda who smiles and says, "How's the little witch?"

"Not dead," Rachel answers.

Rachel's father looks at her as if she has a knife in her head.

They go from house to house begging for candy. The witches of Stone drop M&M's, peanut butter cups, and popcorn balls into Rachel's plastic pumpkin. Once, a ghost answers the door, and once, when she reaches into a bowl for a small Hershey's bar, a green hand pops up through the candy and tries to grab her. Little monsters, giant spiders, made-up witches, and bats weave gaily around Rachel and her father. The pumpkins, lit from within, grin at her. Rachel thinks of Wilmot Redd standing on Old Burial Hill watching all of them, waiting for her to bring the bones.

But when Rachel gets home, the bones are gone. The pillowcase, filled with most of her collection and shoved under her bed, is missing. Rachel runs into the living room, just in time to see Melinda leaving with a white bundle under her arm. Rachel stands there, in her fake witch costume and thinks, *I wish you were dead.* She has a lot of trouble getting to sleep that night. She cries and cries and her father asks her over and over again if it's because of her mother. Rachel doesn't tell him about the bones. She doesn't know why. She just doesn't.

Two days later, Melinda is killed in a car accident. Rachel's father wipes tears from his eyes when he tells her. Mrs. Williamson cries when she thinks Peter and Rachel aren't watching. But Peter and Rachel don't cry.

"She stole my bones," Rachel says.

"Mine too," says Peter. "She stole a bunch of them."

Melinda's school picture is on the front page of the newspaper, beside a photograph of the fiery wreck.

"That's what she gets," Rachel says, "for stealing."

Peter frowns at Rachel.

"Wanna trade?" she asks.

He nods. Rachel trades a marshmallow pumpkin for a small bone shaped like a toe.

That night, after her father kisses her on the forehead and turns off the light, she takes her small collection of bones and tries to make them dance, but the shape is all wrong. It just lies there and doesn't do anything at all.

The day of Melinda's funeral, Rachel's father doesn't go to work. He's a lawyer in Boston and it isn't easy, the way it is for some parents, to stay home on a workday, but he does. He picks Rachel up at school just after lunch.

The funeral is in a church in the new section of Stone, far from the harbor and Old Burial Hill. On the way there, they pass a group of people carrying signs.

"Close your eyes," her father says.

Rachel closes her eyes. "What are they doing?"

"They're protesting. They're against abortion."

"What's abortion?"

"Okay, you can open them. Abortion is when a woman is pregnant and decides she doesn't want to be pregnant."

"You mean like magic?"

"No, it's not magic. She has a procedure. The procedure is called having an abortion. When that's over, she's not pregnant anymore."

Rachel looks out the car window at the pumpkins with collapsed faces, the falling ghosts, a giant spiderweb dangling in a tree. "Dad?"

"Mmhm?"

"Can we move back to Boston?"

Her father glances down at her. "Don't you feel safer here? And you already have so many friends. Mrs. Williamson says you and Peter get along great. And there's your friend, Jack. Maybe we can have him over some Saturday."

"Melinda said there are a lot of witches in Stone."

Her father whistles, one long low sound. "Well, she was probably just trying to be funny. Here we are." They are parked next to a church. "This is where Melinda's funeral is."

"Okay," says Rachel but neither of them move to get out of the car.

"Let's say a prayer for Melinda," her father says.

"Here?"

He closes his eyes and bows his head while Rachel watches a group of teenage girls in cheerleading uniforms hugging on the church steps.

"Now, do you wanna get ice cream?"

Rachel can't believe she's heard right. She knows about funerals and they don't have anything to do with ice cream, but she nods, and he turns the car around, right in the middle of the street, just as the church bells ring. Rachel's father drives all the way back to the old section of Stone, where they stop for ice cream. Rachel has peppermint stick and her father has vanilla. They walk on the sidewalk next to the water and watch the seagulls. Rachel tries not to think about Wilmot Redd who stands on Old Burial Hill, waiting.

Her father looks at his watch. "We have to get going," he says. "It's almost time for Peter to get off the bus."

"Peter?"

"His mother has to go to the doctor's. I told her he could come to our house."

Rachel's father goes out to meet Peter when he gets off the bus and they walk in together, talking about the Red Sox. They walk right past Rachel. "Dad?" she says but he doesn't answer. She follows them into the kitchen. Her father is spreading cream cheese on a bagel for Peter. Later, when she is playing in her bedroom with him, Rachel says, "I wish your mom had an abortion," which makes Peter cry. When her father comes into the room he makes her tell him what she did and she tells him she didn't do anything but Peter tells on her and her father says she is grounded.

*

Miss Engstrom tells them that they are very lucky to live in Stone, so near to Danvers and Salem and the history of witches. Rachel says that she knows there are a lot of witches in Stone and Miss Engstrom laughs and then all the children laugh too. Later, on the playground, Stella Miner and Leanne Green hold hands and stick out their tongues at Rachel, and Minnity Dover throws pebbles at her. Miss Engstrom catches Minnity and makes her sit on the bench for the rest of recess. Rachel swings so high that she can imagine she is flying. When the bell rings, she comes back to Earth where Bret and Steve Keeter, the twins, and Peter Williamson wait for her. "We wish your mom had an abortion," Peter says. The twins nod their golden heads.

"You don't even know what that means," says Rachel, and runs past them, toward Miss Engstrom who stands beside the open door, frowning.

"Rachel," she says, "You're late." But she doesn't say anything to the boys, who come in behind Rachel, whispering.

"Shut up!" Rachel shouts.

Miss Engstrom sends Rachel to the office. The principal says he is going to call her father. Rachel sits in the office until it's almost time to go home, and then she goes back to the classroom for her books and lunchbox.

"Wanna know what we did while you were gone?" Clara Vanmeer whispers when they line up for the bus.

Rachel ignores her. She knows what they did. They are witches, all of them, and they put some kind of spell on her. *I wish you were all dead*, Rachel thinks, and she really means it. It worked with Melinda, didn't it? But not her mom. She never wished her mom would die. Never never never. Who did? Who wished that for her mother who used to call her Rae-Rae and made chocolate chip pancakes and was beautiful? Rachel hugs her backpack and stares out the window at the witches of Stone, picking their kids up from school. The bus drives past rotten pumpkins and fallen graveyards. Rachel's head hurts. She hopes Mrs. Williamson will let her take a nap but when they get there, the house is locked. Peter rings the doorbell five hundred times, and pulls on the door but Rachel just sits on the step. Nobody is home, why can't he just get that through his head? Finally, Peter starts to cry. "Shut up," Rachel says. She has to say it twice before he does.

"Where's my mother?" Peter asks, wiping his nose with the sleeve of his jacket.

"How should I know?" Rachel watches a small black cat with a tiny silver bell around its neck emerge from the bush at the neighbor's house. Unfortunately, it is not carrying a dead bird or mouse.

Peter starts crying again. Loudly. Rachel's head hurts. "Shut up!" she says, but he just keeps crying. She stands up and readjusts her backpack.

Rachel is already walking down the tiny sidewalk when Peter calls for her to wait. They walk to Rachel's house, but of course that is locked as well. Peter starts crying again. Rachel takes off the backpack and sets it on the step. The afternoon sun is low, the sky gray and fuzzy like a sweater. Her head hurts and she's hungry. Also, Peter is really annoying her. "I want my mother," he says.

"Well, I want my mother too," Rachel says. "But that doesn't help. She's dead, okay? She's dead."

"My mom's dead?" Peter screams, so loud that Rachel has to cover her ears with her hands. That's when Mrs. Williamson comes running up the sidewalk. Peter doesn't even see her at first because he's so hysterical. Mrs. Williamson runs to Peter. She sits down beside him, says his name, and touches him on the shoulder. He looks up and shouts, "Mom!" He wraps his arms around her, saying over and over again, "You're not dead." Rachel resists the temptation to look down the sidewalk to see if her own mother is coming. She knows she is not.

They walk back to the Williamsons' house together. Rachel, trying not to drag her backpack, follows. "I'm sorry," she hears Mrs. Williamson say. "I had a doctor's appointment and I got caught in traffic. I tried to call the school, but I was too late, and then I tried to find someone to come to the house, but no one was home."

Peter says something to Mrs. Williamson. She can't hear him and she leans over so he can whisper in her ear. Rachel stands behind them, watching. Mrs. Williamson turns and stares at Rachel. "Did you tell him I was dead?" she asks.

Rachel shakes her head no, but she can tell Mrs. Williamson doesn't believe her.

"When the Pilgrims came to America they wanted to live in a place where they could practice their religion. They were trying to be good people. So when they saw someone doing something they thought was bad, they wanted to stop it. Bad meant the devil to them. They didn't want to be around the devil. They wanted to be around God." Miss Engstrom stands at the front of the room dressed as a Puritan. She puts the Puritan dress on every day for Social Studies. Her cheeks are pink and her hair is sticking to her face. She is trying to help them understand what happened, she says, but Cindi Becker has said, more than once, that her mom doesn't want Miss Engstrom teaching them religion. "It's not religion," Miss Engstrom says, "it's History."

Every day Miss Engstrom puts on the Pilgrim dress and pretends she's a Puritan. The children are supposed to pretend they are witches. "Act natural," she tells them. "Just be yourselves." But when they do, they get in trouble; they have to stand in the stockade or go to the jail in the back of the room. The stockade is made out of cardboard, and the jail is just chairs in a circle. Rachel hates to be put in either place. By the fourth lesson, she has figured out how to sit at her desk with her hands neatly folded. When Miss Engstrom asks Rachel what she is doing, she says, "Praying," and Miss Engstrom tells her what a good Puritan she is. By the sixth lesson the class is filled with good Puritans, sitting with neatly folded hands. Only Charlie Dexter is stuck in the stockade and Cindi Becker is in the jail in the back of the room. Miss Engstrom says that they are probably witches. Rachel decides that Social Studies is her favorite subject. She looks forward to the next lesson. What will happen to the witches when they go on trial? But the next day they have a substitute and the day after that, another. They have so many substitutes Rachel can't remember their names. One day, one of the substitutes tells the class that she is their new teacher.

"What happened to Miss Engstrom?" Rachel asks.

"My mother had her fired," says Cindi Becker.

"She's not coming back," the teacher says. "Now, let's talk about Thanksgiving."

Rachel is so excited about Thanksgiving she can't stand it. A whole turkey! Think of the bones! Each night Rachel rearranges her bone collection. It is a difficult time of year for it. Cats still wander the crooked streets of Stone but they are either eating everything they kill, or killing less, because there are few bones to be found. Rachel arranges and rearranges, trying to form the shape that will dance for her. Damn that Melinda, Rachel thinks. What would happen if Rachel had bones like that in her collection? Human bones?

Rachel has a fit when her father tells her they are going to the Williamsons' house for Thanksgiving. "This will be better," he says. "You can play with Peter and his cousins. Don't you think it would be lonely with just you and me at our house?"

"The bones!" Rachel cries. "I want the bones!"

"What are you talking about?" her father asks.

Rachel sniffs. "I want the turkey bones."

Rachel's father stares at her. He is cutting an apple and he stands, holding the knife, staring at her.

"You know, for my project."

"Are you still doing that, now that Miss Engstrom is gone?"

Rachel nods. Her father says, "Well, we can make a turkey. But not on Thursday. On Thursday we're going to the Williamsons'."

The night before Thanksgiving though, her father gets a phone call. He says, "Oh, I am so sorry." And, "No, no please don't even worry about us." He nods his head a lot. "Please know you are in our prayers. Let us know if we can do anything." After he hangs up the phone he sits in his chair and stares at the TV screen. Finally, he says, "It looks like you got your wish."

He looks at his watch, and then, all in a hurry, they drive to the grocery store, where he buys a turkey, bags of stuffing, and pumpkin pie. He throws the food into the cart. Rachel can tell that he is angry but she doesn't ask him what's wrong. She'd rather not know. Besides, she has other stuff to worry about. Like is there a bad man in this store? Will he shoot them the way he shot her mother?

When they get home her father says, "Mrs. Williamson lost the baby."

"What baby?" Rachel asks.

"She was pregnant. But she lost it."

Rachel remembers, once, when Mrs. Williamson got angry at Peter when he came home from school without his sweater. "You can't be so careless all the time," Rachel remembers her saying.

"Well, she shouldn't be so careless," Rachel says.

"Rachel, you have to start learning to think about other people's feelings once in a while."

Rachel thinks about the lost baby, out in the dark somewhere. "Mrs. Williamson is stupid," she says.

Rachel's father, holding a can of cranberry sauce with one hand, points toward her room with the other. "You go to your room," he says. "And think about what you're saying."

Rachel runs to her room. She slams the door shut. She throws herself on her bed and cries herself to sleep. When she wakes up there is no light shining under the door. She doesn't know what time it is, but she thinks it is very late. She gets up and begins collecting bones from all the hiding places; bones in her socks, bones in her underwear drawer, bones in a box under the bed, bones in her jewelry box, and bones in her stuffed animals, cut open with the scissors she's not supposed to use. She hums as she assembles and reassembles the bones until at last they quiver and shake. She thinks they are going to dance for her but instead, they stab her with their sharp little points.

"Stop it," Rachel says. She takes them apart again, stores them in separate places and goes to sleep, crying for her mother.

The next morning, Rachel watches the parade on TV while her father makes stuffing and cleans the turkey. When the phone rings, he brings it to Rachel, and turns the TV sound off. The Grandma asks her how school is going and how she likes living in Stone, and finally, how is she? Rachel answers each question, "Fine," while watching a silent band march across the TV. The Grandma asks to speak to her father again and Rachel goes to the kitchen. Her father reaches for the phone and says, "My God, Rachel, what happened to your arms?" Rachel looks down at her arms. There are small red spots and tiny bruises all over them.

"She has bruises all over her arms," her father says.

Rachel grabs a stick of celery and walks toward the living room. Her father follows, still holding the phone. "Rachel, what happened to your arms?"

Rachel turns and smiles at him. Ever since her mom died, her dad has been trying hard. Rachel knows this, and she knows that he doesn't know she knows this. But there are certain things he isn't very good at. Rachel is positive that if her mom were still alive, she wouldn't even have to ask what had happened, she'd know. Rachel feels sorry for her dad but she doesn't want to tell him about the bones. Look what happened when she barely even mentioned them to Melinda. So Rachel makes something up instead. "Miss Engstrom," she says.

"What are you talking about? Miss Engstrom? She isn't even your teacher anymore."

Rachel only smiles, sweetly, at her father. He repeats what she told him, into the phone. Rachel walks into the living room. She wraps herself in the red throw and sits in front of the TV, watching the balloon man fill up the screen as she munches on celery. How many bones does it take, anyway? Miss Engstrom never did answer her question.

Later, when the doorbell rings, her father shouts, "I'll get it," which is sort of strange because she is never allowed to answer the door. She hears voices and then her father comes into the room with a policeman and a policewoman. Rachel thinks they've come to arrest her. She's a liar, a thief, and a murderer, so it had to happen. Still, she feels like crying now that it has.

Her father has been talking to her, she realizes, but she has no idea what he's said. He turns the sound off the TV and he and the policeman walk out of the room together. The policewoman stays with Rachel. She sits right next to Rachel on the couch. For a while they watch the silent parade, until the policewoman says, "Can you tell me what happened to your arms, Rachel?"

"I already told my dad," Rachel says.

The policewoman nods. "The thing is, I just want to make sure he didn't leave anything out."

"I don't want to get in trouble."

"You're not in trouble. We are here to help. Okay, honey? Can I see your arms?"

Rachel shakes her head, no.

The policewoman nods. "Who hurt you, Rachel?"

Rachel turns to look at her. She has blonde hair and brown eyes with yellow flecks in them. She looks at Rachel very closely. As if she knows the truth about her.

"You can tell me," she says.

"The bones," Rachel whispers.

"What about the bones?"

"But you can't tell anyone."

"I might have to tell someone," the policewoman says.

So Rachel refuses to speak further. She shows the lady her arms, but only because she figures it will make her go away, and it does. After she looks at Rachel's arms the policewoman goes out in the kitchen with her dad and the policeman. Rachel turns up the volume. Jessica Simpson, dressed in white fur, like a kitten without the whiskers, is singing. Her voice fills up the room, but Rachel can still hear the murmuring sound of the grownups talking in the kitchen. Then the door opens and closes and she hears her father saying good-bye. Rachel's father comes and stands in the room, watching her. He doesn't say anything and Rachel doesn't either but later, when they are eating turkey together he says, "You might still be just a little girl but you can get grownups in a lot of trouble by telling lies."

Rachel nods. She knows this. Miss Engstrom taught them all about the history of witches. Rachel chews the turkey leg clean. It was huge and she is quite full, but now she has a turkey leg, almost as big as a human bone, to add to her collection. She sets it on her napkin next to her plate. As if he can read her mind her father says, "Rachel, no more bones."

"What?"

"Your bone collection. It's done. Over. Find something else to collect. Seashells. Buttons. Barbie dolls. No more bones."

Rachel knows better than to argue. Instead, she asks to be excused. Her father doesn't even look at her; he just nods. Rachel goes to her bedroom and searches through the mess of clothes in the wicker chair until she finds her Halloween costume. When her father comes to tell her it's time for bed, he says, "You can wear that one last time but then we're putting it away until next year."

"Can I sleep in it?" Rachel asks.

Her father shrugs. "Sure, why not?" He smiles, but it is a pretend smile. Rachel smiles a pretend smile back. She crawls into bed, dressed like a pretend witch. Her father kisses her on the forehead and turns out the light. Rachel lies there until she counts to a hundred and then she sits up. She gathers the bones, whispering in the dark.

A few days later, the witch costume has been packed away, the first dusting of snow has sprinkled the crooked streets and picket fences of Stone, and Rachel has forgotten all about how angry she was at her father. Since Mrs. Williamson lost the baby, she no longer watches Rachel. Rachel thinks this is a good idea because she doesn't feel safe with Mrs. Williamson, but she hates being in school all day. All the other children have been picked up from the after school program and it's just Rachel and Miss Carrie who keep looking out the school window, saying, "Boy, your dad sure is late."

Rachel sits at the play table, making a design with the purple, blue, green, and yellow plastic shapes. She is good at putting things together and Miss Carrie compliments her work. Rachel remembers putting the spell on her father and she regrets it. She pretends the shapes are bones, she puts them together and then she takes them apart, she whispers, trying to say the words backward, but it is hard to do and Miss Carrie, who isn't a real grownup at all, but a high school girl like Melinda, says, "Uh, you're starting to creep me out."

Miss Carrie calls her mother, using the purple cell phone she carries in the special cell phone pocket of her jeans. "I don't know what to do," she says. "Rachel is still here. Her dad is really late. Hey, Rache, what's your last name again?" Rachel tells Carrie and Carrie tells her mom. Just then, Mrs. Williamson arrives. She is wearing a raincoat, even though it isn't raining, and her hair is a mess. She tells Carrie that she is taking Rachel home. Rachel doesn't want to go with Mrs. Williamson, the baby loser, but Carrie says, "Oh, great," to Mrs. Williamson and then says into the phone, "Never mind, someone finally came to pick her up." She is still talking to her mother when Rachel leaves with Mrs. Williamson who doesn't say anything until they are in the car.

"Peter told me what you said, Rachel, about how I should have had an abortion, and I want you to know, that sort of talk is not allowed in our house. I really don't even want you playing with Peter anymore. Not one word about abortion or dead mothers or anything else you have up your sleeve, do you understand?"

Rachel nods. She is looking out the window at a house decorated with tiny white icicle lights hanging over the windows. "Where's my dad?" she asks.

Mrs. Williamson sighs, "He's been delayed."

Rachel is afraid to ask what that means. When they get to the Williamsons' house, Mrs. Williamson pretends to be nice. She asks Rachel if her book bag is too heavy and offers to carry it. Rachel shakes her head. She is afraid to say anything for fear that it will be the wrong thing. There is a big wreath on the back door of the Williamsons' house and it has a bell on it that rings when they go inside. Mr. Williamson and Peter are eating at the kitchen table. The house is deliciously warm but it smells strange.

Mrs. Williamson takes off her raincoat and hangs it from a peg in the wall. Rachel drops her book bag below the coats, and stands there until Mrs. Williamson tells her to hang up her coat and sit at the table.

When Rachel sits down Mr. Williamson points a chicken leg at her and says, "Now listen here, young lady – " but Mrs. Williamson interrupts him.

"I already talked to her," she says.

Rachel is mashing her peas into her potatoes when her father arrives. He thanks Mr. and Mrs. Williamson and he says, "How you doing?" to Peter though Peter doesn't answer. Mrs. Williamson invites him to stay for dinner but he says thank you, he can't. Rachel leaves her plate on the table and no one tells her to clear it. She puts on her coat. Her father picks up her backpack. He thanks the Williamsons again and then taps Rachel's shoulder. Hard.

"Thank you," Rachel says.

They walk out to the car together, their shoes squeaking on the snow. The Williamsons' house is decorated with white lights; the neighbors have colored lights and two big plastic snowmen with frozen grins and strange eyes on their front porch.

"What did you say to that policewoman?" Rachel's father asks.

He isn't looking at Rachel. He is staring out the window, the way he does when he is driving in Boston.

"Miss Engstrom didn't do it," she says.

"They seem to think I hurt you, do you understand – " He doesn't finish what he is saying. He pulls into their driveway, but instead of getting out of the car to open the garage door, he sits there. "Just tell the truth, Rachel, okay? Just tell the truth. You know what that is, don't you?"

"I did," Rachel says. She feels like crying and also, she thinks she might throw up.

"Who did that to you, then? Who did that to your arms?"

"The bones."

"The bones?"

Rachel nods.

"What bones?"

"You know."

Her father makes a strange noise. He is bent over, and his eyes are shut. Praying, Rachel thinks. The car is still running. Rachel looks out the window. She cranes her neck so she can see the Sheekles' yard. They have it decorated with six reindeer made out of white lights. The car door slams. Rachel watches her father open the garage door. She watches him walk back to the car, lit by the headlights, his neck bent as if he is looking for something very important that he has lost.

"Dad?" Rachel says when he gets back in the car. "Are you mad?"

He shakes his head. He eases the car into the garage, turns off the ignition. They walk to the house together. When they get inside, he says, "Okay, I want all of them."

"All of what?" Rachel says, though she thinks she knows.

"That bone collection of yours. I want it."

"No, Dad."

He shakes his head. He stands there in his best winter coat, his gloves still on, shaking his head. "Rachel, why would you want to keep them, if they are hurting you?"

It's a good question. Rachel has to think for a moment before she answers. "Not all the time," she says. "Mostly they don't. They used to be my friend."

"The bones?"

Rachel nods.

"The bones used to be your friend?"

"Jack," she says.

He doesn't look at her. He is angry! He lied when he said he wasn't.

"Rachel," he says, softly, "honey? Let's get the bones. Okay? Let's put them away...where they can't...bones aren't...Jesus Christ." He slams his fist on the kitchen table. Rachel jumps. He covers his face with his hands. "Jesus Christ, Marla," he says.

Marla is Rachel's mother's name.

Rachel isn't sure what to do. She takes off her hat and coat. Then she walks into her bedroom and begins gathering the bones. After a while she realizes her father is standing in the doorway, watching.

Rachel hands her father all the bones. "Be careful," she says." They killed Melinda." He doesn't say anything. That night he forgets to tell Rachel when to go to sleep. She changes into her pajamas, crawls into bed, and waits but he forgets to kiss her. He sits in the living room, making phone calls. The words drift into Rachel's room, "bones, mother murdered, lies, problems in school." Rachel thinks about Christmas. What will she get this year? Will she get a new Barbie? Will she get anything? Or has she been a bad girl? Will someone kill her father? Will Mrs. Williamson come to take care of her, and then lose her the way she lost the baby? Will Santa Claus save her? Will God? Will anyone? Will they get white lights for their tree or colored? Every year they switch but Rachel can't remember what they had last year. Rachel hopes it's a colored light year, because she likes the colored lights best. The last thing she hears before she falls asleep is her father's distant voice. "Bones," he says. "Yes that's right, bones."

The next morning, Rachel's father tells her she isn't going to school. She's going with him to Boston. "I made an appointment for you, okay, honey? I think you need a woman to talk to. So I made an appointment with Dr. Trentwerth."

Rachel is happy not to go to school with the nasty children of Stone. She is happy not to have to sit in the classroom and listen to Mrs. Fizzure who never dresses like a Puritan and doesn't put anyone in the stockade or jail. Rachel is happy to go to Boston. They listen to Christmas music the whole way there. Rachel's appointment isn't until ten o'clock, so she has to sit in her dad's office and be very quiet while he does his work. He gives her paper and pens and she draws pictures of Christmas trees and ghosts while she waits. When it's time to go to her appointment, her father looks at her pictures and says, "These are very nice, Rachel." Rachel actually thinks they are sort of scary though she didn't draw the ghosts the way a kindergartner would, all squiggly lines and black spot eyes. She made them the way they really are, a lady smiling next to a Christmas tree, a baby asleep on a floor, a cat grinning.

Dr. Trentwerth has a long gray braid that snakes down the side of her neck. She's wearing an orange sweater and black pants. Her earrings are triangles of tiny gold bells. She says hello to Rachel's father but she doesn't shake his hand. She shakes Rachel's hand, as if she might be someone important. They leave her father sitting on the couch looking at a magazine.

Rachel is disappointed by the doctor's office. There are little kid toys everywhere. A stuffed giraffe, a dollhouse, blocks, trucks, and baby dolls with pink baby bottles. Rachel doesn't know what she's supposed to do. "Be polite," she remembers her father telling her.

"You have a nice room," Rachel says.

"Would you like some tea?" the doctor asks. "Or hot cocoa?"

Rachel walks past all the baby toys and sits in the chair by the window. "Cocoa please," she says.

Dr. Trentwerth turns the electric teakettle on. "Your father tells me you've been having some trouble with your bone collection," she says.

"He doesn't believe me."

"He said the bones hurt you."

Rachel nods. Shrugs. "But not all the time. Like I said. Just once."

The doctor tears open a packet of hot cocoa, which she empties into a plain white mug. She pours the water into it. "Let's just let that sit for a while," she says. "It's very hot. Whose bones hurt you, Rachel?"

Rachel sighs. "Cat bones, mice bones, chicken bones, you know."

Dr. Trentwerth nods. "Your father says you moved to Stone after your mother died. What was that like?"

"We were both really sad, me and Dad. Everyone was. We got a lot of flowers."

Dr. Trentwerth hands the mug to Rachel. "Careful, it's still hot."

Dr. Trentwerth is right. It is hot. Rachel brings it toward her mouth but it is too hot. She sets it, carefully, on the table next to the chair.

"Tell me about where you live," the doctor says as she sits down across from Rachel.

"Well, everyone is a witch," Rachel says. "Okay, not everyone, but almost everyone and one time, a long time ago, there was a woman there named Wilmot Redd and some people came and took her away 'cause they said all witches had to die. They hung her and no one did anything about it. Miss Engstrom, she was my teacher, got taken away too, and Melinda, my babysitter, died, but that's because she stole the bones and now my father has them and I don't want him to die but he probably will. Mrs. Williamson is this lady who sometimes takes care of me and she looks real nice but she loses babies and she lost one and no one even is looking for it. If my mom was still alive she would rescue me."

"And the bones?"

"They used to keep me company at night."

"Where would you be when the bones kept you company, Rachel?"

"In my room."

"In your bedroom?

"Mmhm."

"I see."

"But then they stopped being nice and started hurting me."

"Whose bones, Rachel?"

"My dad has them now."

"Where did your dad's bones hurt you?"

"They were still mine then."

"Where did the bones hurt you, Rachel?"

"On my body."

"Where on your body?"

Suddenly, Rachel has a bad feeling. How does she know Dr. Trentwerth isn't one of them too? Rachel reaches for her mug and sips the hot cocoa. Dr. Trentwerth sits there, watching.

The moon is not a bone. Rachel knows this, but when the moon stares down at her, like an eye socket, Rachel wonders if she is just a small insect rattling around inside a giant skull. She knows this isn't true. She's not a baby, after all. She knows this isn't how reality works, but she can't help herself. Sometimes she imagines flying up to the moon, and climbing right through that hole to find everyone she's ever lost on the other side. She doesn't care about Melinda but she cares a lot about her mom and dad.

Rachel no longer lives in Stone and she no longer lives with her father. A lady and two policemen came to school one day and took Rachel away. She was cutting paper snowflakes at the time, and little bits of paper fluttered from her clothes as they walked to the car. Now Rachel lives with the Freemans. Big plastic candy canes line the walk up to the Freemans' front porch, which is decorated with blinking colored lights. A wreath with tiny gift-wrapped packages glued to it hangs on the front door. (But there are no gifts inside, Rachel checked.) The house smells sweet with the scent of holiday candles. Mrs. Freeman tells Rachel to be careful around the candles and not to bother Mr. Freeman when he is watching TV, which is most of the time.

Rachel's bedroom is in the back of the house. It has green itchy carpet and two twin beds and a dresser that is mostly blue, with some patches of yellow and lime green, as though someone started to paint it and then gave up on the project. The curtains on Rachel's window are faded tiny blue flowers with yellow centers and they are Rachel's favorite things in the room. Lying in her bed, Rachel can look out the window at the moon and imagine crawling right out of her world into a better one.

On the first night, Mrs. Freeman came into the bedroom and held Rachel while she cried and told her things would get better. In the morning, Mr. Freeman drove Rachel to school. He walked with a limp and he burped a lot, but before he left her in the school office he told her she was a brave girl and everything was going to be better soon.

"The Freemans are nice," the lady who took Rachel away from Stone told her. "Mrs. Freeman was once in the same situation you are in. She understands just what you're going through. And Mr. Freeman is a retired police officer. He got shot a few years ago. You're lucky to go there."

But Rachel didn't feel like a lucky girl, even when the Freemans took her to the Christmas tree lot and let her choose their tree, or when Mrs. Freeman put lotion on Rachel's chapped hands, or when they took her to an attorney's office, a very important woman who acted as if everything Rachel said mattered.

Rachel doesn't feel lucky until the day Mr. Freeman says, "Rachel, the lawyers think you should go back and live with your father." Mrs. Freeman cries and says, "Tomorrow's Christmas Eve, how can they do this?" But Rachel is so happy she almost pees in her pants. When the lady comes to pick Rachel up, Mrs. Freeman says, "I have half a mind not to let you take her." But Mr. Freeman says, "Rachel, get your suitcase." Mrs. Freeman hugs Rachel so tightly that for a second she is afraid she really isn't going to let her go, but then she does. The lady who waits for Rachel says, "This isn't my fault. This is hard for all of us." "It's hardest for her," Mrs. Freeman says and after that, Rachel doesn't hear the rest. Down the street the Mauley kids are building a snowman. "I hate you, George Mauley," Rachel screams at the top of her lungs. "What did you do that for?" the lady asks. "Get in the car." But Rachel has no idea why she did it. As they drive past the Mauley children, Rachel turns her face toward the window, so her back is to the lady. She sticks her tongue out at George Mauley but he is busy putting stones in the snowman's eyes and doesn't notice. "I want you to know, you are not alone," the woman says. "Maybe things didn't work out this time, but we are watching. You just keep telling the truth, Rachel, and I promise you things will get better."

It starts snowing. Not a lot, just tiny flakes fluttering down the white sky. Rachel remembers the snowflake she had been cutting when the lady took her away from Stone. What happened to her snowflake?

"Here we are then," the lady says. "Don't forget your suitcase." They walk into a big restaurant with orange booths along the wall and tiny Christmas trees on the tables. The waitresses wear brown dresses with white aprons and little half-circle hats that look like miniature spaceships crashed into all their heads. A woman is standing in one of the booths, waving and calling Rachel's name. The lady walks toward her. Rachel follows.

The woman wraps her arms around Rachel. She smells like soap. When she lets go of Rachel, she doesn't stand up but stays at Rachel's level, staring at her. Pink lipstick is smeared above her lips so she looks a little bit like she has three lips. Her eyebrows are drawn high on her forehead, beneath curls that are a strange shade of pink and orange, and she wears poinsettia earrings. "You remember me, don't you, honey?" she says. Then she looks up at the lady and frowns. "You can go now." She pulls Rachel close; together they pivot away from the lady. "Here, let me take that." She leans over and takes Rachel's suitcase. Rachel looks over her shoulder at the lady who is already walking away. "You don't remember me, do you? It's me. Grandma."

"Where's Dad?"

The Grandma sighs. "Are you hungry?" She guides Rachel into the booth and then slides in across from her. "This has all been expensive, you know. The lawyers and everything. He's at work. But he'll be home by the time we get there. Do you want a hamburger? A chocolate shake? What did you say to those people? Okay, I promised I wouldn't talk about it. Don't touch the little tree, Rachel, can't you just sit still for five minutes? It's just for looking."

Rachel's stomach feels funny. "Can I have an egg?"

"An egg? What kind of egg? Don't you want a hamburger?"

Rachel shakes her head. She starts to cry.

"Don't cry," the Grandma says. "It's over, all right? If you want an egg, you can have an egg. Were the people mean to you, Rachel? Did anyone hurt you?"

"Fried, please," Rachel says. "And can I have toast?"

"You can tell me, you know," the Grandma says. "Did anything happen to you while you were gone? Did anyone touch you in a bad way?"

Rachel is tired of the questions about bad touch. She is tired of grownups. Also she is cold. She just looks at the Grandma and after a while the Grandma says, "We decorated the tree last night. Your father hadn't even bought one yet. But don't worry; I set him straight about that. After everything you've been through! Well, he just wasn't thinking clearly. He's been through a lot too. Blue Spruce. It looks real nice."

The waitress comes and the Grandma orders a fried egg and toast for Rachel and the fish platter for herself. The waitress says, "Rachel?"

Miss Engstrom! Dressed as a waitress!

"Do you know each other?" the Grandma says.

"I used to be Rachel's teacher," Miss Engstrom says.

"In Boston?" asks the Grandma.

Miss Engstrom shakes her head, "No, in Stone. How are you, Rachel? Are you having a good holiday? Do you like your new teacher?"

"Wait, I know who you are. I know all about you."

"I wish you would come back," Rachel says.

"I forbid you to speak to my granddaughter, do you hear me? Where's the manager?"

Miss Engstrom's face does something strange, it sort of collapses, like an old jack-o'-lantern, but she shakes her head and everything goes back to normal. She smiles a fake smile at Rachel and walks away. The Grandma says, "She's the one who hurt you, isn't she? Where's that social worker when you need her? Why didn't you tell them about her, Rachel? Could you just tell me that?"

"Miss Engstrom never hurt me," Rachel says. "She was nice."

"Nice? She left bruises on your arms, Rachel."

Rachel sighs. She is sooo tired of stupid grownups and their stupid questions. "I told everyone," she says, "it wasn't her. It wasn't my dad, okay? It was the bones that did it."

"What bones? What are you talking about?"

But Rachel doesn't answer. She's learned a thing or two about answering adults' questions. Instead, she picks up the salt shaker and salts the table. The Grandmother grabs the shaker. "Just sit and wait for your egg," she says. "Maybe you could use this time to think about what you've done."

Rachel folds her hands neatly in front of her, just as she learned to do in Miss Engstrom's class. She is still sitting like that when Miss Engstrom returns with their order.

"You can eat now, Rachel," the Grandmother says. Rachel unfolds her hands and cuts her egg. The yellow yolk breaks open and smears across her plate. She can feel both Miss Engstrom and the Grandmother watching, but she pretends not to notice. The music is "Frosty the Snowman." Rachel eats her egg and hums along.

"Stop humming," says the Grandma, then, to Miss Engstrom, "You can go. We don't want anything else."

Miss Engstrom touches Rachel's head, softly. Rachel looks up at Miss Engstrom and sees that she is crying. Miss Engstrom nods at Rachel, one quick nod, as if they have agreed on something, then she sets the bill down on the table and walks away.

"Your father will be happy to see you," the Grandmother says. "Eat your egg. We've still got a long drive ahead of us."

★

Rachel's father does act happy to see her. He says, "I am so happy you are home," but he hugs her as if she is covered in mud and he doesn't want to get his clothes dirty.

The Christmas tree is already decorated. Rachel stares at it and the Grandma says, "Do you like it? We did it last night to surprise you." It is lit with tiny white lights, and oddly decorated with gold and white balls.

"Where are our ornaments?" Rachel asks.

"We decided to do something different this year," the Grandma says. "Don't you just love white and gold?"

Rachel doesn't know what to say. Clearly she is not expected to tell the truth. "Why don't you go unpack," the Grandma says, nodding at the suitcase. "Make yourself at home," she laughs.

Rachel is surprised, when she enters her bedroom, to discover that her bed is gone, replaced by two twin beds, just like at the Freemans'. One bed is covered with Rachel's old stuffed animals; they stare at her with their black eyes. She assumes this is her bed. Rachel inspects the animals and discovers that the ones she had cut open and stuffed with bones have been sewn shut, all except her white bear and he is missing. The other bed is covered with a pink lacy spread and several fat pillows. Next to it is a small table with a lamp, a glass of water, a few wadded tissues, and a stack of books.

"Surprise!" the Grandma says. "We're roomies now. Isn't this fun?"

Rachel nods. Apparently this is the right thing to do. The Grandma lifts the suitcase onto Rachel's bed. "Now, let's unpack your things and we can just forget about your little adventure and get on with our lives." The Grandma begins unpacking Rachel's suitcase, refolding the clothes before she puts them in the dresser. "Didn't anyone there help you with your clothes?" she says, frowning.

Rachel shrugs.

The Grandma closes the suitcase, clasps it shut, and puts it in the closet, right next to a set of plaid luggage. "Do you want a cookie? How about a gingerbread man? I've been baking up a storm, let me tell you."

Rachel follows the Grandma into the kitchen. Baking up a storm? she thinks. Maybe the Grandma is a witch; that would explain a lot. Her father is in the kitchen, talking on the phone, but when he sees her, he stops. He smiles at her, with the new smile of his, and then he says, "She just walked into the kitchen. Can I call you back?" The Grandma is talking at the same time, something about chocolate chip eyes. Rachel's father says, "I love you too," softly, into the phone but Rachel stares at him in shock. Is he talking to her mother? Rachel knows that doesn't make sense. She's not a baby, after all, but who is he talking to?

"Here," the Grandma says, "choose."

Rachel looks down into the cookie tin the Grandma has thrust before her. Gingerbread men lie there with chocolate chip eyes and wrinkled red mouths. ("Dried cranberry," the Grandma says.) Rachel chooses the one at the top and immediately begins eating his face. Her father sits across from her and shakes his head when the Grandma thrusts the tin toward him. "I missed you," he says.

The gingerbread man is spicy but the eyes and nose are sweet. Rachel doesn't care for the mouth but that part is gone fast enough.

"Your grandmother has been nice enough to come here to live with us."

The Grandmother sets a glass of milk down in front of Rachel. "Oh, I was ready for a change. Who needs Milwaukee?"

Rachel doesn't know what to say about any of it. She chews her gingerbread man and drinks her milk. Her father and the Grandma seem to have run out of ideas as well. They simply watch her eat. When she's finished, she yawns and the Grandmother says, "Time for bed."

Rachel looks at her father, expecting him to do something. Just because she yawned doesn't mean she's ready for bed! But her father isn't any help.

"Say good night," the Grandma says.

"Good night," says Rachel. She gets up, pushes the chair in, and rinses her glass. The Grandma follows her into the bedroom. She stays there the whole time Rachel is getting undressed. Rachel feels embarrassed but she doesn't know what else to do, so she pretends she doesn't mind the Grandma sitting on her bed talking about how much fun it's going to be to share the room. "Every night just like a slumber party," she says. After Rachel goes to the bathroom, brushes her teeth, and washes her face and hands, the Grandma tells her to kneel by her bed. The Grandma, complaining the whole time about how difficult it is, kneels down beside her.

"Lord," she says. "Please help Rachel understand right from wrong, reality from imagination, truth from lies and all that. Thank you for sending her home. Do you have anything to add? Rachel?"

Rachel can't think of anything to say. She shakes her head. The Grandma makes a lot of noise as she stands up again.

Rachel crawls into bed and the Grandma tucks the covers tight. So tight that Rachel feels like she can't breathe, then the Grandma kisses Rachel's forehead and turns out the light. Rachel waits, for a long time, for her father to come in to kiss her good night but he never does.

It is very dark when Rachel wakes up. The room is dark and there is no light shining under the door. It takes a moment for Rachel to realize why she's woken up. A soft rustling sound is coming from the closet.

"Grandma?" Rachel whispers, and then, louder, "Grandma?"

The Grandma wakes up, sputtering, "Marla? Is that you?"

"No. It's me, Rachel. Do you hear that noise?"

They listen for a while. It seems, to Rachel, a very long time and she is just starting to worry that the Grandma will think she is lying when the rustling starts again.

"We've got a mouse," the Grandma says. "Don't worry, I have a feeling Santa Claus might bring you a cat this year."

Very soon the Grandma is snoring in her bed. The rustling sound stops and then, just as Rachel is falling asleep, starts again. Rachel stares into the dark with burning eyes. It doesn't matter what the grownups do, she realizes, she's not safe anywhere.

Carefully, Rachel feels around in the dark for her bunny slippers. She picks up a shoe by mistake, and is startled by how large it is until she realizes it must belong to the Grandmother. She sets it down and picks up first one slipper, and then the other.

Her bunny slippers on, Rachel tiptoes out of the bedroom into the hallway, which is softly lit by the white glow of the Sheekles' Christmas-light reindeer. Rachel isn't sleepwalking, she is completely awake, but she feels strange, as though somehow she is both entirely awake and asleep at the same time. Rachel feels like she hears a voice calling from a great distance. But she isn't hearing it with her ears; it's more like a feeling inside, a feeling inside and outside of herself too. This doesn't make sense, Rachel knows, but this is what is happening. Maybe the grownups aren't right about anything, about what is real, or what is possible.

When she walks outside, the bitter cold hits Rachel hard. But she does not go back to her warm bed, instead she walks in the deadly dark of Stone, lit by occasional Christmas lights, and the few cars from which she hides, all the way to Old Burial Hill where the graves stand in the oddly blue snow, marking the dead who once lived there.

Rachel isn't afraid. She lies down. It is cold. Well, of course it is. She shivers, staring up at the stars, which, come to think of it, look like chips of bones. Maybe the skull she's been trapped in has been smashed open by some giant child who is, even now, searching through the pieces, hoping to find her. She closes her eyes.

"No, no. Not your bones. You've misunderstood everything."

Rachel opens her eyes. Standing before her is the old woman.

"Get up. Stamp your feet."

Rachel just lies there so the woman pulls her up.

"Are you a witch?" Rachel asks.

"Clap your hands and stamp your feet."

"Are you real?"

But the old woman is gone and Rachel's father is running toward her. "What are you doing here?" he says. "Rachel, what is happening to you?"

He wraps her tight in his arms and picks her up. One of her bunny slippers falls from her foot and lands softly on the snow-covered grave but he doesn't notice. He is running down the hill. Rachel, bouncing in his arms, watches the bunny slipper get smaller and smaller. She holds her father tight.

The Grandma is waiting for them in the kitchen where she is heating milk on the stove. She has on a flowered robe; her pinky-red hair, sparkling in the light, circles her face like a clown.

"She was in the graveyard," Rachel's father says.

The Grandma touches Rachel's bare arm with her own icy fingers. "Get a blanket. She's chilled to the bone."

Rachel's father sets her on the kitchen chair. He gently pries her fingers from around his neck. "I'll be right back," he says. "You have to let me go."

Rachel watches the doorway until he returns, carrying the white comforter from his bed. He wraps Rachel in it ("like a sausage," he used to say in happier times) then sits down with her on his lap.

Rachel's father kisses her head. She starts to feel warm. "Rachel," her father says, "never do that again. We'll visit your mother's grave in Boston more often, if that's what you want, but don't just leave in the middle of the night. Don't scare us like that."

Rachel nods. The Grandmother hands her a Santa-Claus-face mug of hot chocolate, and sets another on the table in front of Rachel's father.

Rachel sips her hot chocolate, gives the Grandma a close look.

"Good, isn't it?" the Grandma says.

Rachel nods.

"Milk. That's the secret ingredient. None of that watery stuff."

The Grandmother sets the tin of gingerbread men on the table and Rachel reaches for one, teetering on her father's lap. He hands her a gingerbread man and takes one for himself.

"Well, it's a good thing you didn't fall asleep out there," the Grandma says.

Rachel swallows the gingerbread foot. "I started to but someone woke me up. I think it was that witch, Wilmot Redd. She found me and she made me stand up. She told me she didn't want my bones."

Rachel's father and the Grandmother look at each other. Rachel stops chewing and stares straight ahead, waiting to see if her father will make her get off his lap or if the Grandma will call the lady to come and take her away again.

"Rachel, Wilmot Redd was just some old lady. A fisherman's wife," Rachel's father says, gently.

The Grandma sits down at the kitchen table. She looks at Rachel so hard that Rachel finally has to look back at her. The Grandma's face is extraordinarily white and Rachel thinks it looks just a little bit like a paper snowflake.

"I think I know who it might have been," she says. "Have you ever heard of La Befana? She's an old woman. Much older than me. And scary looking. Ugly. She carries around a big old sack filled with gifts that she gives to children. A long time ago the three wise men stopped by her house to get directions to Bethlehem, to see the Christ Child, you know. And after she gave them directions they invited her along but she didn't go with them 'cause she had too much housework to do. Of course she immediately regretted being so stupid and she's been trying to catch up ever since, so she goes around giving gifts to all the children just in case one of them is the Savior she neglected to visit, all those years ago, just 'cause she had dirty laundry to take care of. I bet that's who helped you tonight. Old La Befana herself." The Grandmother turns to look at Rachel's father. "It's about time this family had some luck, right? And what could be luckier than to be part of a real live Christmas miracle?"

Rachel's father hugs her and says, "Well, this little miracle better go to bed. Tomorrow is Christmas Eve, you don't want to sleep through it, do you?"

The Grandmother takes the mug of hot chocolate and the half-eaten gingerbread man from Rachel. Her father carries her to bed, tucks her in, and kisses her forehead. Rachel is falling asleep, listening to the faint murmuring voices of her father and the Grandmother, when she hears the noise. She goes to the closet, opens it, and sees right away, the Halloween treat bag in the corner, rustling as though the mouse is trapped inside. She is just about to shut the door when the small hand reaches out of the bag, grasps the paper edge, and another hand appears, and then, a tiny, bone head.

"Is that you?" Rachel whispers.

The bones don't answer. They just come walking toward her, their sharp points squeaking.

Rachel slams the closet door shut. She runs out of her room. The Grandma and her father are sitting next to the tree. When they turn to her, their faces are flicked with yellow, blue and green, they grin the wide skeletal grin of skulls. "Honey, is something the matter?" her father asks. Rachel shakes her head. "Are you sure? You look like you've seen – "

The Grandma interrupts, "Is it the mouse? Did you see the mouse?"

Rachel nods.

"Don't worry about it," the Grandma says, "Maybe Santa Claus will bring you a kitty this year."

Rachel refuses to go back to bed until her father and the Grandmother walk with her. They tuck her in, and again her father kisses her forehead, and the Grandma does the same, and then they leave her alone in the dark. After a while she hears the bones squeaking across the floor. Rachel feels around in the dark until she finds the Grandmother's big shoe. Rachel waits until she hears the squeaking start once more. When it does, she pounds where the sound comes from, and the first two times, she hits only the floor but the next five or six, she hears the breaking of bones, the small cries and curses. Her father and Grandmother run into the room and turn on the light. "Well, you killed it," the Grandma says, looking at her, strangely. "I'll go get the broom and dustpan."

Rachel's father doesn't say anything. They just stand there, looking at the mess on the floor, and then at the mess on the bottom of the Grandmother's shoe.

Later, after it's all cleaned up, Rachel crawls back into bed. She pulls the blankets to her chin, and rolls to her side. Her father and the Grandmother stand there for a while before they walk out of the room. For a long time Rachel listens in the dark but all she hears is her own breathing, and she falls asleep to the comforting sound.

When she wakes again it is Christmas Eve and snowing outside, glistening white flakes that tumble down the sky from the snow queen's garden, the Grandma says.

Because it is a special day the Grandma lets Rachel have gingerbread cookies and hot chocolate for breakfast on the couch while her father sleeps late. "He's worn out after everything you've been through," the Grandma says. Occasionally Rachel thinks she hears mewing from her father's room but the Grandma says, "Anyone can sound like a cat. It's probably just a sound he makes in his sleep. You, for instance, last night you were singing in your sleep."

"I was?" Rachel asks.

"Didn't anyone ever tell you that before? You sing in your sleep."

"I do?"

The Grandma nods. "You're a very strange little girl, you know," she says.

Rachel chews the gingerbread face and sighs.

"Now what do you suppose this is all about?"

The Grandma stands next to the Christmas tree, looking out the window. Rachel gets off the couch and squeezes between the Grandma and the tree. A gray cat meanders down the crooked sidewalk in front of the house. In its mouth it holds a limp mouse. Walking behind the cat is a straggling line of children in half-buttoned winter coats and loosely tied scarves, tiptoeing in boots and wet sneakers, not talking to each other or catching snowflakes on their tongues, only intently watching the cat with their bright eyes.

"Like the Pied Piper," the Grandma says.

Rachel shrugs and goes back to the couch. "It's just a bunch of the little kids," she says. "Who's the Pied Piper?"

The Grandma sighs. "Don't they teach you anything important these days?"

Rachel shakes her head.

"Well, it looks like I'll have to," the Grandma says.

And she does.

The Roaming Forest

Michael Moorcock

Michael Moorcock (*www.multiverse.org* and *www.eclipse.co.uk/sweetdespise/moorcock*) lives in Bastrop, Texas, though he has declared his intention to move to France. Once the firebrand editor of *New Worlds*, and the polemicist behind the British New Wave of the 1960s, and still one of the great living SF and fantasy writers, Moorcock is now known more for his avant-garde work, and his support of other writers pushing the boundaries of genre, than for his genre work. He is now a recognized literary figure in the UK, a significant contemporary writer. But his fantasy adventures in the cycle of the Eternal Champion are still the basis of his popularity in the USA. To most genre readers, Moorcock still means the creator of Elric.

One of Moorcock's key strengths is his ability to create setting, and he is well known for his "multiverse," and his settings have been used by a number of other writers. He is also highly attuned to mythic imagery being used in the here-and-now. In an interview with 3:AM, he discusses political uses of the language of the blood feud: "I've...quoted in 'Firing the Cathedral'...Cromwell's justification of the brutal massacres in Ireland 'spilling blood so that no more blood shall be spilled in future.' England was still paying the price of that logic, which also moved Cromwell's co-religionists into Irish territory as a matter of policy, the last I heard.... When Reagan began to use the language of the blood feud (Old Testament language if you prefer) in the 1980s, I predicted that this was setting the terms both domestically and abroad. Domestically the blood feud has become about the only law of the 'ghettoes,' and abroad it is being followed through Clinton's bombing of the Sudanese pharmaceutical plant (also the 'subject' of a Jerry Cornelius story, 'Cheering for the Rockets,' which is online at *Fantastic Metropolis*, *The Edge*, and maybe *Revolution SF*)."

"The Roaming Forest" was published in *Cross Plains Universe*, edited by Scott A. Cupp and Joe R. Lansdale, the Robert E. Howard memorial anthology released at the 2006 World Fantasy Convention in Austin, Texas. For those of you in the know, it is a story of Rackhir, the Red Archer, and his quest for Tana Lorn – and of a forest that feasts on blood. For readers not yet familiar with the Moorcock multiverse, it is an intense adventure tale bathed in fabulous imagery, of a hero and a beautiful woman, and their battle to escape the place and world that entraps them.

GREEN DEATH FOR THE RED ARCHER!!

The First Chapter
A Long Way From Phum

The night was a shrieking chaos of ragged clouds racing across a sky of bruised red, green and gold. All about the scarlet-clad rider the earth moved like the ocean, wind whipping grass and trees into a madman's dance. Bolts of lightning, slashing down from every point of the compass, made the man's horse snort and flatten its ears, white-eyed, nostrils flaring, as it bore its bowman master on at a killing gallop.

Some old terror buried within the archer warned him that this was no normal tempest. It was not the first he had ever encountered, whipped up by sorcery. He had not known such a storm on this island, but he knew it spoke of a powerful evil at play. He was anxious to ride out of it as swiftly as he could.

At last he mounted a hill. The sky was still in turmoil but, as the first fingers of dawn came creeping under the night, the main storm was now behind him, hanging above the valley where the dark mass of a forest somehow seemed to absorb the disturbance as he watched. The red-clad archer frowned. He could have sworn that the forest had been further away the last time he looked back.

On this island, the archer was known as Red Ronan. He had lived here for over a year. He wiped a mixture of water and sweat from his face and neck, throwing back his hood to catch the cool following breeze. The stallion, a big, healthy roan, was exhausted. His coat steaming, he bent to crop the lush grass. Ronan dismounted. Grey light spread through the beginning morning and the storm subsided, falling into the forest like smoke sucked through a window. Sunrise, and the sky became its normal pale cloudy canopy. In the distance, in the next valley, Ronan heard pipes and drums. He wondered if they were celebrating the end of the storm or hoping to drive something off. As he led his horse down a well-marked sheep-track he murmured the words of a tune which had become familiar to him since he had found himself living amongst these people.

They called him Ronan because his given name defeated their familiar tongue. They had misheard him when he first introduced himself and "Ronan" was what they thought he had said. In fact he was Rakhir in his own land of Phum. There he ranked high amongst the warrior-priests who served Phum's patriarch. "Ronan" resembled r'nan, his own people's word for archer. Though by training more warrior than priest he was, by disposition, more priest than warrior. A curiosity about the world and a quest for a mysterious city had brought him accidentally to this island nation where he originally understood no language and whose culture was alien to a well-educated man like himself, who felt he had read every existing account of the Young Kingdoms of the West.

He dressed in the scarlet jerkin and breeks of his caste, a covered quiver of arrows on his back, an unstrung bow slung over his shoulder, a long, light sword at his side. To the people of this island, he passed for what they called a "Templar'," though they were surprised he carried no cross insignia on his cloak. That cross was popular here. The mark of the chief god of their pantheon.

Ronan/Rakhir followed the music down into the valley, where a fast-flowing river ran, leading him into a grey stone village over whose roofs hung a haze of peat-smoke. He knew enough of their language and customs now to give his horse up to an ostler at the village inn and fling him one of the copper pieces he had earned here after his encounter with the seabear which attacked his boat off the coast of Lormyr. In the fight, the bear had virtually destroyed his little craft and all but killed him, giving him such a swipe with its massive flipper that he had lost consciousness, to awaken on a beach at the estuary of a river the locals called "Liffé."

He was beginning to suspect that since that encounter with the seabear he had slipped into some unearthly realm, though this island was otherwise as real as anything he had experienced before. If a little wet. It had scarcely stopped raining since he had awakened on a shingle beach to be met by a group of strangely dressed children. They had been friendly enough. They had led him to their village and fed him food, which though unpalatable was nourishing. Since then he had travelled on, finding work in the nearest large port. There some of the other soldiers had taken exception to his foreign ways and inability to understand them, forcing him to travel further and further afield, accepting whatever work he could, mostly as bodyguard, forever hoping to find a ship to take him off the island and on his way to seek a city he knew as Tana Lorn. He cursed himself for giving credence to the old Filkarian wine merchant who had advised him to travel by sea, rather than continue on his way by land.

Unhappily, the seabear had ripped away Ronan's purse, well-stocked with gold from his previous adventure in Oi Oi, City of the Pearl Kings. He kept a few pieces in the folds of his belt, but he wanted to preserve them as long as possible. The boat had been blown off course, into the path of the seabear and ultimately to the shore of Eerin, this island. Here, he had been surprised that no one had heard of Phum, let alone the city of Tana Lorn which he sought partly from curiosity and partly because he had heard he might find rest there. He had been told that gods dwelled in the city – gods willing to debate with mortals on the nature of the Seven Spheres, which, apart from the realm of Man, were those of Chaos, Law, Limbo, Dwarves, Giants and

Eternals. Only Phum's paramount god, Krim, existed in all those spheres. Throughout his conscious life Ronan had thought about these seven realms and had entered the priesthood, accepting the harsh training administered to all would-be adepts, in order to learn whatever there was to know, read whatever had been written. And, though they disagreed on many things, all agreed that it was Tana Lorn, where Law and Chaos were forever held in balance that guarded the secrets of the Seven Spheres. The great wise lords who ruled there would be able, he was sure, to impart the knowledge he desired.

For almost five years, since leaving Phum, Ronan/Rakhir had sought that city. He had been sure he was nearing it when he had taken bad advice and decided to shorten his journey by the sea route. Instead of growing closer to Tana Lorn, he was borne further away. Now, he was becoming convinced, was not even his own sphere, though it closely resembled it. Could there be *eight* realms of existence, as some in Phum believed? Or were there even more? And was this one of those? Or had he died in his own world, slain by the seabear? Was this some deceptively familiar version of Limbo?

While the people of Eerin Island were willing to drink at his expense, teach him their language and debate his ideas until much of his remaining gold was exhausted, he met no one who knew any more than did he. Now his silver, too, was running low. With the hasty departure for the mainland of his last merchant master, Ronan could find no further work for an itinerant archer. The priests of Eerin were already over-employed, so he had decided to retrace his journey, on a fresh-bought horse. He would see if he could hire a boat to take him back to the general area of ocean where he had first encountered the seabear.

But, in the last village where he had stopped, others had seen his money while he rested. He soon became aware of being followed by six or seven wolfsheads who clearly intended to enrich themselves at his expense. Thus, rather than shelter when the storm came up, he had ridden into its teeth, anxious to put distance between himself and the ruffians. He had enjoyed the satisfaction of seeing them pull back, over in the far valley as he had neared the dense, dark green wood. At the last moment he had instinctively skirted those old, heavy trees, feeling eyes upon him. Had it been his imagination, or had the trees themselves seemed to be watching? Only now he felt he could afford to rest a little.

Pushing open the heavy side door of the tavern, Ronan found himself in a familiar enough place, with rough-hewn benches and tables at which sat a handful of farmers who, for reasons best known to themselves, had armed themselves with swords and axes. When they saw him they became visibly relaxed and greeted him pleasantly enough. He ordered ale and meat in his strange, lilting accent. To their questions he gave them the answer he had learned satisfied them most readily.

"I'm from France," he explained, "lately in the service of the O'Dowd, who trades between here and there."

"And what brings ye to Ballycochub?" one red-faced cattleman wanted to know. "Since ye're the wrong side of the water for England and so too for France?"

"I was followed by robbers and sought to escape them. I'm lost and heading coastwards to find a boat."

"Ah, then ye'll want to head east," growled the landlord, putting down a mug of porter and a plate of coarse bread and half-raw meat before him. "But be careful, for English reavers plague the waters between here and that damned godless land. Ye'll serve yerself well if ye take a ship that travels with a fleet. What's more, there's the Roaming Forest to fear. Will ye be staying with us for the night, sir?"

Ronan shook his head, incurious about any fearsome forest. All country people feared dense trees, which their superstitions populated with every kind of imp and demon. He did not wish to spend a night at the inn because the more speed he made, the less chance there would be of any pursuing thieves catching him. "I'll rest for a few hours here," he said, "and give my horse time to recover himself, then I'll be riding on."

"This is not the best time of the year for that, sir." The landlord glanced at the other shifty-eyed customers. "Which is why we are all gathered here to wait until it's safe to travel again."

"What's the danger?" Narrowing his eyes, for he suspected them of wanting him to stay so that they could rob him in his sleep, he pulled on his ale-pot.

"Did ye pass by a forest on the way to our valley?" asked another of the farmers, his features troubled.

"I skirted it. I know outlaws prefer the deeps of a wood for their hiding places. I took the high road, but I passed near it. I think that's where I lost the would-be thieves pursuing me."

"Ah, well, that's as maybe, my master." The landlord gestured with his rag. "We call that forest Huntingwood."

"What do you hunt there?"

"It's not what's hunted among those trees but what the trees and their creatures hunt," declared the cattleman. "For these are the nights when the forest seeks fresh sustenance. And the wood-serpent, which guards the old treasure, must have blood, as must the witch who is the serpent's mistress. These are the nights when the forest roams..."

But when Ronan tried to question them further, they would tell him no more. One or two of the farming men clearly wanted to talk, but others forced them to silence. The idea of a forest which could uproot itself and travel where it willed was so nonsensical that Ronan gave it not a minute of his thoughts. He himself had seen trees sliding down a loose embankment, seeming to march, but he knew that had to do with the shallowness of their roots. He shook his head at these credulous provincials and longed to be back in some familiar city of the Young Kingdoms.

Thus it was before sunset the Red Archer mounted his refreshed horse, paid the ostler handsomely, tied a bundle of food and beer to his saddle-bow, and continued the journey east, up the shallow flank of the valley towards the distant ridge which, he'd been told, marked the highway to the coast. The moon was full when he crested the peak and looking back he was surprised to see no lights. It was as if the village had vanished completely from the valley and where it had stood was the thick foliage of a summer forest. The moon was high in a cloudless sky. He knew a sudden thrill of superstitious fear. There was no doubt that it was a forest he saw. Somehow, he decided, he had lost his bearings, but search where he could, he saw no village. He needed sleep more than he realised. Ronan decided he could afford to rest for a couple of hours before moving on. He lit no fire but, wrapping himself in a blanket, was soon snoring gently in a shallow slumber, one hand on his sword-hilt, the other on his bow-staff.

The Second Chapter
Reivers in Green

Out of that surrounding forest they came, shrieking through the moonlight, their faces painted with indigo dye, their bodies clothed in fur. They had big, round wooden shields. Their fists were full of bronze and iron. Moonlight glanced off axeblade, sword and spear. Ronan had time to note with astonishment that he had somehow made camp in the middle of a forest, when he had been sure he had settled on a bare hillside, then he was fighting for his life, bow used as a quarter staff, sword darting in and out, quick as a cobra, to send another soul to hell.

Outnumbered as he was, Ronan the Red had been trained from childhood in the arts of war and even as he stabbed his second man he reached forward to grab the war-axe from his useless hand. The bow staff was dropped and the axe split a head from crown to jaw. For a fleeting moment, he could have sworn he recognised the face of the man he slew. This one had no warpaint but his skin bore a green tinge. Ronan was sure the man was one of those who had been in the tavern in the last village in which he'd rested. And there were others, now he realized – all with faintly glowing green complexions! Had they posed as honest country workers to deceive him, to discover where he was headed? Was it they who had brought the forest to him?

But there was no time to think. For one of Ronan's subtle skills this was butcher's work. He sheathed his slender sword as he fought, snatching up a massive claymore and using it one handed. Axe in the other fist, he swung them together and two more barbarians died, yelling their terror as death engulfed them. To his horror, green blood spattered, drenching the archer's clothing, making the turf slippery beneath his feet. His terrified disgust gave him greater strength. He ducked and swung, severing limbs and slicing into necks and thighs until his attackers had become little more than a pile of green, writhing meat. But as many of them as Ronan slew, more kept coming at him. He knew that weariness, if nothing else, would eventually defeat him. Still his heavy axe and sword rose and fell. Streams of blood glittered in the yellow light of the full moon. His sword swung in an arc, first before him, then behind him, and every time more warriors dropped before that deadly arc. He leapt this way and that. For a moment it seemed he walked up the trunk of a tree to stand on a limb before leaping again into the thick of his enemies. He had no time to pause to think, no time to wonder how he had reached this forest or how the men had known where to find him.

Gradually, they began to press in on him, blue-painted faces grinning with triumphant expectation, green eyes glaring in the moonlight, full of fierce bloodlust, green bodies tensed to spring at him. He cursed the bad luck which had brought him to this alien land, to die without benefit of his own deities, the grim gods of Phum, without ever knowing where he was or whether he might ever have found the city he sought. And he called out to Krim, Lord of the Seven Spheres, to aid him. But Krim, as was conventional, sent no aid. Indeed, he might not have existed in this sphere at all.

Then, suddenly, the moonlight disappeared and glancing up he saw that clouds were spreading across it. It would be even harder to fight in darkness, but he was determined to take as many with him as he could.

To his astonishment, they began to fall back, muttering amongst themselves. They were conferring in a language he had never heard before. He stepped back and saw his bow where he had dropped it. Quickly, he bent to snatch it up and string it. From the quiver that never left his belt he drew four arrows, sending one after another with unerring speed into their ranks. This seemed to be enough to cause them to fall back, slinking into the darkness of the trees.

"Stand, you painted cowards!" he cried in his own language, letting fly another brace of arrows. But, as the two men fell, their companions grunted, yelled, then stumbled off into the undergrowth. He heard them crashing through the wood and then there was sudden silence. In the darkness, he heard the rasping breath of the dying, the thump of his own heart and – something else...

It was a woman's voice, sweet, almost a whisper. "I must thank you for your aid, stranger. What are you called?"

"I am Rakhir, the Red Archer, Warrior Priest of Phum." He answered automatically in his own language and then he added. "Men call me in these parts Ronan the Red."

"Ah, Phum," murmured the unseen woman in another language altogether. "Such redness there is in Phum. They say it's a city built of blood, do they not?"

"Those who do not know us, aye." Rakhir/Ronan was suspicious.

Her voice was mellow, slightly mocking. "It's centuries since I last saw her rust-coloured towers rising from the desert like a mirage. Do the ruby fountains still play in her squares and do the maidens still bathe themselves there on the Night of the Nomad Nuptials?"

"You know Phum?" He turned, seeking the source of the voice.

"I know all the lands called by my kin the Young Kingdoms. But it is nigh on a millennium since I last saw them. For I am O'indura of Imrryr, the Dreaming City, and it is my doom to dream forever, trapped in this place which the folk of Eerin call the Roaming Forest."

Now he knew the language she spoke. It was High Melnibonéan, the common speech of all who dwelled in his sphere. He answered in the same tongue. "Who were those men?"

"They belong to a tribe called the Nishut, which means 'No tribe.' They are the miners of emeralds and some say their skins take on the hue of the jewels they seek. They are the milkers of blood, who feed she who guards the Original Seed. They belong to the forest and defend her and do her bidding."

"And you are their mistress? You defend this Seed?"

She laughed then. Her voice was sweet silver. "If only I did, Red Archer. I am sustained by what the forest herself grows. For centuries now I have lived on bloodberries, sap and dew. But those warriors are kept alive by moonlight

and when the moon is dark, they must seek the comfort of the great barrow. For they are not truly alive as you are alive. Like me, they are vitalised by
dreams. But where their fellows dream of them, I dream only of myself. I am
kept from complete annihilation by the power of my own mind."

An almost primeval growl rose in Ronan's throat. Though trained in the
mystic arts, he yet felt deep suspicion of unexplained supernatural things.
"Show yourself, madam," he demanded. "Show yourself or, by Krim, I'll…"
But his voice trailed off, for he knew there was no threat he could offer her
while she remained invisible to him.

And then it seemed that sudden silver blossomed on the edge of the
glade, a brilliance which all but blinded him so that, with an oath, he covered his eyes. Then she stepped out of the light and he gasped at her beauty.
She was tall, slender and her hair was the colour of polished brass. Her blue-
grey eyes were slightly slanted and she had the finest cheekbones he had ever
seen. Almost too beautiful to be real, she stepped towards him, her white
garments drifting in a faint breeze, and he could easily believe that she was
the figment of a dream. At her side, however, was a scabbarded longsword
and matching it on her other hip, a thin dagger in a silver filigree sheath.

Instinctively, Ronan bowed, a tribute to her beauty as much as to her fem-
ininity.

"My lady."

"Well, Sir Rakhir of Phum, what mischance brings you to the floating
forest? Or do you, like me, travel the dream-roads, seeking a return to your
homeland?"

"This is not the sphere where Melniboné yet rules the world, I assume?"

"By your answer, I understand that you travelled here unwillingly. I can-
not say the same for myself. I was foolish enough to take a dream quest.
Melniboné never existed here and maybe never will. My corporeal body is as
real, if not more real, than this one. It still lies on the dream couches of the
Dreaming City. We have a skill, unknown to you humans, which allows us to
send a form, as real in blood, bones and flesh as our own, into other spheres.
One hour might pass on the dream couches, but centuries go by elsewhere.
That is how we learn so much and why our sorcerers are so powerful, for
they carry the knowledge of a hundred lifetimes. As a cousin to Melniboné's
empress, I was allowed access to the dream couches. I longed to explore all
the realms of what our wise men call 'the multiverse' and which an adept
can investigate only by travelling the moonbeam roads, the roads between the
worlds. But in my multiplicity of dreams, I became confused and lost the
secrets of how to gain those paths. I made the mistake of trusting a minor

deity of these parts, who said she would help me. Instead, she stole much of my memory and trapped me here in the Roaming Forest. Where I move, the forest moves. If I seek the sanctuary of a temple, the forest engulfs that temple. If I try to find safety in a village, that village is – is eaten. Her inhabitants are slain or made into warriors serving the semi-sentient creature which lives in the deep barrow. So, if I do not wish to destroy those whose help I seek, I can only move when the Roaming Forest moves. Moreover, even when I have been able to escape its confines by some trick of my magic, I grow less and less substantial. The closer I stay within the forest, the more my flesh feels like real flesh, the more alive I am."

As an adept of Phum, Ronan understood more of this than most men would. "And what of these?" he asked, pointing at the heaps of green bodies which still surrounded him. "Why have they not killed you?"

"They dare not. Their superstitions have made me their goddess. They believe that if I die, so will the forest die. And if the forest dies, so will they."

Ronan wondered privately if there was more to what she said. What if the forest could only move when she moved? What if she herself sought villages whose inhabitants would feed these unholy trees?

She moved a step or two closer. "We are all of a supernatural piece, you see, Sir Rakhir."

It was only when she used his true name, that the archer's suspicion of her increased. He had heard of the wiles of these unhuman people who ruled all the kingdoms of the west. He had been taught not to trust them, that reptilian blood, the blood of the ancient dragon folk called the Phoorn, ran in their veins, that they had the power to converse with serpents. Yet she was very beautiful and he wanted very much to believe her. He looked hard into her blue-grey eyes. She stared back frankly. He could do nothing, he realised, but believe her.

"Lady, I would rescue you from this if I could," he said.

"And I would be rescued. We both belong to the same realm. Believe me, I have waited for centuries in the hope that such a one as you would come to the Roaming Forest and save me, make me real again."

"How may I do that, lady?"

"There is only one way I know. You must find the Original Seed and destroy it. That will have the effect of destroying both the forest and its natives and opening up the moonbeam path which, with my guidance, you can cross back to your own realm again."

"And have you tried yourself to find and destroy this Seed?"

"Of course. And you are not the only man – or, indeed, woman – whose help I have sought. All died or were otherwise destroyed in pursuit of the Original Seed."

"And why should I have any better chance of succeeding?"

"Because you are a Warrior Priest of Phum and I am an Imperial Princess of Melniboné."

Rakhir had discovered the corpse of his horse. What kind of barbarians slew a horse for no good reason? A valuable horse? He stood over the beast, frowning. His saddle bags were untouched. There had been no attempt to rob him. What had they wanted? He turned, putting this question to O'indura.

"They wanted your blood," she said. "They wanted your blood to feed the Seed. That was why they fought so cautiously and why you defeated so many with such relative ease."

This made sense to Rakhir. Then another question came to him. "Do you live amongst these people?"

"I do not. I have to maintain their superstition, their fear of me, or they would use my blood to feed the Seed. Yet they believe I am the spirit of the Seed. Its personification, if you like. With a variety of allies I have made many attempts to get close to it, but it lies deep underground, in a chamber I have never been able to negotiate and it is guarded by the creature who lured me here in the first place, whose language I spoke, a monstrous three-eyed serpent, one bite from which entails an agonised death. She claimed to be the forest's victim, but now I understand she is its life."

"You do not make the prospect attractive," he declared.

"I have no intention of doing so. You are still able to leave this forest and you would best leave while the moon is hidden. I, however, cannot do so, as I've explained. Unless I can make a moonbeam road to lead us out of here, I am trapped forever. If you go, go soon. For you can be sure that the forest will follow you now that it has your scent and the moon stays high."

Ronan sighed. Thinking deeply, he went from corpse to corpse, skillfully removing his arrows, wiping them and replacing them in his quiver. How he longed for home. And he knew he must believe most of her story, since she spoke the common tongue of his world. For some odd reason his spirits were lifting. He turned to the silver princess, a strange battle-grin on his handsome features.

"Very well, lady. I am mightily tired of this island and would continue on my way to Tana Lorn. If you know a way to escape and return to our own sphere, we have a mutual motive. Let's rest in the shelter of the trees for a short while and then we'll seek this Seed of yours or die in the attempt."

The Third Chapter
The Original Seed

Later that morning Ronan awoke to a rustling in the trees and reached for his bow, but then he realised the sound was made by birds, a black flock with strange, golden eyes, which hopped along the lower branches, heads to one side as they regarded him, he thought, with a certain hunger.

The forest had not moved. Waking, the silver woman, O'indura, stretched and wiped her hands in the dew. She yawned, pushing back her long hair to expose slightly pointed, delicate ears, proving her origin. Rakhir-called-Ronan knew the appearance of Melnibonéans. They appeared on bas-reliefs in the temples of Phum. In the daylight her almost translucent skin seemed to shine and he drew a sharp breath as he experienced her full beauty. She turned and smiled at him, as if she knew she had entranced him.

From his purse the archer priest took a packet of dried sheep meat and offered some to her, but she shook her head, patiently waiting for him to chew the tough stuff before she stepped closer to him across the dark green turf.

"Tonight the moon will still be strong enough to move the forest," she said. "So we must do what we can during the day. Come nightfall, it will be more dangerous. We should act quickly. I will lead you to the Place of the Seed." She stretched out her hand.

Ronan took the soft fingers in his own hard, suspicious grasp. He wondered how many other warriors like him had been lured to their deaths or worse by this sorceress...

"Tell me," he said, as she led him past all the corpses of those he had slain in last night's battle. They were black with the same golden-eyed birds which filled the trees, no doubt waiting their own turn to feast. "Tell me, lady. Have others sought to help you find this Seed?"

"Oh, yes," she replied. "Many."

"And they have all perished?"

"They were not archer-priests of Phum," she told him. Her reply gave him little comfort as he padded beside her, looking hard at the old trunks and wondering if they had any means of harming him. More than once, he felt he saw a branch move in an unnatural way, but when he stared back, there seemed nothing amiss.

"Who are these warriors who move with the forest?" he asked her. "What's their bargain with it?"

"They guard and feed the Seed and for this they are repaid with a form of life. Did you pass through a village a night or so ago?"

"I did."

"Few of those villagers live. They formed the Feast of Blood. It was my fault. I saw you from the trees and thought to seek your help. I had hoped the forest would not follow, that I could reach you before my form faded to nothing. But the forest did follow. And it feasted, sparing some, who elected to serve the forest and were amongst the warriors who attacked you." There was a genuine agony in her eyes. And Ronan found himself increasingly convinced by her.

The undergrowth grew thick and the two of them were forced to use captured broadswords to cut their way through. But a path was faintly visible beneath the shrubs and saplings.

"We are almost at the Barrow of the Seed," she murmured. "A few days ago this path was cleared. That's how quickly the forest grows when it has blood to feed it."

And then they had passed through a narrow gap and entered a gloomy glade, an arena of heaped earthworks in which red clay lay exposed from the turf like the wounds of battle and on which low bushes grew, like patches of hair.

"This is the Barrow," she said. "Now we go underground."

But Red Ronan hesitated, every instinct in him refusing further movement. He felt that once he descended into the earth, into the very bowels of this beast that took on the appearance of a forest, he could be trapped forever.

"I am not sure – " he began.

She lifted her silvery arm and put soft fingers to his lips, staring hard into his eyes. "You must be sure, Red Archer. Your gaze must be as steady as never before. Your aim must be true and your confidence complete. For unless we possess the Seed we shall both of us surely die here today. We cannot hold off such a weight of fighting men forever. And if we fail? We die and are already buried. But if we succeed, we walk the moonbeam roads. I will lead you back to your own realm – our own world – and set you on the path to Tana Lorn, this I promise."

So he took hold of his strength and his courage and he said: "Lady, I believe your promise and I yearn to go home. So I will do this thing."

And at her bidding they approached the tallest part of the earthworks and there, hidden from casual view, they found a mouth of a cave into which a great stone arch had been built and the arch filled with ancient oaken gates. He sensed that this was a familiar action for her as she pushed open the gates.

They swung back silently and revealed a profound, impenetrable darkness.

This time Ronan did not hesitate, but strode forward with an almost animal growl on his lips, while she held to his arm. And he smelled blood and filth – the stink of men and of other fouler things – and again he was forced to control his fear. And then the gates swung shut behind them and they stood in pitch blackness and he realised that her scent was stronger than all the terrible stench assailing his nostrils. He felt her warm softness against him and he knew that even if this were, indeed, an inescapable hell, he would follow her anywhere. But he took a tighter grip on his captured broadsword and was glad he had decided to stick one of the war-axes in his belt.

The tunnel twisted like a beast in pain, back and forth, and the archer knew that if he ever had to find his way back again he would be lost here forever. An unidentifiable stink blended with that of men, damp, rooty soil and ordure until every breath he caught was thick in his throat, threatening to choke him. Yet her soft hand led him further and further into the belly of the earth.

At last he sensed rather than saw light ahead and he began to recognise the stink. He had not experienced it since he had been on this island, but it was yet familiar and the strongest he had ever known. The stink was reptilian. And it raised his hackles. Every instinct told him to turn back. But he knew he could not. His only choice was to continue and pray the Melnibonéan woman had not lied to him.

She was whispering in his ear now. "We are nearing the Chamber of the Seed. Remember that its guardians know no more than to die protecting it. There will be no parleying with them. But you are an archer and the first chance you have you must string your bow and let fly three arrows."

"Three? Why..."

"You will see."

And then they were in the chamber, a sphere whose walls curved beneath their feet. The source of the light came from three spots near the centre – a steady, greenish glow. But now, emerging from the floor were the silhouettes of men and the archer readied himself as they began to lumber towards him. He glimpsed glittering green eyes, open green mouths, bared green-grey teeth and he knew these were the survivors of the fight in the forest.

He prepared to stand against them but she murmured in his ear. "Quick. Your bow. Those three points of light. While you can. Three arrows."

And reluctantly he stuck the sword in his belt and strung his bow, nocking one arrow to the string, the other two held against the staff. In that darkness he wondered if he could possibly strike his targets. The first arrow flew and to his great relief it struck the central glowing orb. Immediately the chamber was filled with a horrific shrieking and wailing, a hissing and thrashing, and the warriors paused, as if uncertain. A second arrow, and a second orb pierced. Again the terrible hissing and convulsions. The noise grew, at once deafening and deep, shrill as the cry of some enormous seabird.

Then the warriors were upon him and he was forced to tug the axe free of his belt and strike two down, ducking beneath the sweep of their swords. A third fell, head split in two by the bright, bronze blade. Blood spattered against the Red Archer's face and he spat it out in disgust, carrying the attack to two more of the warriors who, he realised, could see hardly any better than he could. He lost contact with the woman. Where was she? Had she betrayed him, leaving him to his death? Was this what she had done with all the others who had come here seeking what she called the Original Seed?

One brilliant orb was coming closer and closer at astonishing speed. Yet all around him he felt the press of the warrior defenders of the Seed. Stinking breath struck his face. He continued to hack blindly, this way and that. His arm rose and fell and he knew he bathed in that thick, green, unnatural blood.

"Ronan!" She no longer whispered. There was tangible terror in her voice. "Shoot! Shoot! If you do not, we are both doomed!"

He stepped to one side, slammed his battle axe into another body and, using it as a temporary shield, raised his bow and his remaining arrow. Drawing the long shaft back, he let fly in one, instinctive movement.

Immediately an unhuman scream shrilled loud enough to threaten his ear-drums and his sanity. He saw the outline of the arrow plunge everywhere, with light streaming behind it, thrashing first to one side, then to another, then overhead. Filthy liquid stung his skin. The stench grew stronger and stronger and he staggered, retching, fearing he must surely pass out.

"Now, Ronan! Guard my back!"

Black shadows moved towards him and he sensed red rage threatening again. He had a glimpse of a lithe body against the failing light and resisted an urge to clap his hands over his ears. Again his hand gripped the long-shafted war-axe. Again he swung the blade deep into flesh, then swung backwards to catch the warrior threatening him from behind. A huge body was thrashing from side to side now, flinging corpses and living men indiscriminately about the earthen sphere. And all the while that deafening, hellish screaming.

Then she was beside him and he smelled something infinitely sweet. In the dying light of the last orb he saw her pale features and knew she had succeeded in getting what she sought.

"They are distracted by the beast's death-throes now, and hardly know whether to fight or flee. This is our moment to leave."

She took his arm and he backed along the serpentine corridor, striking out at more shadows as they approached.

As the passages narrowed, it was easier to defend them. His eyes were now much better accustomed to the gloom and he glimpsed his enemies by the faint, reflected green light in their eyes.

And then at last they were bursting out from the mound into air that was heavy with dense rain. Ronan was glad of the rain. It washed the worst of the viridian blood from his body. He lifted his head and let the water pour down on him. But she was still in haste. He saw that she cradled in her arms a tall, wooden beaker carved with strange, alien forms. The thing did not look as if it had been fashioned to be held by human hands.

Now the remaining warriors were gathering under the stone arch of the entrance. Ronan felt almost sorry for them as they looked in wonder at the cup O'indura held. They could not believe it was being taken from them by the woman they had worshipped as its spirit. He nocked another arrow to his bow and shot an attacker through the throat. This did not stop the warrior at once. He came stumbling forward, bronze sword raised, his other hand reaching for the beaker, then his feet gradually moved faster and faster over the ground as his body fell and he died sprawling at Ronan's feet. But more warriors were pouring from the entrance. Too many for him to fight in this natural arena.

The archer still did not wholly trust the Melnibonéan woman. He kept half an eye on her as he watched the warriors. He had no arrows left in his quiver. He felt a knot in his stomach, a sense of deep failure. Had he done all this just to die in a predatory supernatural?

Then she was at his side again, clutching his arm and leading him backwards. "We have the Seed," she said. "With it we can return to our home realm." Then she reached into the beaker and took out something about the size of a walnut.

"What's that?" He flung a battle-axe. A green-skinned warrior fell. How many more had filled that horrible chamber?

"The Seed," she said. "Put it into your mouth. But be sure not to swallow."

He could hardly believe what he heard. "Put that in my mouth? Why, by Krim, would I do that?"

"Have I failed you yet, Red Archer?"

"Why don't you – ?"

"I am not a man, nor a warrior. Do it, Priest of Phum. You'll not regret this!"

So he took the Seed and placed it gingerly in his mouth. He expected the taste to be unpleasant, but it was strangely sweet and delicate. He began to feel a very unfamiliar energy coursing through him. He was hallucinating, surely?

He felt that he himself had kinship with the surrounding trees and he had more than two arms, more than two legs but instead a number of sturdy branches. And each branch ended in something like a weapon. He swung one of his branches and knew at once that if he was hallucinating, then so were the green warriors. The man went flying back towards the entrance of the barrow. He swung again. Another warrior was sent hurtling backwards. He sensed that she had climbed onto his back as he gradually moved out of the glade, scattering warrior after warrior, until at last their antagonists became afraid and followed them no longer. He felt her long, warm fingers reaching into his mouth.

And he was a mortal man again, standing beside her as she replaced the Seed in the cup and then spat into it. Suddenly her other hand, which did not hold the cup, shot out and in it was a silver knife.

"So – you'd betray me, after all," he growled, lurching to seize her wrist, but she was too swift for him. He yelled in sudden, extraordinary pain as the cold knife sliced through his wrist and she held the cup to catch his gushing blood. "You hell-bitch! I'll – "

She grinned into his face. "You'll do nothing. I am saving your life, Red Archer!"

With the speed of a striking snake she sliced through her own wrist and now her blood mingled with his in the cup.

"The Seed needs our nourishment. It will take us home!"

The warriors were regrouping now. He saw them through the trees.

"Look," she murmured and he saw that, even as he staunched his own blood with his kerchief, something was forming in the cup. The Seed was glowing like a ruby and pulsing within the beaker. It was growing bigger.

He heard a creaking groan and saw a huge tree fall into the glade and pin several warriors to the ground. Then another tree fell. Then another. And this time when a tree fell it sent up a vast cloud of dust into the rainy air. The trees around him were petrifying, crumbling. The whole forest was dying in a few moments when it would have normally taken centuries.

O'indura looked down. He followed her gaze. The grass itself was turning to dust. The blood which had kept the forest alive had ceased to retain its power. Whatever she had done to the Seed had sucked the very essence from the predatory forest.

Then the Melnibonéan woman dashed the cup through the air and the liquid within streamed out into the air, turning from scarlet to green and then to gold before their eyes.

The thing spread into the air and hung there like a long-veined leaf, shimmering and curling in the cool rain. The forest continued to collapse, becoming almost as vaporous as smoke.

"Climb onto it," she said. "Help me."

He handed her up until she was standing on the huge leaf, which curled its edges to support her. Then with her help, letting the axe and the sword fall, he, too clambered to join her. She said something quietly in a language he did not recognise and made a motion with her hand and the world around him began to fade while the leaf stretched further and further ahead of them until it was like a long, many-tendrilled vine sending its shoots into the dark blue depths now surrounding them.

Rakhir, the Warrior-Priest of Phum, looked ahead at the wide tendrils, thick as the thickest tree trunks, which now stretched in all directions.

"Lady," he murmured, "what sorcery is this? What have you made?"

She smiled, linking her arm in his. "I have made a pathway," she said. "With a little luck, Red Archer, it will carry us to the moonbeam roads and from there we shall find a way which, with inspiration, courage and intelligence, will carry me to Melniboné and you to your Tana Lorn.... See?"

And he saw that there were many more long roads, like tendrils of a vine spreading through the dark blue depths. And there were other beings, not all of them human, walking on the wide, thick vines, back and forth at every level, above and below, walking through the multiverse.

"We have reached the moonbeam paths," she said. "We have found the roads between the worlds. Now comes the hardest task."

"What is that, lady?"

She laughed and pressed her warmth and her softness against his hard warrior's body. "To discover which of these roads, Rakhir the Red Archer, will carry us home."

Show Me Yours

Robert Reed

Robert Reed (tribute site: *www.starbaseandromeda.com/reed*.html) lives in Lincoln, Nebraska, where he turns out story after high-quality story, both fantasy and science fiction, seemingly inexhaustible. He is perhaps the Poul Anderson – whom James Blish once called "The continuing explosion, the most prolific writer of high quality in the field" – of his generation. He has published a steady stream of novels since 1987, the most recent of which is *The Well of Stars* (2005), a sequel to his most famous SF novel, *Marrow* (2000). His collections are *The Dragons of Springplace* (1999), and *The Cuckoo's Boys* (2005). In a review of *The Dragons of Springplace*, Claude Lalumière characterizes Reed's diverse body of short fiction: "In these carefully structured stories, sadness, deceit, revenge, pettiness, and beauty all intermingle to create unexpected emotions and surprising scenarios. Their potent interlocking juxtaposition of speculative setting, scientific extrapolation, exuberant imagination, and human drama exemplify what science fiction does better than anything else – and what Robert Reed pulls off with artful finesse." This year he appears in both our *Year's Best Fantasy* and our *Year's Best SF* volumes, and he had several stories in consideration for each.

"Show Me Yours" was published in *The Magazine of Fantasy & Science Fiction*, and is a weird revenge science-fantasy (although the science is only implied, as is the future). And it is of course about the present, and the problem of how one might deal with a sociopath. Perhaps it is psychological horror, but it is certainly about the inner life of character. It is an interesting comparison to the Rickert story.

SHE WEARS A BLACK FELT ROBE long enough to cover her bare knees and pale pink socks pulled over her ankles; her calves are white and freshly shaved and her shins are even whiter and nicked in two places by razor blades. A red belt is cinched tight, making her waist appear narrow and her hips broad. She isn't a tall woman. By most measures, she is slender, though the body has a roundness that marks five stubborn pounds – pounds sure to grow over time. She isn't lovely in the traditional ways, but youth and a good complexion help. Her fine black hair is long enough to kiss her shoulders; her eyes appear dark and exceptionally large. On stocking feet, she stands in the middle of a long hallway, her head tilted forward while her mouth opens and closes and again opens. The door to her left – the door she came out of – is slightly ajar. She pulls it shut now, applying pressure until the old latch catches with a sudden sharp click. Then she stares at the opposite door, drifting closer to it, listening. The loudest sound in the world is her soft, slow breathing. But then some little noise catches her attention, and on tiptoes, she glides down to the end of the hallway, into the only room in the apartment where a light still burns.

Metal moves, and the second door pops open. At that moment, the young woman is sitting on a hard chair, her back to the kitchen table. She watches a young man step out into the hallway. He wears jeans and nothing else, and judging by his manner, he wants something. He examines the door she just closed, then drifts a few steps to his left, finding nothing but the darkened living room. That most definitely is not what he needs. So he finally turns in her direction and notices her sitting alone in the kitchen, sitting with her legs crossed, illuminated from behind by the weak bulb above the sink.

"The john?" he whispers.

She nods and tilts her head.

The bathroom is beside the kitchen. He starts to fumble for the switch, closing the door all but the last little bit before clicking the light on.

The girl doesn't move, except to scratch the back of an ear and then drop the same finger down the front of her neck, tugging at the warmth of the old black felt. That slight pressure pulls open the robe enough to expose the tops of her breasts. While she waits, a seemingly endless stream of urine echoes inside the toilet bowl. Then comes the hard flush and the light goes off, and the man steps back into the hallway. He already wears a big smile, as if he spent his time in the bathroom rehearsing this moment. "So you're the roommate," he says.

She says, "Hi."

He steps into the kitchen, stops. "Did we wake you?"

"No."

"Good," he says.

She leans against the hard back of the chair, her chest lifting. "No, you didn't wake me." Her voice is deep for a woman and pleasantly rough. Then she shows him a half-wink, asking, "What do you think?"

He almost laughs. "Think about what?"

She doesn't answer.

He takes another little step forward.

"About my roommate," she says. "What do you think?"

The man scratches his bare navel and then his sternum, smiling as he phrases his response. "Sweet."

"My roommate is?"

Again, he says, "Sweet."

Which makes her laugh, and she stands up now and runs one hand through her black hair and flips her head twice and says, "You aren't."

"I'm not what?"

"You know what I mean," she says.

He is barefoot and shirtless and maybe in his middle twenties – a fit, strong young man with pale hair and abdominal muscles and jeans that could be tighter but not much so. "I'm not what?" he asks again.

"Fooling me," she says.

"No?"

"Not at all."

He shakes his head. "I didn't know I was trying to."

She says nothing.

He gestures over his shoulder. "She's sleeping."

"Is she?"

He doesn't answer.

"Sleep is good," she allows.

He watches her face, her body.

Again she uses her index finger, touching herself beneath her pale neck before pulling down, slowly dividing the robe until the inner faces of her breasts show in that gloomy yellow light. She is well-built and naked under the robe and her smile is girlish and warm and her deep rough voice says, "Show me yours, and I'll show you mine."

The young man takes a deep breath and holds it.

"No?" she asks.

"Maybe," he says.

"Maybe is the same as no," she says. "If you think about it."

"How's that?"

"Because every 'no' is just a maybe. It's attached to something you haven't gotten around to doing yet."

"Okay," he says.

She waits.

He puts a hand to his mouth, for an instant.

"Are you going to show me?" she asks.

"Why not?"

"Okay then."

With both hands, he unbuttons his jeans and unzips them and opens them until he is thoroughly exposed.

She studies nothing but his face.

"Now you," he mutters.

Very quickly, she pulls open the robe and then closes it again, in a blur, her face not quite smiling while she does it.

The young man blinks for a moment, as if trying to decide what he saw. Then he yanks up his pants and zips them.

"Do you hear her?" she asks.

He doesn't look back. He doesn't even blink now, watching her. With his face changing – smiling but with a grim, determined quality about the mouth and eyes – he says, "No, I don't hear anything. Nothing at all."

Just the same, he puts a finger to his mouth and turns abruptly, slipping back into the roommate's bedroom.

She waits now, counting to five. Then on tiptoes, she moves back down the hallway, balancing speed with stealth. The house is old and a floorboard groans, but not too loudly. The door has been closed but not quite latched. She hears someone moving; a light shows beneath the door. Somebody says a few soft words – the young man asks a question, judging by the tone. But no answer comes. Standing with her head tilted forward, the girl breathes through her nose, big eyes dancing and her mouth pressed tiny as her right hand turns the old glass knob, lifting the workings until she can push at the door without making much noise.

The young man stands beside a narrow bed – a woman's bed with a headboard made of iron and a flowery bedspread pulled against the wall and embroidered pillows stacked haphazardly on the floor. With considerable care, he holds a long bare foot in the crook of one arm. With a fingertip, he brushes at the foot's sole, working to elicit a reflexive flinch. Nothing happens. The woman on the bed is naked, lying on her stomach, her face turned toward the watching girl. Like the door, her eyes are just a little open. But nothing seems to register in her mind. When the man drops the foot, the bare leg collapses. When he slides his hand over her rump and between her legs, she doesn't react. And when he fishes a lighter out of a back pocket and makes a tall flame and holds it close to the dreamy, drugged eyes, she does nothing to show that she sees anything at all.

Satisfied, he straightens and reaches for the lamp.

The girl in the black robe backs away from the door as the light goes out. Then she moves to the opposite end of the brief hallway, into the darkened living room, sitting on an old upholstered chair. She breathes hard now, even when she only sits. Nearly a minute passes. Her dimly lit face is a little wet with perspiration and her mouth is open, gulping at the air. When the man appears, she says nothing. She watches him return to the kitchen, watches him look around for a moment before glancing into the open bathroom. Has she slipped out of the apartment? He must be asking himself that question.

Then he decides to investigate the other bedroom, giving the wooden door a little rap before putting his hand on the knob.

"Here," she calls out.

He jumps, just slightly. Then he steps into the living room, his face obscured by shadow but something in his posture implying a large, consuming smile. Quietly, he says, "Hey."

"What are you thinking?" she asks.

He shakes his head, laughing softly. "Guess."

"What's funny?"

"You."

She says nothing.

"Your roommate...she told me you don't like men that much...."

"She said that?"

"Just now," he lies.

"Some men are nice," she says. "On the right occasion, I might."

"Really?"

She crosses her pink socks.

"Hey," he says. "Want a drink?"

"Maybe."

"What do you have?"

"Whatever you find," she says.

He acts satisfied, even smug. With a quick walk, he returns to the kitchen. A new light comes on when he opens the refrigerator, and there is the musical clink of bottles and the woosh of seals being broken. Then comes a pause, and he returns with the two beers held in one hand. One bottle is foaming slightly, while his free hand pushes into the front pocket of his jeans.

She breathes deeply and says, "Thanks," as she takes the foamy beer.

"No problem."

She sets the beer on the old carpet between her pink socks. "If you want," she says, "turn on a light."

He fumbles with a floor lamp until the switch clicks once, the bulb glowing at its weakest setting. Then he looks at her for a long moment before saying, "Let's do that game again."

"Show me yours?"

"Yeah."

She nods but then says, "I don't know." She picks up her beer and takes a long drink. "Maybe later."

"Maybe is the same thing as no. Is that right?"

"Good job," she replies.

"Got any other lessons for me?"

"If you want to hear them."

He settles on the nearest chair, on its edge, staring at her robe and the pale, razor-nicked legs. "Yeah, sure."

"Well, first of all, there's no such word as 'sure.'" Grinning at the floor between them, she says, "Nothing is ever sure, or certain, or guaranteed."

"Never?"

"Not in my experience," she reports, taking another long sip of the beer. "You can never know the full consequences of anything you do. Not before you do it. And most of the time, not even afterwards."

The young man leans back in his chair, smiling at everything.

"Suppose it's fifty years from tonight," she says.

"Oh, yeah?"

"Imagine you're an old man looking back. What do you see? Fifty years later, and if you had to describe the consequences of your actions...if you had to explain your life to others...how would you do it?"

"Know what?" he says. "You're just a little bit weird."

She doesn't respond.

"Not that weird is a bad thing." He drinks part of his beer. "I don't know. I guess I'd say, 'In my life, everybody had some fun.'"

"'Fun'?" She takes a last long drink and sets the bottle out of the way. "Is that what you call it?"

He shrugs. Laughs.

"Fifty years," she repeats. "It's going to be a different world. Full of changes, rich with possibilities. I think you'd agree to that, right?"

"I suppose."

"And you'll have led this long life where you said, 'Yeah, sure,' to every whim and desire that came into your head. Which is how a sociopath exists. But I bet that doesn't bother you, does it? Hearing yourself referred to as a sociopath. And you've probably never noticed the worst consequences of your actions. The misery, the waste. The plain ugliness that you leave in your wake."

The young man closes his mouth and stares. After a moment, he asks, "Aren't you getting sleepy?"

"Should I be?"

He glances at her half-finished beer.

"Half a century," she says. "If you think about it, you can appreciate that there's going to be a wealth of new pills available. More powerful than any barbiturate, and infinitely more imaginative in their effects."

He squirms in his chair.

"Believe me, there are some amazing pharmaceutical products in that world. Pills that will make a person believe anything. Feel anything. Do anything, practically." She sits back, smiling with keen pleasure. "If a person were sufficiently clever, she could feed an old man a series of potent medications, and he would suddenly believe that he was young again, sitting inside an apartment that he hasn't visited for years. A young stallion enjoying an evening with two trusting, unfortunate women."

A tight, fearful voice asks, "Who are you?"

"The roommate," she replies. "I had been drinking that night, and when you came out of her room, we played our little game of 'Show Me.' Then you slipped a Mickey in my beer, and I fell asleep in this chair, and I woke up the next day, in my bed, with a miserable headache."

The man kicks with his legs, flails with his arms. But he doesn't possess the simple coordination to lift up off the chair.

"My friend, the first girl you drugged...she eventually killed herself, you know. Three years later, with an entire bottle of pills." In an instant, the woman has become a seventy-year-old, a little heavy and shamelessly gray, staring down the hallway as if waiting for a door to open. "Maybe you weren't directly responsible for her death. I'll give you that much. Maybe she would have killed herself anyway. But I'll tell you this: I find it hard to believe that you made the life she had left any better."

He isn't young anymore. Speckled hands hang in front of his eyes, then he covers a still-handsome face. "So you slipped me something," he mutters. "So what're you going to do? Have your fun with me, is that it?"

"But I already have," she says.

Then she stands and with a calm slow voice explains, "Your body will carry you to one of two places now. You can return to her bedroom, if you want. You'll find her dead body waiting there. She'll look exactly as she did when I found her. And if you go there, you'll never wake up. You'll live out your days in a deep coma, and the only thing inside your head will be that room and a cold pale corpse.

"Or you can step into my room, which would be much, much worse."

He drops his hands. "How?"

"All of your victims...the ones I could find who are still alive...they're waiting behind my door. Silver-haired ladies, and young girls. Faces you'll know very well, and faces you probably won't even remember."

He glares at her.

"It's your choice," she tells him, walking slowly toward the hallway.

"What'll they do to me?" he squeaks.

She pauses. For a long moment, she stands on her tiptoes, letting a wide rich smile spread across her face. Then she pulls her red belt snug, and with genuine delight, she says, "What will they do? I don't think they know. Really, this will be the first time they've ever played the game."

The Lepidopterist

Lucius Shepard

Lucius Shepard (www.lucius-shepard.com) lives in Vancouver, Washington, and is a self-described "connoisseur of desolation." His body of fiction is a sort of World's Most Dangerous Places of Fantasy and SF. His protagonists often attempt escape themselves by traveling to exotic locales. His own bio, on his web site, details a similar odyssey: "So when it's written that Lucius Shepard was born in August of 1947 [it] gives you nothing of the difficult childhood from which he frequently attempted to escape, eventually succeeding at the age of fifteen, when he traveled to Ireland aboard a freighter and thereafter spent several years in Europe, North Africa, and Asia, working in a cigarette factory in Germany, in the black market of Cairo's Khan al Khalili bazaar, as a night club bouncer in Spain, and in numerous other countries at numerous other occupations." Myth or autobiography? Who can tell. But escape to a place one perhaps should not have gone is a major theme of his fiction. He's a poet and rock musician who began to write SF and fantasy fiction in the early 1980s, and became prominent with his first book, Green Eyes, one of the six New Ace Science Fiction Special group of first novels published in 1984. His collections include The Jaguar Hunter (1987) and The Ends of the Earth (1991), and Two Trains Running (2004), and Trujillo (2004).

His recent books include the novels Viator (2005), and Softspoken (2007). In 2005, he had two collections out: Eternity and Other Stories, collecting his short fiction, and Weapons of Mass Seduction, collecting his film reviews and essays.

"The Lepidopterist" appeared in Salon Fantastique, an anthology notable for its darker stories. This one is in the classic frame of the story told by an old man in a bar, the ramblings of a bad old man, among some of the worst low-lifes in Central America, powerless people just trying to get by – in other words, standard Shepard. There is some marvelous hallucinatory butterfly imagery. The voice is so strong and convincing that it carries us in the manner of a Joseph Conrad story, taking us close and leaving us at a distance.

I FOUND THIS in a box of microcassettes recorded almost thirty years ago; on it I had written, "J. A. McCrae – the bar at Sandy Bay, Roatan." All I recall of the night was the wind off the water tearing the thatch, the generator thudding, people walking the moonless beach, their flashlights sawing the dark, and a wicked-looking barman with stiletto sideburns. McCrae himself was short, in his sixties, as wizened and brown as an apricot seed, and he was very drunk, his voice veering between a feeble whisper and a dramatic growl:

I'm goin to tell you bout a storm, cause it please me to do so. You cotch me in the tellin mood, and when John Anderson McCrae get in the tellin mood, ain't nobody on this little island better suited for the job. I been foolin with storms one way or the other since time first came to town, and this storm I goin to speak of, it ain't the biggest, it don't have the stiffest winds, but it bring a strange cargo to our shores.

Fetch me another Salvavida, Clifton...if the gentleman's willing. Thank you, sir. Thank you.

Now Mitch and Fifi were the worst of the hurricanes round these parts. And the worst of them come after the wind and rain. Ain't that right, Clifton? Ain't that always the case? Worst t'ing bout any storm is what come along afterwards. Mitch flattened this poor island. Must have kill four, five hundred people, and the most of them die in the weeks followin. Coxxen Hole come t'rough all right, but there weren't scarcely a tree standing on this side. And Fifi...after Fifi there's people livin in nests, a few boards piled around them to keep out the crabs and a scrap of tin over they head. Millions of dollars in relief is just settin over in Teguz. There's warehouses full, but don't none of it get to the island. Word have it this fella work for Wal-Mart bought it off the military for ten cent on the dollar. I don't know what for sure he do with it, but I spect there be some Yankees payin for the same blankets and T-shirts and bottled water that they government givin away for free. I ain't blamin nothin on America, now. God Bless America! That's what I say. God Bless America! They gots the good intention to be sending aid in the first place. But the way t'ings look to some, these storms ain't nothin but an excuse to slip the generals a nice paycheck.

The mon don't want to hear bout your business, Clifton! Slide me down that bottle. I needs somet'ing to wash down with this beer. That's right, he payin! Don't you t'ink he can afford it? Well, then, slide me that bottle.

Many of these Yankees that go rushing in on the heels of disaster, these so-called do-gooders, they all tryin to find something cheap enough they can steal it. Land, mostly. But rarely do it bode well for them. You take this mon bought up twenty thousand acres of jungle down around Trujillo right after Mitch. He cotching animals on it. Iguana, parrots, jaguar. Snakes. Whatever he cotch, he export to Europe. My nephew Jacob work for him, and he say the mon doing real good business, but he act like he the king of creation. Yellin and cursin everybody. Jacob tell him, you keep cursin these boys, one night they get to drinkin and come see you with they machete. The mon laugh at that. He ain't worry bout no machetes. He gots a big gun. Huh! We been havin funerals for big Yankee guns in Honduras since before I were born.

This storm I'm talkin about, it were in the back time. 1925, '26. Somewhere long in there. Round the time United Fruit and Standard Fruit fight the Banana War over on the mainland. And it weren't no hurricane, it were a norther. Northers be worse than a hurricane in some ways. They can hang round a week and more, and they always starts with fog. The fog roll in like a ledge of gray smoke and sets til it almost solid. That's how you know a big norther's due. My daddy, he were what we call down here a wrecker. He out in the fury of the storm with he friends, and they be swingin they lanterns on the shore, trying to lure a ship onto the reef so they can grab the cargo. You don't want to be on the water durin a norther ceptin you got somet'ing the size of the Queen Mary under you. Many's the gun runner or tourist boat, or a turtler headin home from the Chinchorro Bank, gets heself lost in bad weather. And when they see the lantern, they makes for it in a hurry. Cause they desperate, you know. They bout to lose their lives. A light is hope to them, and they bear straight in onto the reef.

That night, the night of the storm, were the first time my daddy took me wreckin. I had no wish to be with him, but the mon fierce. He say, John, I needs you tonight and I hops to it or he lay me out cold. Times he drinkin and he feel a rage comin, he say, John, get under the table. I gets under the table quick, cause I know and he spy me when the rage upon him, nothin good can happen. So I stays low and out of he sight. I too little to stand with him. I born in the summer and never get no bigger than what you seein now.

We took our stand round St. Ant'ony's Key. There wasn't no resort back then. No dive shop, no bungalows. Just cashew trees, sea grape, palm. It were a good spot cause the reef close in to shore, and that old motor launch we use for boarding, it ain't goin to get too far in rough water. My daddy, he keep checkin' he pistol. That were how he did when t'ings were pressin him. He check he pistol and yell at ever'body to swing they lanterns. We only have the one pistol mongst the five of us. You might t'ink we needs more to take on an entire crew, but no matter how tough that crew be, they been t'rough hell, and if they any left alive, they ain't got much left in them, they can barely stand. One pistol more than enough to do the job. If it ain't, we gots our machetes.

The night wild, mon. Lord, that night wild. The bushes lashing and the palms tearin and the waves crashin so loud, you t'ink the world must have gone to spinnin faster. And dark...We can't see nothin cept what the lantern shine up. A piece of a wave, a frond slashin at your face. Even t'ough I wearin a poncho, I wet to the bone. I hear my daddy cry, Hold your lantern high,

Bynum! Over to the left! He hollerin at Bynum Saint John, who were a fisherman fore he take up wreckin. Bynum the tallest of us. Six foot seven if he an inch. So when he hold he lantern high, it seem to me like a star fell low in the heavens. With the wind howlin and blood to come, I were afraid. I fix on that lantern, cause it the only steady t'ing in all that uncertainty, and it give me some comfort. Then my daddy shout again and I look to where the light shinin and that's when I see there's a yacht stuck on the reef.

Everybody's scramblin for the launch. They eager to get out to the reef fore the yacht start breakin up. But I were stricken. I don't want to see no killin and the yacht have a duppy look, way half its keel is ridin out of the water and its sails furled neat and not a soul on deck. Like it were set down on the rocks and have not come to this fate by ordinary means...

You t'ink you can tell this story better than me, Clifton? Then you can damn well quit interruptin! I don't care you heared Devlin Walker tell a story sound just like it. If Devlin tellin this story, he heared it from me. Devlin's daddy never were a wrecker. And even if dat de case, what a boy born with two left feet goin to do in the middle of a norther? He can't hardly get around and it dry.

Yes, sir! Two left feet. The mon born that way. Now Devlin, I admit, he good with a tale, but that due to the fact that he never done a day's work in he life. All he gots to do is set around collectin other folks' stories.

The *Santa Caterina*, that were the name on the yacht's bow...it were still sittin pretty by the time we reached it. But big waves is breakin over the stern, and it just a matter of minutes fore they get to chewin it up. I were the first over the rail, t'ough it were not of my doin. I t'ought I would stay with the launch, but my daddy lift me by the waist and I had no choice but to climb aboard. The yacht were tipped to starboard, the deck so wet, I go slidin across and fetch up against the opposite rail. I could feel the keel startin to slip. Then Bynum come over the rail, and Deaver Ebanks follow him. The sight of them steady me and I has a look around...and that's when I spy this white mon standing in the stern. He not swayin or nothin, and it were all I could do to keep my feet. He wearing a suit and tie, and a funny kind of hat with a round top were jammed down so low, all I could see of he face were he smile. That's right. The boat on the rocks and wreckers has boarded her, and he smilin. It were like a razor, that smile, all teeth and no good wishes. Cut the heart right out of me. The roar of the storm dwindle and I hear a ringin in my ears and it like I'm lookin at the world t'rough the wrong end of a telescope.

I'm t'inking he no a natural mon, that he have hexed me, but maybe I just scared, for Bynum run at him, waving he machete. The mon whip a pistol from he waist and shoot him dead. And he do the same for Deaver Ebanks. The shots don't hardly make a sound in all that wind. Now there's a box resting on deck beside the mon. I were lookin at it end-on, and I judged it to be a coffin. It were made of mahogany and carved up right pretty. It resemble the coffin the McNabbs send that Yankee who try to cut in on they business. What were he name, Clifton? I can't recollect. It were an Italian name.

Who the McNabbs? Hear that, Clifton? Who the McNabbs? Wellsir, you stay on the island for any time and you goin to know the McNabbs. The worst of them, White Man McNabb, he in jail up in Alabama, but the ones that remain is bad enough. They own that big resort out toward the east end, Pirate Cove. But most of they money derived from smugglin. Ain't an ounce of heroin or cocaine passes t'rough Roatan don't bear they mark. They don't appreciate people messin in their business, and when that Italian Yankee... Antonelli. That's he name. When this Antonelli move down from New York and gets to messin, they send him that coffin and not long after, he back in New York.

So this box I'm tellin you about, I realize it ain't much bigger than a hatbox when the man pick it up, and it can't weigh much – he totin it with the one hand. He step to the port rail and fire two shots toward the launch. I can't see where they strike. He beckon to me and t'ough I'm still scared I walk to him like he got me on a string. There's only my daddy in the launch.

He gots a hand on the tiller and the other hand in the air, and he gun lyin in the bilge. Ain't no sign of Jerry Worthing – he the other man in our party. I'm guessin he gone under the water. The mon pass me the box and tell me to hold on tight with both hands. He lift me up and lower me into the launch, then scramble down after me. Then he gesture with he pistol and my daddy unhook us from the *Santa Caterina* and turn the launch toward shore. It look like he can't get over bein surprised at what have happened.

My daddy were a talker. Always gots somet'ing to say about nothin. But he don't say a word til after we home. Even then, he don't say much. We had us a shotgun shack back from the water, with coco palms and bananas all around, and once de mon have settled us in the front room, he ask me if I good with knots. I say, I'm all right. So he tell me to lash my daddy to the chair. I goes to it, with him checkin the ropes now and again, and when I finish he pat me on the head. My daddy starin hateful at me, and I gots to admit I weren't all that unhappy with him being tied up. What you goin to do with us? he ask, and the mon tell him he ain't in no position to be askin nothin, considerin what he done.

The mon proceed to remove he hat and he coat, cause they wet t'rough. Shirt, shoes, and socks, too. He head shaved and he torso white as a fish belly, but he all muscle. Thick arms and chest. He take a chair, restin the pistol on his knee, and ask how old I am. I don't exactly know, I tell him, and my daddy say, He bout ten. Bout ten? the mon say. This boy's no more than eight! He actin horrified, like he t'ink the worst t'ing a man can not know about heself is how old he is. He tell my daddy to shut up, cause he must not be no kind of father and he don't want to hear another peep out of him. I goes to fiddlin with the mon's hat. It hard, you know. Like it made of horn. The mon tell me it's a pith helmet and he would give it to me, cause I such a brave boy, but he need it to keep he head from burnin.

By the next morning, the storm have passed. Daddy's asleep in the chair when I wakes and the mon sitting at the table, eating salt pork and bananas. He offer me some and I joins him at the table. When Daddy come round, the mon don't offer him none, and that wake me to the fact that t'ings might not go good for us. See, I been t'inkin with a child's mind. The mon peared to have taken a shine to me and that somet'ing my daddy never done. So him takin a shine to me outweigh the killin he done. But the cool style he had of doing it...A mon that good at killin weren't nobody to trust.

After breakfast, he carry my daddy some water, then he gag him. He pick up that box and tell me to come with him, we goin for a walk. We head off into the hills, with him draggin me along. The box, I'm noticing, ain't solid. It gots tiny holes drilled into the wood. Pinholes. Must be a thousand of them. I ask what he keepin inside it, but he don't answer. That were his custom. Times he seem like an ordinary Yankee, but other times it like he in a trance and the most you goin to get out of him is dat dead mon's smile.

Twenty minutes after we set out, we arrives at this glade. A real pretty place, roofed with banana fronds and wild hibiscus everywhere. The mon cast he eye up and around, and make a satisfied noise. Then he kneel down and open the box. Out come fluttering dozens of moths...least I t'ink they moths. Later, when he in a talking mood, he tells me they's butterflies. Gray butterflies. And he a butterfly scientist. What you calls a lepidopterist.

The butterflies, now, they flutterin around he head, like they fraid to leave him. He sit cross-legged on the ground and pull out from he trousers a wood flute and start tootlin on it. That were a curious sight, he shirtless and piping away, wearin that pith helmet, and the butterflies fluttering round in the green shade. It were a curious melody he were playin, too. Thin, twistin in and out, never goin nowhere. The kind of t'ing you liable to hear over in Puerto Morales, where all them Hindus livin.

That's what I sayin. Hindus. The English brung them over last century to work the sugar plantations. They's settled along the Rio Dulce, most of them. But there some in Puerto Morales, too. That's how they always do, the English. When they go from a place, they always leavin t'ings behind they got no more use for. Remember after Fifi, Clifton? They left them bulldozers so we can rebuild the airport? And the Sponnish soldiers drive them into the hills and shoot at them for sport, then leave them to rust. Yeah, mon. Them Sponnish have the right idea. Damn airport, when they finally builds it, been the ruin of this island. The money it bring in don't never sift down to the poor folks, that for sure. We still poor and now we polluted with tourists and gots people like the McNabbs runnin t'ings.

By the time the mon finish playing, the butterflies has vanished into the canopy, and I gots that same feelin I have the night previous on the deck of the *Santa Caterina*. My ears ringing, everyt'ing have a distant look, and the mon have to steer me some on the walk back. We strop my daddy to the bed in the back room, so he more comfortable, and the mon sit in he chair, and I foolin with a ball I find on the beach. And that's how the days pass. Mornin, noon, and night we walks out to the glade and the mon play some more on he flute. But mainly we just sittin in the front room and doin nothin. I learn he name is Arthur Jessup and that he have carried the butterflies up from Panama and were on the way to La Ceiba when the storm cotch him. He tell me he have to allow the butterflies to spin their cocoons here on the island, cause he can't reach he place in Ceiba soon enough.

I t'ought it was caterpillars turned into butterflies, I says. Not the other way round.

These be unusual butterflies, he say. I don't know what else they be. Whether they the Devil's work or one of God's miracles, I cannot tell you. But it for certain they unusual butterflies.

My daddy didn't have no friends to speak of, now he men been shot dead, but there's this old woman, Maud Green, that look in on us now and then, cause she t'ink it the Christian t'ing to do. Daddy hate the sight of her, and he always hustle her out quick. But Mister Jessup invite her in and make over her like she a queen. He tell her he a missionary doctor and he after curin Daddy of a contagious disease. Butterfly fever, he call it, and gives me a wink. It a terrible affliction, he say. Your hair fall out, like mine, and it don't never come back. The eye grow dim, and the pain...The pain excrutiatin. Maud Green cock her ear and hear Daddy strainin against the gag in the back room, moanin. He at heaven's gate, Mister Jessup say, but I believe, with the Lord's help, we can pull the mon back. He ask Maud to join him in prayin over

Daddy and Maud say, I needs to carry this cashew fruit to my daughter, so I be pushing along, and we don't see no more of her after that. We has a couple of visitors the followin day who heared about the missionary doctor and wants some curin done. Mister Jessup tell them to bide they time. Won't be long, he say, fore my daddy back on he feet, and then he goin to take care of they ills. It occur to me, when these folks visitin, that I might say somet'ing bout my predicament or steal away, but I remembers Mister Jessup's skill with the pistol. It take a dead shot to pick a man off a launch when the sea bouncin her round like it were. And I fears for my daddy, too. He may not be no kind of father, but he all the parent I gots, what with my mama dying directly after I were born.

Must be the ninth, tenth day since Mister Jessup come to the island, and on that mornin, after he play he flute in the glade, he cut a long piece of bamboo and go to pokin the banana fronds overhead. He beat the fronds back and I see four cocoons hangin from the limbs of an aguacate tree. They big, these cocoons. Each one big as a hammock. And they not white, but gray, with gray threads fraying off dem. Mister Jessup act real excited and, after we returned home, he say, Pears I'll be out of your hair in a day or two, son. I spect you be glad to see my backside goin down the road.

I don't know what to say, so I keeps quiet.

Yes sir, he say. You not goin to believe your eyes and you see what busts out of them cocoons. That subject been pressin on my mind, so I ask him what were goin to happen.

Just you wait, he say. But I tell you this much. The man ain't born can stand against what's in those cocoons. You goin to hear the name Arthur Jessup again, son. Mark my words. A few years from now, you be hearin that name mentioned in the same breath with presidents and kings.

I takes that to mean Mister Jessup believe he goin to have some power in the world. He a smart mon...least he do a fine job pretendin he smart. Still, I ain't too sure I hold with that. Bout half the time he act like somet'ing have power over him. Grinnin like a skull. Sittin and starin for hours, with a blink every now and then to let you know he alive. Pears to me somebody gots they hand on him. A garifuna witch, maybe. Maybe the butterfly duppy.

You want to hear duppy stories, Clifton be your man. When he a boy, he mama cotch sight of the hummingbird duppy hovering in a cashew tree, and ever after there's hummingbirds all around he house. Whether that a curse or a blessing, I leave for Clifton to say, but...

Oh, yeah. Everyt'ing gots a duppy. Sun gots a duppy. The moon, the wind, the coconut, the ant. Even Yankees gots they duppy. They gots a fierce duppy, a real big shot, but since they never lay eyes on it, it difficult for them to understand they ain't always in control.

Where you hail from in America, sir?

Florida? I been to Miami twice, and I here to testify that even Florida gots a duppy.

Evenin of the next day and we proceed to the glade. The cocoons, they busted open. There's gray strings spillin out of dem...remind me of old dried-up fish guts. But there's nothin to show what have come forth. It don't seem to bother Mister Jessup none. He sit down in the weeds and get to playin he flute. He play for a while with no result, but long about twilight, a mon with long black hair slip from the margins of the glade and stand before us. He the palest mon I ever seen, and the prettiest. Prettier than most girls. Not much bigger than a girl, neither. He staring at us with these gray eyes, and he make a whispery sound with he mouth and step toward me, but Mister Jessup hold up a hand to stay him. Then he goes to pipin on the flute again. Time he done, there three more of them standin in the glade. Two womens and one mon. All with black hair and pale skin. The mon look kind of sickly, and he skin gray in patches. They all of them has gray silky stuff clinging to their bodies, which they washes off once we back home. But you could see everyt'ing there were to see, and watchin that silky stuff slide about on the women's skin, it give me a tingle even t'ough I not old enough to be interested. And they faces...You live a thousand years, you never come across no faces like them. Little pointy chins and pouty lips and eyes bout to drink you up. Delicate faces. Wise faces. And yet I has the idea they ain't faces at all, but patterns like you finds on a butterfly's wing.

Mister Jessup herds them toward the shack at a rapid pace, cause he don't want nobody else seein them. They talking this whispery talk to one another, cept for the sickly mon. The others glidin along, they have this snaky style of walkin, but it all he can do to stagger and stumble. When we reach the shack, he slump down against a wall, while the rest go to pokin around the front room, touchin and liftin pots and glasses, knifes and forks, the cow skull that prop open the window. I seen Japanese tourists do less pokin. Mister Jessup install heself in a chair and he watchin over them like a mon prideful of he children.

Few months in La Ceiba, little spit and polish, he say, and they be ready. What you t'ink, boy? Well, I don't know what to t'ink, but I allow they some right pretty girls.

Pretty? he say, and chuckle. Oh, yeah. They pretty and a piece more. They pretty like the Hope Diamond, like the Taj Mahal. They pretty all right.

I ask what he goin to do for the sick one and he say, Nothin I can do cept hope he improve. But I doubt he goin to come t'rough.

He had the right of that. Weren't a half-hour fore the mon slump over dead and straightaway we buries him out in back. There weren't hardly nothin to him. Judgin from the way Mister Jessup toss him about, he can't weigh ten pounds, and when I dig he up a few days later, all I finds is some strands of silk.

We watches the butterfly girls and the mon a bit longer, then Mister Jessup start braggin about what a clever mon he be, but I suspect he anxious about somet'ing. An anxious mon tend to lose control of he mouth, to take comfort from the sound of he voice. He say six months under he lamps, with the nutrients he goin to provide, and won't nobody be able to tell the difference between the butterflies and real folks. He say the world ain't ready for these three. They goin to cut a swath, they are. Can you imagine, he ask, these little ladies walkin in the halls of power on the arm of a senator or the president of a company? Or the mon in a queen's bedchamber? The secrets they'll come to know. They hands on the reigns of power. I can imagine it, boy. I know you can't. You a brave little soldier, but you ain't got the imagination God give a tick.

He run on in that vein, buildin heself a fancy future, sayin he might just take me along and show me how sweet the world be when you occupies a grand position in it. While he talkin, the women and the man keeps circulatin, movin round the shack, whispering and touchin, like they findin our world all strange and new. When they pass behind Mister Jessup, sometimes they touch the back of he neck and he freeze up for a moment and that peculiar smile flicker on; but then he go right on talking as if he don't notice. And I'm t'inkin these ain't no kind of butterflies. Mister Jessup may believe they is, he may think he know all about them. And maybe they like he say, a freak of nature. I ain't disallowin that be true in part. Yet when I recall he playin that flute, playing like them Hindus in Puerto Morales does when they sits on a satin pillow and summons colors from the air, I know, whether he do or not, that he be summonin somet'ing, too. He callin spirits to be born inside them cocoons. Cause, you see, these butterfly people, they ain't no babies been alive a few hours. That not how they act. They ware of too much. They hears a dog barkin in the distance, a coconut thumpin on the sand, and they alert to it. When they put they eye on you...I can't say how I knows this, but there somet'ing old about them, somet'ing older than the years of Mister Jessup and me and my daddy all added up together.

Eventually Mister Jessup reach a point in he fancifyin where he standin

atop the world, decidin whether or not to let it spin, and that pear to satisfy
him. He lead me back to where my daddy stropped down. Daddy he starin at
me like he get loose, the island not goin to be big enough for me to hide in.

Don't you worry, boy, Mister Jessup say. He ain't goin to harm you none.

He slip Daddy's gag and inquire of him if the launch can make it to La
Ceiba and the weather calm. Daddy reckon it can. Take most of a day, he figures.

Well, that's how we'll go, say Mister Jessup.

He puts a match to the kerosene lamp by the bed and brings the butterfly
people in. Daddy gets to strugglin when he spies them. He callin on Jesus to
save him from these devils, but Jesus must be havin the night off.

The light lend the butterfly people some color and that make them look
more regular. But maybe I just accustomed to seein them, cause Daddy he
thrash about harder and goes to yellin fierce. Then the one woman touch a
hand gainst he cheek, and that calm him of an instant. Mister Jessup push
me away from the bed, so I can't see much, just the three of them gatherin
round my daddy and his legs stiffening and then relaxin as they touch he
face.

I goes out in the front room and sits on the stoop, not knowin what else to
do. There weren't no spirit in me to run. Where I goin to run to? Stay or go, it
the same story. I either winds up beggin in Coxxen Hole or gettin pounded by
my daddy. The lights of Wilton James' shack shining t'rough the palms, not
a hundred feet away, but Wilton a drunk and he can't cure he own troubles,
so what he goin to do for mine? I sits and toes the sand, and the world come
to seem an easy place. Waves sloppin on the shingle, and the moon, ridin
almost full over a palm crown, look like it taken a faceful of buckshot. The
wind carry a fresh smell and stir the sea grape growin beside the stoop.

Soon Mister Jessup call me in and direct me to a chair. Flanked by the butterfly people, my daddy leanin by the bedroom door. He keep passin a hand
before his eyes, rubbin he brow. He don't say nothin, and that tell me they
done somet'ing to him with they touches, cause a few minutes earlier he
been dyin to curse me. Mister Jessup kneel beside the chair and say, We goin
off to La Ceiba, boy. I know I say I'm takin you with me, but I can't be doin
that. I gots too much to deal with and I havin to worry bout you on top of it.
But you showed me somet'ing, you did. Boy young as you, faced with all this,
you never shed a tear. Not one. So I'm goin to give you a present.

A present sound like a fine idea, and I don't let on that my daddy have
beat the weepin out of me, or that I small for my age. I can't be certain, but I
pretty sure I goin on eleven, t'ough I could not have told him the day I were

born. But eleven or eight, either way I too young to recognize that any present given with that kind of misunderstandin ain't likely to please.

You a brave boy, say Mister Jessup. That's not always a good t'ing, not in these parts. I fraid you gonna wind up a wrecker like your daddy...or worse. You be gettin yourself killed fore you old enough to realize what livin is worth. So I'm goin to take away some of your courage.

He beckon to one of the women and she come forward with that glidin walk. I shrinks from her, but she smile and that smile smooth out my fear. It have an effect similar to Mister Jessup's pats-on-the-head. She swayin before me. It almost a dance she doin. And she hummin deep in she throat, the sound some of Daddy's girlfriends make after he climb atop them. Then she bendin close, bringin with her a sweet, dry scent, and she touch a finger to my cheek. The touch leave a little electric trail, like my cheek sparklin and sparkin both. Cept for that, I all over numb. She eye draw me in til that gray crystal all I seein. I so far in, pear the eye enormous and I floatin in front of it, bout the size of a mite. And what lookin back at me ain't no butterfly. The woman she may have a pleasin shape, but behind she eye there's another shape pressin forward, peekin into the world and yearnin to bust out the way the butterfly people busted out of they cocoon. I feels a pulse that ain't the measure of a beatin heart. It registerin an unnatural rhythm. And yet for all that, I drawn in deeper. I wants her to touch me again, I wants to see the true evil shape of her, and I reckon I'm smiling like Mister Jessup, with that same mixture of terror and delight.

When I rouse myself, the shack empty. I runs down to the beach and I spies the launch passin t'ough a break in the reef. Ain't no use yellin after them. They too far off, but I yells anyway, t'hough who I yellin to, my daddy or the butterfly girl, be a matter for conjecture. And then they swallowed up in the night. I stand there a time, hopin they turn back. It thirty miles and more to La Ceiba, and crossin that much water at night in a leaky launch, that a fearsome t'ing. I falls asleep on the sand waitin for them and in the mornin Fredo Jolly wake me when he drive his cows long the shore to they pasture.

My daddy return to the island a couple weeks later, but by then I over in Coxxen Hole, doin odd jobs and beggin, and he don't have the hold on me that once he did. He beat me, but I can tell he heart ain't in it, and he take up wreckin again, but he heart ain't in that, neither. He say he can't find no decent mens to help, but Sandy Bay and Punta Palmetto full of men do that kind of work. Pretty soon, three or four years, it were, I lose track of him, and I never hear of him again, not even on the day he die.

Mister Jessup have predicted I be hearin bout him in a few years, but it weren't a week after they leave, word come that a Yankee name of Jessup been found dead in La Ceiba, the top half of he head chopped off by a machete. There ain't no news of the butterfly people, but the feelin I gots, then and now, they still in the world, and maybe that's one reason the world how it is. Could be they bust out of they shapes and acquire another, one more reflectin of they nature. There no way of knowin. But one t'ing I do know. All my days, I never show a lick of ambition. I never took no risks, always playin it safe. If there a fight in an alley or riot in a bar, I gone, I out the door. The John Anderson McCrae you sees before you is the same I been every day of my life. Doin odd jobs and beggin. And once the years fill me up sufficient, tellin stories for the tourists. So if Mister Jessup make me a present, it were like most Yankee presents and take away more than it give. But that's a story been told a thousand times and it be told a thousand more. You won't cotch me blamin he for my troubles. God Bless America is what I say. Yankees gots they own brand of troubles, and who can say which is the worse.

Yes, sir. I believe I will have another.

Naw, that ain't what makin me sad. God knows, I been livin almost seventy years. That more than a mon can expect. Ain't no good in regrettin or wishin I had a million dollars or that I been to China and Brazil. One way or another, the world whittle a mon down to he proper size. That's what it done for Mister Jessup, that's what it done for me. It just tellin that story set me to rememberin the butterfly girl. How she look in the lantern light, pale and glowin, with hair so black, where it lie across she shoulder, it like an absence in the flesh. How it feel when she touch me and what that say to a mon, even to a boy. It say I knows you, the heart of you, and soon you goin to know bout me. It say I never stray from you, and I goin to show you t'ings whose shadows are the glories of this world. Now here it is, all these years later, and I still longin for that touch.

The Double-Edged Sword

Sharon Shinn

Sharon Shinn (*www.user.cs.rose-hulman.edu/~thomass/shinn*) lives in St. Louis, Missouri. She works as a journalist for a trade magazine. Her first novel, *The Shape-Changer's Wife* (1995), won her the Crawford/IAFA Award, given for a first book by a fantasy writer. She is now the author of *Archangel* (1997), and four other novels set in the world of Samaria, seven additional SF and fantasy novels for adults, and three young adult novels in a shared setting, *The Safe-Keeper's Secret* (2004; an American Library Association Best Book for Young Adults), *The Truth-Teller's Tale* (2005), and *The Dream-Maker's Magic* (2006).

"The Double-Edged Sword" was published in *Elemental*. A healer suspected of killing the king spends more than a decade away from her former life in the court, but is pulled back into court intrigues because of her reputation for bringing death. The story, she says, "takes place in a world I created for an unpublished fantasy novel. The fact that the whole world already existed in my head helped me give a certain richness to the details of the story. One of my Wiccan friends gave me a blank deck of cards so I could draw the zafo images that were described in the book."

I SAT AT THE BACK of the dark tavern at the table that, in the past five years, had come to be known as mine. Even on the days when I did not bother to leave my house, or leave my bed, no one sat in this booth except me. The townspeople knew better, and strangers who made the mistake of sitting in my place would be told politely by Samuel that the table was reserved. I was the only one who ever sat there, and Samuel was the only one who would approach me while I was in possession.

I idly shuffled my zafo cards and began laying out an unspecified fortune. It would be my own, of course; these days, I did not read for anyone except myself. And even then, I was rarely satisfied with the pictures I saw in the cards.

The swinging door to the back room swept open wide, admitting the appetizing smell of meat and onions as well as Samuel's tall, spare figure. Catching sight of me in the dim corner, he checked abruptly and came my way.

"Aesara. I didn't know you were here," he said. "What will you have to drink?"

"Wine, maybe. Do you have time to drink it with me?"

"In an hour or so, I will."

"A glass of ale, then, until you are free," I said.

"Will you eat with me?" he asked.

I squinted up at him in the insufficient light. I had not been awake more than an hour and could not have said with any certainty what time it had been when I rose. "Is it almost dinnertime?" I asked.

"For you, it is," he said firmly. I laughed out loud. Samuel was convinced that I never ate unless he fed me. "Of course, I'm always hungry," he added with a smile.

This was meant to coax me to eat, for his sake. "I'll eat with you," I said. "It smells good."

"I'll get your ale, then."

He disappeared, returning in a minute with a glass of cold ale and a plate of bread. The bread made me laugh again. He grinned crookedly. He was sandy-haired and freckle-faced, with weathered skin and an unchanging ruddy coloring that made it hard to place his exact age. I knew it, though. He was fifty-eight, seven years older than I was, and he had been a widower for five years.

I had laid my zafo cards out in the standard grid – one card in the top row, four cards in each of the next two rows, and a single card in the bottom row – but I had not turned them face-up yet. Now, with the ale and bread arrived as a diversion, I did not feel like reading the cards after all. I swept them back into a pile, reshuffled the deck, and laid the cards aside.

The activity of the tavern went on quietly around me. I leaned back on my padded bench and watched. Although I talked to no one except Samuel, I knew all the employees and all the habitués by name. Sam's eldest son Groyce handled most of the up-front business, greeting customers, making sure everyone was attended, watching out for trouble. Groyce's wife, a small pretty girl, waited on tables and flirted mildly with the local patrons. Two other young women served customers, and an old man cooked in the back.

At this early hour, there were only half a dozen people in the bar, talking quietly, playing board games, or teasing the young girls. I had lived in Salla City for five years now, and I could tell you the name of every man and woman who inhabited it, but I had yet to get closer to a single one of them than I was at this exact moment.

Except for Samuel, of course, and we were only close because of the bargain we had struck one night five years ago. At that, it was not true friendship. He felt grateful and I felt secure; and so he let me stay, and I stayed.

I sipped at my ale and watched Samuel confer briefly with Groyce before disappearing again into the back room. This was the table I had taken that night five years ago, when I had just paused in Salla City to break my aimless journey for one night. Samuel had served me then, but absently, with clumsy, choppy motions that irritated me because some of the wine had spilled from his unsteady hands to the table. I was laying out the cards then, too, and I had been afraid of staining one of them – although it didn't matter if the whole deck was ruined, if the whole deck was lost.

"Could you bring me a cloth, please," I had said coldly, "so I can wipe this up?"

He had immediately done so; but instead of handing me the linen, he had stood beside me wrapping the white napkin around and around his hands.

"You are a halana," he said, when I finally looked up with a scowl.

"Yes," I snapped. "What of it?"

"I have – my wife is next door. She is dying. That is – we have a halana in the city who has done what she can. She says my wife is dying."

Anger and fear had risen in me, for I knew what was coming next. Knew, and did not want to deal with it. "She is probably right, then," I said.

"But you are a halana," he said almost stupidly.

Halana. Wise woman; healer. We have varied powers, we who are filled with the magical blood of Leith and Egeva. Some of us are very skilled and some of us are merely well-taught, and I had no way of knowing just how good the local practitioner was.

"There is nothing I can do for you," I said.

He went on as if I had not spoken. "She is in such pain. Her head – her lungs – her whole body. She has begged me to take her life because she is in such terrible agony. But I can't do that."

I wanted to put my hands over my ears and shut out the sound of his voice; I also wanted to put them over my eyes to block out the sight of his face. I could not do both.

"There is nothing I can do for you," I said again. In the six years that I had been wandering through Sorretis – from the throne room of Verallis to the rocky hills of Limbeth – this was the response I had given to everyone who had asked a favor of me. There had not been many. I did not look, with my grim face and darkling expression, like a woman of kindly disposition.

"But she is dying," he said.

I opened my mouth to refuse him again, but somehow the words went unsaid. Perhaps it was the dazed grief in his gray eyes, or perhaps it was the dormant power in my own body that made me say what I had no intention of saying. "I will look at her," I said, rising. "But I make no guarantees. I doubt if there is anything I can do."

And so I accompanied him to the small house behind the big tavern, the house that, under other circumstances, would have been pervaded with a welcoming charm. But a woman lay dying inside, and so the house was filled with fear instead.

I knew as soon as I entered the sickroom that the woman was ill beyond my powers of healing. The chamber was shallowly lit by clusters of tapers shielded behind brightly painted screens. Someone had brought in fresh flowers in an attempt to cheer up the sick woman; everywhere were similar evidences of hopeful affection. But there were not enough flowers or candles in Sorretis to bring this woman back to life.

I did not say so, of course. She was conscious, but barely; she turned uneasily when I entered the room. "Sam?" she said faintly, and the lanky man crossed to her side. He took her hand so gently he could have been imprisoning butterflies. Nonetheless, she had to bite back a cry of pain. The look upon his face was sheer desolation.

"I've brought a halana to look at you, Mari," he said, in a low voice. I supposed her fever had made her ears sensitive to sound as well. "Can you say hello?"

"Halana?" she said drowsily and turned her eyes blindly my way. But I could see from the cloudy irises that she could not make out my features – nor, if it came to that, her husband's. I crossed the room quietly and held my hands on either side of her face. I did not quite touch her skin, and she did not moan aloud. Even without touching her, I could feel the heat from her cheeks burn against my palms.

I stayed in the room a few moments, trying to determine what her disease was, while Samuel talked nonsense to distract her. A few minutes was all I could stand; I left as soon as I could have been expected to make a diagnosis. Samuel followed me shortly. On his face was a look of fugitive hope.

"Well?" he said. "Do you think – what do you think?"

I was wont to be blunt at times like these, but he looked so vulnerable that I tried to temper my words. "There are some diseases that can be cured, and some that cannot," I said. "Hers is an illness for which there is no remedy."

He stared at me steadily, while all the light seemed to die slowly from his plain, good-natured face. I had not meant to add even this much, but his expression of despair moved me more than I wished. "I have something I can give her that will ease her pain," I said. "It will not make her well, but it will make her dying less terrible."

"You are sure she will die?"

"In less than a week. Yes, I am sure."

He had flinched when I named the time, but I saw no reason to spare him from the knowledge. "But you can lessen her suffering? With some potion?"

It was not a potion, exactly. I would speak a complex spell over a simple glass of water, and its very essence would change. But I did not explain this to him. Those who are not halani prefer to believe in philtres and potions. It makes them uneasy to rely upon incantations. "That is exactly it," I said. "Wait here, and I will return with the drug."

And so I had gone to the bar and requested water, and paused a moment to pour it into one of the small glass vials I always carried. Shortly thereafter, the medicine had been administered. I had not stayed to see the efficacy of my drug. I was hungry, and I had gone back to the tavern to eat my interrupted meal.

Sam had rejoined me in something less than an hour, his face transformed with wonder. Mari was lucid, she who had been raving before. She had allowed him to take her hand, to kiss her face, without crying out from the agony his lightest touch inflicted. He had told her that she was dying, that this blessed surcease was a gift but not the greatest gift, and even so she had laughed. "I feel so good," Mari had exclaimed. "Even the gift of my life could not make me so happy." Sam related this whole conversation to me.

"I am glad to hear it," I had said somewhat sourly, trying to finish my meal.

"How can I thank you?" he demanded. "Such a wondrous thing you've done – "

"I have not saved her," I warned him. "Don't be deceived. Her body is careening headlong toward death, and I can do nothing to arrest that journey."

He watched me steadily again with those gray eyes. I thought somewhat irrelevantly that this man was nobody's fool. "I understand that," he said almost patiently. "But you don't understand. She was in such pain and now she is at peace. There is nothing I would not do to thank you."

"Let me finish my dinner in solitude," I said. "And tell no one what I have done for you tonight."

"But – "

"No one," I interrupted. "If you want to thank me, leave me alone. I am not much interested in interfering in the lives of others. And I do not want them interfering in mine."

He had continued to watch me with that narrowed, intelligent gaze, and I had the sudden feeling that I had told him, in a few simple sentences, the whole story of my tangled life. But all he said was, "I understand. I will say nothing to anyone. You will be free from importunity as long as you stay."

Mari had died six nights later. I did not attend the funeral services; Samuel did not ask me to. He did not ask me how long I planned to stay in Salla City. He never asked me to intercede for the life or health of any other citizen, and I was relatively certain that he knew of others, over the years, who could have used my help. He did ask me, the day after Mari died, what my name was. *Aesara*, I said. If he recognized it, he gave no sign.

Samuel himself brought two steaming plates of food to the table about an hour later. Groyce's pretty wife followed with a bottle of wine and two glasses. She smiled at me shyly but said nothing, and fled as soon as she had set the pieces upon the table. Samuel decanted and poured.

"She's afraid of me," I observed.

He looked after his daughter-in-law. "Who, Lina? She thinks you're a crazy old woman. Everyone does."

"I'm not that old," I said.

"But crazy?"

I shrugged. "Who isn't?"

The food was delicious, as always. After Lina had cleared our dishes away, Sam leaned back and stretched his arms. Out of habit, I pulled out my zafo cards again and began shuffling. Sam and I never talked much during meals or after them, but our silences were filled with a wordless companionship.

Now he spoke, surprising me. "Do you ever look at them?" he said.

I glanced up. "What?"

He gestured to the cards that I had laid out again, absent-mindedly, in the standard grid. "Your cards. You always place them on the table this way, but you never turn them over and look at them."

I made a wry face. "Sometimes I do. I don't like the pictures I see."

"What pictures do you see?"

"What pictures does one ever see in a zafo deck?"

"I don't know. I've never seen one."

Now I was amused. "You've never had your fortune told? Not even once, just for fun?"

"No, never. I have too much respect for the powers of the halani to approach one lightly."

"Now you do, perhaps," I scoffed. "Since you have such high respect for me."

He grinned. "So do you want to read my fortune?"

I shook my head. "I never read for anyone but myself."

He motioned at the cards again. "Then read one for yourself. I would like to see the pictures."

I hesitated a moment. He caught my reluctance. "Then don't," he said swiftly.

I shrugged and smiled. "Why not? They can't tell me anything I don't know already. But if you have never seen this done, I will have to explain everything."

I turned over the top card, alone in the upper row. "This is called the primary significator," I told him. "It represents me as I am or as I was."

No surprise, the top card was the black queen. I was dark-eyed and dark-haired, but the card meant more than that; it spoke of a somber personality weighted with heavy cares. The brooding queen invariably turned up in my fortune, either as my present or my future.

"Now, most halani read the cards in the order in which they are laid out, but I like to skip around," I told him, reaching for the last card, the single one in the fourth row. "This card will tell us who I will become."

The image revealed was not one I was expecting. It was the hooded figure, a dark, faceless form with its hands outstretched.

"It looks somewhat threatening," Samuel observed.

"Indeed. This card means many things, most of them ominous. It stands for the shadowed future, the as-yet-to-be-revealed. Sometimes it is an intimation of death. At other times, it is a warning of a change to come." I gave Sam a twisted smile. "I told you I do not much care for the readings I do."

"You do not have to go on, then," he said seriously.

"No, now I am curious."

I indicated the four cards in the second row. "Fortune, home, heart, career," I recited. "The pictures of my past."

I turned over the cards in order. Fortune: the open box, everything the soul could desire. Home: the lord's castle, with its white stone walls and graceful gables. Heart...but here my own heart nearly stopped beating. The black king, reversed.

"What does it mean when a card is upside down?" Sam wanted to know.

"It means the opposite of whatever the card usually means," I said through a constricted throat. "Or that something has gone wrong with – that person or that thing – "

The last card in this row was scarcely any more comfort. Career: the spilled wine. Promise gone awry...

"None of this makes any sense to me," Sam said.

Perhaps it would not seem so terrible said aloud. "The cards say that at one time I lived a grand life, in a grand house, and my every wish was indulged," I said. "I cared for a dark-haired man but he – something happened to him. And my career from that point on became something of a waste."

He lifted his eyes to my face, his eyebrows raised, but he did not ask me if any of this was true. "And what about your future?"

I was more cautious this time, and turned the cards over one at a time. "Fortune," I murmured. "The double-edged sword. What I have is equally likely to be used for good or for evil. Home." I smiled. "The roadside tavern. Any place of well-being or cheer."

Sam was pleased. "My bar is in your cards?"

"It looks that way." I turned over the third card: the battling twins. "Interesting."

"What? What does that mean?"

"My heart is in conflict. My dreads and my desires pull me in two."

He was watching me again, as if trying to assess the truth of that. "I suppose you know whether or not any of this has any relevance to you," he remarked.

I laughed shortly. "I suppose I do." I turned over the last card. "Career," I named it. "The white queen. It seems a fair-haired woman, or a very good woman, is going to become my patron."

Now Sam was smiling. "That does not seem too likely, at least," he said.

"No," I replied.

Just then the front door opened, and a phalanx of uniformed guards strode in, their feet making a rhythmic tattoo on the wooden floor. It was late spring, and cold, and they wore fur-edged cloaks over their blue-and-gold livery. Behind them, her silk-white hair haloed by the low afternoon sun, entered a small blond woman with an unmistakably noble face. Everyone in the bar stared at her during the few minutes it took her eyes to adjust to the dimness inside. After my first quick look, I turned my eyes back to the table and pushed all my cards together. I knew even before I heard her hesitant footsteps crossing the floor that she had come to Salla City looking for me.

She wanted to speak to me privately, but I insisted that Sam stay to hear our conference. "Whatever you tell me, I will repeat to him," I said listlessly. "He may as well hear everything as you say it."

So Sam moved to my side of the table, and the stranger seated herself across from us, and her five guards arranged themselves as a screen between us and the rest of the tavern. Groyce brought a fresh bottle and a third glass, and Sam poured for us all.

She just touched her lips to the amber liquid and laid the glass aside. "I know who you are," she said.

I felt Sam physically restrain himself from looking at me. He thought I would ask him to leave now, but why should I? He had not betrayed me in the five years he had known me. No matter what was revealed now, it seemed unlikely he would repeat it to anyone.

"How did you find me?" I wanted to know.

She was not ready to drop the discussion of my identity. "Aesara Vega," she said, as if it was a challenge. "Halana rex."

The king's halana. I closed my eyes briefly. "Former halana rex," I corrected, looking at her again. She was very beautiful. She had pale skin over delicate bones; her eyes were a flawless blue. On every finger of her left hand, she wore a ring that looked impossibly expensive. On her right hand, she wore only two rings, but neither of them looked cheap, either. "How did you find me?" I asked again.

"Someone who had been in Verallis passed through here several months ago," the woman said. "She recognized you."

It had been eleven years since I had lived at the king's palace in Verallis, and I had changed since then. Whoever had recognized me must have had very sharp eyesight. "I can only suppose," I said quite dryly, "that you have come to me because you need a favor."

"It is a terrible favor to ask," she said. Her voice was low and sweet, and she pitched it most persuasively. The blue eyes looked dense with sadness. I braced myself for what she was going to say, because I knew what it would be, and I was right.

"I want you to kill a man," she said.

I heard Sam inhale sharply. I glanced over at him and smiled. He was trying hard to keep his face under control, but her words had undoubtedly shocked him. "She asks me this," I explained kindly, "because it is believed that I once killed a man in Verallis."

"The king," she said.

Her name, she told us, was Leonora Kessington. Her husband was Sir Errol Kessington, son of Sir Havan of Kessing, a wealthy territory not far from Salla City.

"Six months ago, Sir Havan was in a terrible hunting accident," she said. She could scarcely look at us while she told the story; instead, her eyes were fixed on her interlaced fingers. "Something frightened his horse, and the animal bolted. Sir Havan was thrown from the saddle, but his – his foot caught in the stirrup, and he was dragged along the ground..." When she resumed speaking her voice was even softer than before. "When they found him, his leg was broken, and his collar was broken and his neck – was broken – "

Samuel gave her one of the linen napkins. She pressed it to her eyes and it came away damp. She still did not look at us.

"They did not think he would live," she continued. "But he did. His leg healed and all the cuts and bruises healed – but something else had broken, something in his neck. He cannot feel anything anywhere in his body – or, at least, they do not think he can. He does not react when his body is touched. But he cannot speak and tell us what he feels and what he does not feel – "

"He can't speak?" Samuel asked her. "Can he hear you? Can he think and see?"

"His eyes are open, and sometimes he moves them to follow activity. He can grunt and make noises, but they cannot be understood. We can't ever be sure he understands us, but Bella believes he can."

"Bella?"

"His wife. My husband's mother. She tends him night and day, she dribbles food down his throat and cleans him – " Leonora shuddered delicately. I took that to mean that caring for the invalid was no easy task. "She is devoted to him," she whispered.

"Who is looking after the affairs of Kessing?" Samuel wanted to know. It was a fair question. Kessing was a good-sized territory and its lord was absolute law for several thousand souls.

"Lady Bella and my husband divide much of the work between them," Leonora said. Once she had finished the harrowing tale of Sir Havan's accident, Leonora felt capable of facing us again. She lifted her drowned blue eyes and fixed them on Samuel. I wondered what sort of effect their limpid sweetness would have on him. "But at Kessing, we maintain the fiction that Sir Havan still rules."

"How is that done?" I asked.

She looked at me. "Sir Havan has always held a public audience twice a month at which any vassal or tenant could air a grievance or sue for a favor," she said. "He still holds these open meetings – we carry him out and set him upon a chair, and people recite their petitions. Bella and Errol actually decide the cases, but if they make a ruling with which he disagrees, he grunts and moans and twists in his chair. So they call back the petitioner and revise their original judgment."

"So he is able to communicate," Sam said thoughtfully.

"In a way."

"And he is able to understand what goes on around him."

"He seems to be."

"And yet his condition has not improved for six months?"

"It has not improved, it has not deteriorated. It has not changed at all."

"And what do your halani say? I assume you have consulted one or two."

A smile touched her sad lips. "Dozens. They have fed him no end of potions and chanted hundreds of spells over his head. Nothing has availed. His body remains broken and his spirit remains trapped."

"And so you want me to kill him," I said evenly.

She looked at me quickly, her blue eyes utterly serious. "I have always loved Sir Havan," she said. "He is a good man and he has done many good things. But I cannot bear to see him suffer so much, day after day, dependent on another's hand to feed him and bathe him and tend him. You don't understand – you never knew him – he was so alive, so active, so sure of himself. To see him like this...I would not want to live in such a way. I would not condemn anyone to such a life."

"And why should Aesara be the one to murder him?" Sam asked bluntly. "If you have dozens of halani already at your fortress – "

"It is a terrible thing to ask another human being to take a life," she said quietly. "And it is, as you say, murder. If one of the resident halani were to commit such an act, and be discovered, he or she would be put to death as well. I cannot ask them to do it."

"And Aesara? What if someone discovered *she* had poured the poison into the lord's drink?" Sam asked. "You've asked it of *her*."

"No one knows her at Kessing," Leonora replied quickly.

"One person has already recognized her," he pointed out.

"But Aesara could come in disguise. No one would ever know she had been the one to kill him."

I smiled at Sam again. He was such an innocent. All the years of intrigue that I had witnessed at Verallis would stand me in good stead now. "No, and no one would ever be certain if he had been murdered or if he had merely died at last," I told Sam. "That is the other reason the lady would like to hire my services."

Sam looked from me to Leonora and back at me. "I don't understand."

I kept my eyes on Leonora and my voice casual. "It has been eleven years, but surely you remember the scandal that attended King Raever's death?" I asked. "He had been unwell for a few days – everyone knew this, for there are no secrets at Verallis – and I had mixed him a batch of potions to restore him to good health. Shortly after taking one of them, one night, he died. Did I kill him? Was he much sicker than anyone had supposed? Did some prince or courtier, knowing I might be blamed, mix a deadly philtre and administer it in place of mine? No one was ever completely certain – which is why, Samuel, my friend, I sit here with you today in Salla City instead of drifting over the scattered lands of Sorretis as smoke and ashes, having been burned at the stake for treason."

There was a short silence. Leonora did not like to say baldly that she was sure I had killed my king, although clearly she believed it. Sam offered no comment at all.

"I'm interested in knowing," I said, "what the lord's wife and son think about this idea of yours."

The blue eyes were utterly guileless; she met my gaze openly. "It was Bella's idea," she said softly. "She is the one who recognized you here a few months back."

My eyes narrowed. That could very well be the truth. I had seen the traveling coach bowl through Salla City and recognized the heraldry on the door, for all of Raever's vassals were known to me, at least by reputation. I had not gone to the trouble of ducking behind a doorway as the horses slowed and passed. I had not expected to be identified.

"And your husband?" I asked.

"He is not convinced. But he has said to me in private that it would be a blessing for his father if he should die."

"And who rules Kessing when Sir Havan is gone?"

"Errol. And if Errol should die without heirs, his sister."

"And what does she think of this scheme to dispatch her father?"

"She has not been informed."

I picked up my glass of wine, which, like Leonora's, was almost untouched. Even Sam had only taken one or two swallows. I sipped the sweet, heavy liquid meditatively and thought it over. Well, clearly this angelically fair woman would profit if the murder were carried out, but as the case was presented, it was hard to tell if that was her motive. Giving all the participants the benefit of the doubt, it could be that they truly planned a mercy killing for which the corpse itself would thank me. For which all of Kessing would thank me, no doubt. I knew how uneasy subjects and vassals could become when their leader fell ill or grew uncertain. But to coolly and with calculated forethought kill a man...

"When is the next public audience?" I asked her.

She tried to smother her hopeful look. "A week from today, halana," she said. "Will you come?"

I nodded slowly. "I think so. I want to see Sir Havan for myself. At that point I will decide whether I will help you or not."

"And if you decide to help me?"

"I will give you a potion to give to your lord."

It was nearly full dark by the time Leonora left. Sam escorted her out; when he returned to my table, he was carrying a fresh bottle of wine. We had drunk very little of the sweet, fruity stuff he had brought for his visitor, but this was a dry red wine Sam usually chose for his serious drinking. He had finished two glasses before either of us said a word.

"Why don't you go ahead and ask me?" I said finally. I had elected to stay with the sweeter vintage, and I was sipping it much more slowly.

He poured himself another glass. "Why did you agree to go to Kessing and look this lord over?"

I was surprised into a laugh. "That's not the question," I said.

"It's the question I'm interested in the answer to."

I raised my own glass and inhaled the heavy, honeyed aroma. I said, "The real question is: Did you kill King Raever, or did you not?"

"That's not something I would ask you," Sam said quietly.

"I have always wanted to know," I said, "if you recognized my name when I arrived here five years ago."

"I recognized it."

"And so you must have known the scandal that followed me across Sorretis?"

"I had heard it."

"And yet you never wondered whether or not you harbored a murderer in your establishment?"

"I did not care," he said deliberately. I had erased pain from his wife's body, and so he did not care what I had done to others. He added, "Then."

I pounced on the word. "Then? And now?"

He raised his eyes and regarded me steadily. It was a familiar look; he often studied me this way. I was never sure what he hoped to learn. "I have always thought that you probably know how to kill a man."

I swallowed some of my wine. "I do."

"And that you have probably, in fact, killed one or two in your life."

I took another swallow. "I have."

"And it has seemed to me that whatever reasons you would have had for such actions would satisfy me. So I didn't worry about it."

That easily. I had won a man's trust merely by keeping silence for five years. I leaned back against the bench and closed my eyes. "When I was first named halana rex," I said, "I was known more for healing than for killing. For I had quite extraordinary abilities. Some halani are born healers – they need only to lay their fingers upon a man to cure his disease or to knit together the severed fibers of his bones. I had such skills, in those days. I radiated power – my hands seemed to glow at night when I watched them in the dark."

I had consumed more of the wine than I had thought, for my head was beginning to ache and behind my closed eyes I felt the bar rock gently around me. "Five summers after I joined Raever's court," I said, "there was an epidemic. A plague. It swept through the villages on the roads leading to Verallis – it rampaged through the royal household – it laid low guards and servants and noble ladies and faithful vassals and visiting dignitaries. No one was safe. No one was spared.

"Except me. So strong were my healing powers that I never succumbed to illness. Naturally, I ran through the castle, wherever the sickness took root, laying my hands upon the afflicted ones and exorcising the plague. I went to the guardhouses and the guesthouses and the nearby inns and villas, to find felled bodies writhing on the beds and on the floors. On each hot cheek I laid my cool hands, and the disease was routed. I rode like a madwoman through the night to the nearest villages, and stretched my arms out so that twenty people at a time could crowd around me and scratch at my flesh and be healed just by touching me. So exhausted was I, after three days of riding, that I collapsed in the square of one of these villages, unconscious and unmoving. And still they brought the ill and the helpless to my side, and still they reached out to touch me, and still they were cured."

I was silent for a long moment. I had not noticed Sam finishing his last glass of wine, but now I heard him pour another one. "Yet it is not healing for which I am remembered," I said finally. "But for killing."

"You never answered my question," he said.

I opened my eyes and looked at him. The wine or the memories or the dim lighting of the bar made him look softer and younger than usual. "What question was that?"

"Why did you agree to go to Kessing and see the lord? You have not raised a hand to help a soul since the night you gave peace to my Mari."

I closed my eyes again. "Because Leonora was wrong," I said. "I did know Sir Havan of Kessing. Eleven years ago, when I lived at Verallis."

★

I had expected the public audience at Kessing to be gruesome, and it was. Like most of the major fortress holdings of Sorretis, Kessing was built of a heavy gray stone that even on sunny days seemed to enclose a gloomy chill. Inside was a huge chamber where all the supplicants gathered twice a month to make their requests of their lord. Such public audiences were often loud and boisterous affairs; but at Kessing, where the petitioners spoke to a pitiful shell of a man, the mood was sober and deeply depressing.

Sam had casually offered to accompany me on the journey, and I had casually accepted, but inwardly I had been extremely grateful for his escort. I was doubly grateful for his presence now, a solid bulk in this sea of strangers. We stood at the back of the enormous room, gazing over perhaps two hundred bodies, staring toward the dais at the far end where Sir Havan of Kessing had been installed.

Everything Leonora had said of him was true. His head lolled back on his unsupportive neck; his arms and legs hung uselessly down. He had been tied to a large, cushioned chair so that he seemed, at least, to be sitting up and facing us. But his slack mouth and unfocused eyes gave little evidence that his mind was engaged.

Beside him, Lady Bella knelt on an embroidered stool. Leonora stood behind him, gazing down at the inexpressive face. Sir Errol stood at the head of the stage, a herald beside him to call out names, and gravely listened to each petition. It was not a cheery or inspiring scene.

"What do you think of the lord's wife?" I whispered in Sam's ear, as we watched the slow procession.

"She seems to genuinely love the man," he whispered back. "It's a hard thing to counterfeit under such conditions."

I nodded. "And his son?"

"He seems capable enough, but not a happy man."

"Does he want his father dead?"

"Wouldn't you," Sam said slowly, "if your father lived like this?"

"And the son's wife?"

Only once had Leonora lifted her head and surveyed the crowd. Within minutes, she had spotted us. I could see the color of her eyes even across the wide stone floor. She had not smiled or nodded, but merely dropped her gaze again to her father-in-law's face.

"She's ambitious, I think," Sam said slowly. "But she does not look cruel."

"Tell me," I said. "What would you choose, if you were Sir Havan of Kessing? Would you want to continue to live, imprisoned in such a wreck of a body? Or would you want some kind soul to mete out the poison that would let you die, quietly and in peace?"

"I would drink the poison, and gladly," Sam said.

"So would I."

For a few moments longer, I watched Sir Havan across the room. As I had told Sam, I had known Havan and Lady Bella, but not well, and that had been eleven years ago. He had been a laughing, virile, confrontational man who had had as many friends as enemies at Verallis. Raever had trusted him, though they had disagreed often enough, and spectacularly enough, to be considered wary allies. I had not dealt much with court politics, but of course I had met most of the personalities of the day, and Havan had been one of the brightest.

He had not been at Verallis when Raever died. He had not been one of those who accused me or defended me. I wondered what opinion he had, in fact, held of me – not that the knowledge would influence me one way or the other now.

We had been there maybe an hour when a strange commotion erupted on the dais. Sir Errol had just pronounced some sentence on a cowed-looking yokel, when the mangled body of Sir Havan made a violent reaction. Even from this distance, we could hear the formless grunts and whines. We could see the head shake and the shoulders twitch against the sides of the chair. Leonora's hands flew to her cheeks. Bella's fingers wrapped themselves around her husband's wrist. Errol crossed to his father's side and bent over the shivering body as if to try and understand the indecipherable sounds. He turned back to the man he had just dismissed.

"Wait!" he called out. "My father has reversed the judgment."

On the words, Sir Havan grew calm again. The dejected man straightened and made a field-hand's salute toward the stage. "My lord," he said, and backed into the crowd. All around us the audience murmured in a muffled unease.

"I can't stand this," I said. I found that my fingers had clutched Samuel's arm in a grip that must have been painful; I dropped my hand.

"Do you want to leave?" he asked.

I shook my head. "I owe Havan the courtesy of staying long enough to be certain."

And so we stayed, through each grim petition, each inaudible argument. Havan did not again attempt to communicate. It was with indescribable relief that I saw the last petitioner make his case, hear his judgment, bow, and rejoin the assembly. Now what? Everyone appeared to be waiting for some cue, some gesture of release. I saw activity on the dais and realized that four footman had lifted the lord's chair and now were carrying it carefully off the stage, down through the ranks of petitioners, and toward the exit. No one would leave the room before the lord. As the crowd divided, Sam and I found ourselves along the aisle that opened between the dais and the door. Wordlessly, we watched as Havan was carried toward us, his arms flopping against the sides of the chair, his gaze running wildly around the circle of watching faces.

He saw me and his eyes locked on mine.

It was as if he tried to lunge from the chair. His body spasmed and one of his feet kicked out, landing with considerable force against a footman's chin. The servant stumbled, lost his grip, and came to his knees, desperately trying to keep his hold. Bella screamed from the stage. The crowd loosed a collective gasp of dismay and stepped backward as if to avoid contamination.

The other footmen hastily settled the chair on the floor as Sam strode over to offer assistance. I trailed reluctantly behind. "Shall I call for help?" Sam asked. "Do you want me to carry one leg?"

"No, no, I just lost my balance," said the shaken servant.

I paid little attention to the conference between Sam and the footmen; I ignored the sound of Bella's footsteps hurrying across the hall. Havan was still staring at me, still trembling in his seat. His mouth worked as if he would speak the most urgent message. He recognized me, that was clear. He knew what I was capable of. Did he want to shriek at me to go away, to leave him alone, to take my sorcerous potions elsewhere?

Did he want to beg me to release him?

I knelt before him and took one nerveless hand in mine, feeling the fingers lax and chilly. As soon as I touched him, he grew still; he stopped his frantic jerking. Even his eyes seemed more serene, though they never wavered from my face. I could read that look, I thought. Do what you can for me. I squeezed his fingers, then dropped his hand as Bella came skidding to a halt beside him. I did not want her to see me again, to guess why I had come. I stepped back into the silent crowd and turned my face away until Havan had finally been carried out the door.

We had agreed to meet Leonora at a small inn just outside the fortress gates. She came to us that evening with another cadre of guards in the blue-and-gold livery of Kessing.

"Well?" she asked the instant she was shown into our room. "Do you believe now that I told you the truth?"

"I believe you," I said wearily. I had mixed up a potion as soon as we entered the inn. I had sworn to never again interfere in the lives of others, but it is easier to break a promise to yourself than to break a promise to someone else. "No one should have to live like that."

I handed her the vial, wrapped in blue silk, the color of her eyes. She took it from me with those eyes at their widest. "This is it? Already? This is the potion?" she asked, almost stammering. "What must be done?"

"He must drink all of it," I said. "There is not much and it has no flavor. It can be mixed in wine or water. He will not know what he is taking."

She unwrapped the vial and stared at the clear liquid through the glass. "And it will not hurt him?" she whispered. "He will feel no pain?"

"None, I swear to you," I said.

Quickly she rewrapped the philtre and tucked it inside her reticule. I wondered exactly how she planned to administer this to him, but decided not to ask. She seemed quite resourceful. "What do I owe you?" she wanted to know.

I shook my head. "I want nothing from you."

"But – surely – I have brought gold with me, and jewels – "

"This is not a service for which I wish to be paid," I said quietly.

She hesitated a moment, then nodded. "Very well," she said. "On behalf of Sir Havan and his family, I thank you."

"I don't want thanks, either," I said.

She could see that I would not take her hand, but she required something more of a leavetaking, so she offered her hand to Sam. He took it gravely, shook it, and released her. "Goodbye, my lady," he said, and ushered her toward the door.

I was staring out the single small window, but I knew he had turned back to watch me once he locked Leonora out. "Do you want to leave for Salla City first thing in the morning?" he asked.

It was not quite dusk, and the trek would take us several hours. "No," I said, "I want to leave tonight. Now."

We did not push the horses, and in fact the cool, starlit journey was almost pleasant. In the night air, sounds seemed to be invested with a strange significance; each hoofbeat, each jingle of the bridle sounded distinct and mysterious in the plush silence. We encountered no other travelers on the way.

We had been riding for nearly two hours when I began, without prompting, to tell my story. "Raever was dying," I said. "I was the only one who knew it. He had contracted a disease of the blood for which I did not have the remedy. I tried – Leith and Egeva, how I tried – to produce an antidote that would save him, but there are some diseases, I have learned, for which there are no cures. He was not in great pain – that much, as you know, I could do for him – but his body was growing frail and his memory had become unreliable. As I said, no one but me knew just how sick he was, and me he had sworn to secrecy.

"Raever did not fear many things, but he had an absolute abhorrence of weakness, of dependency. He hated to see someone beg – he did not even care much for humility. The idea of a gradual, wasting illness, which would leave him utterly at the mercy of others, was terrible to him. And so he asked me for a philtre that would release him early into death."

I fell silent a moment. Samuel made no comment. Had I not seen his fingers shift upon the reins, I would have thought he was asleep. "At first, I refused, for he was my king and I did not want him to die. Also, I had not yet despaired of finding a cure. But no more than he could, could I bear to see him fall into faintness and delirium, and we agreed that if he were to die by his own hand, it should be while he was still able to rationally choose such a death.

"It was Raever who came up with the plan. He had me mix up a month's supply of potions, all in separate, identical bottles. Twenty-nine of them would be filled with a few harmless ounces of water – only one would carry the death dosage inside. He would drink one every night before he went to bed, destroying the bottle before he slept so that no one would find it and later suspect that I had given him poison. He chose this method," I added, "because he said that no man, even one who wanted to die, should know with certainty the hour of his death."

"And did you in fact present him with the thirty bottles?" Samuel asked at last.

"I did."

"And upon which night did he die?"

I whispered, "The twenty-third."

"It seems to me," Sam said, his voice slow and comforting in the dark, "that a king as clever as Raever was said to be would know that suspicion would fall on you, no matter how careful he was with these bottles."

"Oh, he knew it. I knew it. He wanted me to leave Verallis a few days before he began taking his nightly potions, so I would not be there for any inquisition. But I could not bear to leave him while he was still alive, while

there still might be something I could do for him, however small. I was prepared for the maelstrom that followed. At that, I did not greatly care if they
condemned me to death or allowed me to live. Not much really mattered to
me once Raever was dead."

"You loved him," Sam said.

"He had a wife and three daughters, and he was twenty years older than
I was."

"Yet you loved him," Sam repeated stubbornly.

"I *believed* in him," I said. "He was an autocratic and domineering man,
but he had such vision and strength of purpose. There was nothing he could
have asked me to do that I would not have done, for it seemed to me that this
man, more clearly than anyone I had ever met, understood right and wrong
in the largest sense. I am not the only one from whom he commanded great
devotion. We were a court of disciples, and we fell apart when our leader
died."

"And yet I hear good things about his daughter, who is now the queen."

"Yes," I said wearily. "She is an intelligent woman and she rules well. But
she is not Raever. Something went out of the world when Raever died."

"Something went out of you," he said.

I looked over at him, but I could not see much in the dark. "What do you
mean?"

"You're the healer," he said. "Mend your own broken heart."

"*Your* heart has been broken," I said swiftly. "Do you think it is an easy
thing to fix?"

"I think," he replied carefully, "that someone with the right skills could
heal me."

I faced forward again. The road ahead looked endless. "There are some
things for which there are no cures," I said.

It might have been my imagination, but I thought I heard him sigh. We
rode on into the unchanging darkness.

Naturally, I slept late the next day. It had only been a few hours before dawn
when Sam and I arrived in Salla City. He had accompanied me to the cottage
I had rented on the edge of town, watched me dismount, and taken the reins
of my horse. It was, after all, his horse. He did not say goodbye as he rode
away, and I did not look back at him as I let myself into my unlit house.

Now it was late afternoon, and I was, surprisingly, hungry. I had not eaten
for nearly twenty-four hours, but still, hunger was a sensation I rarely experienced. I rose and moved aimlessly about my cottage, but there was very little

in the cupboards which could be turned into a meal. I felt a curious reluctance to go to Sam's for dinner, certain as I was that he would join me for the meal. I knew better than to rely on the gentleness and seeming strength of any man. I had gone so long without yielding my burdens to anyone. What made me long now to take my comfort from somebody else's heart?

I shook my head and concentrated on putting together a makeshift meal from some moldy biscuits and a vinegary jug of wine. Out of habit, I pulled out my zafo cards and shuffled them. Mostly to distract myself, I laid out a standard grid and turned the cards over in my own unconventional order.

The primary significator: the hooded figure. The final outcome: the black queen. I smiled faintly. These same two cards had appeared in the last reading I had done, only then their positions had been reversed. Now the shadowy, unformed image was in my past, and in my future was the assured, powerful, dark-haired woman. What had I left behind, then, and what was I to become?

The four cards in the second row, the pictures of my past, showed more hazy and undefined images. There, the secretive moon that refused to answer questions; there, the locked box, showing that treasures had been denied. Again, the black king reversed. Beside him, the roan stallion, who bespoke restlessness, travel and change.

In the third row, all was altered. A stack of twelve coins indicated the richness of my fortune, and a blazing sun shone upon my home. The white king appeared to answer the questions of my heart, and in the position that indicated career, the winged horse spread its alabaster wings. This last card was the elemental symbol for air and had been taken by the halani to mean magical ability. A rebirth of my power; a professional renaissance.

I chewed on another stale biscuit and thought for a moment. Clearly, it was going to be impossible to keep the events of Kessing a secret. I had known that before I undertook the journey. Bella had recognized me on the street and had spoken my name at least once. She would be even more likely to mention it again after all this. If I stayed in Salla City, I would be found. If I was found, there were others who would bring requests to me of a dangerous and highly emotional nature. I had sworn never to interfere again in the lives of others, but Raever had made me take another vow.

"Promise me you will not kill yourself after I am dead," he had said. I had been amazed. How had he known about the second vial I had mixed up, giving one to him and keeping one for myself? "Promise me this disease will only take one life."

And because I had been unable to refuse him anything, I had promised, but I had only in the most rudimentary way kept my vow. You could not say I had really lived in the past eleven years.

Except for the last couple of days, when once again I had held life and death in my hands, and shuddered at the responsibility.

I picked up the white king and studied it a moment. A fair-haired man, or a good man, or an old man; the card meant all of these things. I had not looked for such a card in such a position at such a time in my life.

Outside, I heard the gate squeal on the unoiled hinges, and running footsteps crossed the gravel walk. I did not have much time to debate whether or not I would answer the door before it was flung open and Sam strode into the room. He had never before entered my house, for he had never been invited in, and I stared at him in astonishment.

He was laughing. Before I could move toward him or away, he was upon me. He grabbed me around the waist and lifted me in the air. I clutched at his shoulders to keep my balance, staring down at him in excitement and alarm.

"Samuel Berris!" I cried out. "What are you doing?"

He actually tossed me once in the air once before setting me on my feet. Then he hugged me and finally let me go.

"The news from Kessing arrived this morning," he said.

I made a big show of smoothing my hair down after the unexpected rough treatment. "It did?" I said coldly.

"It was a miracle, they say. None of the halani can explain it. Sir Havan of Kessing awoke this morning a whole man, with all his limbs answering the call of his will and his mind completely sharp. He is weak, of course, and they think it will be some time before he walks again under his own power, but he is well, he is healed. There has been a general rejoicing throughout Kessing."

"I'm sure there has been," I said. "Who brought the news to Salla City?"

"Some peddler. Not the Lady Leonora."

"I wonder how she reacted to the news this morning," I said.

Sam grinned. "She is a most dutiful and loving daughter-in-law," he said. "I'm sure she fell to her knees in gratitude."

"I doubt she will ever thank me personally," I said.

Sam was watching me, some of his elation tempered now with speculation. "Lady Bella will, though," he said. "Or the lord himself. You cannot expect this secret to be kept."

"No," I said. "I can't."

"And will you be here when they come?" he asked. "And when the others come, with terrible stories of dying lords and sick children and beloved mothers wracked with pain? Will you be here when travelers come to Salla City, looking for you?"

I glanced around the rented cottage. Perhaps I could have done more with it, changed the curtains or stocked the larder. "I don't care much for this place," I said. "That's why I spent so much time in your tavern."

"I have a house that is too big for one," he said. "And it's very close to the tavern."

I looked at him. "I thought your heart was broken," I said.

"I know a healer," he replied.

"I will be traveling a lot," I said. "None of these sick mothers and crying babies will be able to journey to Salla City."

"I like to travel," he said. "Groyce can mind the bar."

"Then I suppose I will stay in Salla City," I said.

"Good," he said, "I'll help you pack."

Not that there was much to transfer to the small, welcoming house behind the tavern. Groyce and Sam carried the heavier items I elected to keep. Lina helped me organize my clothes. She smiled at me shyly, and for the first time in the five years that I had known her, I attempted to make conversation.

"I'm glad you're staying," she told me when I asked her how she was. "I'm going to have a baby."

It was not quite dark yet, and we had just moved the last of my things into Sam's house, when one of the girls from the tavern ran over with more news. A delegation had been spotted on the road, led by a virtual army of blue-and-gold-clad guards.

"So soon?" I murmured, wiping dust from my face.

"They're late," Sam said. "They should have been here by noon."

"Who are they?" Groyce asked. "Friends of the noblewoman who was here?"

"Friends of Aesara's," Sam said. He took my hand, and we went outside together to greet the travelers.

Hallucigenia

Laird Barron

Laird Barron (*www.benjamindesign.com/lairdbarron*) lives in Olympia, Washington. Barron was born in Alaska, where he raised and trained huskies for many years and moved to Seattle in the mid-'90s, where he began to concentrate on writing poetry and fiction. He has published stories since 2000, characteristically horrific, in *Sci-Fiction*, *The Magazine of Fantasy & Science Fiction*, and his stories have been reprinted in *The Year's Best Fantasy and Horror* and in our *Year's Best Fantasy 6* last year. We think he is a major talent.

"Hallucigenia" was published in *The Magazine of Fantasy & Science Fiction*, the source for more stories in this year's volume than any other. In our opinion, *Fantasy & Science Fiction* had a great year most especially for fantasy, and is now in a leading position. Barron's story is a fine long piece of post-Lovecraftian cosmic horror reminiscent of H. P. Lovecraft's classic novella "The Case of Charles Dexter Ward." Barron gives us glimpses, through the central character's drugged and maddened consciousness, of things too horrific to remember, too evil to be merely natural. As Robert Frost remarked, "What but design of darkness to apall?" This is a story that gets darker, and darker, and darker, and darker.

> And I remembered the cry of the peacocks.
>
> — WALLACE STEVENS

I.

THE BENTLEY NOSED INTO the weeds along the shoulder of the road and died. No fuss, no rising steam, nothing. Just the tick, tick, tick of cooling metal, the abrupt silence of the car's occupants. Outside was the shimmering country road, a desolate field, and a universe of humidity and suffocating heat.

Delaney was at the wheel, playing chauffeur for the Boss and the Boss's wife, Helen. He said to Helen, "She does this when it's hot. Vapor lock, probably." He yanked the lever, got out, and lighted a cigarette. His greased crewcut, distorted by the curve of the windshield, ducked beneath the hood.

Helen twisted, smiled at Wallace. "Let's walk around." She waggled her camera and did the eyebrow thing.

"Who are you, Newt Helmut?" Wallace was frying in the backseat, sweating like a bull, khakis welded to his hocks, thinking maybe he had married an alien. His big, lumpen nose was peeling. He was cranky.

Fresh from Arizona, Helen loved the bloody heat; loved tramping in briars and blackberry tangles where there were no lurking scorpions or snakes. She was a dynamo. Meanwhile, Wallace suffered the inevitable lobster sunburns of his Irish heritage. Bugs were furiously attracted to him. Strange plants gave him rashes. He wondered how fate could be so sadistic to arrange such a pairing.

Maybe Dad had been right. When he received the news of the impending nuptials, Wallace's father had worn an expression of a man who has been stabbed in the back and was mostly pained by the fact his own son's hand gripped the dagger. Paxton women were off limits! The families, though distanced by geography, were intertwined, dating back to when Dalton Smith and George Paxton served as officers during WWII. Dalton quailed at the very notion of his maverick sons mucking about with George's beloved granddaughter and obliterating a familial alliance decades in the forging. Well, maybe brother Payton could bag one, Payton was at least respectable, although that was hardly indemnity against foolishness – after all, his French actress was a neurotic mess. But Wallace? Out of the question entirely. Wallace Smith, eldest scion of the former senior senator of Washington State, was modestly wealthy from birth by virtue of a trust fund and no mean allowance from his father. Wallace, while having no particular interest in amassing a fortune, had always rankled at the notion he was anything less than a self-made man and proved utterly ingenious in the wide world of high finance and speculation. He dabbled in an assortment of ventures, but made his killing in real estate development. Most of his investments occurred offshore in poor, Asian countries like Vietnam and Thailand and Korea where dirt was cheap but not as cheap as the lives of peasant tenants who were inevitably dispossessed by their own hungry governments to make way for American-controlled shoe factories, four-star hotels and high-class casinos.

The trouble was, Wallace had been too successful too soon; he had lived the early life of any ten normal men. He had done the great white hunter bit in the heart of darkest Africa; had floated the Yellow River and hiked across the Gobi desert; climbed glaciers in Alaska and went skin diving in Polynesia. The whole time he just kept getting richer and the feats and stunts and adventures went cold for him, bit by bit, each mountain conquered. Eventually he pulled in his horns and became alarmingly sedentary and complacent. In a manner of speaking, he became fat and content. Oh, the handsome, charismatic man of action was there, the high stakes gambler, the financial lion, the exotic lover – they were simply buried under forty extra pounds of suet following a decade of rich food and boredom. It was that professional ennui that provoked a midlife crisis and led him into the reckless pursuits of avocations best reserved for youngsters. Surfing and sweat lodges. Avant-garde poetry and experimental art. Psychedelic drugs, and plenty of them. He went so far as to have his dick pierced while under the influence. Most reckless of all, love. Specifically love for a college girl with world-beater ambitions. A college girl who could have been a daughter in another life.

Wallace returned Helen's smile in an act of will. "Why not? But I'm not doing anything kinky, no matter how much you pay me."

"Shucks," Helen said, and bounced. Dressed in faded blue overalls, she resembled a slightly oversized Christmas elf.

Wallace grunted and followed. Hot as a kiln. It slapped him across florid jowls, doubled his vision momentarily. He absently unglued his tropical shirt from his paunch and took a survey. On the passenger side, below the gravel slope and rail, spread the field: a dead farm overrun with brittle grass and mustard-yellow clusters of dandelions on tall stalks. Centered in the morass, a solitary barn, reduced to postcard dimensions, half-collapsed. Farther on, more forest and hills.

He had lived around these parts, just west of Olympia, for ages. The field and its decaying barn were foreign. This was a spur, a scenic detour through a valley of failed farmland. He did not come this way often, had not ever really looked. It had been Helen's idea. She was eager to travel every back road, see what was over every new hill. They were not in a hurry – cocktails with the Langans at The Mud Shack were not for another hour and it was nothing formal. No business; Helen forbade it on this, their pseudo-honeymoon. The real deal would come in August, hopefully. Wallace's wrangling with certain offshore accounts and recalcitrant foreign officials had delayed the works long enough, which was why he did not argue, did not press his luck. They could do a loop on the Alcan if it made her happy.

Caw-ca-caw! A crow drifted toward the pucker brush. Wallace tracked it with his index finger and cocked thumb.

"You think somebody owns that?" Helen swept the field with a gesture. She uncapped the camera. Beneath denim straps her muscular shoulders shone slick as walnut.

"Yeah." Wallace was pretty sure what was coming. He glanced at his Gucci loafers with a trace of sadness. He called to Delaney. "What d'ya got, Dee?" Stalling.

Delaney muttered something about crabs. Then, "It ain't a vapor lock. Grab my tools. They're by the spare."

Wallace sprang the trunk, found the oily rag with the wrenches. He went around front, where a scowling Delaney sucked on another cigarette. The short, dusky man accepted the tools without comment. Greasy fingerprints marred his trousers. His lucky disco pants, tragically.

"Want me to call a wrecker?" Wallace tapped the cell phone at his hip. He made a note to send Delaney's pants to Mr. Woo, owner of the best dry cleaners this side of Tacoma. Mr. Woo was a magician with solvents.

Delaney considered, dismissed the idea with a shrug. "Screw it. I've got some electric tape, I'll fix it. If not, we'll get Triple-A out here in a bit."

"What can I do?"

"Stand there looking sexy, Boss. Or corral your woman before she wanders off into the woods."

Wallace noticed that his darling wife waded waist-deep in the grass, halfway across the clearing, her braids flopping merrily. He sighed, rolled his shoulders, and started trudging. Yelling at this distance was undignified. Lord, keeping track of her was worse than raising a puppy.

The crumbling grade almost tripped him. At the bottom, remnants of a fence – rotted posts, snares of wire. Barbs dug a red zigzag in his calf. He cursed, lumbered into the grass. It rose, coarse and brown, slapped his legs and buttocks. A dry breeze awoke and the yellow dandelion blooms swayed toward him.

Wallace's breath came too hard too quickly. Every step crackled. Bad place to drop a match. He remembered staring, mesmerized, at a California brushfire in the news. No way on God's green Earth – or in His dead grass sea – a walrus in loafers would outrace such a blaze. "Helen!" The shout emerged as a wheeze.

The barn loomed, blanked a span of the sky. Gray planks, roof gone to seed wherever it hadn't crumpled. Jagged windows. In its long shadow lay the tottered frame of a truck, mostly disintegrated and entangled in brambles. Wallace shaded his eyes, looking for the ruins of the house that must be nearby, spotted a foundation several yards away where the weeds thinned. Nothing left but shattered concrete and charred bits of timber.

No sign of Helen.

Wallace wiped his face, hoped she had not fallen into a hole. He opened his mouth to call again and stopped. Something gleamed near his feet, small and white. Squirrel bones caught in a bush. A mild surprise that the skeleton was intact. From his hunting experience, he knew scavengers reliably scattered such remains.

Wallace stood still then. Became aware of the silence, the pulse in his temple. Thirst gnawed him. He suddenly, completely, craved a drink. Whiskey.

And now it struck him, the absence of insects. He strained to detect the hum of bees among the flowers, the drone of flies among the droppings. Zero. The old world had receded, deposited him into a sterile microcosm of itself, a Chinese puzzle box. Over Wallace's shoulder, Delaney and the car glinted, miniature images on a miniature screen. A few dusty clouds dragged shadows across the field. The field flickered, flickered.

"Hey, Old Man River, you having a heart attack, or what?" Helen materialized in the vicinity of the defunct truck. The silver camera was welded to her right eye. Click, click.

"Don't make me sorry I bought that little toy of yours." Wallace shielded his eyes to catch her expression. "Unless maybe you're planning to ditch poetry and shoot a spread for *National Geographic*."

Helen snapped another picture. "Why, yes. I'm photographing the albino boor in its native habitat." She smiled coyly.

"Yah, okay. We came, we saw, we got rubbed by poison sumac. Time to move along before we bake our brains."

"I didn't see any sumac."

"Like you'd recognize it if it bit you on the ass, lady."

"Oh, I would, I would. I wanna take some pictures of that." Helen thrust the camera at the barn. Here was her indefatigable fascination – the girl collected relics and fragments, then let the images of sinister Americana stew in her brain until inspiration gave birth to something essay-worthy. The formula worked, without question. She was on her way to the top, according to the buzz. *Harper's*; *Poetry*; *The New Yorker*, and *Granta* – she was a force to be reckoned with and it was early in the game.

"There it is, fire when ready."

"I want to go inside for a quick peek."

"Ah, shit on that." Wallace's nose itched. The folds of his neck hung loose and raw. A migraine laid bricks in the base of his skull. "It isn't safe. I bet there's some big honking spiders, too. Black widows." He hissed feebly and made pinching motions.

"Well, yeah. That's why I want you to come with me, sweetness. Protect me from the giant, honking spiders."

"What's in it for me?"

She batted her lashes.

"A quick peek, you say."

"Two shakes of a lamb's tail," she said.

"Oh, in that case." Wallace approached the barn. "Interesting."

"What." Helen sounded preoccupied. She fiddled with the camera, frowning. "This thing is going hinky on me – I hope my batteries aren't dying."

"Huh. There's the driveway, and it's been used recently." The track was overgrown. It curved across the field like a hidden scar and joined the main road yonder. Boot prints sank into softer ground near the barn, tire treads and faint marks, as if something flat had swept the area incompletely. The boot prints were impressive – Wallace wore a thirteen wide, and his shoe resembled a child's alongside one.

"Kids. Bet this is a groovy spot to party," Helen said. "My senior year in high school, we used to cruise out to the gravel pits after dark and have bonfire parties. Mmm-mm, Black Label and Coors Light. I can still taste the vomit!"

Wallace did not see any cans, or bottles, or cigarette butts. "Yeah, guess so," he said. "Saw a squirrel skeleton. Damned thing was in one piece, too."

"Really. There're bird bones all over the place, just hanging in the bushes."

"Whole birds?"

"Yup. I shot pictures of a couple. Kinda weird, huh?"

Wallace hesitated at the entrance of the barn, peering through a wedge between the slat doors. The wood smelled of ancient tar, its warps steeped in decades of smoke and brutal sunlight, marinated in manure and urine. Another odor lurked beneath this – ripe and sharp. The interior was a blue-black aquarium. Dust revolved in sluggish shafts.

Helen nudged him and they crossed over.

The structure was immense. Beams ribbed the roof like a cathedral. Squared posts provided additional support. The dirt floor was packed tight as asphalt and littered with withered straw and boards. Obscured by gloom, a partition divided the vault; beyond that the murky impression of a hayloft.

"My god, this is amazing." Helen turned a circle, drinking in the ambience, her face butter-soft.

Along the near wall were ranks of shelves and cabinets. Fouled implements cluttered the pegboard and hooks – pitchforks, shovels, double-headed axes, mattocks, a scythe; all manner of equipment, much of it caked in the gray sediment of antiquity and unrecognizable. Wallace studied what he took to be a curiously shaped bear trap, knew its serrated teeth could pulp a man's thighbone. Rust welded its mouth shut. He had seen traps like it in Argentina and Bengal. A diesel generator squatted in a notch between shelves, bolted to a concrete foot. Fresh grease welled in the battered case.

Was it cooler in here? Sweat dried on Wallace's face, his nipples stiffened magically. He shivered. His eyes traveled up and fixed upon letters chalked above the main doors. Thin and spiky and black, they spelled:

THEY WHO DWELL IN THE CRACKS

"Whoa," Wallace said. There was more, the writing was everywhere. Some blurred by grease and grit, some clear as:

FOOL

Or:

LUCTOR ET EMERGO

And corroded gibberish:

GODOFBLOATCHEMOSHBAALPEEORBELPHEGOR

"Honey? Yoo-hoo?" Wallace backed away from the yokel graffiti. He was sweating again. It oozed, stung his lips. His guts sloshed and prickles chased across his body. Kids partying? He thought not. Not kids.

"Wallace, come here!" Helen called from the opposite side of the partition. "You gotta check this out!"

He went, forcing his gaze from the profane and disturbing phrases. Had to watch for boards; some were studded with nails and wouldn't that take the cake, to get tetanus from this madcap adventure. "Helen, it's time to go."

"Okay, but look. I mean, Jesus." Her tone was flat.

He passed through a pool of light thrown down from a gap in the roof. Blue sky filled the hole. A sucker hole, that's what pilots called them. Sucker holes.

The stench thickened.

Three low stone pylons were erected as a triangle that marked the perimeter of a shallow depression. The pylons were rude phalluses carved with lunatic symbols. Within the hollow, a dead horse lay on its side, mired in filthy, stagnant water. The reek of feces was magnificently awful.

Helen touched his shoulder and pointed. Up.

The progenitor of all wasp nests sprawled across the ceiling like a fantastic alien city. An inverse complex of domes and humps and dangling paper streamers. Wallace estimated the hive to be fully twelve feet in diameter. A prodigy of nature, a primordial specimen miraculously preserved in the depths of the barn. The depending strands jiggled from a swirl of air through a broken window. Some were pink as flesh; others a rich scarlet or lusterless purple-black like the bed of a crushed thumbnail.

Oddly, no wasps darted among the convolutions of the nest, nor did flies or beetles make merry among the feculent quagmire or upon the carcass of the horse. Silence ruled this roost surely as it did the field.

Wallace wished for a flashlight, because the longer he squinted the more he became convinced he was not looking at a wasp nest. This was a polyp, as if the very fabric of the wooden ceiling had nurtured a cancer, a tumor swollen on the bloody juices of unspeakable feasts. The texture was translucent in portions, and its membranous girth enfolded a mass of indistinct shapes. Knotty loops of rope, gourds, hanks of kelp.

Click, click.

Helen knelt on the rim of the hollow, aiming her camera at the horse. Her mouth was a slit in a pallid mask. Her exposed eye rolled.

Wallace pivoted slowly, too slowly, as though slogging through wet concrete. *She shouldn't be doing that. We really should be going.*

Click, click.

The horse trembled. Wallace groaned a warning. The horse kicked Helen in the face. She sat down hard, legs splayed, forehead a dented eggshell. And the horse was thrashing now, heeling over, breaching in its shallow cistern, a blackened whale, legs churning, hooves whipping. It shrieked from a dripping muzzle bound in razor wire. Wallace made an ungainly leap for his wife as she toppled sideways into the threshing chaos. A sledgehammer caught him in the hip and the barn began turning, its many gaps of light spinning like a carousel. He flung a hand out.

Blood and shit and mud, flowing. The sucker holes closed, one by one.

2.

"You're a violent man," Helen said without emphasis. Her eyes were large and cool. "Ever hurt anyone?"

Wallace had barely recovered his wits from sex. Their first time, and in a hot tub no less. He was certainly a little drunk, more than a little adrenalized, flushed and heaving. They had eventually clambered onto the deck and lay as the stars whirled.

Helen pinched him, hard. "Don't you even think about lying to me," she hissed. "Who was it?"

"It's going to be you if you do that again," he growled.

She pinched him again, left a purple thumbprint on his bicep.

Wallace yelled, put her in a mock headlock, kissed her.

Helen said, "I'm serious. Who was it?"

"It's not important."

Helen sat up, wrapped herself in a towel. "I'm going inside."

"What?"

"I'm going inside."

"Harold Carter. We were dorm mates," Wallace said, finally. He was sinking into himself, then, seeing it again with the clarity of fire. "Friend of ours hosted an off-campus poker club. Harold took me once. I wasn't a gambler and it was a rough crowd aiming to trim the fat off rich college kids like ourselves. I wouldn't go back, but Harold did. He went two, three nights a week, sometimes spent the entire weekend. Lost his shirt. Deeper he got, the harder he clawed. Addiction, right? After a while, his dad's checks weren't enough. He borrowed money – from me, from his other buddies, his sister. Still not enough. One day, when he was very desperate, he stole my wallet. It was the week after Christmas vacation and I had three hundred bucks. He blew it at a strip club. Didn't even pay off his gambling marker. I remember waiting up for him when he straggled in at dawn, looking pale and beat. He had glitter on his cheeks from the dancers, for God's sake. He smiled at me with the game face, said hi, and I busted him in the mouth. He lost his uppers, needed stitches. I drove him to the hospital. Only time I ever punched anyone." Which skirted being a lie only by definition. He had flattened a porter in Kenya with the butt of a rifle and had smashed a big, dumb Briton in the face with a bottle of Jameson during a pub brawl in Dublin. They'd had it coming. The porter had tried to abscond with some money and an antique Bowie knife. The Brit was just plain crazy-mean and drunk as a bull in rut. Wallace was not going to talk about that, though.

They lay, watching constellations burn. Helen said, "I'll go to Washington, if I'm still invited."

"Yes! What changed your mind?"

She didn't say anything for a while. When she spoke, her tone was troubled. "You're a magnet. Arizona sucks. It just feels right."

"Don't sound so happy about it."

"It's not that. My parents hate you. Mother ordered me to dump your ass, find somebody not waiting in line for a heart bypass. Not in those words, but there it was." Helen laughed. "So let's get the hell out of here tomorrow – don't tell anybody. I'll call my folks after we settle in."

Wallace's chest ballooned with such joy he was afraid his eyes were going to spring leaks. "Sounds good," he said gruffly. "Sounds good."

Wallace stood in the gaping cargo door of a Huey. The helicopter cruised above a sandy coast, perhaps the thin edge of a desert. The sea was rigid blue like a watercolor. A white car rolled on the winding road and the rotor shadow chopped it in half. He recognized the car as his own from college –

he had sold it to an Iranian immigrant for seventy-five dollars, had forgotten to retrieve a bag of grass from the trunk and spent a few sweaty months praying the Iranian would not know what it was if he ever found it. Was Delaney driving? Wallace wondered why a Huey – he had never served in the military, not even the reserves or the Coast Guard. Too young by a couple of years for Vietnam, and too old for anything that came about during the bitter end of the Cold War. Then he remembered – after the horse broke his leg, he had been airlifted to Harbor View in Seattle.

Soundless, except for Mr. Woo's voice, coming from everywhere and nowhere. God had acquired a Cantonese accent, apparently.

"Mr. Wallace, you are very unlucky in love, I think," Mr. Woo said from the shining air. He was not unkind.

"Three strikes," Wallace said with a smile. He smiled constantly. No one mentioned it, but he was aware. His face ached and he could not stop. "Gracie divorced me. Right out of college, so it doesn't count. A practice run. Beth was hell on wheels. She skinned me alive for what – ten years? If I'd known what kind of chicks glom onto real estate tycoons, I would've jumped a freight train and lived the hobo life. You have no idea, my friend. I didn't really divorce her, I escaped. After Beth, I made a solemn vow to never marry again. Every few years I'd just find some mean, ugly woman and buy her a house. Helen's different. The real deal."

"Oh, Mr. Wallace? I thought you live in big house in Olympia."

"I owned several, in the old days. She took the villa in Cancun. Too warm for me anyway."

"But this one, this young girl. You killed her."

"She's not dead. The doctors say she might come 'round any day. Besides, she's faster than I am. I can't keep up."

"A young girl needs discipline, Mr. Wallace. You must watch over her like a child. She should not be permitted to wander. You are very unlucky."

The chopper melted. Mr. Woo's wrinkled hands appeared first, then a plastic bag with Wallace's suit on a hanger. A wobbly fan rattled above the counter. "Here is your ticket, Mr. Wallace. Here is some Reishi mushroom for Mrs. Wallace. Take it, please."

"Thanks, Woo." Wallace carefully accepted his clothes, carried them from the dingy, chemical-rich shop with the ginger gait of a man bearing holy artifacts. It was a ritual he clung to as the universe quaked around him. With so much shaking and quaking he wondered how the birds balanced on the wire, how leaves stayed green upon their branches.

Delaney met him at the car, took the clothes and held the door. He handed

Wallace his walking stick, waited for him to settle in the passenger seat. Delaney had bought Wallace an Irish blackthorn as a welcome home present. An elegant cane, it made Wallace appear more distinguished than he deserved, Delaney said. Wallace had to agree – his flesh sagged like a cheap gorilla suit, minus the hair, and his bones were too prominent. His eyes were the color of bad liver, and his broad face was a garden of broken veins.

There were reasons. Two hip operations, a brutal physical therapy regimen. Pain was a faithful companion. Except, what was with the angry weals on his neck and shoulders? Keloid stripes, reminiscent of burns or lashes. Helen was similarly afflicted; one had festered on her scalp and taken a swath of hair. Their origin was on the tip of Wallace's tongue, but his mind was in neutral, gears stripped, belts whirring, and nothing stuck. He knocked back a quart of vodka a day, no problem, and had started smoking again. A pack here or there – who was counting? He only ate when Delaney forced the issue. Hells bells, if he drank enough martinis he could live on the olives.

Delaney drove him home. They did not talk. Their relationship had evolved far beyond the necessity of conversation. Wallace stared at the trees, the buildings. These familiar things seemed brand new each time he revisited them. The details were exquisitely rendered, but did not con him into accepting the fishbowl. Artificial: the trees, the houses, the windup people on the shaded streets. Wallace examined his hands: artificial too. The sinews, the soft tissues and skeletal framework were right there in the X-ray sunlight. He was Death waiting to dance as the guest of honor at Día de los Muertos.

Wallace was no longer in the car. The car melted. It did not perturb him. He was accustomed to jumpcuts, seamless transitions, waking dreams. Doctor Green said he required more sleep or the hallucinatory episodes would intensify, destroy his ability to function. Wallace wondered if he ever slept at all. There was no way to be certain. The gaps in his short-term memory were chasms.

He was at home in the big house his fortune built, seated stiffly on the sofa Beth, ex-wife number two, had procured from Malaysia along with numerous throw rugs, vases, and some disturbing artwork depicting fertility goddesses and hapless mortals. He did not like the décor, had never gotten around to selling it at auction. Funny that Beth took half of everything and abandoned these items so punctiliously selected and obtained at prohibitive expense. Wallace's closest friend, Skip Arden, suggested that Beth always hoped things would change for the better, that she might regain favor. Skip offered to burn the collection for him.

Wallace's house was a distorted reflection of the home he had grown up in, a kind of anti-mirror. This modern house was designed by a famous German architect that Beth read of in a foreign art directory. Multi-tiered in the fashion of an antique citadel, and, as a proper citadel, it occupied a hill. There was an ivy-covered wall, a garden, and maple trees. Mt. Rainier fumed patiently in its quarter of the horizon. At night, lights twinkled in the town and inched along the highway. Wallace's personal possessions countered the overwhelming Baroque overtones – his hunting trophies, which included a den crammed with the mounted heads of wild boars, jaguars, and gazelles; and his gun collection, a formidable floor-to-ceiling chestnut-paneled cabinet that contained a brace of armament ranging from an assortment of knives and daggers native to three dozen nationalities, to an even greater array of guns – from WWII American issue Browning .45 automatics up to show-stopping big-game rifles: the Model 76 African .416 and his pride and joy, a Holland & Holland .500, which had come to him from the private collection of a certain Indian prince, and was capable of sitting a bull elephant on its ass. Littered throughout the rambling mansion was the photographic evidence of his rough and wild youth; mostly black and white and shot by compatriots long dead or succumbed to stultified existences similar to his own. The weapons and the photographs grounded his little hot air balloon of sanity, but they also led to thinking, and he had never been one to dwell on the past, to suffer introspection. They were damning, these flybuzz whispers that built and built with each stroke of the minute hand, each wallowing undulation of the ice in his drink. *You always wanted to be Hemingway. Run with the bulls; fire big guns and drink the cantinas dry. Maybe you'll end up like the old man, after all. Let's look at those pistols again, hmm?* And when such thoughts grew too noisy, he took another snort of bourbon and quieted the crowd in his skull.

Outside his skull, all was peaceful. Just Wallace, Helen, Helen's aides, Cecil and Kate, Delaney, and Bruno and Thor, a pair of mastiffs that had been trained by Earl Hutchison out in Yelm. The dogs were quietly ubiquitous as they patrolled the house and the grounds. The gardener called on Friday; the housecleaner and her team every other weekend. They had keys; no one else bothered Wallace except Wallace's friends.

These friends came and went unexpectedly. Ghosts flapping in skins. Who? Skip and Randy Freeman made frequent guest appearances. Barret and Macy Langan; Manfred and Elizabeth Steiner. Wallace thought he had seen his own father, though that was unlikely. Dad divided his time between the VFW, the Masonic Temple, and the Elks Lodge, and according to reports, his participation at social gatherings was relegated to playing canasta, drinking gin, and rambling about "The Big One" as if he had jubilantly kissed a nurse in Times Square to celebrate v-j Day only last week.

"She's getting worse," Skip said as he helped himself to Wallace's liquor. "You should ship her to Saint Pete's and be done with it. Or send her home to ma and pa. Whatever you've got to do to get out from under this mess." He was talking about Helen, although he could have been discussing a prize Hereford, or an expensive piece of furniture. His own wife hated him and refused to live under his roof, it was said. Skip, a reformed attorney-at-law, was older and fatter than Wallace. Skip drank more, too, but somehow appeared to be in much better shape. His craggy features were ruddy as Satan under thick, white hair. Egregiously blunt, he got away with tons of indiscretions because he was a basso profundo who made Perry Mason sound like a Vienna choirboy. Jaws slackened when he started rumbling.

"Is she?" Wallace nodded abstractedly. "I hadn't noticed."

"Yes she is, and yes you have," said Randy Freeman, the radical biologist. Radical was accurate – he had bought *The Anarchist Cookbook* and conducted some experiments in a gravel pit up past the Mima Mounds. Which was how he had blown off his right hand. His flesh-tone prosthesis was nice, but it was not fooling anybody. He had recently completed a study of the behavior of crows in urban environments and planned to write a book. Randy was a proponent of human cloning for spare parts.

Skip said, "Nine months. Enough is enough, for the love of Pete, you could've given birth. Pull yourself together, get back on the horse. Uh, so to speak. You should work." He gestured broadly. "Do *something* besides grow roots on your couch and gawk."

"Yeah," said Randy.

"I do things, Skip. Look, I got my dry cleaning. Here it is. I pick it up every Thursday." Wallace patted the crinkly plastic, rubbed it between his fingers.

"You're taking those pills Green prescribed."

"Sure, sure," Wallace said. Delaney sorted the pills and brought them with a glass of water at the right hour. Good thing, too. There were so many, Wallace would have been confused as to which, where, and when.

"Well, stop taking them. Now."

"Okay." It was all the same to Wallace.

"He can't stop taking them – not all at once," Randy said. "Wallace, what you gotta do is cut back. I'll talk to Delaney."

"We'll talk to Delaney about this, all right. That crap is eating your brain," Skip said. "I'll give you some more free advice. You sue those sonsofbitches that own that Black Hills property. Jerry Premus is champing at the bit to file a claim."

"Yeah...he keeps calling me," Wallace said. "I'm not suing anybody. We shouldn't have been there."

"Go on thinking that, Sparky. Premus will keep the papers warm in case your goddamned senses return," Skip said.

Wallace said, "She is getting worse. I hear strange noises at night, too." It was more than strange noises, wasn't it? What about the figure he glimpsed in the garden after dusk? A hulking shadow in a robe and a tall, conical hat. The getup was similar to but infinitely worse than the ceremonial garb a Grand Dragon of the Ku Klux Klan might wear. The costumed figure blurred in his mind and he was not certain if it existed as anything other than a hallucination, an amalgam of childhood demons, trauma, and drugs.

He looked from his reflection in the dark window and his friends were already gone, slipped away while he was gathering wool. Ice cubes collapsed in his glass. The glass tilted slackly in his hand. "Nine months. Maybe Skipperoo's got a point. Maybe I need to wheel and deal, get into the old groove. What do you think, Mr. Smith?" Wallace spoke to his glum reflection and his reflection was stonily silent.

"Mr. Smith?" Cecil's voice crackled over the intercom, eerily distorted. They had installed the system long ago, but never used it much until after the accident. It was handy, despite the fact it almost gave Wallace a coronary whenever it started unexpectedly broadcasting. "Do you want to see Helen?"

Wallace said, "Yes; be right up," although he was sickened by the prospect. Helen's face was a mess, a terrible, terrible mess, and it was not the only thing. Whenever Wallace looked at her, if he really looked at her a bit more closely after the initial knee-jerk revulsion, the clouds in his memory began to dissolve. Wallace did not like that, did not like the funhouse parade of disjointed imagery, the shocking volume of the animal's screams, the phantom reek of putrescence. The triple pop of Delaney's nickel-plated automatic as he fired into the horse's head. Wallace preferred his thick comforter of pill- and alcohol-fueled numbness.

Dalton had asked him, *You really love this girl? She isn't like one of your chippies you can bang for a few years and buy off with a divorce settlement. This is serious, sonny boy.*

Yeah, Dad. Course, I do.

She a trophy? Better goddamn well not be. Don't shit where you eat.

Dad, I love her.

Good God. You must have it bad. Never heard a Smith say that before....

Wallace pressed the button again. "Is she awake?"

"Uh, yes. I just finished feeding her."

"Oh, good." Wallace walked slowly, not acknowledging Delaney's sudden presence at his elbow. Delaney was afraid he would fall, shatter his fragile hip.

One of Wallace's private contractors had converted a guestroom into Helen's quarters. A rectangular suite with a long terrace over the garden. Hardwood floors and vaulted ceilings. They needed ample space to house her therapy equipment – the hydraulic lift and cargo net to transport her into the changing room, the prototype stander which was a device designed to prevent muscle atrophy by elevating her to a vertical plane on a rectangular board. She screamed torture when they did this every other afternoon and wouldn't quit until Cecil stuck headphones over her ears and piped in Disney music.

Helen lay in bed, propped by a rubber wedge and pillows. During the accident, her brain was deprived of sufficient oxygen for several minutes. Coupled with the initial blunt trauma, skull fractures, and bacterial contamination, the effects were devastating. Essentially, the accident had rendered Helen an adult fetus. Her right hand, curled tight as a hardwood knot, was callused from habitual gnawing. She possessed minimal control of her left hand, could gesture randomly and convulsively grasp objects. Cecil splinted it a few hours a day, as he did her twisted feet, to prevent her tendons from shortening. Her lack of a swallow reflex made tube-feeding a necessity. She choked on drool. It was often impossible to tell if she could distinguish one visitor from another, or if she could see anything at all. Cortical blindness, the doctors said. The worst part was the staph infection she contracted from her open head wound. The dent in her skull would not heal. It refused to scab and was constantly inflamed. The doctors kept changing her medication and predicting a breakthrough, but Wallace could tell they were worried. She had caught a strain resistant to antibiotics and was essentially screwed.

"Hi, Mr. Smith." Cecil carefully placed the feeding apparatus into a dish tub. He was a rugged fellow, close to Helen's age. Built like a linebacker, he was surprisingly gentle and unobtrusive. He faithfully performed his myriad duties and retreated into the adjoining chamber. It was always he or his counterpart, the RN Kate, a burly woman who said even less than Cecil. She dressed in an official starched white pinafore over her conservative dresses with a white hat. Wallace knew when she was around because she favored quaint, polished wooden shoes that click-clocked on the bare floors. Ginger

Rogers, he privately called her. Ginger Rogers tapping through the halls.

Helen flinched and moaned when Wallace took her hand. Startle reflex, was the medical term. She smiled flaccidly, eyes vacant as buttons. She smelled of baby powder and antiseptic.

Wallace heard himself say, "Hey, darling, how was dinner?" Meanwhile, it was the raw wound in her forehead that commanded his attention, drew him with grim certainty, compounded his sense of futility and doom.

Abruptly exhausted, he whispered farewell to Helen and shuffled upstairs and crawled into bed.

3.

After the world waned fuzzy and velvet-dim, he was roused by the noises he had mentioned to Skip and Ken. The night noises.

He pretended it was a dream – the blankets were heavy, his flesh was heavy, he was paralyzed but for the darting of his eyes, the staccato drum roll in his chest. The noises came through the walls and surrounded his bed. Faint sounds, muffled sounds. Scratching and scrabbling, hiccupping and slithering. Soft, hoarse laughter floated up to his window from the garden.

Wallace stashed a .357 magnum in the dresser an arm's length from his bed. He could grab that pistol and unload it at the awful giant he imagined was prowling among the rosebushes and forsythia and snowball trees. He closed his eyes and made fists. Could not raise them to his ears. The room became black as pitch and settled over him and pressed down upon him like a leaden shroud. Grains of plaster dusted the coverlet. *Pitter-pat, pitter-pat.*

4.

Detective Adams caught Wallace on a good morning. It was Wallace's fifty-first birthday and unseasonably cold, with a threat of rain. Wallace was killing a bottle of Hennessy Private Reserve he'd received from Skip as an early present and shaking from a chill that had no name. However, Wallace was coherent for the first time in months. Delaney had reduced the pills per Skip's orders and it was working. He was death-warmed-over, but his faculties were tripping along the tracks right on schedule. He toyed with the idea of strangling Delaney, of hanging him by the heels. His mood was mitigated solely by the fact he was not scheduled for therapy until Thursday. Possibly he hated therapy more than poor shrieking Helen did.

Detective Adams arrived unannounced and joined Wallace on the garden patio at the glass table with the forlorn umbrella. Adams actually resembled a cop to Wallace, which meant he dressed like the homicide cops on the television dramas. He wore a gray wool coat that matched the streaks in his hair. A square guy, sturdy and genial, though it was plain this latter was an affectation, an icebreaker. His stony eyes were too frank for any implication of friendliness to survive long. He flicked a glance at the mostly empty bottle by Wallace's wrist. "Hey there, Mr. Smith, you're looking better every time I swing by. Seriously though, it's cold. Sure you should be hanging around like this? You might get pneumonia or something. My aunt lives over in Jersey. She almost croaked a couple years ago."

"Pneumonia?"

"Nah, breast cancer. Her cousin died of pneumonia. Longshoreman."

Wallace was smoking unfiltered Cheyenne cigarettes in his plushest tiger-striped bathrobe. His feet were tinged blue as day-old fish. His teeth chattered. "Just when you think spring is here, winter comes back to whack us in the balls. One for the road, eh?"

Detective Adams smiled. "How's everything? Your hip...?"

"Mostly better. Bones are healed, so they say. Hurts like hell."

"How's your wife?"

"Helen's parents are angry. They want me to send her to Arizona, pay for a home. They're...yeah, it's screwed up."

"Ah. Are you planning to do that?"

"Do what?"

"Send her home."

"She's got a lot of family in the southwest.... Lot of family." Wallace lighted another cigarette after a few false starts.

"Maybe sending your wife to Arizona is a good idea, Mr. Smith. Heck, a familiar setting with familiar faces, she might snap out of this. Never know."

Wallace smoked. "Fuck 'em. What's new with you, Detective?"

"Not a darned thing, which is pretty normal in my field. I just thought I'd touch base, see if any more details had occurred to you since our last palaver."

"When was that?"

"Huh? Oh, let me check." Adams flipped open a notebook. "About three weeks. You don't remember."

"I do now," Wallace said. "I'm still a little mixed up, you see. My brain is kind of woozy."

"Yeah," Adams turned up the wattage of his smile. "I boxed some. Know what you mean."

"You talk to Delaney? Delaney saw the whole thing."

"I've spoken to everyone. But, to be perfectly clear, Delaney didn't actually see *everything*. Did he?"

"Delaney shot the horse."

"Yes, I saw the casings. A fine job under pressure."

This had also been present in each interview; an undercurrent of suspicion. Wallace said, "So, Detective, I wonder. You think I smashed her head in with a mallet, or what?"

"Then broke your own hip and somehow disposed of the weapon before Mr. Delaney made the scene? Nah, I don't suppose I think anything along those lines. The case bothers me, is all. It's a burr under my saddle blanket, heh. We examined the scene thoroughly. And...without a horse carcass, we're kinda stuck."

"You think Delaney did it." Wallace nodded and took a drag. "You think me and Delaney are in it together. Hey, maybe we're lovers and Helen was cramping our style. Or maybe I wanted Helen's money. Oops, I have plenty of my own. Let me ponder this, I'll come up with a motive." He chuckled and lighted another cigarette from the dwindling stub of his current smoke.

Wallace's humor must have been contagious. Detective Adams laughed wryly. He raised his blocky cop hands. "Peace, Mr. Smith. Nothing like that. The evidence was crystal – that horse, wherever it went, just about did for the two of you. Lucky things turned out as well as they did."

"I don't feel so lucky, Detective."

"I guess not. My problem is, well, heck, it's not actually a problem. There's something odd about what happened to you, Mr. Smith. Something weird about that property. It's pretty easy to forget how it was, standing in there, in the barn, screening the area for evidence. Too easy. Those pylons were a trip. Boy howdy!"

"Don't," Wallace said. He did not want to consider the pylons, the traps, or the graffiti. The imagery played havoc with his guts.

"Lately, I get the feeling someone is messing with my investigation."

"Please don't," Wallace said, louder.

"My report was altered, Mr. Smith. Know what that means? Somebody went into the files and rewrote portions of the paperwork. That doesn't happen at the department. Ever."

"Goddamn it!" Wallace slammed his fist on the table, sent the whiskey bottle clattering. His mind went crashing back to the barn where he had regained consciousness for several seconds – Helen beside him in the muck, dark blood pulsing over her exposed brain, surging with her heartbeat. He covered his eyes. "Sorry. But I can't handle talking about this. I don't like to think about what happened. I do whatever I can to not think about it."

"Don't be offended – I need to ask this." Adams was implacable as an android, or a good telemarketer. "You aren't into any sort of cult activity, are you? Rich folks get bored, sometimes they get mixed up with stuff they shouldn't. I've seen it before. There's a history in these parts."

"There's history wherever you go, detective. You ought to ask the people who own that property – "

"The Choates. Morgan Choate."

"They're the ones with all the freaky cult bullshit going on."

"Believe me, I'd love to find Aleister Crowley's nephew was shacking there, something like that. Solve all my headaches. The Choate place was foreclosed on three years ago. Developer from Snoqualmie holds the deed. This guy doesn't know squat – he bought the land at auction, never set foot on it in his life. Anybody could be messing around out there."

Wallace did not give a tinker's damn about who or what might be going on, he was simply grateful they would be grinding that barn into dust and fairly soon.

Detective Adams waited a moment. Then, softly as a conspirator, "Strange business is going on, Mr. Smith. Like I said – we checked your story very carefully. The Smith name carries weight in this neck of the woods, I assure you. My boss would have my balls if I hassled you."

"Come on, my pappy isn't a senator anymore. I'm not exactly his favorite, anyway."

"Just doing my job, and all that."

"I understand, Detective. Hell, bad apples even fell off the Kennedy tree. Right?"

"I'm sure you're not a bad apple. You seem to be a solid citizen. You pay your taxes, you hire locally, and you give to charity."

"Don't forget, I donated to the Policeman's Ball five years running."

"That's a write-off, sure, but it's worth what you paid. Ask me, your involvement is purely happenstance. You're a victim. I don't understand the whole picture, yet. If there's anything you haven't told me, if you saw something.... Well, I'd appreciate any help you might give me."

Wallace lifted his head, studied Adams closely. The cop was frayed – bulging eyes latticed with red veins, a twitch, cheeks rough as Brillo. Adams's cologne masked the sour musk of hard liquor. His clothes were wrinkled as if he'd slept in them. Wallace said, "As far as I'm concerned, it's over. I want to move on."

"Understandable, Mr. Smith. You've got my number. You know the drill."

The detective stood, peered across the landscaped grounds to the forest. A peacock strutted back and forth. A neighbor had raised them in the distant past; the man lost his farm and the peacocks escaped into the wild. The remaining few haunted the woods. The bird's movements were mechanical. Back and forth. "Do me a favor. Be careful, Mr. Smith. It's a mean world."

Wallace watched Adams climb into a brown sedan, drive off with the caution of an elderly woman. The brake lights flashed, and Adams leaned from the window and appeared to vomit.

Daylight drained fast after that.

5.

Wallace pulled on the loosest fitting suit in his wardrobe, which was not difficult considering how the pounds had melted from him during his long recovery. He knotted a tie and splashed his face with cologne and crippled his way downstairs to the liquor cabinet and fixed himself a double scotch on the rocks. He downed that and decided on another for the road. Sweat dripped from him and his shirt stuck to the small of his back and hips. He sweated nonstop, it seemed, as if the house were a giant sauna and yet he routinely dialed the thermostat down to the point where he could see his own breath.

Pain nibbled at him, worried at his will. He resisted the urge to swallow some of the heavy-duty pills in his coat pocket – promises to keep. Then he went somewhat unsteadily to the foyer with its granite tiles and a marble statue of some nameless Greek wrestler and the chandelier on its black chain, a mass of tiered crystal as unwieldy as any that ever graced the ballroom of a Transylvanian castle or a doomed luxury liner, and reported to Delaney. Delaney eyed him critically, dusted lint from his shoulder and straightened his tie while Wallace dabbed his face with a silk, monogrammed handkerchief, one of a trove received on birthdays and Christmases past, and still the sweat rilled from his brow and his neck and he wilted in his handsome suit. Delaney finally opened the front door and escorted him to the car. The air was cold and tasted of smog from the distant highway. Delaney started the engine and drove via the darkened back roads into Olympia. They crossed the new Fourth Avenue Bridge with its extra-wide sidewalks and faux Gaslight Era lampposts that conveyed a gauzy and oh so cozy glow and continued downtown past unlit shop windows and locked doors to a swanky restaurant called The Marlin. The Marlin was old as money and had been the It spot of discerning socialites since Wallace's esteemed father was a junior senator taking lobbyists and fellow lawmakers out for highballs and graft.

Everyone was waiting inside at a collection of candlelit tables near the recessed end of the great varnished bar. People, already flushed with their martinis and bourbons and cocktails, rose to shake his hand and clap his back or hug him outright and they reeked of booze and perfume and hairspray and cigarettes and talked too loudly as they jostled for position around him. The Johnsons and Steiners attended as a unit, which made sense since so many of their kids were intermarried – it was exceedingly difficult to determine where the branches and the roots of the respective family trees ended or began; Barb and Michael Cotter; old man Bloomfield, the former city councilman, and his nephew Regis, a tobacco lobbyist who kept rubbing his eyes and professing irritation at all the secondhand smoke; Skip Arden, doing his best John Huston as The Man from the South, in a vanilla suit hand-sewn by a Hong Kong tailor of legendary distinction; Jacob Wilson, recent heir to the Wilson fortune, who matched Skip in girth and verbosity, if not in taste or wit, and Jacob's bodyguard, Frank, a swarthy man in a bomber jacket who sat at the bar with Delaney and pretended inattentiveness to anything but the lone Rolling Rock beer he would order for the duration of the evening; Randy Freeman, wild-eyed behind rimless glasses and dressed way down in a wrinkled polo shirt, khaki pants, and sandals, and his lovely, staid wife, Janice; the Jenson twins down from Bellevue, Ted and Russell, who worked for Microsoft's public relations department – they were smooth as honey and slippery as eels; Jerry Premus, Wallace's hired gun in matters legal, who was twice as smooth and twice as slippery as the Jenson brothers combined; a couple of youngish unidentified women with big hair and skimpy gowns, glittering with the kind of semi-valuable jewelry Malloy's on State Avenue might rent by the evening (Wallace forgot their names on contact and figured they must be with a couple of the unattached men); and dear old Dad himself lurched from the confusion to kiss Wallace's cheek and mutter a gruff how do ye do? Wallace looked over Dalton Smith's shoulder, counting faces, and there were another half dozen that he did not recognize, and who knew if they were hangers-on or if his faculties were still utterly short-circuited? He decided to play it safe and put on his biggest movie-star grin for all concerned and bluff his way to the finish line.

Skip took charge of the event, dinging his glass of champagne to summon collective attention. He proposed a toast to Wallace's regenerative capabilities, his abundance of stalwart comrades, and his continued speedy recovery, upon which all assembled cried, "Here, here!" and drank. No one mentioned Helen. She sat amongst them, nonetheless. Wallace, ensconced at the head of the main table like a king, with his most loyal advisers, Skip and

Randy, at either hand, saw her shadow in the faces that smiled too merrily and then concentrated with abject diligence on their salmon and baked potatoes in sour cream, or in the pitying expressions blocked by swiftly raised glasses of wine or the backs of hands as heads swiveled to engage neighbors in hushed conversation. Not that such clandestine tactics were necessary: Wallace's exhaustion, his entrenched apathy, precluded any intemperate outburst, and Skip's thunderous elocution mercifully drowned out the details anyway.

Wallace was fairly saturated and so nursed his drink and picked at his birthday prime rib and tried to appear at least a ghost of his former gregarious self. Matters were proceeding apace until the fifth or six round of drinks arrived and Mel Redfield started in on Vietnam and the encroachment of French and American factories upon traditional indigenous agrarian cultures. Wallace suddenly feared he might do something rash. He set aside his glimmering knife, grinned and told Mel to hold that thought. He lurched to his feet, miraculously without upsetting a mass of tableware and half-full glasses, and made for the restrooms farther back where it was sure to be dim and quiet. Delaney, alert as any guard dog, cocked his head and then rose to follow, and subsided at a look from Wallace.

Wallace hesitated at the men's room, limped past it and pushed through the big metal door that let into the alley. The exit landing faced a narrow, dirty street and the sooty, featureless rear wall of Gossen's Fine Furniture. A sodium lamp illuminated a Dumpster and a mound of black garbage bags piled at the bottom of the metal stairs. He sagged against the railing, fumbled out his cigarettes, got one going and smoked it almost convulsively. Restaurant noises pulsed dimly through the wall. Water dripped from the gutters and occasionally car horns echoed from blocks farther off, tires screeched and a woman laughed, high and maniacal – the mating cry of the hopelessly sloshed female.

He finished his cigarette and began another and was almost human again when someone called to him.

"Hey." The voice floated from the thicker shadows of the alley. It was a husky voice, its sex muted by the acoustics of the asphalt and concrete. "Hey, mister."

Wallace dragged on his cigarette and peered into the darkness. The muscles in his neck and shoulders bunched. His hand shook. He opened his mouth to answer that odd, muffled voice and could not speak. His throat was too tight. What did it remind him of? Something bad, something tickling the periphery of his consciousness, a warning. A certain quality of the voice, its inflection and cadence, harkened recollections of hunting for tigers in the high grass in India, of chopping like Pizarro through the Peruvian jungles on the trail of jaguars – of *being* hunted.

"Mister." The voice was close now. "I can see you. Please. *Prease.*" The last word emerged in a patently affected accent, a mockery of the Asian dialect. A low, wheezy chuckle accompanied this. "*Prease, mistuh. You put a hotel in my rice paddy, mistuh.*"

Wallace dropped his cigarette. He turned and groped for the door handle and it was slick with condensation. He pushed hard and the handle refused to budge. Locked. "Ah, sonofabitch!" He slumped against the door, face to the alley, and clutched his cane, wished like hell he had not been too lazy and vain to strap on one of his revolvers, which he never carried after the accident because the weight dragged on his shoulder. His heart lay thick and heavy. He gulped to catch his breath.

The sodium lamp dimmed. "*Mistuh Smith. Where you goin' Mistuh Smith?*" Someone stood across the way, partially hidden by the angle of the building.

Jesus Christ, what is he wearing? Wallace could not quite resolve the details because everything was mired in varying shades of black, but the figure loomed very tall and very broad and was most definitely crowned with bizarre headgear reminiscent of a miter or a witch's hat. Wallace's drunkenness and terror peeled back in an instant of horrible clarity. Here was the figure that had appeared in his fever dreams – the ghastly, robed specter haunting the grounds of his estate. The lamp flickered and snuffed and Wallace was trapped in a cold black box. He reached back and began to slap the door feebly with his left hand.

"Wally. It is *soo* nice to meet you in the flesh." The voice emanated from a spot near Wallace's foot and it was easy to imagine the flabby, deranged face of a country bumpkin grinning up between the stairs. "Are you afraid? Are you afraid, sweetheart? Don't be afraid...*boss man*. They're about to cut the cake."

Wallace slapped the door, slapped the door. It was as futile as tapping the hull of a battleship. A rancid odor wafted to him – the stench of fleshy rot and blood blackening in the belly of a sluice. "W-what do you want?"

"I want to show you something beautiful."

"I'm – I'm not interested. No cash."

"Father saw you that day. What Father sees, He covets. He covets you, Wally-dear."

Wallace's stomach dropped into his shoes. "Who are you?"

The other laughed, a low, moist chuckle of unwholesome satisfaction. "Me? A sorcerer. The shade of Tommy Tune. The Devil's left hand. One of the inheritors of the Earth." Something rattled on the steps. Fingernails, perhaps. "I am a digger of holes, an opener of doors. I am here to usher in the dark." The odor grew more pungent. Glutted intestines left to swell in greenhouse heat; a city stockyard in July. Flies droned and complained. Flies were suddenly everywhere. "He lives in the cracks, Wally. The ones that run through everything. In the cracks between yesterday and tomorrow. Crawl into the dark, and there He is, waiting...."

"Look, I – just leave me alone, okay. Okay?" Wallace brushed flies from his hair, his lips, and nose. "Don't push me, fella."

"Wifey met Him and you shall too. Everyone shall meet Him in good, sweet time. You'll scream a hymn to the black joy He brings."

Wallace lunged and thrust at the voice with his cane and struck a yielding surface. The cane was wrenched from his fingers with such violence his hand tore and bled. He stumbled and his traitorous hip gave way. He went to his knees, bruised them on the grating. Pain telescoped from his hip and stabbed his eyes – not quite the sense of broken bone, but it hurt, sweet Christ did it ever. Fingers clamped onto his wrist and yanked him flat. The hand was huge and impossibly powerful and Wallace was stuck fast, his arm stretched over the edge of the landing and to the limits of his shoulder socket, his cheek pressed against metal. The dying remnants of his cigarette smoldered several inches from his eye. Sloppy, avaricious lips opened against his palm. The tongue was clammy and large as a preposterously gravid slug and it lapped between Wallace's fingers and sucked them into a cavernous mouth.

Wallace thrashed and lowed like a cow that has been hamstrung. Teeth nicked him, might have snipped his fingers at the knuckle, he could tell from the size and sharpness of them. A great, Neolithic cannibal was making love to his hand. Then his hand slipped deeper, as the beast grunted and gulped and the mouth closed softly over his forearm, his elbow, and this couldn't be possible, no way the esophageal sheath of a monstrous throat constricted around his biceps with such force his bones creaked together, no way that he was being swallowed alive, that he was going to disappear into the belly of a giant –

The world skewed out of focus.

The door jarred open and light and music surged from the restaurant interior. "Boss, they want to cut the cake...Boss! What the hell?" Delaney knelt beside him and rolled him over.

Wallace clutched his slick fingers against the breast of his suit and laughed hysterically. "I dropped my cane," he said.

"What are you doing out here?" Delaney gripped Wallace's forearms and lifted him to his feet. "You okay? Oh, jeez – you're bleeding! You break anything?"

"Needed some air...I'm fine." Wallace smiled weakly and sneaked a glance at the alley as he hurriedly wiped his face with his left sleeve. The lamp was still dead and the wedge of light from the open door did not travel far. He considered spilling his guts. Delaney would call the cops and the cops would find what? Nothing, and then they would ask to see his prescription and probably ask if he should be mixing Demerol with ten different kinds of booze. Oh, and by the way, what really happened in that barn. Go on: you can tell us. "I'm okay. Slipped is all."

Delaney leaned over the railing and peered down. "I'll go find your cane – "

"No! I, uh, busted it. Cheap wood."

"Cheap wood! Know what I shelled out for that?"

"No, really. I'm freezing. We'll get a new one tomorrow."

Delaney did not appear convinced. "It broke?"

"Yeah. C'mon, Dee. Let's go and get this party over with, huh?"

"That's the spirit, Mr. S," Delaney steadied him and said no more, but Wallace noticed he did not remove his hand from his pocket until they were safely inside and among friends.

6.

The remainder of the evening dragged to pieces like old fearful Hector come undone behind Achilles' cart and eventually Wallace was home and unpacked from the car. He collapsed into bed and was asleep before Delaney clicked off the lights.

Wallace dreamt of making love to Helen again.

They occupied a rocky shelf above Sun Devil Stadium, screwing like animals on a scratchy Navajo blanket. It was dusk, the stadium was deserted. Helen muttered into the blanket. Wallace pulled her ponytail to raise her head, because he thought he heard a familiar syllable or phrase. Something guttural, something darksome. His passion cooled to a ball of pig iron in his belly. The night air grew bitter, the stars sharp.

Helen said in a metallic voice, *There is a hole no man can fill.*

Wallace flew awake and sat pop-eyed and gasping. Clock said 3:39 A.M. He got out of bed, switched on the lamp, and slumped in its bell of dull light, right hand tucked against his chest. His hand was thickly bandaged and it itched. The contours of the bedroom seemed slightly warped, window frames and doorways were too skinny and pointy. The floor was cold. The lamp bulb imploded with a sizzle that nearly stopped his heart and darkness rushed in like black water filling a muddy boot print.

He did not feel welcome.

Delaney stood in the kitchen eating a sandwich over the sink. He was stripped to the waist. "You want me to fix you one?" he asked when Wallace padded in. He lived in the old gardener's cottage, used a second key to come and go as he pleased. Wallace had contemplated asking him to move into the downstairs guestroom and decided it was too much of an imposition. Delaney had women over from the clubs; he enjoyed loud music. Best to leave him at the end of a long leash.

Wallace waved him off, awkwardly poured a glass of milk with his left hand, sloshed in some rum from an emergency bottle in a counter drawer. He held his glass with trembling fingers, eyeballing the slimy bubbles before they slid into his mouth; poured another. He leaned against the stainless steel refrigerator. The kitchen was designed for professional use – Beth had retained a chef on the payroll for a while. That was when the Smith House was the epicenter of cocktail socials and formal banquets. The Mayor and his entourage had attended on several occasions. The middleweight champion of the world. A porn star and his best girl. With people like that dropping in, you had better have a chef. Anymore, Delaney did the cooking. Delaney, king of cold cuts.

Wallace said, "How'd you get that one?" He meant the puckered welt on Delaney's ribcage.

Delaney scraped his plate in the sink, ran the tap. "I was a pretty stupid kid," he said.

"And all that's changed?"

Delaney said, "Des Moines is a tough town. We were tough kids. A big crew. We caused some trouble. People got hurt."

Wallace knew about Delaney's record, his history of violence, the prisons he had toured. He knew all that in a peripheral way, but had never pried into Delaney's past, never dug up the nitty-gritty details. Guys like him, you left well enough alone. The confession did not surprise him. It was Delaney's nature and a large reason why Wallace hired him when the investment money began to attract unwanted attention. Delaney knew exactly how to deal with people who gave Wallace grief.

Delaney sat on a stool, arms crossed. He directed his gaze at the solid black window, which gave back only curved reflections of the room and its haggard occupants. "Most of us went to the pen, or died. Lots of drinking, lots of dope. Everybody carried. I got shot for the first time when I was sixteen. We knocked over this pool hall on the South End – me and Lonnie Chavez and Ruby Pharaoh. Some guy popped up and put two .32 slugs through my chest. The hospital was a no-go, so Ruby Pharaoh and Chavez loaded me in Ruby's caddy and took me to a field. Chavez's dad was an Army corpsman; he lifted some of his old man's meds and performed home surgery." The small man shook his head with a wry grin. "Hell, it was like the old Saturday matinee westerns we watched as kids – Chavez heating up his knife with a Zippo and Ruby pouring Wild Turkey all over my chest. Hurt like a sonofabitch, let me say. Chavez hid me in a chicken coop until the whole thing blew over. I was real weak, so he fed me. Changed my bandages, brought me comic books and cigs. I never had a brother."

"Me either," Wallace said. "Mine was too young and I left home before he got outta diapers. But I gotta be honest, I always thought of you as a son."

"You ain't my daddy, Mr. S. You're too rich to be my daddy. You like the young pussy, though. He did too and it caused him no end of trouble."

"That cop was by today."

"Yeah."

"He seems edgy. Seems worried."

"Yeah."

"Dee, when you came into the barn, did you see anything, I don't know, weird?" Wallace hesitated. "Besides the obvious, I mean. These burns on my back; I can't figure how I got them. And what happened to the horse?"

Delaney shrugged. "What's the matter, Mr. S? Cop got you spooked too?"

"I don't need him for that." Wallace placed his glass in the sink. "What happened to the horse, Dee?"

"I blew its head off, Boss." Delaney lighted a cigarette, passed it to Wallace, fired another and smoked it between his middle and fourth fingers, palm slightly cupped to his lips. During the reign of Beth, smoking had been forbidden in the house. Didn't matter anymore.

"I want cameras in tomorrow. Get Savage over here, tell him I've seen the light," Wallace said.

"Cameras, huh."

"Look...I've seen somebody sneaking around at night. I suspected I was hallucinating and maybe that's all it is. I think one of the Choates is around."

"Dogs woulda ripped his balls off."

"I want the cameras. That's it."

"Okay. Where?"

"Where...the gate, for certain. Front door. Pool building. Back yard. We don't use the tool shed. Savage can run everything through there. Guess I'll need to hire a security guy – "

"A couple of guys."

"A couple of guys, right. Savage can take care of that too."

"It'll be a job. A few days, at least."

"Yeah? Well, sooner he gets started...."

"Okay. Is that all?"

Wallace nodded. "For now. I haven't decided. Night, Dee."

"Night, Boss."

7.

Billy Savage of Savage and Sons came in before noon the following day and talked to Delaney about Wallace's latest security needs. Savage had silver, greased-down hair, a golfer's tan, and a denture-perfect smile. Wallace watched from his office window as Savage and Delaney walked around the property. Savage took notes on a palm-sized computer while Delaney pointed at things. It took about an hour. Savage left and returned after lunch with three vans loaded with men and equipment. Delaney came into the office and gave Wallace a status report. The guys would be around for two or three days if all went according to plan. Savage had provided him a list of reliable candidates for security guards. Wallace nodded blearily. He was deep into a bottle of blue label Stoli by then. He'd told Delaney he trusted his judgment – *Hire whoever you want, Dee. Tell Cecil to leave Helen be for a while. I'm sick of that screaming.*

She's asleep, Mr. S. They doped her up last night and she's been dead to the world ever since.

Oh. Wallace rubbed his eyes and it was night again. He lolled in his leather pilot's chair and stared out at the cruel stars and the shadows of the trees. "You have to do something, Wally, old bean. You really do." He nodded solemnly and took another swig. He fumbled around in the dark for the phone and finally managed to thumb the right number on his speed dialer. Lance Pride, of the infamous Pride Agency, sounded as if he had been going a few rounds with a bottle himself. But the man sobered rather swiftly when he realized who had called him at this *god-awful* hour. "Wallace. What's wrong?"

Wallace said, "It's about the accident."

"Yeah. I thought it might be." And after nearly thirty seconds of silence, Pride said, "Exactly what do you want? Maybe we should do this in person – "

"No, no, nothing heavy," Wallace said. "Write me the book on the Choates. Forward and back."

Pride laughed bleakly and replied that would make for some unpleasant bedtime reading, but not to worry. "Are we looking at...ahem, payback?" He had visited the hospital, sent flowers, et cetera. Back in the olden days, when Wallace was between wives and Pride had only gotten started, they frequented a few of the same seedy haunts and closed down their share. Of course, if Wallace wanted satisfaction over what had happened to Helen, he need but ask. Friend discount and everything. The detective was not a strong-arm specialist per se, however he had a reputation for diligence and adaptation. Before the arrival of Delaney, Wallace had employed Pride to acquire the goods on more than one recalcitrant landowner – and run off a couple that became overly vengeful. Pride was not fussy about his methods; a quality that rendered him indispensable. "I'll skin your cat, all right," was his motto.

Wallace thanked him and disconnected. He stared into darkness, listening for the strange, intermittent cries from his wife's room.

8.

It was a busy week. On Tuesday, Doctor Green paid a visit, shined a light in his eyes and took his pulse and asked him a lot of pointed questions and wrote a prescription for sleeping pills and valium. Doctor Green wagged his finger and admonished him to return to physical therapy – Hesse, the massively thewed therapist at the Drover Clinic, had tattled regarding Wallace's spotty attendance. Wednesday, the hospital sent a private ambulance for Helen and whisked her off to her monthly neurological examination. She came home in the afternoon with a heart monitor attached to her chest. Kate told Wallace it was strictly routine, they simply wanted to collect data. She smiled a fake smile when she said it and he was grateful.

He sat with Helen for a couple of hours in the afternoons while Kate did laundry and made the bed and filled out the reams of paperwork necessary to the documentation of Helen's health care service. Helen was losing weight. There were circles beneath her vacant eyes and she smelled sick in the way an animal does when it stops eating and begins to waste from the inside. There was also the crack in her face. The original small fracture had elongated into a moist fissure. Wallace gazed in queasy fascination at the pink, crusty furrow that began at her hairline and closed her right eye and blighted her cheek-bone. The doctors had no explanation for the wound or its steady encroach-ment. They had taken more blood and run more scans, changed some medi-cations and increased the dosage of others and indicated in the elegant man-ner of professional bearers of bad tidings that it was a crap shoot.

Meanwhile, men in coveralls traipsed all over the grounds setting up alarms and cameras; Delaney interviewed a dozen or so security guard appli-cants from the agency Billy Savage recommended.

Wallace observed from the wings, ear glued to the phone while his sub-ordinates in Seattle and abroad informed him about the status of his various acquisitions and investments. His team was soldiering on quite adequately and he found his attention wandering to more immediate matters: securing his property from the depredations of that ghoulish figure and getting to the bottom of the Choate mystery.

Pride had the instincts of a blue ribbon bird dog and he did not disappoint Wallace's expectations. The detective only required three days to track down an eyewitness to history, one Kurt Bruenig of the Otter Creek Bruenigs.

"The Choates were unsavory, you bet." Kurt Bruenig wiped his mustache, took a long sip of ice tea. A barrel of a man, with blunt fingers, his name stitched on the breast of an oil-stained coverall. His wrecker was parked out-side their window booth of the Lucky Bucket in downtown Olympia. "Nasty folk, if you must know. Why do you want to know, Mr. Smith?"

Wallace punched the speed dial on his cell. It rang, rang, rang. "Damn," he muttered. His head felt like a soccer ball. He cracked the seal on a packet of aspirin and stirred seltzer water in a shabby plastic drinking glass. He swallowed the aspirin, chased them with the seltzer, and held on tight while his guts seesawed into the base of his throat.

"Somethin' wrong?"

"How's your lunch?" Wallace gestured at the man's demolished fish and chips basket.

"Fine."

"Yes? How's the fat check you got in your pocket? Look, there's more in it for you, but I'm asking, and my business is mine." Wallace caught Delaney's eye at the bar, and Delaney resumed watching the Dodgers clobber the Red Sox on the big screen.

"Hey, no problem." Bruenig shrugged affably. Tow truck drivers dealt with madmen on a daily basis. "The Choates...our homestead was the next one over, butted up against Otter Creek."

"Pretty area," Wallace said. He placed a small recorder on the table and adjusted the volume. "Please speak clearly, Mr. Bruenig. You don't mind, do you?"

"Uh, no. Sure. It went to hell. Anyways, they were around before us, 'bout 1895. My great-granddaddy pitched his tent in 1910. Those old boys were cats 'n dogs from the get go. The Choates were Jews – claimed to be Jews. Had some peculiar customs that didn't sit well with my kin, what with my kin bein' Baptists and all. Not that my great-granddaddy was the salt of the earth, mind you – he swindled his way into our land from what I've been told. I suppose a fair amount of chicanery watered my family tree. We come from Oklahoma and Texas, originally. Those as stayed behind got rich off of cattle and oil. Those of us as headed west, you see what we did with ourselves." He nodded at the wrecker, wiped his greasy fingers on a napkin. "My dad and his tried their hands at farmin'. Pumpkins, cabbage. Had a Christmas tree farm for a few years. Nothin' ever came of it. My sister inherited when my dad passed away. She decided it wasn't worth much, sold out to an East Coast fella. Same as bought the Choate place. But the Choates, they packed it in first. Back in '83 – right after their house burned down. We heard one of 'em got drunk and knocked over a lantern. Only thing survived was the barn. Like us, there weren't many of them around at the end. Morgan, he was the eldest. His kids, Hank and Carlotta – they were middle-aged, dead now. Didn't see 'em much. Then there was Josh and Tyler. I was in school with those two. Big, big boys. They played line on a couple football teams that took state."

"How big would you say they were?" Wallace asked.

"Aw, that's hard to say. Josh, he was the older one, the biggest. Damned near seven foot tall. And thick – pig farmers. I remember bumpin' into Josh at the fillin' station, probably four years outta high school. He was a monster. I saw him load a fifty-five-gallon drum into the back of his flatbed. Hugged it to his chest and dropped it on the tailgate like nothin'. He moved out to the Midwest, somewhere. Lost his job when the brewery went tits-up. Tyler, he's doin' a hard stretch in Walla Walla. Used to be a deputy in the Thurston County Sheriff's department. Got nailed for accessory to murder and child pornography. You remember that brouhaha about the ring of devil worshippers supposed to operate all over Olympia and Centralia? They say a quarter of the department was involved, though most of it got hushed by the powers that be. He was one of those unlucky assholes they let dangle in the wind."

Wallace hadn't paid much attention to that scandal. In those days he had been in the throes of empire building and messy divorces. He said, "That's what you meant by nasty folk?"

"I mean they were dirty. Not dirt under the nails from honest labor, either. I'm talkin' 'bout sour-piss and blood and old grotty shit on their coveralls. Josh and Tyler came to school smellin' half dead, like they'd slaughtered pigs over the weekend and not bothered to change. Nobody wanted to handle their filthy money when they paid down to the feed store. As for the devil worshipping, maybe it's true, maybe not. The Satanist rap was sort of the cherry on top, you might say. The family patriarch, Kaleb Choate, was a scientist, graduated from a university in Europe. It was a big deal in the 1890s and people in these parts were leery on account of that. A Jew and a scientist? That was askin' a bit much. He worked with Tesla – y'know, the Tesla Coil guy. My understanding is Tesla brought him to America to work in his laboratory and didn't cotton to him and they had a fallin' out, but I dunno much about all that. One more weird fact, y'know? Wasn't long before rumors were circulatin' 'bout how old man Choate was robbin' crypts down to the Oddfellows Cemetery and performin' unnatural experiments on farm animals and Chinamen. We had a whole community of those Chinese and they weren't popular, so nobody got too riled if one turned up missin', or what-have-you. And a bunch of 'em did disappear. Authorities claimed they moved to Seattle and Tacoma where the big Chinese communities were, or that they sailed back to China and just forgot to tell anybody, or that they ran off and got themselves killed trespassing. Still, there were rumors, and by the time my great-granddaddy arrived, Kaleb Choate's farm was considered off limits for good honest Christians. 'Course there was more. Some people took it into their heads that Choate was a wizard or a warlock, that he came from a long line of black magicians. There were a few, like the Teagues on Waddel Creek and the Bakkers over to the eastern Knob Hills, who swore he could mesmerize a fella by lookin' into his eyes, that he could fly, that he fed those Chinamen to demons in return for...well, there it kinda falls apart. The Choates had land and that was about it. They were dirt poor when I was a kid – sorta fallen into ruin, y'might say. If Old Poger made a bargain with 'em, then they got royally screwed from the looks of it. I wonder 'bout the flyin' part on account of my sister and her boyfriend, Wooly Clark, claimed Josh could levitate like those yogis in the Far East, swore to Jesus they saw him do it in the woods behind the school once when they were necking. But hell, I dunno. My sister, she's a little soft in the brain, so there's no tellin' what she did or didn't see....

"Anyhow, the Bruenigs and the Choates had this sort of simmerin' feud through the years – Kaleb kicked the bucket in the forties, but our families kept fightin'. Property squabbles, mainly. Their pigs caused some problems, came onto our land and destroyed my grandma's garden more than once. The kids on both sides liked to cause trouble, beat hell out of each other whenever they could. I guess the grown men pulled that too. My uncles got in a brawl with some of the Choates at the Lucky Badger; all of 'em were eighty-six'd for life and Uncle Clover did a month in the county lockup for bustin' a guy over the noggin with a chair."

Wallace said, "So, did you ever notice anything unusual going on?"

"You mean, like was the deal with Tyler an isolated incident or were the old rumors all true? Maybe we had a bona fide witch coven next door?" Bruenig shook his head. "There were some strange happenin's, I'll grant. More complicated than witches, though."

"Complicated?"

"That's right, partner. Look at the history, you'll notice a few of the Choates were eggheads. Heck of a deal to be an egghead yet spend your whole life on a farm, isn't it? Buncha friggin' cloistered monks – unnatural. You had Kaleb's son, Morgan, he owned the land until they sold out and he was a recluse, nobody ever saw him, but I heard tell he was an astronomer, wrote a book or somethin'. Then you got Paul Choate – Dr. Creepy, the kids called him; he taught physics at Evergreen in the seventies and did some research for NASA. But he wasn't even the smartest of the litter. We knew at least three more of those guys coulda done the same. Hell, Josh was a genius in school. He just hated class; bored him. Me, I always thought they were contacted by aliens. That's why they all acted so weird."

"You're shitting me," Wallace said.

"No, sir. You gonna sit there and tell me you don't believe in the ETs? This is the twenty-first century, pal. You oughta read Carl Sagan."

"You read Carl Sagan?"

"'Cause I drive a wrecker I'm a dumbass? Read Sagan, there's plenty of funky stuff goin' on in the universe."

"Okay, okay," Wallace said. "Tell me about the aliens."

"Like I said, it goes all the way back to the beginnin', if you pay attention. Within a decade of Kaleb Choate's arrival, folks started reportin' peculiar sightin's. Goat men in the Waddel Creek area, two-headed calves, lights over the Capitol Forest – no airplanes to explain that away. Not then. People saw UFOs floatin' around the Choate fields month after month in 1915 and 1916, right when the action in Europe was gettin' heavy. Some of it's in the papers, some it was recorded by the police department and private citizens, the library. It's a puzzle. You find a piece here and there, pretty quick things take shape. Anyhow, this went on into the fifties and sixties, but by then the entire country was in the middle of the saucer scare, so the authorities assumed mass hysteria. There were still disappearances too, except now it wasn't the Chinese – the Chinese had moseyed to greener pastures by the late forties. Nope, this was mostly run-of-the-mill, God-fearin' townies. Don't get me wrong, we aren't talking 'bout bus loads. Three or four kids, a couple wives, a game warden and a census taker, some campers. More than our share of bums dropped off the face of the earth, but you know that didn't amount to a hill of beans. These disappearances are spread thin. Like somebody, or somethin', was bein' damn careful not to rouse the natives.

"Of course, as a kid I was all-fired curious 'bout morbid crap, pestered my dad constantly. I pried a little out of him; more I learned Hardy Boys style. Got to tell you, my daddy wouldn't talk 'bout the Choates if he could help it; he'd spit when someone mentioned 'em. Me and my sister got ambitious and dug into the dirty laundry. We even spied on 'em. Mighty funny how often they used to get visitors from town. Rich folks. Suits from the Capitol drove out there. Real odd, considerin' the Choates have always been looked down on as white trash – homegrown eggheads or not. That's what got me thinkin'. That and I saw Morgan and his boys diggin' in their fields at night."

"Mass graves?" Wallace said dryly.

Bruenig barked a wad of phlegm into his basket. "Huh! Better believe it crossed my mind. Told my pappy and his eyes got hard. Seems Granddad saw 'em doin' the same thing in his day. *Near as we could tell they were laying pipe or cable, all across their property.* They owned about three thousand acres, so there's miles of it, whatever it is. Then there were the pylons – "

"Pylons. Where'd you see those?" Wallace's interest sharpened.

"Farther back on their land. Long time ago a road wound around there – it's overgrown now, but when it was cleared there were these rocks sittin' out in the middle of nowhere. Sorta like that Stonehenge deal, except it was just one or two in each field. Jesse, my sister, counted twenty of 'em scattered 'round. She said they looked like peckers, and I have to admit they did bear a resemblance."

"Any idea who made them?"

"No. I mentioned it to a young geologist fella, worked for the BLM. He got interested, said he was gonna interview the Choates, see if they'd built on tribal grounds. Never heard from him again, though. He was barkin' up the wrong tree anyway. Those rocks are huge: least two tons each. How the Indians supposed to move that kinda load? Otter Creek – *puhlease*. Not in your lifetime. Plus, I never seen rock looked like those pylons. We don't have obsidian 'round here. Naw, those things are ancient and the ETs shipped

'em in from somewhere else. Probably markers, like pyramids and crop circles. Then the Choates come along and use 'em to communicate with the
aliens. Help 'em with their cattle mutilations and their abductions. Don't
ask me why the aliens need accomplices. No way we'll ever understand what
makes a Gray tick."

Wallace turned off the recorder, slipped it in his pocket. "Is that all, Mr.
Bruenig? Anything else you want to add that I might find useful?"

"Well, sir, I reckon I don't truly know what that could be. My advice is to
steer clear of the Choate place, if you're thinkin' of muckin' 'round that way.
You aren't gonna find any arrowheads or souvenirs worth your time. Don't
know that I hold with curses, but that land's got a shadow over it. I sure as
hell don't poke my nose around there."

9.

Wallace's favorite was the dead woman on the rocker.

Beth had hated it, said the artist, a local celebrity named Miranda Carson,
used too much wax. The sculpture was indeed heavy; it required two burly
movers to install it in the gallery. Wallace did not care, he took morbid pleasure in admiring the milky eyes, the tangled strands of real hair the artist collected from her combs. In low light, the wax figure animated, transformed
into a young woman, knees drawn to chin, meditating upon the woods
behind the house, the peacocks and the other things that lurked. Wallace
once loaned the piece, entitled Remembrance, to the UW library; brought it
home after an earthquake shattered an arm and damaged the torso. Carson
had even driven over and performed a hasty repair job. The cracks were still
evident, like scars. Macabre and beautiful.

The gallery was populated by a dozen other sculptures, a menagerie
orphaned by Beth's departure and Wallace's general disinterest. Wallace
wandered among them, cell phone glued to his ear, partially aware of Skip's
buzzing baritone. Wallace thought the split in the dead girl's body seemed
deeper. More jagged.

" – so Randy and I'll go today. Unless you want to come. Might be what
you need."

"Say again?" Wallace allowed himself to be drawn into the cathode. It
dawned on him that he had made a serious tactical error in confiding the
Bruenig interview to Skip. They had discussed the Choate legend over drinks
the prior evening and Wallace more than half expected his friend to laugh,
shake his snowy head and call him a damn fool for chasing his tail. Instead,
Skip had kept mum and sat stroking his beard with a grim, thoughtful

expression. Now, after a night's sleep, the story had gestated and hatched as a rather dubious scheme to nip Wallace's anxieties at their roots.

"Randy and I'll scope out that property this afternoon. He wants to see that nest you were going on about at the hospital. He said it sounds weird. I told him it's dried up. He refuses to listen, of course."

"Wait-wait." Wallace rubbed his temple. "You plan to go to the barn."

"Uh-hmm, right."

"To what – look at the nest?"

"That's what I've been saying. I'm thinking noon, one o'clock. We'll have dinner at the Oyster House. It's lobster night."

"Lobster night, yeah. Skip?"

"What?"

"Forget about the nest. You're right, it won't be there, they migrate, I think. And the barn's condemnable, man. It's dangerous. Scary people hang around – maybe druggies, I dunno. Bad types." Wallace's hand was slippery. He was afraid he might drop the phone.

"Oh yeah? Well it just so happens I called Lyle Ferguson – your old pal Lyle, remember him? He landed the bid and he says they're planning to commence tearing down the barn and all that sort of thing on Monday or Tuesday. So time is of the essence, as they say."

"Skip – "

"Hey, Wally. I'm driving here. You don't want to come with us?" Skip's voice crackled.

"No. Uh, say hi to Fergie, if you see him."

"Okay, buddy. I'm driving, I gotta go. Call you tomorrow." Click.

"Uh, huh." Wallace regarded a bust on a plinth. It was the half-finished head of a woman wearing thick lipstick. A crack had begun to divide the plaster face.

He had had Pride check into Bruenig's story about the BLM geologist and the monoliths. The geologist was named Chuck Doolittle and he abruptly quit his post six years ago, dropped everything and departed the state of Washington, although nobody at the department had a handle on where he might have emigrated. As for the so-called monoliths, the bureau disavowed knowledge of any such structures, and while the former Choate property did overlap tribal grounds, it had long ago been legally ceded to the county. No mystery at all.

The only hitch, insomuch as Pride was concerned, was the fact certain records pertaining to the Choate farm were missing from the county clerk's office. According to a truncated file index, the Choate folder once contained numerous photos of unidentified geological formations, or possibly man-made constructs of unknown origin. The series began in 1927, the latter photographs being dated as late as 1971. Pride located eight black-and-white pictures taken in 1954 through 1959 that displayed some boulders and indistinct earth heaves akin to the Mima Mounds. Unfortunately, the remainder of the series, some ninety-eight photos, was missing and unaccounted for since an office fire at the old courthouse in '79.

Wallace went into Helen's suite, waited near the door while Cecil massaged Helen's cramped thigh muscles. Kate had arrived early. The burly nurse dabbed Helen's brow with a washcloth and murmured encouragement. Helen's fish-black eyes rolled with blindness and fear. There was nothing of comprehension or sanity in them, and the cleft in her forehead and cheek was livid as a gangrenous brand. She howled and howled without inflection, the flat repeating utterance of an institutionalized mind.

Wallace limped upstairs to his office, turned up the radio. His hip throbbed fiercely – sympathy pangs. His hand itched with fading scabs. What had happened to him that night in the alley behind the Marlin? What was happening now? He found some Quaaludes in a drawer, chased them with a healthy belt of JD, and put his head down in his arms, a kindergartner again.

10.

Wallace was standing in Skip's dining room. Wallace's feet were nailed down with railroad spikes.

"Why'd you let them go?" Delaney asked. He slouched against a cabinet and smoked a cigarette.

Watery light washed out the details. Randy's prosthesis shone upon the table, plastic fingers blooming in a vase. A two-inch crack separated the fancy tiled ceiling. There was movement inside. Squirming.

Skip swaggered from the kitchen and plunged oversized hands into a bowl of limp, yellow noodles. He drew forth a clump, steaming and dripping, plopped it on his head as a wig. Grinned the wacky grin of a five-year-old stoned out of his gourd on cough syrup.

"Why are you doing that?" Wallace tried to modulate his voice; his voice was scratchy, was traitorously shrill.

Skip drooled and capered, shook fistfuls of noodles like pom-poms.

Wallace said, "Where's Randy? Skip, is Randy here?"

"Nope."

"Where is he?"

"With the god of the barn-b-barn – b-barn barn barn barn!"

"Skip, where's Randy?"

"In the barn with Bay-el, Bay-el, Bay-el. Playing a game." Skip hummed a ditty to his noodles, cast Wallace a sidelong glance of infinite slyness. "Snu-falupagus LOVES raw spaghetti. No sauce, no way! I pretend it's worms. Worms get big, Wallace. You wouldn't believe how big some worms get. Worms crawl inside your guts and make babies. They crawl up your nose, your ears, into your mouth. If somebody grinds you into itty-bitty pieces and a worm eats you, it'll know all the stuff you did." He lowered his voice. "They can crawl up your butt and make ya do the hula dance and jabber like Margie Thatcher on crank!"

"Where's Randy?"

"Playing sock puppets." Skip began ramming noodles down his throat. "He's Kermit de Frog!"

"Should've stopped them, Boss. Now they've stirred up the wasps' nest. You're fucked." Delaney stubbed his cigarette and walked through the wall.

Wallace awoke in darkness, fearful and disoriented. He had drunkenly migrated to his bedroom at some fuzzy period and burrowed into the covers. He remembered long, narrow corridors, bloody nebulas splattered against leaded glass, and Kirlian figures scorched into the walls: skeletal fragments of clawing hands and gaping mouths.

Wallace, Helen said. She was there with him in the room, wedged high in the corner of the walls where they joined the ceiling. She gleamed white as bone and her eyes and mouth and the crack in her face were black as the pits between the stars. *There's a hole you can't fill*, she said.

Wallace screamed in his throat, a mangled, pathetic cry. The clouds moved across the moon and reshaped the shadows on the wall and Helen was not hanging there with her black black eyes, her covetous mouth, or the stygian worm that fed on her face. There were only moonbeams and the reflections of branches like skinned fingers against the plaster.

Wallace lay trembling. Eventually he drifted away and slept with the covers over his head. He flinched at the chorus of night sounds, each knock upon the door.

II.

"Skip. Are you eating? Where've you been?"

"Nothing, Wallace. I'm tired."

"Skip, it's three. I've been calling for hours. Why don't you come over."

"Ahh, no thanks. I'm gonna sleep a while. I'm tired."

"Skip."

"Yeah?"

"Where's Randy? He doesn't answer his phone."

"Dunno. Try him at the office. Little bastard's always working late."

"I tried his office, Skip."

"Okay. That's right. He's out of town. On business."

"Business. What kind of business?"

"Dunno. Business."

"Where did he go, exactly? Skip? Skip, you still there?"

"Dunno. He won't be around much, I guess. There's a lot of business."

"Skip –"

"Wallace, I gotta sleep, now. Talk to you later. I'm very tired."

12.

Wallace sat on the steps, new cane across his knees, Bruno and Thor poised at his flanks like statuary come alive. The sun bled red and gold. The trees would be getting green buds any day now. He listened to the birds mating in the branches. The graveyard-shift security guard, a gray, melancholy fellow named Tom, was going off-duty. He came over to smoke a cigarette and introduce himself to his new boss. He was a talker, this dour, gaunt Tom. He used to drive school buses until his back went south – lower lumbar was a killer, yessiree. He was an expert security technician. Twenty-four years on the job; he had seen everything. The other two guys, Charlie and Dante, were kids, according to Tom. He promised to keep an eye on them for Wallace, make certain they were up to standard. Wallace said thanks and asked Tom to bring him the nightly surveillance video. The guard asked if he meant all four of them and Wallace considered that a moment before deciding, no, only the video feed from the garden area. Tom fetched it from the guard shack and handed it over without comment. The look on his face sufficed – he was working for a lunatic.

Wallace plugged the CD into the player on his theater-sized plasma television in the den. He called Randy's house and talked to Janice while silent, grainy night images flickered on the screen. Janice said Randy had left a cryptic message on the answering machine and nothing since. He had rambled about taking a trip and signed off by yelling, *Hallucigenia! Hallucigenia sparsa! It's a piece of something bigger – waaay bigger, honey!* Janice was unhappy. Randy had pulled crazy stunts before. He dodged lengthy stays in Federal penitentiaries as a college student and she had been there for the entire, wild ride. She expected the phone to ring at any moment and him to be in prison, or a hospital. What if he tried to sneak into Cuba again? What if he blew off his other hand? Who was going to wipe his ass then? Wallace reassured her that nothing of the sort was going to happen and made her promise to call when she heard anything.

Lance Pride dropped in to report his progress. Pride was lanky, a one-time NBA benchwarmer back in the seventies. He dressed in stale tweeds and emanated a palpable sense of repressed viciousness. His eyes were hard and small. He glanced at the video on the television and did not comment.

Pride confessed Joshua Choate appeared to be a dead end. His last known residence was a trailer court on the West Side of Olympia and he had abandoned the premises about three years ago. The former Ph.D. farm boy had not applied for a driver's license, a credit card, a job application, or anything else. Maybe he was living on the street somewhere, maybe he had skipped the country, maybe he was dead. Nobody had seen him lately, of that much Pride was certain.

Pride strewed a bundle of newspaper clippings on the coffee table, artifacts he had unearthed pertaining to Paul, Tyler, and Josh: stories detailing the promotion of Tyler Choate and a file picture of the young deputy sheriff grinning as he loomed near a Thurston County police cruiser, and another of him shackled and bracketed by guards after he had been exposed as a mastermind cultist; a shot of Joshua when he had been selected as an All-American tackle – his wide, flabby face was nearly identical to his brother's; articles from the mid-sixties following Paul Choate's hiring at the newly founded Evergreen State College and his brief and largely undocumented collaboration with NASA regarding cosmic microwave background radiation. There were school records for Tyler and Josh – four-point-oh students and standout football players. Major universities had courted them with every brand of scholarship. Tyler did his time at Washington State, majored in psychology, perfect grades, but no sports, and joined the sheriff's department. Meanwhile, Josh earned a degree in physics at Northwestern, advanced degrees in theoretical physics from Caltech and MIT, and then dropped off the radar forever. Tyler eventually became implicated in a never-fully-explained scandal involving Satanism and rape and got dropped in a deep, dark hole. The only other curious detail regarding the younger brothers was the fact both of them had been banned from every casino within two hundred miles of Olympia. None of the joints ever caught them cheating, but they were unstoppable at the blackjack tables, and the houses became convinced the boys counted cards.

None of it seemed too useful and Wallace barely skimmed the surface items before conceding defeat and shoving the pile aside. Pride just smiled dryly and said he'd make another pass at things. He had a lead on the company that had sold the Choates a ton of fabricated metals in the sixties and seventies. Unfortunately the company had gone under, but he was looking into former employees. He told Wallace to hang onto the newspaper clippings and left with a promise to check in soon.

Wallace moped around the house, mixing his vodka with lots of orange juice in a feeble genuflection toward sobriety. He picked up the newspaper photo of Josh Choate aged seventeen, in profile with his shoulder pads on. He wore a slight smile, and his pixelated eye was inscrutable. *I am a loyal son. I am here to usher in the dark.*

The day was bright and hot like it often was in Western Washington during the spring. The garden filled the television with static gloom. Upstairs, Helen began to scream. Wallace was out of orange juice.

He called Lyle Ferguson. The contractor was cordial as ever. He was moving crews into the Otter Creek Housing Development, AKA the old Choate place as of that morning. Yeah, Skip Arden had called him, sure; asked whether he could nose around the property. No problem, Ferguson had said, just don't trip and break anything. Pylons? Oh, yeah, they found some rocks on the site. Nothing a bulldozer couldn't handle....

13.

The next day Wallace became impatient and had Delaney drive him to the branch office of Fish and Wildlife. Short visit. Randy Freeman's supervisor told Wallace that Randy had two months' vacation saved. The lady thought perhaps he had gone to Canada. Next, he phoned the number Detective Adams gave him and got the answering machine. He hit the number for the front desk and was told Detective Adams was on sick leave – would he care to leave a message or talk to another officer?

Wallace sat in the rear of the Bentley, forehead pressed against the glass as they waited in traffic beside Sylvester Park. Two lean, sun-dried prostitutes washed each other's hair in the public drinking fountain. Nearby, beat cops with faces the shade of raw flank steak loomed over a shirtless man sprawled in the grass. The man laughed and flipped the cops off and a pug dog yapped raucously at the end of a rope tied to the man's belt.

Delaney chewed on a toothpick. He said, "Boss, where are we going with this?"

Wallace shrugged and wiped his face, his neck. His thoughts were shrill and inchoate.

"Well, I don't think it's a good idea," Delaney said.

"You should've kept feeding me my pills. Then we wouldn't be sitting here."

"You need to see a shrink. This is what they call the grieving process."

"Think I'm in the denial stage?"

"I don't know what stage to call it. You aren't doing so hot. You're running in circles." The car moved again. Delaney drove with the window rolled down, his arm on the frame. "Your wife isn't going to recover. It's a bitch and it hurts, I know. But she isn't going to come around, Mr. S. She won't ever be the woman you married. And you got to face that fact, look it dead in the eye. 'Cause, till you do, whatever screws are rattling loose in your head are going to keep on rattling." He glanced over at Wallace. "I'm sorry to say that. I'm real sorry."

"Don't be sorry." Wallace smiled, thin and sad. "Just stick with me if you can. I'll talk to that Swedish psychiatrist Green recommended. Ha, I've been ducking that guy since I got out of the hospital. I'll do that, but there's something else. I have to find out what the Choates were doing on that property."

"Pit bull, aren't you, Boss?" There was admiration mixed with the melancholy.

"Bruenig said the man moved out of state. He's wrong. Choate's in the neighborhood. Maybe he lives here, maybe he's visiting, hiding under a bridge. Whatever. I saw his tracks at the barn and I think he's been creeping around the garden. I told you." *Saw him in the alley, too, didn't you, Wally?* He shuddered at the recollection of that febrile mouth closing on him.

"Yup, you saw tracks. Almost a year ago," Delaney said. "If they were even his."

"Trust me, they were. Pride's running skips on him, although I'm getting the feeling this fellow isn't the type who's easy to find. That's why I've got Pride tracking down whoever sold the Choates the materials for their projects in the back forty. Maybe you can call in a favor with the Marconi boys, or Cortez, see if you can't turn up some names. I gotta know."

"Maybe you don't wanna know."

"Dee...something's wrong. People are dying."

Delaney looked at him in the rearview mirror.

"You better believe it," Wallace said. "Stop acting like my wet nurse, damn it."

Delaney stared straight ahead. "Okay," he said.

"Thank you," Wallace said, slightly ashamed. He lighted a cigarette as a distraction.

They went to Skip's home, idled at the gate. Delaney leaned out and pressed on the buzzer until, finally, a butler emerged with apologies from the master of the house. The servant, a rigid, ramrod of a bloke, doubtless imported directly from the finest Hampton school of butlery, requested that they vacate the premises at once. Wallace waited until the butler was inside. He hurled a brandy flask Skip gave him some birthday past, watched with sullen pleasure as it punched a hole through a parlor window. Delaney laughed in amazement, shoved Wallace into the car, left rubber smoking on the breeze.

14.

Wallace and Delaney were sitting in the study playing cards and eating a dinner of tuna fish sandwiches and Guinness when Lyle Ferguson called to say the barn had been razed. Ferguson hoped Helen would be more at peace. There was an awkward silence and then the men exchanged meaningless pleasantries and hung up.

"It's done," Wallace said. He drank the last of his beer and set the dead soldier near its mates.

Delaney dragged on his cigarette and tossed his cards down. He said, "Thing is, no matter how much you cut, cancer always comes back."

Wallace chose not to acknowledge that. "Next week, I'll hunt for the rest of those pylons, the ones in the woods, and take a jackhammer to them. I'll dynamite them if it comes to that."

"Not big on respecting cultural artifacts, are we?"

"I have a sneaking suspicion that it's better for us whatever culture they belong to is dead and in the ground." Wallace missed his little brother. The kid was an ace; he would have known what was what with Bruenig's story, the crazy altar in the barn, the pylons.

"I saw Janice yesterday. She's losing her marbles. Randy was supposed to take her and the kids to Yellowstone for spring vacation. She called the cops."

"I have two postcards from him." What Wallace didn't say was that there was something strange about the cards. They were unstamped, for one. And they seemed too old, somehow, their picturesque photographs of Mount Rainier and the Mima Mounds yellowing at the edges, as if they'd lingered on a gift shop rack for decades. Which, in fact, made sense when he checked the photo copyrights and saw the dates 1958 and 1971.

"Sure you do." Delaney dropped his butt into an empty bottle, pulled another cigarette from behind his ear and lighted it. His eyes were bloodshot. "Hate to admit it...but I was a little stoned that day. When everything happened. Nothing major – I wasn't impaired, I mean."

"Hey, it doesn't matter. I'm not going to bust your chops over something stupid like that."

"No. It's important. I wasn't totally fucked up, but I don't completely trust my recollections either. Not *completely*."

"What're you talking about?"

"I pulled you out of the barn first. Then I ran in for Mrs. S. You're not supposed to move a person with injuries. Know why I moved her?"

Wallace's mouth was full of sand. He shook his head.

"Because it took the horse, Mr. S. The horse was already trussed like a fly in a spiderweb and hanging. I still see its hooves twitching. I didn't look too close. Figured I wouldn't have the balls to go under there and grab your wife." Delaney's mouth turned down. "That wasp nest of yours...it had a face," he said, and looked away. "An old man's face."

"Dee – "

"Randy was an okay dude. He deserves a pyre. You gonna deal, or what?"

5.

Night seeped down. It rained. The power came and went, stuttered in the wires. Wallace picked up on the second ring. The caller ID said, UNKNOWN NAME – UNKNOWN NUMBER.

"Hi, Wally. Your friend is right." The mouth on the other end was too close to the receiver, was full, sensual, and malicious.

Wallace's face stiffened. "Josh?"

"Cancer always returns because time is a ring. And a ring...well, that's just a piece of metal around a hole." A wave of crackling interference drowned the connection.

"Josh!" No answer; only low, angry static.

The display said, THEREISAHOLENOMANCANFILLTHEREISAHOLE-NOMANCANFILLTHEREISAHOLENOMANCANFILL. Then nothing.

16.

Friday morning, Charlie, the dayshift security guard, brought Wallace a densely wrapped parcel from Lance Pride. The shipping address was a small town in Eastern Washington called Drummond and it had been written in a thin, backward-slanting style that Wallace didn't recognize.

Wallace cut the package open and found a tape cassette and a battered shoebox jammed with musty papers – personal correspondence from the appearance. It bothered him, this delivery from Pride. Why not in person? Why not a phone call, at least? Goosebumps covered his arms.

Wallace retreated to his office. He made a drink and sat at his desk near the window that looked across the manicured lawn, the sleeping garden, and far out into the woods. He finished his drink without tasting it and fixed another and drank that too. Then he filled his glass again, no ice this time, no frills, and put the tape in the machine and pressed the button. The wall above his desk shifted from red to maroon and a chill breeze fluttered drapes. The afternoon light slid toward the edge of the Earth.

After seconds of static and muffled curses, Pride cleared his throat and began to speak.

"Wallace, hi. This is Wednesday evening and...where am I. Uh, I'm at the Lone Tree Motel outside of Drummond on Highway 32 and I recently finished interviewing Tyler Choate. It's about two in the A.M. and I haven't slept since I dunno, so cut me slack if this starts to drag. The guards confiscated my tape recorder at the door, but Tyler gave me a notepad so I could write it down for later. He wanted to be certain you got your money's worth...I'll try to hit the highlights as best I can. Bear with me....

"Okay, I went looking for the manufacturer that might've sold the Choates aluminum tubes, pipes or what have you. I called some people, did some digging, and came up with a name – Elijah Salter. Salter was a marine, vet of the Korean War; rode with the cavalry as a gunner and engineering specialist – survived Operation Mousetrap and had the Bronze Star and Ike's signature to prove it. This leatherneck Bronze Star-winner came home after the war, started a nice family and went back to school where he discovered he was a real whizbang mechanical engineer. He graduated and signed on with a metal fabrication plant over in Poulsbo. Calaban Industries. This plant makes all kinds of interesting stuff, mostly for aerospace companies and a certain East Coast college that was rigging a twenty-mile-long atom-smasher – more on that later.

"Well, old Sergeant Salter climbed the ladder to plant manager, got the keys to the executive washroom, the Club Med package, free dental. They gave him plenty of slack and he jumped at it, opened a sideline with his own special clientele – among these, the Choates. Struck me as a tad eerie, this overseer of a high tech company keeping a group of hicks in his black book, and I decided to run it to ground. Wasn't tough to track Salter, he'd retired in '84, renovated a villa near here. I kid you not, a dyed-in-the-wool Spanish villa like where Imperial era nobility cooled their heels. I couldn't believe my ex-jarhead could afford a spread that posh – guy had palm trees, marble fountains, you name it. You woulda been jealous. Tell you what: his sidelines musta been lucrative.

"Made it big, made it real big, and after Salter got over the shock of meeting me in his den with my revolver pointed at his gut, he offered me a scotch and soda and praised Kaleb Choate to the heavens. Claimed not to know any of the rest of the clan that was still alive. Oh, he knew of them, he'd corresponded with Paul Choate occasionally, but they hadn't ever met in person or anything like that. I didn't get it – Kaleb's been in the ground since 1947, but what the hell.

"The sergeant had gone soft, the way a lion in a cage goes soft – he still had that bloody gleam in his eye when he gestured at the house and said his patrons took care of their own.

"Patrons? The way it slithered out of his mouth, way he sneered when he said it, didn't make me too comfortable. Also, when he's bragging about all the wonderful things these patrons did for him, I noticed a painting hanging over the piano. Damned thing was so dark it was almost black and that's why it took me a while to make out it wasn't actually a portrait, it was a picture of a demon. Or something. Guy in a suit like muckety-mucks wore in the Roaring Twenties, but his head was sort of, well, deformed, I guess is the best way to put it. Like I said, though, the oil was so dark I couldn't quite figure what I was seeing – just that it reminded me of a beehive sittin' on a man's neck. That, and the hands were about as long as my forearm. Reminded me of spooky stories my granny used to tell about Australia during the Depression. The aborigines have this legend about desert spirits called the Mimis. The Mimis are so thin they turn sideways and slip through a crack in the wall. They grab snotty kids, drag 'em underground. Don't know why I thought of that – maybe the long, snaky hands rang a bell. Granny used to scare the holy shit outta us kids with her campfire tales.

"Now I'm studying Salter's décor a bit more closely and, yep, he's got funky Gothic crap going on everywhere. Salter goes, sure, ya, ya betcha, we laid some aluminum cables on the Choate property; set up a few other gadgets too – but these projects were simply improvements on systems that had been in place for decades. I asked him what the idea was behind these cables, and he titters something about flytraps and keyholes. Kaleb Choate had been investigating alternate forms of energy and that's why he buried pipes and wires everywhere; he was building a superconductor, although his version was different, a breakthrough because it operated at high temperature. He used it to develop a whole bunch of toys. Salter used the word *squid* to describe them, except I don't think that's quite right either. Here it is – superconducting quantum interference device. SQUID, that's cute, huh. Oh, yeah...about the weird rocks you saw. Those pylons scattered around the area have been there for thousands of years. Some ancient tribe set 'em up to achieve a prehistoric version of Kaleb's machine, kinda like the Pyramids were before their time. Those rocks are highly radioactive – but Salter said the radiation is of unknown origin, something today's science boys haven't classified, even.

"Said if I want to know the *dirty details*, I should speak with the Choate brothers. I didn't appreciate that answer much, so I bopped him around. He starts babbling at me in a foreign language – dunno *what* language, probably Korean, but it made my skin prickle – this old savage on his belly by the pool, grinning and yammering and leaking from his nose. Then Salter just stops all of a sudden and stares at me and he's obviously disgusted. I got a gun on him, I ain't afraid to hurt him a little or a lot, and here he is shaking his head as if I'm some brat who's shat his diaper at a dinner party. He says he hopes I live so long as to bear witness and join the great revelry. Says my skin will fly from a flagpole. And all the pistol-whipping in the world wouldn't encourage him to say anything else. Not in English, anyhow. I ransacked his house, found a shoebox of letters and postcards from P., M., and T. Choate to Salter dated 1967 through 2002, and there were some drawings of things the Choates were building; blueprints.... Oh, and I swiped a rolodex chock full of interesting names. Creepy bastard had the Lieutenant Governor's home number, I kid you not. Guy's handwriting was goddamned sloppy, but I spotted one for Tyler Choate, the ex-sheriff's deputy. I decided Salter was right – best to have a chat with Tyler, get it straight from the source.

"Choate was my only choice. According to the records, Tyler and Joshua were the last of the breed, discounting obscure family branches, illegitimate kids, and so on. Since I'd been striking out with Josh, and Tyler's doing twenty to life in the state pen, I went the easy route.

"Tyler's not at Walla Walla anymore; there'd been some razzle-dazzle with the paperwork and he got transferred north to a max security facility. Place called Station 3, between Lind and Marengo on the Rattlesnake Flat.

"Choate surprised me. Friendly. Real damned friendly. Strange accent; spoke very distinctly, as if he were a 'right proper' gentleman, not a con nabbed for assorted nastiness. In fact, I got the impression he was eager for my visit. Lonely. Didn't care what I was after, either. I gave him a cockamamie story, naturally, but I needn't have bothered. Sonofabitch was rubbing his hands together over the phone.

"It was a date. Long drive and I hate going east. Once you climb over the mountains it's nothing but wheat fields, desert, and blowing dust. This Station 3 was on the outskirts of the Hanford Nuclear Reservation. It sat at the end of a dirt road in the middle of a prairie. The earth is black in those parts; salt deposits. Humongous black rocks and pine trees scattered around. Coyotes, jackrabbits, and rattlesnakes.

"I went by an Indian reservation; heard there's a pretty nice casino, but I didn't check. The Station itself was depressing – a bunch of crappy concrete houses inside a storm fence with rusty rolls of barbwire on top. Some buses were parked near the loading docks, the kind that are painted gray and black with mesh on the windows, said FRANKLIN COUNTY CORRECTIONS in big letters. A reject military base is how it looked.

"Way, way out in a field men were hoeing rows in biblical tradition; seems the prison industry, such as it is, revolves around selling potatoes and carrots to the local tribe. A dozen cons in jumpsuits milled in the yard, pulling weeds, busting asphalt to make way for the new parking lot. Don't know why they needed one – the screws and admin parked in a garage and there were maybe three cars in front, counting mine.

"After I handed my I.D. to the guards in the gatehouse, they buzzed me through to a short, uncovered promenade. Heavy gauge chain link made a funnel toward the main complex and as I walked I noticed there's graffiti on the concrete walls. Some of it'd been whitewashed, but only some. I saw SHAITAN IS THE MASTER and PRAISE BELIAL. BOW TO CHEMOSH O MAGGOTS. THE OLD ONE IS COMING. Frankly, it gave me the willies. Told myself they hadn't gotten around to scrubbing those sections. They'd missed a spot or two. Uh-huh.

"I was beginning to regret my impulsive nature. Not as if I'm green, or anything; I've been locked inside the kit kat for a minor beef. More than the graffiti was playing on my nerves, though. The guards seemed off-key. The whole bunch of them were sluggish as hornets drunk on hard cider. Swear to God one was jacking off up in the tower; his rifle kinda bounced on its shoulder strap.

"Warden Loveless, he's this pencil-dick bean counter with thick glasses; he didn't blink while we were jawing. Sounded like one of my undergrad English lit profs, droned through his nose. Don't recall his little list of rules and regs, but I can't forget him drooling on his collar. He kept dabbing it with a fancy handkerchief. I tried not to stare, but damn.

"The warden says he's glad I made it, he thought I had changed my mind, and he sounded relieved, joked about sending some of the boys to bring me in if I hadn't come. Warden Loveless says Tyler Choate is expecting me, that we should go visit him right away, and let me tell you the only reason I didn't turn on my heel and walk out was there were several men holding carbines at half-mast and staring at me with zombie eyes, and I think some of them were drooling too. See, I coulda sworn Loveless said, *Master* instead of Tyler. Acoustics were pretty screwed up in there, though.

"Loveless takes me on a walking tour of the prison. Place probably hadn't been remodeled since the forties or fifties, exposed pipe and those grilled-in bulbs. Damp and foul as a latrine, mildew creeping in every joint. Damned dark; seemed like most of the lights had been busted and never replaced. Another odd detail – three quarters of the cells were empty. We've got the planet's most crowded prison system and this place is deserted.

"We rode an elevator to the sublevels, a steel cage like coal miners crowd into. Down, way down. The cage rattled and groaned and I never realized before that I'm claustrophobic. Okay, something funny happened to me. The walls closed in and my collar got tight. I...started seeing things. No sound, only images, clear as day, like my mind was the Bijou running a matinee horror flick.

"That goddamned barn of yours. My mom and pop squirming in a lake of worms. Helen grinning at me. Jellyfish. I hate those things. Got stung once in Virginia when I spent the summer with my cousin. I nearly drowned. Goddamned things. I saw other stuff, stuff I don't want to remember. So damn real I got vertigo, thought the floor was gonna drop from under me.

"Maybe I'm not claustrophobic, maybe it was something else. Fumes. Stress. My daddy had shellshock when he came home from Korea. Flipped his wig every so often, beat the hell outta his fellow drunks at the tavern. When he was like that, he'd sit in his rocker till the A.M., cleaning his Winchester and staring at nothing, face of a china plate. Said he saw the gooks coming, too many, not enough bullets, stabbed so many his bayonet got dull as a butter knife. My old man drank wood grain alcohol through a funnel; smelled like a refinery before he died.

"Riding down in that elevator, I bet my face looked like his when he was fighting ghosts. I played it cool, gritted my teeth and thought about the Red Sox batting order, getting laid by the chick who used to come by the Mud Shack every Thursday with her sister, whatever happy shit I could dream up on short notice. The vertigo and the visions went away when we hit bottom. A broken circuit. After a few steps it was easy to think the whole episode was a brain fart, my bout with the pink elephants. Yeah, I had DT's. Been trying to kick the sauce, and you know how that is... My hands were doing the Parkinson's polka.

"Loveless called this level the Isolation Ward; told me to follow the lights to H Block; said he'd wait for me. No rush. Choate didn't entertain every day.

"More graffiti. More by a thousand fold. Numbers, symbols, gibberish. It covered the tunnel walls, ceiling, the cell bars. Probably inside the cells too, but those things were black as a well-digger's asshole. Kicker is, I saw one of the fellas responsible for the artwork – this scrawny man in filthy dungarees was doing the honors. Must've been eighty years old; His ribs stuck out and his eyes were milky. Blind as hell. He carted a couple buckets of black and white paint and was slapping brush-loads onto the concrete. After he'd made a nice mess, he'd get a different brush to start turning the shapeless gobs into letters and such. Precise as a surgeon, too. Kind of fascinating except for the parts I could read were little gems like: WORMS OF THE MAW WILL FEED ON THY LIVER and INFIDELS WILL CHOKE ON THE MASTER'S SHIT.

"There was a guard station and a gate. While the gate was grinding open I heard music up ahead, distorted by the echoes of clanging metal and my heart. Thought I was gonna have a coronary right there. A bloody glow oozed from the mouth of a cell. It was the only light after the wimpy fluorescent strip in the guard shack.

"Tyler Choate had himself a cozy pad there in the bowels of Station 3. They'd even removed the door; it was lying farther down the hall, as if somebody had chucked it aside for the recycling man. Chinese paper lamps were everywhere, floating in the dark; that's what gave off the red glow. The bunks had been ripped out, replaced by a hammock and some chairs. Bamboo. Oriental rugs, a humongous vase with a dead fern. Big wooden cabinets loaded with knickknacks, bric-a-bracs and liquor. Sweet Jesus, the old boy loves his liquor. Found out later most of the doodads were from China, the Polynesian Islands, a bunch of places I can't pronounce. Who would've guessed this hick deputy for a traveling man, right?

"Music was coming from an antique record player – the type with a horn and a hand crank. A French diva sang the blues and Tyler Choate soaked her up in a big reed chair, feet propped, eyes closed. Real long hair; oily black in a pony tail looped around his neck. He looked like a Satanic Buddha – skinny on the ends and bloated in the middle.

"I noticed the shoe collection. Dozens and dozens of shoes and boots, lined up neat as you please along the wall and into the shadows of the adjoining cell where the red light didn't quite reach. None of them were the right size for Choate – his slippers were enormous; the size of snowshoes, easy. Tailor-made for sure.

"Then he says to me, *Welcome to the Mandarin Suite, Mr. Pride. Take off your shoes.* His voice was lispy, like the queers that hang around beauty parlors. But not like that either. This was different. He sounded...amused. Smug.

"The elevator ride had rattled me, sure, sure, but not enough to account for the dread that fell on me as I stood in that dungeon and gawped at him. I felt woozy again, same as the elevator, worse than the elevator. Swear, he coulda been beaming these terrible thoughts into my head. I kept seeing Randy Freeman's face, all splattered and buried in mud. Why would I see such a thing, Wally? Doesn't make sense.

"When Choate stood to shake my hand, I nearly crapped my pants. I knew from the files the Choate brothers were tall, but I swear he wasn't much shy of eight feet, and an axe-handle broad. He wore a white silk shirt with stains around the pits. He smelled rank. Rank as sewage, a pail of fish guts gone to the maggots. A fly landed on his wrist, crawled into his sleeve. Bruenig wasn't jiving about those kids being filthy.

"My hand disappeared into Choate's and I decided that I'd really and truly screwed up. Like sticking my hand into a crack in the earth and watching it shut. Except, he didn't pulp my bones, didn't yank me in close for a hillbilly waltz, nothing like that. He said he was happy to meet a real live P.I., made me sit in the best chair and poured Johnny Walker Black in greasy shot glasses, drank to my health. All very cordial and civilized. He asked if I had met his brother, and I said no, but Josh was hanging around your house and it really had to stop. He agreed that Josh was on the rude side – he'd always been a touch wild. Choate asked what you thought about the barn, if you'd figured it out yet. I said no and he laughed, said since you hadn't blown your brains out, you must not know the whole truth, which, to me, sounded like some more hocus pocus crap was in the offing. I wasn't wrong on that count. Did I know anything about String Theory? He thought I looked like a guy who might dabble in particle physics between trailing unfaithful husbands and busting people's heads. I told him I'm more of a Yeats man and he said poetry was an inferior expression of the True Art. What about molecular biology; surely I craved to understand how we apes rose from primordial slime. No? Supersymmetry? Hell no, says I and he chuckled and filled my glass. Guess the Bruenig spiel was right about a few things. The Choate men were scientists, always have been interested in the stars and nature, time travel and all sorts of esoteric shit. Mostly they studied how animals and insects live, how, lemmesee...how *biological organisms adapt and evolve in deep quantum time. The very nature of space time itself.* Choate said the family patriarchs had been prying into that particular branch of scientific research since before the Dark Ages.

"What was Kaleb's interest? Tyler said, *Hypermutation and punctuated equilibrium.* Started in on those SQUIDS Salter told me about. Kaleb wanted to accelerate his own genetic evolution. He grafted these homemade SQUIDS onto his brain and that jumpstarted the process. I can just imagine the operation. Brrr. He survived without lobotomizing himself and it was a roaring success. The implant heightened his mental acuity by an incredible degree, which led to more inventions – *Devices Tesla never dreamt of – never dared!* Jesus Louise...shoulda seen Tyler Choate's face when he said that. He leered at me like he intended to make me his *numero uno bitch.*

"What kind of devices, you may be asking. See, Grandpa figured there was a way to configure electromagnetic pulses to create a black hole, or a kind of controlled tear in subatomic matter, and I heard some think-tank guys in Boston tried the very same thing a few years ago, so between you and me, maybe the geezer wasn't totally bonkers, but anyhow. Kaleb wanted to use this black hole, or whatever the hell it's supposed to be, to access a special radioactive energy. They'd detected traces of it in the pylons, like Salter said, and Tyler confirmed the radiation doesn't exist anywhere in the known spectrum.

"I'm blitzed and feeling a bit kamikaze, so I ask, where's it come from, then? *Out there,* is how Tyler put it. *Out there in the great Dark.* So picture this: this friggin' psycho hillbilly leaning over me with his face painted like blood in the lamplight, sneering about *ineffable mysteries* and flexing his monster hands as if he's practicing to choke a camel. He grins and says Grandpa Kaleb bored a hole in space and crawled through. Tyler started spouting truly wild-ass stuff. Some bizarre mumbo-jumbo about a vast rift, the cosmic version of the Marianas Trench. He said very old and truly awful things are drifting in the dark and it's damned lucky for us apes that these huge, blind things haven't taken any notice of planet Earth.

"Tyler said Kaleb became *The door and the bridge. The mouth of the pit.* And if that wasn't enough, Tyler and Josh are hanging around because the rest of Kaleb's heirs have been taken to His bosom, rejoined the fold. Tyler and Josh had been left with us chickens to, I dunno, guard the henhouse or something. To make things ready. Ready for what? *For the Old Man, of course. For his return.* I didn't press him on that.

"Another thing...The bonus effect of Kaleb's gizmo's electromagnetic pulse is it's real nifty for shutting off car engines and stranding people near the ol' farm...I asked why they wanted to strand people near their property and he just looked at me. Scary, man. He said, *Why? Because it gives Him tremendous pleasure to meet new and interesting people. Grandfather always liked people. Now He loves them. Sadly, folks don't drop by too often. We keep Him company as best we can. We're good boys like that.*

"By this point I was pretty much past wasted and I know he went on and on, but most of it flew over my head. One thing that stuck with me as I got ready to stagger outta there, is he clamped one giant paw on my shoulder and said with that creepy smile of his, *'Out there' is a relative term, it's closer than you might think. Oh my, the great Dark is only as far away as your closet when you kill the light...as your reflection when it thinks you aren't looking. Bye, bye and see you soon.*

"I beat it topside. Barefoot. Bastard kept my shoes...." Pride's narrative faltered and was replaced by a thumping noise in the background. A chair squeaked. He spoke from a distance, perhaps the motel room door. "Yeah? Oh, hey – " His voice degenerated into jags of a garbled conversation followed by a long, blank gap; then a wheeze like water gurgling in a hose. Another gap. Someone coughed and chuckled. Then silence.

17.

Wallace gazed at the rolling wheels as dead air hissed through the speaker. He emptied the dingy shoebox on his desk, pushed the yellow papers like a man shuffling dominos or tarot cards. He poured another drink from the dwindling bottle, squinted at the cramped script done in bleeding ink, whole paragraphs deformed by water stains and stains of other kinds and the depredations of silverfish. There were schematics, as Delaney had promised – arcane, incomprehensible figures with foreign notations.

The house was dark but for the lamp on Wallace's desk. The walls shuddered from a blast of wind. Rain smacked hard against the windows. Floorboards creaked heavily and Wallace strained to detect the other fleeing sound – a rustling, a whisper, an inhalation like a soft, weak moan. He wiped his face and listened, but there was nothing except whistling pipes. He poured another drink and now the bottle was dry.

He sifted through the letters, sprinkling them with vodka because his hands were trembling. He studied one dated February 1971. It was somewhat legible:

Eli,

The expedition has gone remarkably well, thanks to your timely assistance. It is indeed as Grandfather says, "Per aspera ad astra that we seek communion and grace from our patrons of antiquity." I shall keep you apprised of developments. Yours, P. Choate.

Another, from June 1971:

Grandfather has sent word from the gulf, Ab ovo, as it were. It is as they promised…and more. His words to me: "Non sum qualis eram." It is the truth. He is the door and the bridge and we are grateful. On the day all doors are thrown open, you shall be remembered and honored for your service to the Grand Estate. Thank you, dear friend. Yours, P. Choate.

He counted roughly three dozen others, including some photographs, mostly ruined. He paused at a warped and faded postcard picturing a ramshackle barn in a field. It was unclear whether this was an etching or an actual photograph – the perspective featured the southeast face of the barn and the road in the distance. He could barely make out the Bentley on the shoulder, a man working under the raised hood. The back of the card was unstamped and grimy with fingerprints. It had been addressed to Mr. Wallace Smith of 1313 Vineland Drive. October 6, 1926:

Hello, Wallace.

Helen wishes you were here.

Regards, K. Choate.

Wallace's belly sank into itself. What could it possibly mean?

Grandfather always liked people. Now he loves them.

The house shook again and Wallace dropped the card. He was nauseated. "Mr. Smith?" The intercom squawked and he almost pissed himself. " – to say good night?" Kate was nearly unintelligible over the intercom.

"What!" He nearly shattered the plastic from the force of his blow. He took a breath, said in a more reasonable tone, "I'll be there in a minute."

The desk lamp flickered. *I am here to usher in the dark.* Wallace dialed Pride's cell number and received no answer. He pushed away from the desk, stood, and shuffled in a dream to the hallway. A draft ran cold around his ankles and when he thumbed the switch, the lights hesitated in their sockets, grudgingly ignited and shone dim and milky. Shadows spread across the floor and climbed the walls.

Wallace plodded forward and ended up at Helen's door. Helen's door was made of thick oak and decorated with filigreed panels. He stood before the oak door and breathed through his mouth, blowing like a dray horse.

Cancer always returns.

Wallace turned the knob and pushed into Helen's apartment. He slapped the switch and nothing happened. The dimensions were all wrong; the room had become an undersea cavern where a whale had bloated on its gasses and putrefied. Objects assumed phantom shapes in the sleepy murk: the therapy table and its glinting buckles; a pinewood armoire; a scattering of chairs; the unmade bed, a wedge of ivory sheets and iron lattice near the opaque window.

Wallace detected a hushed, sticky sound. The muffled squelch of a piglet snuffling its mother's teat, smacking and slobbering with primal greed. As he turned toward the disturbance, something damp and slender tickled the back of his neck. Then his scalp, his left ear, his cheek. Something like moist jelly strands entangled him. These tendrils floated everywhere, a veritable hanging garden of angel's hair gently undulating in the crosshatched light from the hallway. Wallace cried out and batted the strands like a man flailing at cobwebs.

He gaped up into the blue-black shadows and did not comprehend the puzzle of dangling feet, one in a shoe, the other encased in hosiery; or the legs, also wrapped in nylon hose that terminated at the hem of a skirt. Wallace did not recognize the mannequin extremities, jittering feebly with each impulse of a live current. The left shoe, a square, wooden thing with a blunt nose, plopped onto the hardwood as the legs quivered and slid upward, vanishing to mid-thigh attended by the sound of a squishing sponge.

Wallace was confused; his mind twittered with half-formed memories, fragmented pictures. All circuits busy, please try again. He thought, *Kate's shoe. Kate's shoe is on the floor. Kate's legs. Where's the rest of her. Where oh where oh fuck me.* He beheld it then, an elephantine mass lodged in the ceiling, an obscene scribble of shivering tapioca and multi-jointed limbs. A gory fissure traversed its axis and disgorged the myriad glutinous threads. The behemoth wore a wicked old man's face with a clotted Vandyke, a hooked nose, and wet, staring eyes that shone like cinders of dead stars. The old man patiently sucked Kate the Nurse into his mouth. Ropes of viscid yolk dripped from the corners of the old man's lips and pattered on the floor. Wallace thought with hysterical glee, *Gulper eel, gulper eel!* Which was an eel that lived in the greatest depths and could quite handily unhinge its skull to swallow large prey.

Wallace reeled.

The bloody fissure throbbed and seeped; and following the convulsion, he discovered the abomination's second head. He glimpsed Helen's pallid torso, her drooping breasts and slack face – an alto-relievo sculpted from wax at the apex of the monstrous coagulation of her body. The crack nearly divided her face and skull and it fractured the ceiling with a jagged chasm that traveled far beyond the reach of any light.

Helen opened her eyes and smiled at Wallace. Her smile was sweet and infinitely mindless. Her mouth formed a perfect black circle that began to dilate fantastically and she craned her overlong neck as if to kiss him.

Wallace screamed and stumbled away. He was a man slogging in mud. The vermiculate tendrils boiled around him, coiled in his hair, draped his shoulders and slithered down the collar of his shirt.

He was still screaming when he staggered into the hall and yanked the door shut. He crabbed two steps sideways and tottered. His legs gave way and the floor and walls rolled and then he was prone with his right arm flung out before him in a ghastly imitation of a breast stroke. A wave of lassitude suffused him, as if the doctor had given him a yeoman's dose of morphine, and in its wake, pins and needles, and hollowness. Countless tendrils had oozed through the doorjamb, the spaces between the hinges, the keyhole, and burrowed into him so snugly he was vaguely aware of their insistent twitches and tugs. Dozens were buried in the back of his hand and arm, reshaping the veins and arteries; more filaments nested in his back, neck and skull, everywhere. As he watched, unable to blink, their translucence flushed a rich crimson that flowed back toward their source, drawn inexorably by an imponderable suction.

He went under.

18.

Wallace regained consciousness.

The veins in his hand had collapsed and the flesh was pale and sunken like the cracked hand of a mummy. Near his cheek rested a sandal that surely belonged to a giant. The sandal was caked in filth and blood.

"Are you sleeping, brother Wallace?" Josh said. "I want to show you something beautiful." He opened the door. Wallace's eyes rolled up as he was steadily drawn across the threshold and into darkness.

Oh, sweetheart, Helen said eagerly.

19.

Delaney came in that morning and boiled himself a cup of instant coffee and poured a bowl of cereal and had finished both before he realized something was wrong. The house lay vast and quiet except for small sounds. Where was the hubbub of daily routine? Helen had usually begun shrieking by now, and Cecil inevitably put on one of the old classical heavies like Mozart or Beethoven in hopes of calming her down. Not today – today nothing stirred except the periodic rush of air through the ducts.

Delaney lighted a cigarette and smoked and tried to convince himself he was jumpy over nothing. He went upstairs and found Wallace's bedroom empty. Near Helen's suite, he came across a muddy track. The shoe print was freakishly large. Delaney pulled a switchblade from his pocket and snicked it open. He put his hand on the door knob and now his nerves were jangling full alarm like they sometimes had back in the bad old days of gang battles and liquor store hold-ups and dodging Johnny Law. The air was supercharged. And the doorknob was sticky. He stepped back and regarded, stoic as a wolf in the face of the unknown, his red fingers. A fly hummed and circled his head.

He bounced the switchblade in his palm and decided, to hell with it, he was going in, and then a woman giggled and whispered something and part of the something contained Delaney. He knew that voice. It had been months since he heard it last. "Screw this noise," he said, very matter of fact. He turned and loped for the stairs.

Delaney calmed by degrees once he was outside, and walked swiftly across the waterlogged grounds to his cottage where he threw a few essentials into his ancient sea bag – the very one his daddy brought home from the service – checked his automatic and stuffed it under his shirt. He started his Cadillac and rolled to the gate. His breathing had slowed, he had combed his hair and gotten a grip and was almost normal on the surface. At least his hands had stopped shaking. He forced a cool, detached smile. The smile that said, *Hello, officer. Why, yes, everything is fine.*

Charlie the guard was a pimply twenty-something with disheveled hair and an ill-fitting uniform. He was obviously hung over and scarcely glanced up at Delaney as he buzzed the gate. "See ya, Mr. Dee."

"Hey, any trouble lately? Ya know – anything on the cameras?"

Charlie shrugged. "Nah. Well, uh, the feed's been kinda wonky off 'n' on."

"Wonky?"

"Nothin' to worry 'bout, Mr. Dee. We ain't seen any prowlers."

"What about the night fella?"

"Uh, Tom. He woulda said somethin' if there was a problem. Why?"

"No reason. I figured as much. You take care, partner." Delaney pushed his sunglasses into place and gave the guard a little two-finger salute. He cast a quick, final glance at the house in his rearview mirror, but the view was spoiled by a crack in the glass. Had that been there before? He tacked it on his list of things-to-do once he got wherever he was going. Where was he going? Far away, that was certain.

Delaney gunned the engine and cruised down the driveway. He vanished around the bend as Charlie set aside his copy of *Sports Illustrated* to answer the phone. "Uh, yeah. Oh, mornin', Mr. Smith. Uh.... Okay, sure. Right now? Yessir!" Charlie hung up with a worried expression. It was only his second week on the job. He walked briskly to the big house, opened the door, and hurried inside.

An Episode of Stardust

Michael Swanwick

Michael Swanwick (www.michaelswanwick.com) lives in Philadelphia, Pennsylvania. His most prominent fantasy novels are *The Iron Dragon's Daughter* (1993) and *Jack Faust* (1997). They are examples of what Swanwick in an essay, "In the Tradition…" calls hard fantasy, not like the fantasy worlds of other writers, and in this case dark, technological, and sometimes brutal. His forthcoming fantasy novel is set in the world of *The Iron Dragon's Daughter*. His stories have been collected principally in *Gravity's Angels* (1991), *A Geography of Unknown Lands* (1997), *Moon Dogs* (2000), *Tales of Old Earth* (2000), a pamphlet, *Puck Aleshire's Abecedary* (2000), a collection of short-shorts, *Cigar-Box Faust and Other Miniatures* (2003), and *The Periodic Table of Science Fiction* (2005). His latest short story collection, *The Dog Said Bow-Wow*, is coming out in September 2007 from Tachyon. He has been writing more fantasy than SF in recent years.

"An Episode of Stardust" was published in *Asimov's SF*. It is a light and amusing piece, quite like his Darger and Surplus SF stories in tone, but is in fact set in the Iron Dragon world, apparently an episode from the forthcoming novel but quite satisfying as a fairy tale by itself. Gabbro Hornfelsson, a dwarf with a healthy sense of curiosity, sees Nat Whilk, a "donkey-eared fey," escorted aboard his train by two fey marshals. Naturally, he must investigate.

THE LANKY, DONKEY-EARED FEY got onto the train at a nondescript station deep in the steppes of Fäerie, escorted by two marshals in the uniform of His Absent Majesty's secret service. He smiled easily at the gawking passengers, as though he were a celebrity we had all come to see. One of the marshals was a sharp-featured woman with short red hair. The other was a tough-looking elf-bitch with skin so white it was almost blue. They both scowled in a way that discouraged questions.

The train returned to speed, and wheatfields flowed by the windows. This was the land where horses ate flesh and mice ate iron, if half the tales told of it were true, so doubtless the passing landscape was worth seeing. But I was born with a curiosity bump on the back of my skull, and I couldn't help wondering what the newcomer's crime had been, and what punishment he would receive when he arrived in Babylon.

So when, an hour or two later, the three of them got up from their seats and walked to the saloon car at the end of the train, I followed after them.

The usual mixture of unseelies and commercial travelers thronged the saloon, along with a dinter or two, a pair of flower sprites, and a lone ogre

who weighed four hundred pounds if he was a stone. This last was so anxious to retrieve his beer when the duppy-man came by with a tray, that he
stumbled into me and almost fell. "Watch where you're going, Shorty!" he
barked. "You people are a menace."

"My people mined and smelted the tracks this train moves on," I said
hotly. "We quarried the stone that clads the ziggurats at our destination, and
delved the tunnel under the Gihon that we'll be passing through. If you have
any complaints about us, I suggest you take them up with the Low Court. But
if your problem is against me personally, then Gabbro Hornfelsson backs
down from nobody." I thrust my calling card at his loathsome face. "Be it
pistols, axes, or hand grenades, I'll happily meet you on the field of honor."

The ogre blanched and fled, his beer forgotten. I didn't blame him. A
dwarf in full wrath is a fearsome opponent, no matter how big you may be.

"Well spoken, Master Hornfelsson!" The donkey-eared fey clapped
lightly, perforce pulling the red marshal's hand to which he was cuffed above
their table. She yanked it back down with a glare. "I've convinced my two
companions that, the way to Babylon being long and without further stops,
there's no harm in us having a drink or two together. If you were to join us,
I'd be honored to pick up your tab as well."

I sat down beside him and nodded at the briefcase the white marshal held
in her lap. "That's evidence, I presume. Can you tell me its nature?"

"No, he cannot," the red marshal snapped.

"Stardust, moonstones, rubies the size of plovers' eggs..." the fey said
whimsically. "Or something equally valuable. It might well be promissory
notes. I forget its exact nature but, given how alluring it was, you could
hardly blame me for making a play for it."

"And yet, oddly enough," said the red marshal, "we do."

"My name is Nat Whilk," the fey said without annoyance. I couldn't help
noticing his Armani suit and his manticore-leather shoes. "And I believe
that I may say, without boasting, that in my time I have been both richer
and poorer than anyone in this car. Once, I was both at the same time. It's a
long tale, but – " here he smiled in a self-deprecating way – "if you have the
patience, I certainly have nothing better to do."

A white-jacketed duppy came by then to take our orders. I asked for a
Laphroaig, neat, and the two marshals called for beer. Minutes later, Nat
Whilk took a long sip of his gin-and-tonic, and began to speak:

I was a gentleman in Babel once (Nat began) and not the scoundrel you see
before you now. I ate from a silver trencher, and I speared my food with a

gold knife. If I had to take a leak in the middle of the night, there were two servants to hold the bedpan and a third to shake my stick afterwards. It was no life for a man of my populist sensibilities. So one day I climbed out a window when nobody was looking and escaped.

You who had the good fortune of being born without wealth can have no idea how it felt. The streets were a kaleidoscope of pedestrians, and I was one of them, a moving speck of color, neither better nor worse than anyone else, and blissfully ignored by all. I was dizzy with excitement. My hands kept rising into the air like birds. My eyes danced to and fro, entranced by everything they saw.

It was glorious.

Down one street I went, turned a corner at random, and so by Brownian motion chanced upon a train station where I took a local to ground level. More purposefully then, I caught a rickshaw to the city limits and made my way outside.

The trooping fairies had come to Babel and set up a goblin market just outside the Ivory Gate. Vendors sold shish kabob and cotton candy, T-shirts and pashmina scarves, gris-gris bags and enchanted swords, tame magpies and Fast Luck Uncrossing Power vigil candles. Charango players filled the air with music. I could not have been happier.

"Hey, shithead! Yeah, you – the ass with the ears! *Listen* when a lady speaks to you!"

I looked around.

"Up here, Solomon!"

The voice came from a booth whose brightly painted arch read Rock! The! Fox! At the end of a long canvas-walled alley, a vixen grinned at me from an elevated cage, her front feet tucked neatly under her and her black tongue lolling. Seeing she'd caught my eye, she leapt up and began padding quickly from one end of the cage to the other, talking all the while. "Faggot! Bedwetter! Asshole! Your dick is limp and you throw like a girl!"

"Three for a dollar," a follet said, holding up a baseball. Then, mistaking my confusion for skepticism, he added, "Perfectly honest, monsieur," and lightly tossed the ball into the cage. The vixen nimbly evaded it, then nosed it back out between the bars so that it fell to the ground below. "Hit the fox and win a prize."

There was a trick to it, I later learned. Though they looked evenly spaced, only the one pair of bars was wide enough that a baseball could get through. All the vixen had to do was avoid that spot and she was as safe as houses. But even without knowing the game was rigged, I didn't want to play. I was filled with an irrational love for everyone and everything. Today of all days, I would not see a fellow creature locked in a cage.

"How much for the vixen?" I asked.

"*C'est impossible*," the follet said. "She has a mouth on her, sir. You wouldn't want her."

By then I had my wallet out. "Take it all." The follet's eyes grew large as dinner plates, and by this token I knew that I overpaid. But after all, I reasoned, I had plenty more in my carpetbag.

After the follet had opened the cage and made a fast fade, the vixen genuflected at my feet. Wheedlingly, she said, "I didn't mean none of the things I said, master. That was just patter, you know. Now that I'm yours, I'll serve you faithfully. Command and I'll obey. I shall devote my life to your welfare, if you but allow me to."

I put down my bag so I could remove the vixen's slave collar. Gruffly, I said, "I don't want your obedience. Do whatever you want, obey me in no matters, don't give a thought to my gods-be-damned welfare. You're free now."

"You can't mean that," the vixen said, shocked.

"I can and I do. So if you – "

"Sweet Mother of Beasts!" the vixen gasped, staring over my shoulder. "*Look out!*"

I whirled around, but there was nothing behind me but more booths and fair-goers. Puzzled, I turned back to the vixen, only to discover that she was gone.

And she had stolen my bag.

So it was that I came to learn exactly how freedom tastes when you haven't any money. Cursing the vixen and my own gullibility with equal venom, I put the goblin market behind me. Somehow I wound up on the bank of the Gihon. There I struck up a conversation with a waterman who motored me out to the docks and put me onto a tugboat captained by a friend of his. It was hauling a garbage scow upriver to Whinny Moor Landfill.

As it turned out, the landfill was no good place to be let off. Though there were roads leading up into the trashlands, there were none that led onward, along the river, where I wanted to go. And the smell! Indescribable.

A clutch of buildings huddled by the docks in the shadow of a garbage promontory. These were garages for the dump trucks mostly, but also Quonset hut repair-and-storage facilities and a few leftover brownstones with their windows bricked over that were used for offices and the like. One housed a bar with a sputtering neon sign saying *Brig-O-Doom*. In the parking lot behind it was, incongruously enough, an overflowing dumpster.

Here it was I fetched up.

I had never been hungry before, you must understand – not real, gnaw-at-your-belly hungry. I'd skipped breakfast that morning in my excitement over leaving, and I'd had the lightest of dinners the day before. On the tugboat I'd watched the captain slowly eat two sandwiches and an apple and been too proud to beg a taste from him. What agonies I suffered when he threw the apple core overboard! And now...

Now, to my horror, I found myself moving toward the dumpster. I turned away in disgust when I saw a rat skitter out from behind it. But it called me back. I was like a moth that's discovered a candle. I hoped there would be food in the dumpster, and I feared that if there were I would eat it.

It was then, in that darkest of hours, that I heard the one voice I had expected never to hear again. "Hey, shit-for brains! Aintcha gonna say you're glad to see me?"

Crouched atop a nearby utility truck was the vixen.

"You!" I cried, but did not add *you foul creature*, as my instincts bade me. Already, poverty was teaching me politesse. "How did you follow me here?"

"Oh, I have my ways."

Hope fluttered in my chest like a wild bird. "Do you still have my bag?"

"Of course I don't. What would a fox do with luggage? I threw it away. But I kept the key. Wasn't I a good girl?" She dipped her head, and a small key on a loop of string slipped from her neck and fell to the tarmac with a sharp clink.

"Idiot fox!" I cried. "What possible good is a key to a bag I no longer own?"

She told me.

The Brig o' Doom was a real dive. There was a black-and-white television up in one corner tuned to the fights and a pool table with ripped felt to the back. On the toilet door, some joker had painted *Tir na bOg* in crude white letters. I sat down at the bar. "Beer," I told the tappie.

"Red Stripe or Dragon Stout?"

"Surprise me."

When my drink came, I downed half of it in a single draft. It made my stomach ache and my head spin, but I didn't mind. It was the first sustenance I'd had in twenty-six hours. Then I turned around on the stool and addressed the bar as a whole: "I'm looking for a guide. Someone who can take me to a place in the landfill that I've seen in a vision. A place by a stream where garbage bags float up to the surface and burst with a terrible stench – "

A tokoloshe snorted. He was a particularly nasty piece of business, a hairy brown dwarf with burning eyes and yellow teeth. "Could be anywhere." The fossegrim sitting with him snickered sycophantically. It was clear who was the brains of this outfit.

" – and two bronze legs from the lighthouse of Rhodes lie half-buried in the reeds."

The tokoloshe hesitated, and then moved over to make space for me in his booth. The fossegrim, tall and lean with hair as white as a chimneysweeper's, leaned over the table to listen as he growled *sotto voce*, "What's the pitch?"

"There's a bag that goes with this key," I said quietly. "It's buried out there somewhere. I'll pay to find it again."

"Haughm," the tokoloshe said. "Well, me and my friend know the place you're looking for. And there's an oni I know can do the digging. That's three. Will you pay us a hundred each?"

"Yes. When the bag is found. Not before."

"How about a thousand?"

Carefully, I said, "Not if you're just going to keep jacking up the price until you find the ceiling."

"Here's my final offer: Ten percent of whatever's in the bag. Each." Then, when I hesitated, "We'll pick up your bar tab, too."

It was as the vixen had said. I was dressed as only the rich dressed, yet I was disheveled and dirty. That and my extreme anxiety to regain my bag told my newfound partners everything they needed to know.

"Twenty percent," I said. "Total. Split it however you choose. But first you'll buy me a meal – steak and eggs, if they have it."

The sun had set and the sky was yellow and purple as a bruise, turning to black around the edges. Into the darkness our pickup truck jolted by secret and winding ways. The grim drove and the tokoloshe took occasional swigs from a flask of Jeyes fluid, without offering me any. Nobody spoke. The oni, who could hardly have fit in the cab with us, sat in the bed with his feet dangling over the back. His name was Yoshi.

Miles into the interior of the landfill, we came to a stop above a black stream beside which lay two vast and badly corroded bronze legs. "Can you find a forked stick?" I asked.

The tokoloshe pulled a clothes hanger out of the mingled trash and clay. "Use this."

I twisted the wire into a wishbone, tied the key string to the short end, and took the long ends in my hands. The key hung a good half-inch off true. Then, stumbling over ground that crunched underfoot from buried rusty cans, I walked one way and the other, until the string hung straight down. "Here."

The tokoloshe brought out a bag of flour. "How deep do you think it's buried?"

"Pretty deep," I said. "Ten feet, I'm guessing."

He measured off a square on the ground – or, rather, surface, for the dumpings here were only hours old. At his command, Yoshi passed out shovels, and we all set to work.

When the hole reached six feet, it was too cramped for Yoshi to share. He was a big creature and all muscle. Two small horns spouted from his forehead and a pair of short fangs jutted up from his jaw. He labored mightily, and the pile of excavated trash alongside the hole grew taller and taller. At nine feet, he was sweating like a pig. He threw a washing machine over the lip, and then stopped and grumbled, "Why am I doing all the work here?"

"Because you're stupid," the fossegrim jeered.

The tokoloshe hit him. "Keep digging," he told the oni. "I'm paying you fifty bucks for this gig."

"It's not enough."

"Okay, okay." The tokoloshe pulled a couple of bills from his pocket and gave them to me. "Take the pickup to the Brig-O and bring back a quart of beer for Yoshi."

I did then as stupid a thing as ever I've done in my life.

So far I'd been following the script the vixen had laid out for me, and everything had gone exactly as she'd said it would. Now, rather than playing along with the tokoloshe as she'd advised, I got my back up. We were close to finding the bag and, fool that I was, I thought they would share.

"Just how dumb do you think I am?" I asked. "You won't get rid of me that easily."

The tokoloshe shrugged. "Tough shit, Ichabod."

He and the fossegrim knocked me down. They duct-taped my ankles together and my wrists behind my back. Then they dumped me in the bed of the pickup. "Scream if you want to," the tokoloshe said. "We don't mind, and there's nobody else to hear you."

I was terrified, of course. But I'd barely had time to realize exactly how desperate my situation had become when Yoshi whooped, "I found it!"

The fossegrim and the tokoloshe scurried to the top of the unsteady trash pile. "Did you find it?" cried one, and the other said, "Hand it up."

"Don't do it, Yoshi!" I shouted. "There's money in that bag, a lot more than fifty dollars, and you can have half of it."

"Give me the bag," the tokoloshe said grimly.

By his side, the fossegrim was dancing excitedly. Bottles and cans rolled away from his feet. "Yeah," he said. "Hand it up."

But Yoshi hesitated. "Half?" he said.

"You can have it all!" I screamed. "Just leave me alive and it's yours!"

The tokoloshe stumbled down toward the oni, shovel raised. His buddy followed after in similar stance.

So began a terrible and comic fight, the lesser creatures leaping and falling on the unsteady slope, all the while swinging their shovels murderously, and the great brute enduring their blows and trying to seize hold of his tormentors. I could not see the battle – no more than a few slashes of the shovels – though I managed to struggle to my knees, for the discards from Yoshi's excavations rose too high. But I could hear it, the cursing and threats, the harsh clang of a shovel against Yoshi's head and the fossegrim's scream as one mighty hand finally closed about him.

Simultaneous with that scream there was a great clanking and sliding sound of what I can only assume was the tokoloshe's final charge. In my mind's eye I can see him now, racing downslope with the shovel held like a spear, its point aimed at Yoshi's throat. But whether blade ever connected with flesh or not I do not know, for it set the trash to slipping and sliding in a kind of avalanche.

Once started, the trash was unstoppable. Down it flowed, sliding over itself, all in motion. Down it flowed, rattling and clattering, land made liquid, yet for all that still retaining its brutal mass. Down it flowed, a force of nature, irresistible, burying all three so completely there was no chance that any of them survived.

Then there was silence.

"Well!" said the vixen. "That was a tidy little melodrama. Though I must say it would have gone easier on you if you'd simply done as I told you to in the first place." She was sitting on the roof of the cab.

I had never been so glad to see anybody as I was then. "This is the second time you showed up just when things were looking worst," I said, giddy with relief. "How do you manage it?"

"Oh, I ate a grain of stardust when I was a cub, and ever since then there's been nary a spot I can't get into or out of, if I set my mind to it."

370 MICHAEL SWANWICK

"Good, good, I'm glad. Now, set me free!"

"Oh dear. I wish you hadn't said that."

"What?"

"Years ago and for reasons that are none of your business I swore a mighty oath never again to obey the orders of a man. That's why I've been tagging along after you – because you ordered me not to be concerned with your welfare. So of course I am. But now you've ordered me to free you, and thus I can't."

"Listen to me carefully," I said. "If you disobey an order from me, then you've obeyed my previous order not to obey me. So your oath is meaningless."

"I know. It's quite dizzying." The fox lay down, tucking her paws beneath her chest. "Here's another one: There's a barber in Seville who shaves everyone who doesn't shave himself, but nobody else. Now – "

"Please," I said. "I beg you. Sweet fox, dear creature, most adorable of animals... If you would be so kind as to untie me out of the goodness of your heart and of your own free will, I'd be forever grateful to you."

"That's better. I was beginning to think you had no manners at all."

The vixen tugged and bit at the duct tape on my wrists until it came undone. Then I was able to free my ankles. We both got into the cab. Neither of us suggested we try digging for my bag. As far as I was concerned, it was lost forever.

But driving down out of the landfill, I heard a cough and glanced over at the vixen, sitting on the seat beside me. More than ever, I felt certain that she was laughing at me. "Your money's in a cardboard box under the seat," she said, "along with a fresh change of clothing – which, confidentially, you badly need – and the family signet ring. What's buried out there is only the bag, stuffed full of newspapers."

"My head aches," I said. "If you had my money all along, what was the point of this charade?"

"There's an old saying: Teach a man to fish, and he'll only eat when the fish are biting. Teach him a good scam, and the suckers will always bite." The vixen grinned. "A confidence trickster can always use a partner. We're partners now, you and me, ain't we?"

When the story ended, I stood and bowed. "Truly, sir, thou hast the gift of bullshit."

"Coming from a dwarf," Nat said, "that is high praise indeed."

One of the marshals – the white one – stood. "Too much beer," she said. "I have to use the powder room."

Her comrade looked pointedly at the briefcase, and in that glance and the way the marshal drew herself up at it, I read that the two women neither liked nor trusted each other. "Where could I go?" White asked.

"Where in the regulations does it say that makes any difference?" Red replied. "The evidence case must remain within sight of two designated agents at all times."

With a sigh, the white marshal freed herself from the briefcase and handcuffed it to her red-haired compatriot. Then she put her hand on my shoulder and said, "All right, Short Stuff, I'm deputizing you as a representative of His Absent Majesty's governance. Keep an eye on the case for the duration of my tinkle, okay?"

I didn't think much of her heightist slur, of course. But a gentleman doesn't go picking fights with ladies. "Fine," I said.

As soon as she was gone, Nat Whilk said, "That calls for a smoke." He held out a hand, twisted it about, and a Macanudo appeared between thumb and forefinger. He bit off the end and was about to conjure up a light when our duppy-man appeared at his elbow.

"I'm sorry, sir," the duppy said firmly. "But smoking is not allowed inside the train."

Nat shrugged. "Well, then. It's the rear platform or nothing, I suppose." He turned to his companion and said, "Shall we?" Then, when she hesitated, "I'm hardly likely to throw myself from the train. Not at these speeds."

His words convinced her. A c-note laid down on the table, and Nat's polite direction to the duppy to let me drink my fill and then pocket the change, made our two faces smile. I watched as he and the marshal stepped to the rear of the car, and through the door. Nat leaned against the rail. A wisp of smoke from the cigar was seized by the wind and flung away.

I watched them for a while. Then my second drink came. I had just taken my first sip of it when the white marshal returned.

"Where are they?" she cried.

"They went – " I gestured toward the rear platform, and froze. Through the door windows it could be seen that the platform was empty. Lamely, I said. "They were there a second ago."

"Sweet Mother of Night," the marshal cried, "that case contained over twenty ounces of industrial-grade stardust!"

We ran, the both of us, to the platform. When we got there, we saw two small figures in the distance, standing by the side of the track, waving. As we shouted and gestured, one of the two dwindled in size until it was no larger than a dog. It was red, like a fox, and I got the distinct impression it was laughing at us.

The fox trotted away. Nat Whilk followed it down a sandy track into the scrub. Our shouts dwindled to nothing as we realized how futile they were.

The train turned a bend and the two tricksters disappeared from our ken forever.